Books by Fran Stewart

The Biscuit McKee Mystery Series:

Orange as Marmalade
Yellow as Legal Pads
Green as a Garden Hose
Blue as Blue Jeans
Indigo as an Iris
Violet as an Amethyst
Gray as Ashes

Red as a Rooster
Black as Soot
Pink as a Peony
White as Ice

A Slaying Song Tonight

The Scot Shop Mysteries:

A Wee Murder in My Shop
A Wee Dose of Death
A Wee Homicide in the Hotel

Poetry:

Resolution

For Children:

As Orange As Marmalade/
Tan naranja como Mermelada
(a bilingual book)

Non-Fiction:

From The Tip of My Pen: a workbook for writers

Pink as a Peony

Fran Stewart

Journey of a Dream Press

Pink as a Peony
the 10th Biscuit McKee Mystery
Fran Stewart

1st edition: © 2018 Fran Stewart

ISBN: 978-0-9897142-9-7

This book was printed in the United States of America.

Journey of a Dream Press
Duluth GA 30096
www.JourneyofaDream.com

For Savannah and Aiden

The final four books of the Biscuit McKee Mystery Series began with RED AS A ROOSTER, followed by BLACK AS SOOT. PINK AS A PEONY is the third of the four books, and will be followed by WHITE AS ICE. For your own enjoyment, please read all four in the correct order, as the author makes no attempt to "bring the reader up to speed" with the story so far.

If you enjoy reading the usual "Author's Note," you will find a all-inclusive one at the end of RED AS A ROOSTER. Each book contains a list of the original Martin Clan members, a chart showing the town coiuncil chairs, a list of the inhabitants of Beechnut House, and a list of who's in Biscuit and Bob's house.

Finally, Janice Adams Beene flew to Georgia from Indiana for the launch of RED AS A ROOSTER, thereby earning the use of her name in PINK AS A PEONY and WHITE AS ICE.

5 December 1741

HUBBARD BRANDT WOKE to unimaginable pain. He knew his brother had dragged him from the coals. He remembered the water dashed onto his head and shoulders. But after that, he could recall no more until this very moment. His belly felt empty, but the pain of hunger was as nothing compared to this other agony.

He reached toward his head, toward the source of the pain, but something, someone, stayed his hand. "You must not touch my clumsy bandaging, brother. I fear it may fall off if you move too much."

Ira? The voice sounded like Ira's, but Hubbard had never heard it so gentle. It could not, therefore, be Ira. Who was it, though?

He tried to open his eyes to see, but all was darkness. He tried to speak, but his pain at the simple act of opening his mouth was almost more than he could bear. He heard someone whimpering, and wondered who it might be.

That voice—who could it belong to?—cut across the moans.

"Hush now, brother. Hush. I boiled the last of the hare in some water. I know you cannot open your mouth much because of the burns on the side of your face, but if you will allow me to raise your shoulders a bit, I will try to spoon some of the broth into you. Hush. Just open a bit. Just a bit. Damnation! Open your mouth!"

Oh, good. That sounded more like the Ira he knew. Hubbard spread his lips a scant half-inch apart, trying not to move the right side of his face, and was rewarded with a flood of broth that threatened to choke him.

IRA WATCHED, FEELING helpless, as Hubbard coughed and retched and finally passed out again. Hubbard had been insensible and had eaten nothing for four days. If the burns did not kill him, starvation would. Had Ira not been able to see the labored rise and fall of his brother's chest, he might have thought Hubbard had died. The bucket of water had put out the fire that had consumed the side of Hubbard's face and most of his hair, but nothing would extinguish the despair Ira felt.

For the first three days, Ira had done little other than dribble cooling water over the burns. On the third day, he could stand the sight of the charred skin no longer. He sacrificed his one other shirt to make a rough bandage. He almost despaired of cutting it, one-handed, into strips, and he ran through his well-used stock of curses—thrice—before he finally managed to hold the homespun linen in place with his left elbow while he wielded his knife with his right hand. His good hand. His only hand.

It was a poor bandage indeed, but the only one Ira could scrape together.

Ira dripped more water onto the cloth, hoping that the cooling effect of the water would at least ease Hubbard's pain a bit. Thanks be that Hubbard had managed to turn his head to one side as he had fallen toward the coals, else his entire face would have been burnt. As it was, almost all Hubbard's hair had burned off, and despite repeated trips to the well for cooling water—curses on this missing arm of his!—blisters and charring covered Hubbard's scalp, and one entire side of his face was raw.

Ira felt certain that Hubbard had lost the use of his right eye altogether, for the eyelid was not only scorched, but was fused shut. He spared a moment to consider how they would hunt for their food from now on. What was left of the two enormous hares Hubbard had trapped four days ago even now simmered in the pot of broth on the coals. Once those hares were gone, how would they live? He with only one hand and Hubbard with only one eye. If Hubbard even survived. Their saddlebags contained enough dried and smoked meat for more than a fortnight, meat that Hubbard had insisted they not eat as they traveled after the Martins. "We may have need of it farther along the road," he had urged. Thank God Ira had been swayed by his brother's argument.

But Hubbard could not eat dried meat. He could not chew. He could barely open his mouth wide enough to admit a gnat, much less a spoonful of … of anything.

Damn the Martins. If that first Martin had never come to Brandtburg, none of this would have happened.

Assuming he could care for Hubbard enough to get him back on his feet and onto Star, should they return to Brandtburg? Should they continue to follow the Martin trail?

Nothing could be decided for the now. Hubbard was his brother, after all. Ira needed to care for his brother. Nothing else mattered. For now.

Awkwardly, he lifted Hubbard's head and shoulders away from today's puddle of ash-coated water. Once he was on a drier surface, Ira covered Hubbard with his sleeping blanket as best he could and tucked it in, careful to avoid the burned chin and the few droplets that still dripped from the bandage on Hubbard's head. Then he added a dense oak log and several smaller pine logs to the fire, stoking them carefully until they caught.

The oak would last the night. There would be no way to warm themselves or to heat water for more broth if this fire went out, for Ira had not yet been able to strike a flint with just one hand, and his brother was in no condition to do anything. Ira was desperately aware that if the fire went out, they might freeze to death.

He brought in kindling and logs—it took him five trips, for he could not carry much at a time—until there was enough to last through this night and into the morning.

He unrolled his own blanket and stretched out, as he had each night, on the floor close beside his brother, trying to warm Hubbard with his own body's heat. He was reminded of when they were small boys, sharing a narrow bed in Brandtburg. Except that then there had been no stench of burnt flesh. Nor had Ira felt afraid, back then, as a child, that he might wake to find his brother dead.

Tuesday, September 26, 2000

WHAT CLARA SAID to him, what she did to him, how hard she'd pushed him. Hubbard Martin didn't have much time to think about his wife or anyone else before he hit the ground at the bottom of the sixty-foot cliff. He had never felt such unimaginable pain, mostly about what Clara had said to him just before she pushed him.

When the rain began to fall, he didn't feel it. Not really. His body shivered, but Hubbard just wasn't there. Not really.

Thursday, December 7, 2000

I IGNORED THE general conversation at the lunch table for a bit and walked to the bay window. The little round breakfast table, which we hadn't used at all since the hordes descended, held a stack of my TBRs—books I was determined to read, but just hadn't gotten around to yet.

I'd gathered them from the living room, and here in the kitchen, too, trying to make room on counters and coffee tables for all the stuff—for want of a better word—people always seemed to deposit around themselves. The way Bob and I deposited books.

"I hope they had some good books along the trail," I said over my shoulder when there was one of those momentary silences.

"Books were still a fairly rare commodity, except among the well-to-do," Carol said, "but I imagine they had at least a few, and many families had a Bible."

Bob spoke up. "For somebody who read Shakespeare as avidly as Mary Frances did, I can't imagine she'd last without books. Has she mentioned any in her journal yet?"

"You're as up-to-date as we are," I said. "She hasn't mentioned a single one."

"Maybe," Maddy said, "they were safely packed away at the bottom of their boxes to keep them dry."

"And to keep mice from gnawing at them," Ida added.

"It's probably hard to read on a jouncing wagon seat," Dee said.

"Especially," Carol said, "when she was most likely driving the wagon."

"Why do you say that?"

"Think about it, Biscuit. If Homer led the group, he'd have been out front on his horse, which would leave Mary Frances with the job of driving."

Made sense. But if she was pregnant all that time, it couldn't have been much fun.

5 December 1741

MARY FRANCES WOKE that morning with a blinding headache as if every part of her above her neck was on fire. She had felt poorly for the past three—or was it four?—days, an overall sense of malaise, as if she could not throw off—what? She knew not where the feeling came from, for her morning queasiness had ceased to bother her some months before. Other than her despair at having to sleep beside Mister Homer Martin each night, she supposed she was in tolerably good health. Still, her head throbbed. If driving the team had been up to her, she would just as likely have led them off a cliff or into a bog, for she could barely open her eyes against the blinding light of the dawn.

She glanced sideways at Lucius Hastings, who had become the official driver of the Martin wagon.

Almost seven months before, the morning after her supposed wedding, after they buried her dead father, when the company dispersed to their wagons, Lucius had bounced past her, nodding his head respectfully, and began without a murmur to harness Mister Homer Martin's horses. Even with his broken arm in a sling, he managed a tolerably fine job of it. Silas Martin had come along to help the boy, and Mary Frances had heard his quiet instructions.

You have done well with the team, lad. Will you continue to drive, until Mistress Martin is ready to assume the task?

Mistress Martin. How she abhorred that title. Now, seven months later, with her pregnancy increasingly obvious, she still let the boy do the job he so obviously loved. Would that he would forget some morning and drive off without her.

But no, she had need of the company to protect her babe. Since the babe's father was nowhere in evidence.

She put a hand to her head, hoping to alleviate the hurt. Why had Hubbard not come for her?

With Silas Martin on Devil riding up and down the line to make sure everyone was in place, or with him forging ahead to inspect the proposed path, and with Mister Martin slouched at the head of the column on his bay mare, she knew there was no one else to drive the Martin wagon. If Myra Sue had lived, she would have driven the team.

If Myra Sue had lived, none of this … this horror would have happened. Mary Frances would not be here. She would be with her husband. With Hubbard.

Why, oh why did her head hurt her so?

Wednesday, 23 December 1741

IT HAD BEEN three endless weeks since Hubbard had fallen into the fire, and Ira was beginning to despair. He knew not what else he could do for his brother, but the hours were interminable and Ira was sore afraid that what little tending he could do for Hubbard was for naught. His brother still breathed, but little else could be said.

In desperation, Ira rooted through Hubbard's pack and withdrew the smallest of the books Hubbard had taken from the wooden box beside the trail just a month before. "*Advice to a Lady*," he read out loud, "by George Lyttelton, the first Baron Lyttelton." It was a small book, which suited Ira's inclinations perfectly. "Shall I read to you, brother? It appears to be poetry."

The grunt that answered his inquiry could have meant anything from yes to no to something else altogether profane, although Hubbard had never been wont to use profanity.

"I will take that to mean yes." He opened to a page at random.

> Do you, my Fair, endeavour to possess
> An elegance of mind as well as dress;
> Be that your ornament, …

Ira lost his place when Hubbard moaned.

"Shall I stop reading?"

"No."

"Are you in pain?"

"Stupid question."

Ira noticed that Hubbard's lips hardly moved at all as he spoke. Little wonder. Not knowing what else to do, he found his place and went back to reading.

> Nor make to dang'rous wit a vain pretence,

But wisely rest content with modest sense,
For wit like wine intoxicates the brain,
Too strong for feeble woman to sustain.

He quit when Hubbard drew his index finger across his throat in a cutting motion. That was just as well. Ira was not enjoying the book any more than Hubbard appeared to be. Instead, he spoke of the rabbits he hoped to snare soon. They had subsisted on roast hare for these three weeks, and he was heartily tired of the fare, but it was the only meat he was able to procure. He was rather proud of his ability to set a snare with but one hand. Squirrels were far too canny to approach the snares, but hares, fortunately, were less perceptive. The rabbit meat boiled down to a fine broth, too, something that Hubbard was able to swallow, just barely.

HUBBARD MAY HAVE been so miserable he could barely think, but he knew enough to recognize the absurdity of what his brother was reading. He would much rather lie here and think of his wife and her ready wit.

Had he been able to claim her, her tender hands could have nursed him. Had he been able to claim her, she would have read to him with great joy, and he would have listened with great pleasure.

Had he been able to claim her, none of this … this … he searched for a word but could not find it. None of this would have happened.

2000

BOB SPOKE LOUDLY enough for the rest of the conversations to stop. "I wonder if they had many dealings with the Indians back then on their journey."

"I should think so," Carol said.

"This all happened before the Trail of Tears, didn't it? When…?" Pat let her question die away. I couldn't blame her. The Trail of Tears was such a horrible blot in our country's history.

"Late 1830s," Carol said.

"It started in 1839," Maddy clarified.

"Keep an eye out in those journals," Bob said. "You might get us some answers."

"I just hope they had friendly dealings," Melissa said. "I don't think I could endure hearing about too much bloodshed."

Rebecca Jo shivered. "I don't want to hear about *any* bloodshed."

"You know what you need to do," Henry said, "is scout around town in everybody else's attics and see if you can find more diaries."

"Don't think we haven't thought about it already," Pat said. "We're one step ahead of you, though. I volunteered my husband to be the one to do the searching."

"No way in … uh"—Dave looked at me uncertainly. "No way."

"Thank you for maintaining such propriety at our formal dining table," I said in my best countess voice, and we all burst out in various guffaws and giggles.

What is a countiss voice?

Even Marmalade joined in the hilarity.

Thursday, 24 December 1741

IRA BRANDT HAD lost count of the days recently, but he thought it might be close to Christmastide. There had been a fair amount of snow of late, but the roof of saplings and pine boughs had held fairly tight. What few drips there were did not come from directly above where he and his brother slept at night—what little sleep he got considering how Hubbard cried out throughout the dark hours whenever he with inadvertence turned his head or touched his face or scalp.

Now, Hubbard slept fitfully through the dawn hours, and Ira knelt beside him, pondering how to proceed. He knew of nothing else he could do for Hubbard. The bandages he had tried to keep on Hubbard's scalp and forehead appeared to have done more harm than good. He had made the mistake of letting them dry out about a sevenday after the accident, and when he went to remove them, Hubbard screamed in agony as the bandage ripped from his face.

Ira had no weapon close at hand when he heard Blaze whinny a greeting. He reached for his knife, but he had left it sitting just out of reach on the warm hearthstone. Within seconds, before Ira could get his feet under him, a lone Indian opened the door. He held a knife at the ready, but did not advance into the room.

Ira saw at a glance the balance of the man. Sure of himself but wary.

The Indian nodded toward Hubbard's ravaged face. "Fie-yer?" The word was awkwardly accented and took up two distinct syllables, but it was understandable.

"Yes."

"Wait." With that, the man took a step backward, pulled the door closed, and disappeared from sight.

The exchange had been so brief, Ira might almost have thought he had imagined it, but a footprint of snow from the bottom of the man's shoe—moccasin?—remained just inside the doorstep.

The snow print had long melted by the time the man returned, this time with an elderly woman so bundled against the cold, Ira wondered whether she had any shape to her at all under the layers.

She said nothing, but studied him with eyes that seemed to take in everything about him. When she shrugged, as if in dismissal, Ira shivered and wondered if somehow he had been rendered invisible.

The woman glided across the floor, leaving no footprints that Ira could see, although the legs of the man standing beside the now-closed door dripped melting snow onto the wooden floor. She held up her hand in a peremptory gesture, and Ira felt like he had been shoved aside. He moved quickly to give her room.

She knelt beside Hubbard, where he lay on his left side, since he could not bear to have the burned portion of his head in contact with anything. His left ear and cheek nestled into a makeshift pillow of dead grasses covered with Ira's spare breeches. The woman removed the damp cloth Ira had draped over the burn and tossed it aside. It landed with a distinct plop next to Ira's left foot, and he bent to retrieve it. She paid him no mind, but laid a hand on Hubbard's shoulder, speaking softly in words Ira did not understand. Hubbard stirred. "Yes," he said, his lips barely moving.

From some hidden recess of her garments, she withdrew an earthenware jug, plugged with a wad of some sort of greenery, which she removed and set to one side. Tipping it carefully, she poured a few drops into her hand and dribbled them onto the raw surface of Hubbard's ruined face. He gasped, but then subsided as she blew gently on the oily-looking drops. Her breath seemed to spread them a bit. Finally, she produced a sturdy feather from somewhere or other about her. It was black with white splotches, and she used it to smooth the greenish liquid over the entire surface of the burn—face, eye, forehead, scalp, and ear—what little was left of it. The smell of the liquid was … Ira reached for a word, but could not find it. It smelled green, he finally decided. Fresh and green.

The woman laid a hand on Hubbard's chest, right above his heart. Ira watched as her impassive face seemed to darken, to constrict somehow. Her wrinkled skin, which had seemed simply furrowed before, now resembled nothing so much as a withered pumpkin rind.

She said a few more unintelligible words, stood, and thrust the jug into Ira's hands. She bent quickly and swished the feather through the water bucket, tapped it on the side, flicked off the excess water with a practiced wrist movement, and handed Ira the feather as well.

She pointed from him to the jug to Hubbard and back at the feather. Ira nodded dumbly. Yes, he felt confident he could repeat her actions.

Next, she pantomimed lifting the bucket to her lips and drinking, then pointed to Hubbard and to Ira.

Yes, he nodded, he would drink of it himself and would give the water to his brother as well.

He recognized, too, her signs for sunrise and sunset. Twice a day he was to dose Hubbard with the green drops, spread them around with the feather, and transfer what was left on the feather to the water bucket. Then they both were to drink it. Drink it all.

Hubbard lay there quietly, seeming to watch the mime show with his one good eye. Ira thought he looked peaceful, for the first time in well more than a fortnight.

The woman spared one more glance at Hubbard, nodded as if in satisfaction, and brushed past Ira. She opened the door and left. The man who had brought her raised his hand in a brief signal of farewell, and it was in that motion that Ira saw the puckered, scarred skin across the man's palm.

As if in answer to Ira's start of recognition, the man flexed his hand, transferred the knife to that hand, apparently intending to show that it worked well despite the heavy burn scars, and left as suddenly as he had come.

Hubbard muttered something, and Ira knelt close beside him. "I did not know angels wore doeskin," Hubbard said, and fell into a sound and peaceful sleep.

Thursday, 24 December 1741

IT HAD BEEN WEEKS since Mary Frances had been able to sleep through the night. She knew not where her discomfort came from, except that her head had hurt her exceedingly, both day and night. Perhaps that was the cause. Sleep was not forthcoming when one's head felt so horrible.

This night, though, was different. Mister Homer Martin stayed up late, trading stories beside the fire, and when he finally crawled into the wagon, it was to sleep. Mary Frances, knowing she would not be bothered this night, curled into a ball and found that for the first time in well more than a fortnight, her head was free from the pounding burning misery she had been wont to have.

She slept soundly, deeply, peacefully.

2000

"YOU KNOW," RALPH said a little while later, "we've got it pretty good here." He picked a bit of meat off the chicken leg he'd been gnawing on. "We may not have any power, but as long as we've got food, we're okay."

"And water," Ida reminded her husband. "We need that, too."

"And indoor facilities," Sadie said. "Those outhouses were cold as the dickens in the winter when I was a girl, and they'd feel even worse now."

"Let us be thankful," Henry said, just at the same moment Father John said, "Thank God and the people who invented indoor plumbing."

"That would be the Romans," Maddy said.

Sadie looked at her in surprise. "Wait a minute, Maddy. If the Romans invented it, why did we still have outhouses when I was a girl?"

"Blame it on the Middle Ages. We lost a lot of knowledge then."

"Doesn't matter," Ralph said, bringing us back to the current century. "We've got toilets and water and"—he patted his middle—"plenty of grub, and that's all that matters."

Leave it to a grocer to focus on the food.

January 1742

IRA BRANDT WRENCHED off the last bit of meat and threw the leg bone back into the pot simmering on the hearth. He was heartily tired of hare for three meals out of every day, but rabbits were easier to snare than squirrels. Thank Providence the squirrels had never discovered a way to warn the rabbits.

He was tired of wresting pine boughs from trees that seemed to be reluctant to give up their branches, but he had to do it to provide a layer warmer than the bare floor for them to sleep on. He was tired of dragging firewood from the stacks the previous occupants of this desolate cabin had left, but if they had not left so much wood, he did not know how he and his brother could have survived, for he was unable to wield an axe with only the one hand. Thank Providence, as well, that the winter so far had been fairly mild. Blaze and Star could still find enough browse near to the cabin, the creek that ran behind the house served the horses well, and there were rabbits aplenty for Ira and his brother to eat. How grateful he was that the previous inhabitants had dug so dependable a well, too.

He had been pleasantly surprised to find he could balance his rifle on the elbow joint of his left arm and still manage to sight accurately along the barrel, although he had not even tried to shoot one of the deer that had visited the clearing just that morning. He might be able to shoot, but he would be sore pressed to field dress any creature larger than a hare. His store of ammunition had already grown sparse, even before they arrived here, and they would need to move on as soon as spring arrived. By that time, if Hubbard was still alive, he might be better, and might be able to do the butchering.

Ira watched his brother pull another leg from the roasted hare. Hubbard's face, if you saw it only from the left side, was not too badly impaired, but it still turned Ira's stomach to look at the ruined right side. Very little of his hair had regrown, and only in patchy spots. And the tight, mottled red skin of half his face was difficult to view. His right eyelid was fused shut with livid tight scar tissue, and his right ear was horribly misshapen, although the green liquid medicine the Indian woman had left them with had aided Hubbard's healing immensely.

Ira dreaded their reception if and when they made it to a town—and who knew how far the next town would be? Maybe he should improvise some sort of mask that Hubbard could wear to cover the immovable expanse of scarred tissue that kept that side of his face from any sort of expression. It was almost worse than the pitting caused by smallpox. At least people were used to seeing pox scars.

Over the months of their imprisonment here, for so Ira thought about this unwilling sojourn, his stump had finally healed completely. He had been using the Indian woman's green liquid on it, reasoning that if it helped a burn it could surely help an amputation. And had not the end of Ira's arm been burned as well to stop the bleeding? He had found himself more easy of late with cramping the rope of the well in the crook of his left elbow or of wrapping his half-arm around almost anything that needed to be carried.

Hubbard had recovered enough to be able to get himself to the privy and had, only the day before, managed to bring in an armful—a small armful—of wood. He stumbled frequently when he walked and seemed not to know how far his feet were from any object in his path. Each day he seemed to regain more of his strength, but he seemed as well to wallow in despair. And Ira did not like to see the way Hubbard so often pressed his hand to his chest, as if it pained him somehow.

If Ira had only known beforehand what the result of his irritated shove would be.

If only the Martins had never come to Brandtburg.

But in a rare moment of insight and self-examination, Ira realized he could no longer blame every misfortune on the Martin clan. Hubbard had never spoken a word of reproach to him, but Ira knew at his heart's core that he himself, his ready anger and his unwillingness to curb his impulsive actions, had brought about this great tragedy that had disfigured his brother.

We will return to Brandtburg, he thought. *In the spring, when it is easier to travel, I will leave off my hunt for Homer Martin. I will take my brother home.*

2000

REBECCA JO PICKED up one more cookie. "What are we waiting for?"

We whisked the dirty dishes off the table so fast, the men hardly knew what was happening. In no time we had the kitchen clean and everything put away.

"I'm the slowest," Rebecca Jo said. "I'll bring up the rear."

I will wait and walk with you, BookLady.

She stood aside and waited for Maddy and Carol to lead the way. I expected Marmalade to walk upstairs beside me the way she usually did, but this time, she lingered behind. Hoping for more food, perhaps?

Mouse droppings!

Oh dear. It sounded like she was swearing at me. I was going to have to rethink all my opinions about what I thought was her constant complaining for food.

I do not complain about food. I am well fed. Sometimes, though, I have to remind you about chicken.

I needed Carol back here in the middle of the line to interpret for me.

Saturday, 3 January 1742
Somewhere in Pennsylvania, along the Susquehanna River

SILAS MARTIN HELD out his mittened hands toward the roaring central fire. The trouble with such a large fire, he thought, was that the front of a person roasted while the back of that same person froze. He had observed many times when he had come upon groups of Indians, hunting, that their fires were inevitably small, just enough to warm one man who curled himself around it almost as he slept. One small fire per man. Silas had tried it himself on those times when he had been away from the wagons overnight. He had been unable to convince anyone else of the sense of such a practice, though. They would insist that the bigger the fire, the more the warmth would spread.

The bigger the fire, he thought, the less usable it was, unless you wanted to destroy a building.

"I thought we were traveling to a *warmer* place." Charles Hastings pulled his knitted scarf more tightly around his ears and stretched the ends another time around his neck.

"It will be warmer once we are farther south," Silas assured him.

As anxious as he was to find a haven where they could finally end their journey, he knew it was imperative that they remain in one place for now. He had convinced Homer only two days before that there was little sense in continuing to try to travel through such a heavy storm. "We will lose some of the stragglers and many of the livestock unless we can bunch all of us together. We have enough meat to sustain us while we rest and gather our strength for the remainder of the journey. Surely this storm cannot last but another day or two."

Homer had, of course, objected, but Silas continued to reason with him until Homer reached for a bottle. "Be it as you wish," he had growled. "I care not."

At Silas' direction, they had pulled the wagons into a semicircle, with the tail of each wagon pointed into the circle. In the middle was the large fire, ringed with smaller individual cooking fires. The remaining part of the circle was filled in by temporary pens that held the livestock. The smell was intense, but the animals generated a certain amount of warmth, and bunched together like that, they kept each other from freezing.

With the winter winds howling around the wagons, there was little else to do—once the daily chores of tending the stock and gathering firewood were accomplished—except to hunker in to sleep or, as they would be doing this day, attend a wedding.

"At least they will keep each other warm tonight," Daniel Endicott observed with a decided leer, causing three of his brothers to burst into raucous laughter. Silas did not even bother to smile. The Endicotts needed no encouragement.

He lifted his gaze from the fire and settled it on Colton Shipleigh and his intended, Orra Fountain, who had always seemed to Silas to be polar opposites. Colton, so like a squat loosely strung fiddle without a bow and Orra, the gaunt bow without the fiddle. Hopefully, their marriage would bring the two together to make at least a degree of music. His fingers were too cold to handle a pen—and the ink would most likely freeze should he try—but he itched to put those images to paper, Colton's paunchy frame that would stand soon in front of Reverend Russell, next to Orra's stick-thin angularity.

Silas bent his neck and turned to warm his backside. He was not usually prone to such lyrical imaginings, but he indulged himself another moment or two, envisioning himself as the conductor of the numerous instruments around him.

Mary Frances, his brother's wife, was too heavy with pregnancy to be a violin—never a fiddle, that woman. She was too serious for a fiddle. Her face looked strained, and he wondered if she felt much discomfort. He had always felt something akin to awe at the way in which a woman's body could create life within. Someday, someday he would marry and have children, but he shuddered to think of the screams he had heard when women were birthing their babes. Did he have the right to inflict that on any woman? Particularly on the woman to whom he was drawn.

Elias Shipleigh, the father of the groom, was a horn of some sort, always honking on and on. Mistress Charlotte Endicott Ellis over there beside her brother Worthy was—what instrument would she be? A high-pitched piccolo, perhaps, strident but—unlike a piccolo—somehow monotonous, unenthusiastic. Charlotte's brother, Worthy Endicott, was definitely a bass drum, pounding his incessant rhythm without regard to the ears or the cadence of the rest of the group.

Silas longed to get his fingers on paper and ink. These images were too vivid not to record.

He turned around yet again, knowing what he would see. He was so attuned to Louetta Tarkington, he knew instinctively where she stood almost every minute of every day. It was far too early to speak his mind, for she had mourned her dead husband for less than eight months, and he felt fair certain she would not look kindly on any suit of his that came too soon. A cello. That was what instrument she was. Mellow, powerful, soft-spoken but of imminent sense—did a cello have sense? He decided that it did. Those mellifluous strains underlying the sounds produced by any group of musicians, held the entire ensemble together in—

"Silas?" Homer's insistent bark of irritation cut into the picture Silas had composed. "I need you now for … for a conference."

That, Silas knew, meant Homer was going to argue about something—the arrangement of the circle, the need to remain in one place for at least another day, the disposition of the livestock. He left the welcome warmth of the fire and walked aside with his brother. His brother the snare drum.

They had barely reached the edge of the second wagon circle when the voice of Reverend Russell began to call the congregation together for the wedding service. Silas, happy for the reprieve, cocked an eyebrow at Homer. "Later, brother?"

Homer, for once, did not snarl, but merely turned around and headed back from whence he had come. Silas sent up a heartfelt prayer for milder, sunnier weather preferably beginning on the morrow. Homer had ever been a creature who seemed to wither in the dark days of winter. Perhaps going far southward had truly been one of Homer's better ideas.

HARDLY HAD REVEREND Russell proclaimed, "Those whom God hath joined together, let no man put asunder," when Mistress Anthina Shipleigh, the mother of the groom, began to gasp and to claw the multiple scarves away from her scrawny throat.

The women near her instinctively rushed to her side, only to be repulsed when Mistress Shipleigh began the gagging sounds that everyone present knew would result in vomiting. She turned away from her son and his new wife, scorned the help of her neighbors, and clutched with one hand at the wheel of the wagon as she pulled herself off to the side, through the slush of the churned-up snow, away from the recently-concluded wedding ceremony. With her other hand, she held her stomach.

Although the weather warmed somewhat the following day, no one suggested leaving, for Mistress Shipleigh was in dire straits. Even Louetta Tarkington, who had proven to have great healing skills, was unable to alleviate the woman's extreme pain.

The next night after the onset of her distress, Silas stood watch near the Shipleigh wagon as the moon passed beyond its zenith. Louetta Tarkington ducked from under the canvas cover of the wagon and stepped onto one of the wheel hubs and thence to the ground.

"Is she any better?" Silas kept his voice low. He had not—not truly—intended this, but his near-whisper encouraged Mistress Tarkington to lean closer to hear him. He could smell the fresh herbal scent of her hair overlaid with the rancid smell of Mistress Shipleigh's stale vomit.

"I cannot believe she will last the night," Louetta said in just as low a voice. "I find myself surprised that she has survived this long, for I can do naught to stop her puking, and she grows weaker with each breath." She staggered slightly, and Silas reached out to take hold of her elbow and steady her.

"You are practically asleep on your feet. You must rest. Surely there is another woman who can sit with her."

"They all fear that it is the plague or the fever. That is why her husband took their children off to other wagons."

"Is it the fever?" Silas could not help the surge of fear that welled up in him. "Might you be in danger tending her?"

Louetta shook her head wearily. "This is no fever. I am at a loss to tell what has caused it, though. 'Twas almost certainly something she ate, but as far as I can tell, she has eaten nothing that was not eaten by other members of her family, and none of them is poorly."

"Excuse me, Mistress Tarkington."

Silas took a step back and turned to see Charlotte Ellis peering at them in the wavery light of the central fire. "Yes, Mistress?"

Charlotte ignored him. "I fear we women have left too much of the tending to you, Mistress Tarkington. Will you take some rest now and let me sit with poor Anthina?"

"Oh, my thanks, Mistress Ellis. If I could get but a few hours of rest …" The relief in Louetta's voice was unmistakeable. Silas wished he had been able to provide her with such comfort.

"Think nothing of it. I am happy to be of help. Does she any better, think you? No? Well, it is all in God's hands, is it not? Get you off to your sleep and I will see if there is aught I can do." She flapped her hand in a dismissive gesture.

Silas waited to be sure Louetta was safely inside the Russell's wagon before he left the side of the Shipleigh wagon. Before he wrapped himself in his sleeping blanket, he glanced back at Charlotte Ellis who stood still, apparently waiting to see him settled before she went about her charitable duty.

There was something about that woman he did not like.

Once she disappeared into the wagon, he reached for his paper and ink.

CHARLOTTE HAULED HERSELF up into the wagon, steeled herself against the revolting smells, and settled as comfortably as she could at Anthina's side. "Well, now," she whispered, low enough that no one except the dying woman could possibly hear her, "you thought you could make off with the man who should have been mine. You thought you were the winner. You thought that you were safe with Elias Shipleigh. You did not know how I swore revenge all those years ago, and think you I did not laugh to myself as I knitted those soft stockings as such a special gift for you?" She reached inside the pocket tied at her waist and pulled out a small package of tightly woven and heavily waxed linen. "Death's cap mushroom, dried and reduced to a powder." She dangled it above Anthina. "Little did you realize that for two weeks your feet have been taking in this poison with each step you took. What good are all your sons to you now?"

I should have come here sooner, Charlotte thought, for Anthina was too far gone to appreciate the irony. She could not even open her eyes in horror, but Charlotte saw the woman's wasted fingers curl and clench, and knew that Anthina was at least aware that Charlotte had prevailed. Revenge had been a long time in coming, but Charlotte was nothing if not patient.

Mistress Shipleigh died before the morning dawned. When the other women gathered to prepare the body for burial, Charlotte Ellis insisted that Anthina's long knitted stockings remain on her feet. "I made them for her, the poor dear, and she told me just before she died that she hoped to be buried in them. It was the last thing she said." She wiped away a tear that was simply a response to the chilly wind—for Charlotte had never mastered the skill of crying on demand, but the other women had no need to know that. "I have known her for so long a time."

Charlotte excused herself from the onerous task ahead and let the others wipe Anthina Shipleigh's face clean and wrap her body in a linen shroud. "I sat with her all the night," Charlotte explained, "and I am sore exhausted."

"You poor dear."

WHEN THE MEN of the company would have dug a grave in the nearby forest, Mistress Sarah Russell informed her husband—with due respect, of course—that Anthina Shipleigh "had a terrible fear of being buried far from a churchyard. Is there not a town nearby where we might lay her to rest in consecrated ground?"

Reverend Russell consulted briefly with Silas Martin, who rode through the bitter wind, following the well-worn trail ahead to a moderate-sized town, where a white church with an ill-proportioned steeple towered over a motley group of houses. The most imposing structure, besides the church, appeared to be the town tavern, which squatted like a fat toad alongside the road near the outskirts of the town, as if waiting to snare any unwary travelers who might come that way.

Before Silas entered the church, he studied some of the markers in the graveyard, which appeared to be near full. Silas had seen the marks of the smallpox on numerous people as he passed through the town. "You have been plagued by the pox, I see," Silas mentioned to the minister when he found him in the parsonage next door to the church.

"You need have no fear. The last death was more than a year beforehand."

AFTER SOME NEGOTIATION, during which some of the cash money Robert Hastings carried came into play, the Martin troupe laid Anthina Shipleigh to rest in a corner of the church graveyard and placed thereon a wooden cross, which Silas had carved with her name and the date of her death. Nobody could remember exactly what day or which year she had been born. Anthina's closest friends were chagrined to find that neither the Surratts nor the Shipleighs had a family Bible in which such details might have been recorded.

As they left the graveyard to return to their wagons, which were strung across a clearing just outside the town, preparatory to the continuance of their journey, Louetta Tarkington turned away from Silas and spoke to Charlotte Ellis. "The Susquehanna River sings a lovely song, does it not? I am glad Anthina will be able to hear the river for eternity."

Charlotte made a non-committal sound.

"I am sorry, though, that we have to leave her here alone. I did not know her well, of course, but she was always most pleasant to me and to my son, Brand."

"Are you wishing that someone else had died as well, to keep her company?"

"You mistake me, Mistress Ellis. That is not what I meant at all."

Charlotte grunted one more time before she walked away.

Louetta spread her mittened hands, palms upward, once Charlotte Ellis was out of earshot. "Did I say aught to displease her?"

"Not that I could tell," Silas said. "Do not let her distress you. She has ever been a prickly one." He revised his mental image of Mistress Ellis. Not a piccolo, but a strident trumpet, blaring her tune at the cost of the ears around her.

2000

"THAT WAS A good lunch," Pat said, "but I almost wish we could eat up here in the attic and keep on looking and reading and such."

"I know what you mean," Dee said. "It's like there's a whole new world here just waiting for us to open it up."

Amanda cleared her throat. "The advantage of going downstairs to eat is that it gets our blood moving. All this sitting around isn't good for us."

"Spoken like a true therapist," Rebecca Jo said with a laugh. "But then again, who's just sitting?" She reached toward an upper shelf of one of the numerous bookcases and pulled down a stack of ratty paperbacks. They looked almost as disreputable as the ones Clara Martin had donated to the library. After one brief look, Rebecca Jo said, "On second thought, I vote that we sit and let Ida read some more Mary Frances."

"Nope," I said. "It's my turn. Hubbard's turn, that is."

"I hope Ira gets his act together soon," Maddy said. "He's been a pill so far."

I looked ahead a sentence or two. "They're on their way. That's good."

Monday 23 November 1741. We left Brandtburg on the 2nd of this month, and I have found no time to write since then. There has been little sign of the Martins other than the wide track that must have been their path, but this morning we happened upon a cache of boxes that had been thrown from their wagons. I might not have spotted them if it had not been for a black chess piece—a queen—that stood upright on a rock, almost as if she had been waiting for me, beckoning to me. The cache was a treasure indeed, for I gathered seven books. Seven! From the inscriptions, it is clear that they were stolen from Master Ormsby, most likely by the Endicott brood. It is easy to blame them when they are not here to defend themselves. Sayrle is the only one of the group who seemed interested in reading, but from what I knew of him I would not have supposed him to be a thief. Still, some men are tempted beyond their ability to resist. He may have seen a journey without books as a punishment. But if so, I can not imagine why he would dispose of books—if these were indeed his—in such a disrespectful way.

"This is perfect," Dee said. "Remember, Maddy, how you said they might have been like Hansel and Gretel, leaving breadcrumbs along the way?"

"Yeah," Maddy said, obviously no surer than I was of where Dee was headed.

"So, thanks to the Endicotts, they left chess pieces and books. I'd say that's even better than bread crumbs."

"I guess the Endicotts were good for something after all," Rebecca Jo mused.

"It's better than leaving dead bodies," Maddy said.

"What?!"

"Don't pop a cork, Dee. I meant graves. I hope they didn't have to leave too many of those."

"I'm sure there were more than a few," Carol said.

I looked ahead a few lines. "Don't speak so fast, Maddy."

I will keep the books safe until my wife and I can return them to Brandtburg. I know Master Ormsby will be delighted to have them back. In the meantime, I can well imagine how my wife and I will delight in reading to each other by the fire in the evenings.

We have found no more graves past the one we saw on the fifth of this month. My wife's father. His grave was covered with a mound of stones, and there was a small wooden marker etched with his name and dates—the work of Silas Martin, no doubt. Calvin Garner would have been my father-in-law. My heart aches for the pain Mary Frances must feel at having lost her father. I wonder how she fares? Pray God that she knows I am coming at last to find her. Would that there were some angel to convey the message to her.

Blaze and Star both carry extra canvas for tents, for I will need a way to shelter my wife on our journey home. Food has been plentiful, although I become a bit weary of roasted hare. They are surprisingly easy to snare, which is a good thing, for I must do all the work. Ira refuses even to try. He tires easily. I fear the length of this journey. Pray God that my wife keeps faith that I will come to her. Pray God that I will find her soon. My heart aches for her as I write this.

"Good grief," I said. "There's nothing after this until the first of April in 1742."

"What on earth," Ida asked, "could have kept him from writing for that long?" When I looked back at Hubbard's book, she held up a peremptory hand. "No fair peeking. You'll have to wait your turn until we get to then."

Phooey. I didn't like it, but she was right. So I marked the place with a scrap of paper, set Hubbard's journal aside, and took off my white gloves. I wouldn't need them for a while.

Thursday, 7 January 1742

WHEN MARY FRANCES had lain with Hubbard in the loft of Reverend Atherton's barn on their wedding night, she had assumed that if a child resulted, it would be born in a snug house in Brandtburg, not here in a cold wagon jouncing along on an inhospitable trail in the middle of the wilderness, with three women crowded around in attendance. Her mother was not one of the three. Augusta Garner had chosen to stay in her own wagon with young Able, who was ailing, too sick to walk or even sit upright. At the moment, Mary Frances did not care. Her mother had sided with her father to force her to go through with her unlawful wedding to Homer Martin. Mary Frances did not want even to see her mother during this birth, much less to be attended by her.

Nor was Homer hovering beside the wagon or even driving it. He had left Lucius Hastings with that task as soon as he had seen that Mary Frances could not manage the job.

Mary Frances had heard Geonette Black Surratt ask him, "Can we not stop whilst your wife births this child?"

"We have miles still to cover before sundown," he had replied, as if it were not his wife about to birth his child. Of course, thought Mary Frances, I am not truly his wife and this is most certainly not his child, so why should I worry that he does not care for our safety or comfort?

"There is no snow here," Homer had further said to Mistress Surratt. "While the trail is dry and passable, we must make as much progress as we can."

At that point, Geonette had shooed Lucius away from the wagon seat. "You do not want to be this close to a woman birthing a babe. I will drive this day."

Lucius had taken one alarmed look at Mary Frances and disappeared faster than morning haze after a hot sunrise.

She had not been in labor for long—although it felt like an eternity to her. Mistress Hastings sponged off her forehead with a wet cloth. Mary Frances took comfort in the fact that she had asked Mistress Hastings several weeks before to serve as godmother to her babe. If only Myra Sue were still alive, she would have been godmother to this child.

"You are not the first woman to go through this," Mistress Tarkington told her, "nor will you be the last."

"If … if I die …" Mary Frances did not know how to continue. How could she tell them to return to Brandtburg to summon the babe's father?

"Never fear."

Mistress Tarkington had proved to be an effective midwife during other births along the trail, but Mary Frances knew she could not trust the words of that calm voice. She knew she would die soon. She only wished that she might see her husband once more before the end.

"When the mother begins to feel sure she will die, that means the babe will come quickly."

"Is that meant to be a comfort to—" Her exasperation was cut short as another pain gripped her, then another, so close to the last one that she hardly had time to breathe. Sarah Russell slipped a clean rolled-up rag between her teeth, telling her to bite down on it.

"Already, the babe's head is visible," Louetta Tarkington said, and guided Mary Frances' hand so that she might be the first to touch the child. The surface of the baby's head felt warm and slick. Surely it would be a boy. A son for her Hubbard.

A son he would never see.

"There is no need to cry now," Sarah Russell crooned to her. "You have barely made a sound ever since your waters broke forth at mid-morning, and now when it is almost over, you cry? Hush now. Hush, and give one more push."

Mistress Tarkington laid her hands across the linen shift that covered the tight, quivering mound of Mary Frances' belly. "I will help."

Mary Frances supposed she ought to feel grateful that this woman who had only recently joined their band should have been so knowledgeable about birthing, but at that moment, she cared not for anyone or anything other than her urgent need to expel this child and rid herself of the pain.

It took three more pushes to birth the babe, and when he emerged, mewling with hunger, Mary Frances saw that he had the same high forehead as his father. Pain forgotten, she clasped him to her. "Our son," she said. "Our son."

Sarah Russell and Louetta Tarkington busied themselves with the aftermath of the birth. "Homer Martin will be proud indeed," Sarah eventually said as she watched the new babe at its first meal.

Jane Elizabeth Hastings scoffed as she took the bloodstained sheets and rolled them up, to be saved until the travelers tarried beside a cold stream where the blood could be soaked out. "If Homer Martin even deigns to look."

LATER THAT EVENING, after the camp was prepared and the men had been fed, the other women came to see the babe two at a time, for two was all that would fit in the wagon easily, what with their voluminous wrappings against the winter's chill, and with Sarah Russell and Jane Elizabeth Hastings, both of whom had refused to leave Mary Frances. Mary Frances saw with chagrin that Charlotte Ellis lifted an eyebrow when she came into the narrow space, and said in a dry tone, "Does he not look just like his father?"

"For certain," Sarah Russell agreed, although Mary Frances could tell from her tone of voice that she did not truly believe it. "Babes always do, although they can change so much in the first few hours after their birth, one would never know it. By tomorrow he will look even more like his own sweet self." She bundled yet another felted wool blanket over the baby and slipped a knitted woolen cap onto his head as he nestled beside Mary Frances, encircled by her arm.

"It is a shame Mister Martin is too drunk to see him while he still looks like this," Charlotte observed, her eyes slitted so tight in suspicion that Mary Frances could barely see the dark, empty center of them, as bleak and empty as Mary Frances suspected Charlotte's heart was.

Once all the women were gone back to their own wagons, Sarah Russell offered Mary Frances some soothing tea. "I had hoped to attend the birth of my grandchild," she said. "If only …"

She did not finish her sentence.

"Yes," Mary Frances thought. If only. If only Myra Sue Russell Martin had lived. If only Ira Brandt had never been born. If only Hubbard had followed. If only Homer Martin had fallen off his horse into a ravine or a rushing river.

Her baby mewed almost like a tiny kitten, and she loosened her grasp on him. This babe was all she had of her dear husband. She would treasure this child forever.

2000

IDA TOOK UP where she'd left off to cover the time missing from Hubbard's journal, but the next number of entries, written during November and December of 1741, were, quite frankly, much less interesting than the story of the dead bear and the one about how Mary Frances looked forward to the birth of her child. She seemed to be hoarding her precious paper, for the entries had gradually tapered down to only two or three a month. Quite a few newborns died—was every woman on that journey pregnant?—and there were a number of mishaps with broken axles, lost goats, and lamed horses, as well as some hair-raising fights among some of the young men in the company, usually instigated by the Endicott brothers, a fact not lost on our attic company. It was only when Ida reached January of 1742 that our ears truly perked up.

Saturday, 23 January 1742

Anthina Shipleigh died soon after the marriage of her son Colton to Orra Fountain on the third of this month. She was buried in the churchyard of the nearby town of Harrisburg.

I have been unable to write for well more than a fortnight, for my son was born on the seventh of January, a Thursday afternoon, as our wagon bounced over a most inhospitable road. Mister Homer Martin—I will never refer to him as my husband—refused our request to tarry while my babe was birthed, and so my son's first impression of this world must have been that it was constantly moving up and down, rocking backward and forward, bumping from side to side in a most disconcerting way. I will not be surprised if John—for so I have named him, since John is his true father's middle name—becomes an expert horseman, as his sense of balance has been greatly challenged over these first few weeks of his life.

"He wouldn't stop the wagons while his wife had the baby?" Pat sounded as incensed as I felt.

"She wasn't his wife," Maddy reminded her.

"He thought she was."

I couldn't imagine birthing a baby under those circumstances. "Poor woman. Those wagons didn't have shock absorbers, did they?" Without waiting for a reply, I said, "It's a miracle she survived."

"At least we know the baby made it okay," Sadie said, "and so did the mother."

"But who knows what else she had to put up with," Dee said.
"If you'll let me keep reading, we'll find out."

Pray God his life will be a long one—if the prayers of such a sinner as I will even be heard by the Almighty. Homer Martin has insisted on lying with me now that the babe is born, and the pain of it must be my punishment for living in sin with a man to whom I am not truly wedded.

"What a sad story," I said. "None of this was her fault. How could she possibly feel sinful when it was just a matter of circumstances that forced her into—"

Pat interrupted me. "Circumstances? It wasn't circumstances. It was those awful parents of hers."

"Well, think about it," Melissa said. "Her father was trying to see she was provided for. I'm sure he knew he was going to die, with his leg rotting off like that."

"Hmph! He was trying to get her out of his wagon 'cause he couldn't stand her crying. She even said so in her journal. And her mother is the one who really pushed her into it."

"That's the way things were back then," Carol said, effectively silencing Pat's objections. "If her mother suspected Mary Frances was pregnant, marrying her off would have been the best way to protect the whole family from scandal."

"I still think it's a shame Mary Frances felt so guilty about marrying Homer."

"I see your point, Biscuit, but the church was absolutely ironclad about such things." Carol stared at the book in Ida's hands. "Mary Frances obviously believed strongly that her soul was condemned to eternal damnation."

Pat let out an exasperated breath. "Didn't they ever hear about forgiveness?"

Ida just raised an eyebrow and kept reading.

Sarah Russell tells me that women often feel sadness after a birth. That can not explain why I have felt so constantly melancholy, ever since the beginning of December, around the time when I began having such headaches. I did so look forward to my John's birth, so I can not account for my feelings of despondency. Perhaps it is just that I have been constantly worried that Charlotte Ellis might say something that would cause Homer Martin to spurn me

Rebecca Jo motioned to Ida to stop reading, but Ida had already ground to a halt. We all looked at Charlie, but she seemed singularly unaffected.

"So what," she said when she noticed us looking at her. "That was a long time ago. And remember? I'm not that Charlotte."

"That's right," Dee said. "You're Charlie."

Sadie looked like she was going to say something, but she closed her mouth and exhaled deeply.

Ida screwed up her face, but kept reading.

... and to leave me with my babe beside the trail. I know she suspects. Young John looked so much like his father that afternoon when he was born, with the same high forehead and even the same shape to his eyes. She intimated as much, although none of the other women seemed to understand her accusation. She may dress herself in that new cap she has made, with its shirred edging, but the jauntiness of her cap is no reflection of the stony intent of her mind. The term <u>mean-spirited</u> does not even begin to describe her. I do wonder what she expects to get from me, for I am sure her heart is hard, and there is a deceitful set to her mouth that I mistrust intensely.

Rebecca Jo inspected Charlie. "It's a good thing you didn't inherit that deceitful mouth."

I couldn't help wincing, but I tried to hide it. Charlie might not be deceitful, I thought, but the way she took over the chairmanship of the library board showed she had an acquisitive mind of her own. She probably would have managed it even if Sadie hadn't nominated her.

"I don't think I would have trusted her," Sadie said. "Charlotte, I mean."

Carol nodded slowly. "People haven't changed much over the past two hundred and some odd years."

"I think you're right," Pat said. "There're still folks who would undercut someone else every chance they get."

"There are also," Rebecca Jo said with a pointed edge to her voice, "still people who are kind and just, generous and"—here she looked at me—"exceedingly accommodating."

"Loving," Sadie said.

"Tender," Glaze added, and I was amused by her blush. She must have really been looking forward to her wedding night. Certainly I imagined it would be a whole world different from what Mary Frances had gone through with Homer. No wonder Mary Frances wrote backwards so nobody could read her thoughts.

"Entertaining," Maddy suggested with a wry look at Glaze's reddening face.

"Oh, cut the sappiness," Easton said. "There are plenty of people who would just as soon lie or steal or beat their wives or girlfriends or children …" Her voice ran down as she must have noticed the incredulous looks of all the rest of us. Not at her words, for we all knew the unhappy truth of them, but that she was so vociferous about it. I had to wonder yet again at Easton's upbringing by Rupert Hastings, her alcoholic father.

"She's right," Sadie finally said with a gentle voice. "But, Easton dear, I'd rather concentrate on the people who are good."

"And be sure the others get what they deserve," Pat said into the enveloping silence.

I certainly didn't want to say anything to Easton, mainly because I had no idea whether she needed comforting or counseling. Or both. I'd let Sadie handle it.

Ida had obviously been ignoring us all. "Wait till you hear this," she said.

If Charlotte Ellis utters a word of her suspicions, I have no doubt Mister Homer Martin would spurn me, but that woman has little right to scorn me, for her daughters are both less than pristine, if what the women say—and what my own eyes tell me—is true. I am surprised that Reverend Russell continues to shelter Charlotte and her girls, for surely he sees the looks those younger Endicott brothers give the Ellis girls, thinking they are being so casual, when it is obvious to all the women in the circle, except perhaps for Sarah Russell, who is the girls' aunt and the Endicott brothers' sister. Sarah is so pure-minded, I doubt she would suspect anything. And Reverend Russell is so god-fearing, and such a good man himself, he seems to find it hard to see sin in others—a strange set of mind for a minister of the Holy Word. If the Endicott boys are guilty of what I think they are, it is sin indeed—far greater than my sin, for Charlotte is their sister, which means Louisa and Martha are their nieces.

"Good grief," Pat breathed. "That's incest."

Ida closed the book and looked at me. She seemed to be studiously avoiding looking at Charlie, who was after all descended from these Ellis women and their incest-bred daughters. Still, there had been a lot of generations between then and now. Time for all sorts of negative traits to dissipate.

"Mary Frances seems rather forward-thinking for a woman from the seventeen hundreds," Ida said.

"You're right." I was surprised by the undercurrent of anger in my voice.

Marmalade, who was sleeping peacefully curled in my lap, stirred and let out a quiet meow.

"It *is* interesting," Carol said, "that in a time when society in general blamed the woman for any children born out of wedlock, Mary Frances"—she pointed at the journal—"lays the blame at the feet of those Endicott boys."

"Good for her." Dee grimaced. "I wonder if the term testosterone poisoning was in use back then?"

"You must be kidding," Maddy said. "Nobody even knew about—" She stopped abruptly when Dee laughed at her.

"Gotcha!"

"All right, you two," Ida said. "Settle down.

For now I choose to concentrate on the small moments of wonder that come upon me whenever I look at my child. He sleeps now, but I know that if I touch his perfect little hand, he will, even in his sleep, grasp at my finger. His own fingers with their delicate nails cannot yet reach all the way around my much larger finger. I feel so powerful when I hold him. And so helpless as well, for I am overcome with the knowledge that I may not always be here to protect him. Nor do I know what dangers may accost us on this journey and beyond it.

I asked Jane Elizabeth Hastings to stand as godmother to my son. She was, after all, there throughout his birth and has been such a help to me since. When the day came to baptize John, she asked my mother for the christening gown, the one my brothers and sisters and I wore when we were baptized, but my mother said she knew not where it was packed away. I know that to be a falsehood, but I said nothing, for how could I explain my mother's indifference to her first grandchild?

Jane Elizabeth brought out the fine piece of broidered linen that she had wrapped her own children in for their christenings. I can write no more now, for my tears are like to stain the page.

Monday 22 February 1742

IRA BRANDT OPENED the third book, the one by Isaac Watts, and thumbed through it. He recognized Hubbard's script inside the back cover. "You wrote a poem inside the cover of this book."

"I had … hoped the entire … poem would be … in this volume," Hubbard said with a great deal of difficulty through his still healing lips, "but it … was not."

Ira cringed inwardly to hear his usually well-spoken brother speak in such a halting manner. "The book is four hundred and three pages long," he said, hefting the book as if estimating its weight. "Here is the title. Philosophical Essays on Various Subjects Viz." He looked up in some confusion. "What is a viz?"

"V-i-z stands for videlicet." Hubbard managed to get the words out without opening his clenched teeth. "It means *namely*."

Ira huffed in irritation. "Why did he not just say so?" He turned back to the cover and read the entire title.

Philosophical
Essays
On
Various Subjects, Viz.
Space, Substance, Body, Spirit, the Operati-
ons of the Soul in Union with the Body,
Innate Ideas, Perpetual Consciousness, Place
and Motion of Spirits, the Departing Soul,
the Resurrection of the Body, the Producti-
on and Operations of Plants and Animals;
With Some REMARKS on Mr. Locke's Essay on the
Human Understanding.
To which is Subjoined
A Brief Scheme of ONTOLOGY,
OR
The Science of BEING in general
with its Affections.

Ira was silent for quite some time. "That is the longest title I ever read."

"That," Hubbard observed, "is the most you have read in the past ten years."

2000

"KEEP GOING, IDA," Sadie said.

But Ida shook her head. "Her next entry isn't until Christmas of that year. What about you, Biscuit?"

I slipped on the gloves and opened Hubbard's journal. "April. His writing looks a lot sloppier here than it did in the last entry. I wonder why?"

1 April 1742. This morning I told Ira of my marriage. I do believe he has had a true change of heart. I am distressed that my writing is so far degraded, but I find it hard to focus on the page with but one eye.

"Oh no!" I felt something constrict inside me. "Not Hubbard."

This is the first I have written in five months, for I have lived through the greatest hell imaginable. No. That is not so. The greatest hell is knowing that my wife lies ever farther from me and that I have tarried here unable to follow her. This second hell is knowing that she will never now be able to accept me, for my face is scarred and twisted beyond recognition. The burns have left me unable to move much of the right side of my face, and although I have no glass to see myself, my hand reveals the horror of my countenance. I have no hearing in one ear—no ear there at all in fact for the coals into which Ira pushed me

"Pushed him?" Maddy was practically apoplectic. "Ira pushed him into a fire? What kind of monster is that man?"

"We don't know the whole …" Sadie began, but Maddy cut her off.

"Sounds pretty clear to me!"

"Settle down, Maddy. Let me keep reading."

Maddy sank back down onto her pillows, but she twisted and re-twisted her legs, as if she couldn't get settled. No wonder. I felt pretty uncomfortable myself.

… *the coals into which Ira pushed me burned it away completely—and I am blind in one eye. Had it not been for a nearly magical green potion slathered on me by an Indian woman, I feel certain I would have died of my injuries. She spoke to me in her own language, but somehow I understood her. How glad I am that I could see her with my one remaining eye. She was shaped rather like a dumpling, but she looked to me like an angel.*

I gulped and tried to fight back the tears that overwhelmed me. It was a losing battle.

April 1742

"NO," HUBARD SAID, one half of his mouth twisted in the scarred grimace that would be his only expression for the rest of his life. "I will not return to Brandtburg, Ira. Not without having found the Martins."

Ira took a deep breath. Hubbard could tell his brother was troubled, but could not discern the reason for it. He waited, sitting beside Ira on the porch steps of the cabin that had sheltered them through the winter. He looked across the dry, bent winter grasses to the heavy ring of trees, casting dark shadows even now in the mild light of this mid-afternoon. Pale green shoots of new grass sprung up throughout the clearing, and there was a dusting of green on the branches above. Blaze and Star munched contentedly. Hubbard wondered if horses were aware of the passage of time, the movement of the seasons, or did they simply accept the arrival of new grasses each year without worry?

Of course they did not worry. They had no rocking chairs.

Hubbard smiled to himself—the only way he could smile now that his face was largely immoveable. His mother had often told him that worrying was like rocking. It made you think you were doing something, but it never got you anywhere. How he missed her. How he would have loved to see her with Mary Frances.

"We need travel no farther," Ira finally said. "I no longer look for revenge. In all these months of caring for you, I have found that the blood lust in my heart has left me." He rolled a small round stone on the top of his leg with the palm of his right hand. His only hand. "I know now"—and Hubbard could hear the difficulty with which Ira mouthed the words—"that I can no longer blame Homer Martin for all that has happened." He gestured toward Hubbard's face. "I can no longer blame him for that, or"—he held up the stump of his left arm—"or even for this."

Hubbard nodded. He had sensed a change in his brother, but had not known the depth of it. "You cannot blame Homer Martin. It was not

Homer Martin who pushed me into the fire or who killed Homer's wife on the church steps." He had never, before this, voiced any resentment toward Ira. Ira, after all, had always been someone for whom rough-housing seemed to be second nature, someone whose anger simmered always just below the surface, especially since the death of his own wife only two short years ago.

Hubbard ran his open palm carefully across the still-tender scar tissue that was all that remained of the right side of his face. "I do not care to meet up with the Martins. I simply wish to see them, to find where they have gone."

What he truly wished was to see his wife, his Mary Frances, to be sure she had survived the journey, but he knew she would not ever be able to accept him as he now was, with only one eye, a deaf ear, and but half a face. He could not ask her to. But he had to know she was well. If he could but look on her one last time, he would return to Brandt-burg. Not willingly, perhaps, but with resignation and with a calm heart, knowing his wife was well.

He could feel Ira's gaze on the left side of his face—Ira never sat on Hubbard's right—but Hubbard focused his own eye on the dirt a few feet in front of the small stoop. He wondered if Ira's tendency to so position himself was out of consideration, so that Hubbard could more easily see Ira from his one good eye and hear him from his one ear, or whether Ira was still so repelled by the sight of Hubbard's ravaged face that he chose never to look at it.

Ira finally spoke. "Why?"

Hubbard thought, from the sound of his brother's voice, that he did not expect an answer.

And yet, Ira had asked, so Hubbard told him. His marriage almost one year ago, the hopes of Reverend Atherton that such a joining would help to heal the rift between the two communities, his love for Mary Frances, his fears that she might not have survived the journey.

"You came with me, then, not to join in my revenge, but to reclaim your wife?" Ira sounded incredulous.

"Is that so hard to understand? I would have gone after her that very day, or the next, if my nephew had not died and if you had not been so …" He waved a hand, not sure how to express his fear at the time that his brother might have died from the raging fever that had seemed to possess him.

In the end, he said the only thing that seemed to matter. "We are brothers, after all."

Ira swiped at his eyes and walked away, to stand before the two graves of the unknown men at the forest edge. Early spring wildflowers seemed to dance around his feet.

Hubbard picked up the small stone his brother had dropped and rubbed it between his palms. "Mary Frances." He breathed her name, soft as a prayer.

MARY FRANCES COULD not say what caused her heart to lighten, but an errant breeze passed over her face, and she almost heard her husband's voice—her real husband. "Mary Frances," the breeze seemed to say in Hubbard's voice. But then she heard young John coo in the basket on the wagon seat beside her, and she turned to rub her thumb gently along the soft curve of her baby's cheek. The horses needed little guidance, for they were well used to following the Russell wagon in front of them, so she felt comfortable ignoring the reins for several minutes as she studied her boy in the mid-afternoon light.

Mister Homer Martin generally ignored the child, which suited Mary Frances just fine. This was, after all, her baby. Not his. Hubbard's baby. Not Homer's.

2000

WHEN I FINALLY regained my composure—I wasn't the only one crying—the questions came hard and fast.

"I knew Ira was a loser all along," Maddy practically spit the words, "but this is pretty low even for him. Can you imagine pushing your own brother into a bed of coals?"

"I can't believe it," I said. I don't know why I felt compelled to defend Ira Brandt, but Carol looked at me gratefully.

"He might have been drunk," she said. "Maybe it was an accident?"

Rebecca Jo reached up and smoothed her palm over her own face. I noticed how some of her finger joints had begun to swell and stiffen. Why hadn't I paid attention before this? "His face," she said. "You know, we don't really have any idea what he looked liked before this happened. Mary Frances never described him in her diary."

Ida tapped her book thoughtfully. "I think that shows she wasn't much of an artist."

"I think it shows she was more of a thinker," Sadie said. "Hubbard, too. Just think about how so many young people go on and on about the looks of their latest love, but Hubbard and Mary Frances seem to have fallen in love with each other's"—she groped for the right word—"each other's essence rather than their outward appearance."

"He must have found her eventually," Carol said. "Otherwise, his journal couldn't have been tied up with hers, right?"

"But if he looked like that," Pat said, "what would her reaction have been?"

"Doggone it,"—this came from Sadie—"I want answers."

"We have one answer at least," I said. "Remember when Bob asked whether or not they'd had any dealings with Indians?" I held up Hubbard's journal. "Sounds like this woman saved his life with that green goo of hers."

"I wish we had a recipe for it," Sadie said.

"I loved his description of her," Rebecca Jo said. "An angel shaped like a dumpling."

What is a dumbling?

Marmalade put her paws up on Rebecca Jo's lap and demanded a scratch, which Rebecca Jo seemed happy to provide.

Mouse droppings!

"A dumpling," Carol told Marmalade, "is a roundish lump of dough—bread—that's cooked on top of stew. Do you know what stew is?"

Yes. Thank you.

Marmalade jumped up and kneaded Rebecca Jo's tummy.

Rebecca Jo laughed. "Is she saying I'm shaped like a dumpling?"

Sadie smoothed her hand over her green sweatshirt. "I think I'd fit that description better than you, although occasionally I look at myself in the mirror and imagine a fire hydrant."

"And to think how you were always so skinny when you were a

girl," Rebecca Jo said.

"You know," I said, "some of my favorite people ever have been shaped like a dumpling, or"—I smiled at Sadie—"a hydrant."

"They sure can give good hugs." Pat had a wistful look in her eyes. "My Aunt Annette was so … so comforting to snuggle against when I was a little girl."

I happened to glance at Charlie just then. I couldn't interpret the look on her face. It seemed sort of blank. I hoped she didn't have bad memories. Maybe she never got hugs?

January 1996

"MY DAD ALWAYS gave the best hugs," Charlie told Tricia. She crawled into bed and waited to turn out the lamp on her bedside table until her roommate was tucked in across the room. "Dad was tall and strong and so gentle. I remember once when a stray kitten wandered into our yard and I found it and took it inside. Dad didn't even have to think twice about it. He just hugged me and told me I could keep it, and he asked if I wanted to become a vet."

"A vet?"

"Don't sound so incredulous. I probably could have done it. If I could have gotten through chemistry." Charlie laughed at her own silliness. "All right, so I couldn't have been a vet. I'm scared of needles. And blood. I don't think I ever could have operated on anybody, especially not a cat or a dog. But the point is that every time my dad hugged me, it was like he was passing his belief in me right into my brain."

Tricia was quiet for such a long time, Charlie thought she might have dropped off to sleep. Charlie turned over onto her side, but before she could relax fully, Tricia spoke.

"I finally saved enough money to get that dent in my fender repaired."

Charlie laughed again, this time at her roommate. "You're funny," she said, when what she really meant was that she was sorry Tricia never seemed to be able to express her feelings. Charlie wondered if poor Tricia had ever gotten a hug from either of her parents before they died. Maybe she hadn't, and that was why she was more comfortable talking about car repair than about hugging.

1758

PARLEY BREETON LAY next to Lucky while her brother—her half-brother—Willy held Lucky's black and white head and said goodbye. He did not even seem to mind that Parley could see him crying so hard. Maybe it was because Parley was crying, too.

"She is such a good dog," Parley said. "All my life she has protected me."

"Me, too," Willy said through a volley of hiccups, brought on no doubt by his tears.

Lucky whined and tried to lift her old head, but the effort seemed to be too much for her.

"Remember how she used to lie beside your basket and growl at anybody who came near?"

"I could not possibly remember that," Parley reminded him. "I was just a baby."

"Well, I remember it." He lifted Lucky's right front paw and leaned forward to place the unresponsive foot on top of Parley's shoulder. Parley reached up to hold hands with Lucky, something she had done so often in her thirteen years.

"She is seventeen years old," Willy said. "Almost eighteen. I have known her since she was born."

"I know," Parley said. "You were eight. You have told me often enough."

Their tears dwindled as they talked of all the wondrous things Lucky had done over the many years of her extra-long dog life. Just as Willy was recounting the oft-told tale of the turkey leg Lucky stole from old Widow Black's marriage table, the elderly dog slipped away. When Willy realized what had happened, the tears came again. Parley hugged Lucky again and again, and cried as hard as Willy did.

The two of them worked together that day to dig a grave near the Old Church beneath an oak tree where Lucky had once enjoyed chasing squirrels.

Friday, 16 April 1742
Allensburg, Pennsylvania

HUBBARD AND IRA approached Allensburg carefully. Hubbard was not at all sure he should let himself be seen. Thanks to the Indian woman's green medicine, he was no longer in pain, and he could bear having his skin touched by the morning breeze, by the hay-stuffed pillow at night, by the soft enveloping hat he wore, by his own hand. He could tell with his hand how frightening he must look, for he knew his ear had seemed to melt into the side of his face. He knew his right eye was permanently shut. He knew from having seen other burns on other people what the scars must look like. He had studiously avoided looking into any quiet streams or roadside ponds, for he did not wish to see his own countenance.

He dreaded having anyone glimpse his face. He could not bear seeing the revulsion in people's eyes when they looked at him. It was bad enough that his own brother chose never to look him in the face.

But as they rode through the outer limits of the town, Hubbard with the knit hat pulled low across his forehead and Ira with his right hand on the reins and his left arm—half an arm—carefully held against his chest, he found that none of the people paid them much mind. All around them they saw scarred faces and recognized the marks of the smallpox. He hoped they were old disfigurements, from long before the Martin wagons must have passed this way. He sent up a quick prayer that his wife be kept safe from all harm.

They stopped at the tavern to order a noonday meal. Hubbard could not help asking the proprietor, "I see you have had trouble with the pox here. Has it been long over?"

The man eyed him, lifting one brow as if to ask what right Hubbard had to inquire, or perhaps he was simply trying to decipher Hubbard's words, for Hubbard's speech was still impaired by the scarring. Hubbard turned his head so his withered right cheek was clearly visible. The man cleared his throat. "You look as though you have had troubles of your own."

Hubbard nodded.

"You need not worry about the pox as well. It seemed to burn itself out some two years ago." Hubbard let out a sigh of relief, but the innkeeper appeared not to notice. "It left us with more than half the town dead and the rest marked for life."

"But alive," Hubbard said carefully.

"If you can call it that."

Ira drained his cup. "We are following a group of some ninety or more travelers who may have come this way in the past year. Know you aught of them?"

The innkeeper polished the counter, already worn smooth over many years, with a linen cloth. "Aye. I rue the day they ever came to this town. Are they friends of yours?"

"Never," said Ira.

"They took my wife with them," Hubbard said, and he could not keep the bitterness from his voice.

"I hope you find them, then. Three of their young men raised havoc here one night and broke a good many of my cups, and a number of my chairs as well."

Hubbard looked at Ira. "The Endicott brothers, most likely."

"Aye. That is the name they used." He smiled unexpectedly. "I insisted that they pay, and they refused because of a lack of ready money, but they replaced the chairs—and the cups, too—with ones from their own wagon."

As they left the tavern after a substantial noon meal, a small girl ran down the middle of the road, spinning a hoop beside her. Hubbard watched her, but as she came closer, he averted his face. The child might be used by now to the scarring of smallpox, but he had no wish to frighten her with his own face.

She was a lovely child, unmarked with scars. How he had longed to have a child, children, with Mary Frances, but knowing that would now be impossible, he longed instead just to clasp his arms around his wife one more time and to feel her wrap her arms around his neck.

2000

"SHALL I KEEP reading?"

Everybody nodded, so I went on, pulling out my hankie to have it handy just in case.

Friday 16 April 1742. In but two days I will have been a married man for one complete year. There is little reason for celebration. Ira is tossing in his bedroll, no doubt afflicted by dreams of torment, for he has told me he seems at times to feel his missing arm beset by the most terrible gnawings, as if some beast had got hold of it. I feel no such distress over the loss of my ear, for there was nothing left of it but ash, according to what my brother tells me. I must ask him repeatedly for details, for he prefers not to speak of those events of early December. I write by the light of a feeble fire. The night is fairly balmy.

"Last December," I said. "Ida, remember that entry when Mary Frances said she'd been having the most horrible headaches? When was that?"

She quirked an eyebrow at me, but lifted the Mary Frances journal and thumbed back a few pages. "January twenty-third," she said. "Here's what she said. *Ever since the beginning of December, around the time when I began having such headaches.*"

"You're right," Rebecca Jo said. "Mary Frances was feeling Hubbard's pain."

"Don't be ridiculous," Charlie said.

I glared at her. "It's not ridiculous. The two of them were connected in a very special way."

Charlie scratched at her elbow, as if none of this mattered.

It did matter, though.

I looked across the circle at Sadie, who was staring incredulously at Charlie.

It was an accident. I have come to regard it as such. It was but an irritated shove from Ira, one of many he has given me over the years, that sent me headfirst into the coals. Would that I had doused the fire sooner. This noon we stopped in Allensburg in the colony of Pennsylvania. They were beleaguered by the small pox two years ago, but thankfully it burned its way out well before the time my wife came through. The tavern keeper remembered them—and the argumentative Endicott brothers in particular—and pointed us in the right direction. As we left, I saw a small girl spinning her hoop along the road, and I turned my ravaged face away from her, partly to save her tender feelings, but I am loath to admit that part of what I felt was shame, for I feel the revulsion and the pity in the eyes of those few who are brave enough to look at me.

When I finished reading that entry, Ida picked up the Mary Frances journal and turned carefully to the right page. "Humph. He makes such a big deal about their anniversary, and here she can't be bothered even to mention it."

"When's her next entry?"

"May twentieth."

"Maybe she was busy," I said. "After all, she had a baby to care for."

Ida didn't looked convinced, but then again, Ida had never had a child, so she probably had no idea how time consuming a baby could be. Especially back then with no running water, no washing machines, no conveniences of any kind.

Sunday 18 April 1742
Somewhere along the trail

WITH ONE HAND, Mary Frances lifted the bucket of fresh water from the river. With the other, she held the large scarf she had tied around her neck and steadied the baby inside it. Young John was thriving, for which she was grateful indeed, but his increased weight made it ever harder for her to complete her chores in a timely manner. Still, she knew he was less trouble to her like this than he would be when he began to crawl around, for then she would have to be constantly vigilant that he not range too near the fire or stuff his mouth with something noxious from the ground. Even now he was fretting to be fed. This child's appetite was voracious.

She thought with longing of her precious journal, tucked away as it was in the bottom of her sewing basket. There was no time for her to write. There was so little peace in her household—in her wagon—

except when she was alone with John. But even then, her peace was bounded by a nervous fear that Mister Homer Martin might walk in on her when she was unaware. No wonder women rejoiced when they had numerous children, for the older girls could always tend the younger ones, and, of course, the boys would be there to provide homes for their parents as they aged.

Across the camp she espied Mister Homer Martin in close conversation with the other men of the group who had already gathered for the Sunday services, even though they would not begin for another hour. He bothered her seldom, and she had learned to endure it—thankful that, so far at least, she seemed unable to conceive by him. She needed no daughters, and certainly no sons sired by Homer Martin. If she had been with her true husband, with Hubbard, she would have been delighted to bear many children for him.

She handed over the water to Mistress Russell and retreated to the wagon to feed her child. As she bared a breast for him, she thought back to this day exactly one year ago when she had become the wife of Hubbard Brandt. One entire year, and still he had not come for her. Young John did not seem to mind the tears that wet his sweet cheeks as he fed.

IN JUST TWO days, Charlotte Ellis thought as she stirred the pottage, it will be a full year we have been on this God-forsaken trail. She studied the men of the group, who seemed to be in earnest conversation beside the Russell's wagon, but knowing what she did of men's conversation, having overheard many in the barren cabin she had shared with her husband before his death, they were most likely each trying to outdo the other with tales of their own prowess.

She averted her eyes from them, lest they remind her too much of her late husband, the unpalatable Rupell Ellis. She spotted Mary Frances Martin climbing into her wagon, no doubt to feed her mewling bastard. Charlotte scoffed, earning her an inquisitive glance from her sister Sarah, who gestured toward the pot above the fire.

"Is there something amusing about our upcoming meal?"

Charlotte simply stared at Sarah, which was generally effective, but today it did not quiet Sarah's comments.

"I find it hard to believe we have traveled for nigh on a year now." Sarah sounded resigned about it rather than angry, the way Charlotte was.

"With a fool like Homer Martin leading us, it is no wonder we have been this long."

"Hush, Sister." Sarah looked around her, so obviously wanting to be sure none could overhear them. "Such words can only bring dissension."

"I'll thank you not to silence me. Such words are the truth."

Sarah tightened her lips, as if to keep back a ready retort. "Truth or not," she finally said, "they are words that are better left unspoken."

2000

"THE JOHNSONS CAN'T be having nearly as much fun as we are." We'd taken a little break from the journals, and Maddy's head was stuck down inside yet another trunk. Her voice reverberated a bit. "Or any of the other families that have wood stoves."

"Not unless they have an attic to be cleaned out as well," Carol said.

Melissa stepped up next to Carol. "You still don't have a hat of your own."

Carol reached up and pulled her auburn braid around over her shoulder. "That's because hats all make me look like—what did you call it, Ida?—like I sprouted a tail."

"Nonsense!" Sadie pointed to another stack of hatboxes—wherever had that came from? I hadn't noticed it before. "Start at the top and keep looking until you find one. There's bound to be one that will be perfect for you."

I sure hoped Sadie was right. Carol looked both doubtful and hopeful at the same time.

"I'll help," Melissa said. "There has to be something for everybody. Who else doesn't have a hat yet?"

"Besides yourself, you mean?"

"I don't need one, Sadie." She patted her bear claw necklace. "No hat could compete with this. Now, who else needs one?"

Five hands went up. Rebecca Jo, Sadie, Amanda, Sylvia, and my mom. Charlie didn't have a hat, but she didn't raise her hand. Fine with me.

We spent a lot of time laughing as hat after hat went into the reject pile, but then, about half-way through the stack, we hit pay dirt. Sadie picked a light blue cloche, Rebecca Jo chose a straw affair with a wide brim, Amanda found a perky little bright red piece that perched at an angle. I'd never realized just how attractive Amanda was, but the hat seemed to liven her up. Tom's mother was delighted with a dark gray wrap-around turban, and an orange and black houndstooth concoction with a wide orange band was perfect for my mother.

"Ivy," Sadie said when she tried it on, "Do you still have that bright orange caftan you bought in Arizona a couple of years ago?"

Mom grinned. "I sure do. I was planning to wear it to the wedding."

"This will be perfect with it."

"Looks like you're out of luck, Carol," Charlie said. "There's only one hatbox left."

"Only in this stack," Sadie said. She pointed across the attic. "Look over there, between those two dressers." She was right. We still had a lot of hatboxes to go through.

But we didn't have to. This one was perfect, almost as if it had been made for her. It was shaped rather like a fisherman's cap, with a stiff brim that hugged Carol's forehead. Her braid looked completely natural, almost as if the hat had been made for someone with a thick auburn braid. Come to think of it, maybe it had.

1816

CATHARINA FARNER WONDERED if her rather successful millinery business would have to cease after she married next week. After all, she and her new husband would be moving to Garner Creek, and that was a far piece for anyone to travel. Still, the women of her new town would need hats, surely. She knew her skills would be admired. At least, she hoped they would.

It was ironic, she thought, that so many women here in Martin's

Village had ordered new hats to wear to Catharina's wedding, which was planned to be a large affair. She had written and written and written note after note after note, inviting most of the town. They could have had the invitations printed, for the newspaper offices ran a thriving printing business in addition to the publication of the weekly paper, but her husband preferred an old-fashioned approach. He had not volunteered to help her with the writing, though. "Your hand is so much more elegant than mine" had been his excuse.

Still, she had managed to send off every invitation on time. Then, she had been flooded with orders for new hats, which had kept her hands even busier than the invitations had.

This particular order, though, baffled her, which is why she had saved it for the very last. Whatever would she do for her Aunt Betsey? Auntie's unruly hair could be tamed only when it was corralled into a tight braid that hung over her shoulder and looked like nothing so much as a fraying gray rope.

She knew she would have to come up with something new, something daring. She rooted through several piles of fabrics until she found a washed-out looking length of silk that had been used for drapes over the windows in the main room. It had started life as a vibrant coral shade, but exposure to the sun streaming in over the years had drained it of its color where the sun stuck it each day, and left stripes of brighter color where the drapes had bunched together in folds.

Catharina was so glad her mother, Marella Martin Farner, never threw away anything.

Most of the bonnets that were considered to be in high style had wide front brims, almost like a sunbonnet, but much stiffer. They wrapped around the front of the face down as far as the chin. Catharina privately thought they looked like blinders on a horse, but they were in great demand. She laughed, imagining what Aunt Betsey would look like wearing one of those with her rat tail hanging from one side. No, this cap would be completely different. A new fashion altogether.

As she gathered the heavy silk into intricate folds across the entire surface of the cap, she delighted in the ways the coral color seemed to fade in and out, rather like dappled shadows moving across a field of bright wildflowers.

YEARS LATER, BEFORE Betsey died, she directed that her hat, which had caused such a stir at Catharina's wedding all those years before, be given to her niece, Grace Surratt Hoskins. It was completely unsuitable for Grace, of course, as Betsey well knew. Soon after the funeral, Grace consigned the hat to the attic.

2000

"OH!" MADDY EXCLAIMED as she rooted around in her trunk a few minutes after we'd all dispersed. "Look at this christening gown. Isn't it sweet?"

Ida stuck her head over the edge of Maddy's trunk. "It looks like baby what's-his-name threw up all over himself during the service."

Maddy held up what I could see was a long brown-stained dress edged in delicate lace. "And probably all over the minister as well," she said, "considering the size of that stain."

Amanda chuckled. "They should have used some blueing."

"There's another bad spot." Dee pointed to the bottom edge of the long garment where a second stain etched a swath of dull brown over the white lace tatting and halfway up the skirt.

"It's no wonder it's stained," Sadie said. "That thing was most likely passed down from one generation to the next. Wallace was christened in a gown that came from his ten-times-great-grandmother."

"Why not eleven times?" Maddy asked with a chuckle, obviously not expecting an answer.

"There's a good reason." Sadie adjusted the sleeve of her green sweatshirt. "Up until the 1600s, babies were wrapped in what was called a *bearing cloth* for their baptisms. It was usually a large piece of silk or linen with braiding on the edges. Eventually, though, the practice of christening gowns got started, and the gowns became more and more elaborate as the years went on, and fewer and fewer people used the bearing cloths. My mother-in-law gave me Wallace's christening gown, since she didn't have any daughters to pass it on to. It's packed away in my attic. It has very few stains, and it's really lovely."

"I should think you'd want to display it," Carol said.

"Oh no," Sadie said. "I never had it out because … because it wasn't yellow. Maybe I'll have to rethink that."

While we all smiled at Sadie, Maddy spread the stained christening gown across the second card table. "Don't you wonder who this belonged to?"

May 1742
Along the trail, somewhere in northern Pennsylvania

SARAH RUSSELL THREW her hands up in exasperation. "I swear, Charlotte, can you not keep those daughters of yours from bringing shame on our whole family? The Reverend has a hard enough time maintaining decency in his flock without your two girls flaunting their … their wares"—she fairly spit the word—"like this."

Sarah had kept her voice as low as possible, considering her extreme displeasure, but Charlotte noticed a most unflattering redness gathering on Sarah's cheeks.

Charlotte Ellis looked down at Jane, the three-month-old granddaughter she held in her arms. What was a mother to do? They had not been four months on the trail when her Louisa had shown definite signs of being in a family way. And now Martha was growing rotund, unable anymore to hide her advanced pregnancy no matter how much she loosened her stays.

"Are you just going to sit there," Sarah hissed, "and do nothing?"

Charlotte looked down her nose—difficult to do when one was seated and the object being looked at was standing, but Charlotte had perfected that look through many long years of practice—and inspected Sarah in a manner she knew Sarah found to be irritating. "It seems a bit late for me to do anything at all, sister."

"If we lived in any other community than this one, and if your minister was anyone other than my husband, those two daughters of yours would have been turned out into the streets long ago. Why did you not begin some years ago teaching them to keep their hands to themselves and to save their bodies for the sanctity of marriage?"

Charlotte narrowed her eyes. Sanctity of marriage, indeed. If Sarah had been married to Rupell Ellis instead of to the Right Reverend

Anders Russell, she would have changed her tune about just how sanctified such a union had been. Charlotte's arms tightened around young Jane when she saw in her mind—entirely without her own volition, because she tried never to think of it anymore—the way in which her husband's face had turned such a disgusting shade of blue fifteen years ago, only a few hours after she had fed him a stew in which she had ground up seven castor beans. Louisa and Martha had been quite small at the time, but Charlotte often wondered just how much they knew of the things their father had done. Or of what their mother had done. Charlotte had never considered that Louisa and Martha might have had an inkling of what had gone on that long-ago night.

Nonsense. Of course not. They had been far too young.

Was it any wonder, though, that Charlotte had never encouraged them to marry—except for that brief time when she had thought to chain one of them to Homer Martin. What had she been thinking? They were better unmarried. Reverend Anders would never turn them out. They would always have a home. She looked around her at the bleak circle of wagons and carts. Not much of a home at the moment, but once they reached their new settling place in the warmer lands, things would improve.

Was it any wonder, too, that she tried to protect her girls in any way she could? And knowing how Sarah would have berated her, was it any wonder Charlotte had never confided in her sister, Sarah Endicott Russell, wife of the oh-so-upright minister? How could she possibly expect Sarah to understand her need to use the deadly castor beans?

Baby Jane squirmed in her arms and Charlotte, who had never been that fond of children, found that her heart felt differently about this particular child. Whether Martha had a girl-child or a boy-child growing within her, Charlotte was sure she would love it, but she sincerely hoped it was not a boy. Boys grew up into men. And Charlotte had no place for any more men in her life.

WHEN MARTHA GAVE birth to a girl three months later, Charlotte brought out the christening gown she, as the eldest daughter, had inherited. Both she and Sarah had worn it, as had Charlotte's two daughters and all of Sarah's children. And, of course, Louisa's daughter, little Jane. There had been much dissension among the company when Charlotte had insisted that Jane be baptized, but Anders Russell was soft-hearted and believed that the sins of a mother should not be visited upon the head of a small babe—which, as even Charlotte knew, was in direct contradiction to the teachings of many churches. Still, who was she to complain when it suited her purposes that he should believe that way?

It was a rainy October day, but tradition was important, and the christening gown was a tradition going back for quite a few generations. Charlotte ignored the disapproving looks of a number of the women in the company and held a blanket over the child Martha had insisted upon naming Alice.

The baby must have felt the same way about her name as her grandmother did, because at the very moment when Reverend Anders pronounced the child's name, tiny Alice Ellis spewed the not-inconsiderable contents of her fat little tummy all over the gown, her mother, and the minister as well. Charlotte had, of course, stepped back in time to avoid the mess.

Within days, Sarah began working in the evening firelight to fashion a new christening gown, planning for the time her own brood would have children of their own.

Years later, Charlotte's granddaughters Jane and Alice had Ellis daughters of their own—outside the sanctity of marriage so often preached by their great-uncle Anders. They used the gown with the brown Alice Ellis stains, stains that Alice's grandmother Charlotte Ellis had been unable to wash away.

None of Sarah's descendants ever again used the stained gown, for despite the fact that Sarah loved her sister and stood by her husband's decision to baptize the bastard offspring of Charlotte's daughters and granddaughters, Sarah felt at a deep level, which she herself did not even recognize, that the stains on the christening gown went far deeper than a mere blotch on the linen.

Eventually, one of Charlotte's descendants threw the gown away, but it was retrieved from the rubbish pile by an inquisitive child, who brought it home to Beechnut House and tried to clean it so she could dress her cornhusk dolly in it. When that did not work, she left it in the attic.

2000

CHARLIE FINGERED THE edge of the gown and then stepped back away from it. "My mother dropped me on my head the day I was christened," she said, and we all gasped.

"I don't remember that," Sadie said.

Charlie looked confused. "You were there?"

"Well of course, dear. You had the brightest red hair of any baby I'd ever seen. Everybody wanted to touch it, and you smiled at all of us. I saw quite a bit of you when you were a little girl, but I suppose you wouldn't remember that. You were only seven or eight when your mother moved away."

Charlie nodded. "That was when she married my dad. In Atlanta."

Sadie nodded. "That makes sense. Your mom was always something of a rebel." She frowned. "I may be old, but I think I would have remembered if she'd dropped you during your christening."

Charlie pushed a wayward strand of black hair away from her forehead. "She … she told me it happened afterwards, after the christening. She … she never told anybody. I guess she was too embarrassed. And she said I seemed to be fine. I didn't throw up or anything."

Wednesday, September 27, 2000

CLARA THOUGHT SHE was going to throw up. She'd counted on sleeping a good deal later than this. After all that had happened the day before, the argument she'd had with Hubbard, and … and everything else, she needed sleep. When the pounding started on the front door, she stumbled out of bed and didn't even think to ask who was there first.

"Clara," Bob Sheffield said, "may I come in? I have some bad news."

She took a step back, feeling utterly disoriented. "What? What is it?" She hadn't heard her children up and about, but then again they always waited for her to wake them up.

Bob ushered her into the living room. "I'm afraid it's Hubbard.

He seems to have fallen off the cliff. Hoss Cartwright discovered him just a few minutes ago."

"Is he … is he dead?"

"No, he's alive, but he's badly injured."

"Alive?" Clara sat without even thinking about whether or not the couch was directly behind her. Fortunately, Bob grabbed her in time.

Saturday, 1 May 1742

MARY FRANCES CLUTCHED her babe to her breast, hastily wrapping her shawl as tightly around the two of them as she could manage. She placed her hand over the baby's head, and bent forward, hoping to protect him from the heavy, bouncing hailstones that pounded the back of her body with a ferocious intensity, as if some evil genie had been unloosed from the sky and was intent on destruction.

She was glad indeed that Geonette Surratt was driving the team. Had Mary Frances held the reins, her babe would have been in the basket at her feet or beside her and might already have been killed by one of the murderous hailstones.

The sudden storm had come upon them so quickly there had been no time to circle the wagons, and the canvas covers had provided little protection from the pounding of the ice balls.

"Women and children! Under the wagons," Silas shouted. "Men, unhitch your horses. To the shelter of the trees!"

Geonette pulled the horses to a halt, even as Homer and Silas sprang toward the team. "Here, Mary Frances!" Geonette held out her hand. "Let me help you down. You hold the child safe, and I'll steady—" Her words were cut short as an enormous hailstone crashed onto her arm. Geonette screamed and fell backward off the wagon wheel where she had perched to aid Mary Frances.

Mary Frances scrambled down as best she could, supporting her shawl-enclosed baby with one hand and hanging onto the side of the wagon with the other. She managed to help Geonette to her knees but could do little in aid of the obviously broken bone of Geonette's forearm. They both struggled to crawl under the creaking wagon, hampered by their long petticoats, their sodden skirts, and the pelting hail.

Throughout the caravan, women scurried to herd the children, placing the smallest ones directly under the center of each wagon while the older children and the women surrounded them as best they could, their backs turned to the onslaught as they crouched under cover.

The goats, with their built-in good sense, had already scurried beneath the heavy limbs of nearby trees. Thank the good Lord they had been passing through a heavily forested area when the storm hit. Cows, oxen, and horses, though, had run in all directions—some farther along the trail, some back the way they had come, and thankfully, many for the trees. The saddled horses had strained against their riders who tried to steer the terrified livestock toward the leafy shelter. Mary Frances saw Nehemiah Garner half carried away by his panicking stallion, until he managed somehow to bring its head down and bully it into the lee provided by long-branched maples and oaks. Had the storm hit sooner in the year, before the leaves had fully unfurled, there well might have been tragedy indeed.

Beside her, Geonette Surratt cried and cradled her arm.

Young John whimpered in hunger, and Mary Frances left the tending of Geonette to the other women who had sheltered with them. She fed her babe, back braced against the incursion of hailstones that continued to bounce under the wagon, until they had piled up into a barrier two feet high.

2000

"**YOUR MOM MUST** have been really scared when she dropped you," Dee said to Charlie, who shrugged.

Rebecca Jo nodded at Dee's comment. "That just proves you don't have to be traveling in the seventeen hundreds for something scary to happen."

Maddy lifted her elbow into the air and gave an exaggerated sniff at her armpit. "If we're here much longer, something scary's going to happen. Everybody's going to die from asphyxiation."

"I told you how to take a bath with a cup of warm water," Sadie began.

"Bet they didn't have many baths along the trail," Dee said.

"And certainly not with warm water," Carol agreed.

Saturday 8 May 1742

"I DO NOT see why we have to take a bath," Able Garner grumbled loudly enough for all the boys in the loose circle to hear, but not quite loud enough, he hoped, for any of the nearby women's ears to pick up what he said. "We had one last summer after we left Brandtburg, so it hasn't even been a year yet."

Constance, his sister, swished her skirts in that way all the women folk seemed to have. It made Able feel just a little scared, but he tried not to admit it. Maybe not scared, exactly, but his big sister had changed a lot in the past year or two. She was not nearly as much fun anymore, and she was a lot more … he was not sure exactly what had happened to her. But she seemed more grown somehow. Not just rounder in certain places that he tried not to look at but somehow could not quite keep his eyes away from, but like she took up more room than she used to.

"I will not have you smelling like a pig sty during my wedding," Constance said, loud enough for everybody to hear and to laugh about it.

Able stifled a cheeky grin as he considered whether or not he could smuggle a couple of the new piglets into the wagon she'd be moving to tomorrow after she got married. She thought she was all grownup now that she was set to marry Willem Breeton, but Able knew Constance was only a few years older than Mister Breeton's four children.

"Go on, the lot of you," Constance said, and made shooing motions with the bundle of linen clothes she held.

"You will not get a bit of evening food," Mistress Russell said, "until you come back clean and dry and better-smelling than now."

The other women closed in, and the whole group of them advanced with a sense of purpose that set the boys to scattering toward the river. The threat of a delayed meal was more convincing than any other argument, though, and the boys were already persuaded that taking their yearly bath would be in their best interest. The men followed behind the women, with that consciousness of inevitability that came on all of them every year. Everyone knew the women and girls would soon veer off to bathe themselves upstream, around a generous bend, well-shielded by trees and low-growing shrubs from the sight of the men and boys.

It was always like this with the yearly springtime bath, except that back in Brandtburg spring had come later in the year. Able kept hoping as they traveled and the weather became warmer, that maybe they would not find a river that was both deep enough for the bathing and shallow enough not to sweep them all downstream and drown them. Luck was not with him, though, for this land they traveled through now was rife with rivers, all of them seeming to be just the right depth.

By the time they reached the water, though, the boys had forgotten all their objections. They stripped with abandon, ignoring any goose bumps brought on by the late spring day, enjoying the feel of the sun on their winter-bleached bodies, and reveling in the lack of constriction from any sort of clothing. The water was not too cold, even though there had been that unexpected hailstorm just a week before. Able knew this meant the weather upstream must have warmed quite a bit. It was a good sign, even if they did have to have a bath.

Pioneer Breeton pushed his brother Willy into the water. Willy's dog, Lucky, barked at the gleeful sport and plunged into the stream, soon joined by all the other dogs in the company. Charles and Lucius Hastings raced each other to see who could reach the water first, while Thomas Russell and his father, the minister, stepped into the stream with a great deal more dignity. Able privately thought that Thomas, now he had turned twenty, was almost as stuffed as Constance.

Gradually all the men followed into the large pool, good-naturedly shoving each other, dunking anyone they could reach, and bellowing a great deal.

Why did I ever complain about this? Able wondered, but of course, he did not say it out loud. Complaining about the bath every year for all of his thirteen years was a time-honored custom he had learned from his brother and his father. He loved water, truly he did. He had always wanted to live beside a river, or at least a creek. If he lived here, he would name this place Garner River. Baths seemed an unnecessary imposition, but water itself was great fun.

He splashed Willy, dunked Lucius, and forgot about his scheme to put the piglets into Constance's marriage bed.

When three of the Endicott brothers tried to sneak out of the river and worm their way upstream through the bushes to spy on the women, Reverend Russell raised his voice to stentorian tones and ordered them back. Able hoped that someday his own voice could bellow that loudly.

"THANK YOU, EDNA," Constance said as soon as Edna Russell loosened Constance's heavy braid. The two of them, dear friends since early childhood, sat in naught but their shifts on a large boulder that had been pleasantly warmed by the cloudless sun. They watched idly as the older women in the group scrubbed at the younger girls and washed the small children with gentle hands. The laughter spreading through the small dell was a welcome sound, combined though it was with the insistent whine of myriad mosquitoes and overlaid with the muted shouts of the boys and men from downstream beyond the bend.

"I'll just comb this through," Edna said, her own hair hanging limp around her shoulders where Constance had already combed it for her. "Otherwise it will be a terrible tangle once it is wet."

Constance Garner loved the yearly routine of bathing and of washing her hair. She had been known, although it was looked on askance by the other women, to pour water from the rain barrel over her head several times each summer and then to comb her hair dry under the hot sun. There were no rain barrels on this journey, though, and she had spent the past year feeling the want of refreshment. Washing her hands and face—and often enough her feet as well—was all very well and good, but it did nothing to spruce up her hair.

She and the other women had gathered enough spring herbs and roots so they all could refresh themselves, rubbing the sudsy roots over their bodies and ending the ritual with pouring kettles of warm, herb-steeped water over their heads. The fragrance never lasted long enough, to her way of thinking, but for a few precious weeks, all the women—with the exception of the elderly Widow Black who flatly refused to bathe—went about their daily work surrounded by a scented cloud of lemon balm and rosemary.

As if her thought of the elderly widow had taken physical form, Widow Black stomped up beside the rock where Constance and Edna sat. "Humph," she snorted. "All this fuss. Makes no sense." She proceeded to remove her outer clothing, revealing a bedraggled shift that had seen far better days. "Made myself a new shift," she said, sounding as if it were somebody's fault other than her own. "Might as well put it on a clean body."

By this time, the other women had noticed the presence of Widow Black. This was the woman who had spent years telling everyone that bathing was completely unnecessary. They moved back in awe as she loosened the ties on her shift and let it drop to the ground.

There was total silence as the thoroughly naked and thoroughly wrinkled old woman stepped into the water.

Constance turned to look at Edna. "Did you see what I just saw or was it a vision of some sort?"

Edna whispered back at her, "There has to be a reason."

There was nothing wrong with Widow Black's hearing. "Constance," she announced, "is not the only one who is getting hitched. I will marry one week from today."

Eyebrows went up, whispers turned to mutters, which swelled up into full-voiced questions. Constance had to stifle her laughter. Anyone could see that widow Black had determined on old Mister Richard Hastings almost as soon as she was widowed, that horrible day before they left Brandtburg a year gone past. But a bath? For someone who most likely had never had one in all the years since she was a child?

Constance and Edna finally joined a small group of the other women in the water, where Constance endured several minutes of good-natured ribbing about her upcoming wedding night. She had heard such comments before, of course, but after her mother's somewhat garbled instructions earlier this morning as they rode the wagon through a tall heavily-leaved forest of beech and elm and silver maples, she knew—or thought she knew—a bit more of what they laughed about.

Some of the women, though, did not join in. They had bathed quickly and then had withdrawn to the far side of the pool, almost as if they did not want to be a part of the gaiety. Geonette Surratt, of course, was there, her broken arm held still in a sling around her neck. It would have hurt her arm too much to try to get her clothes off. Geonette did not look happy about the arrangement, for she always enjoyed her bath as much as Constance did.

Constance watched her sister for a few moments. Mary Frances sat on the far bank just beyond Geonette, feeding her infant son. Over the past few months, Constance had grown increasingly aware of the fact that Mary Frances never spoke to their mother, nor did Mother ever seem to approach Mary Frances. Augusta Hastings Garner was not the most affable of women, but heretofore—while they lived back in Brandtburg—Mary Frances and their mother had worked together equably enough in the Garner home. Constance thought back over the journey, trying to determine when the rift had developed. A very deep rift it was.

Constance remembered clearly the day John was born. Mother had not set foot in the Martin wagon that day. Why not? Why truly not? She had used some excuse. Able had felt poorly, or some such reason. Had Mother ever held young John? Constance could not call to mind a single instance. She had not attended the baptism, either. Again, some feeble excuse.

Geonette giggled suddenly, and Constance looked in time to see that the other women around Geonette laughed aloud or at the very least, they smiled. Mary Frances, though, hardly changed her expression. Not even a lift of the corners of her mouth. She looked—what? Constance could not place the expression. Unhappy? That was it. She looked ineffably sad. Mary Frances had never confided in Constance, but Constance knew Mary Frances had seldom smiled ever since they had left Brandtburg. The only one who could bring a smile to her sister's face was John, Mary Frances and Homer's first child, and—so far—their only child.

Sunday afternoon, 9 May 1742

SUSAN BREETON STOOD in silence next to the Garner wagon between her sister MaryAnne and her brother Pioneer. Beyond MaryAnne, their father—the bridegroom—stood straight. Susan was aware, though, that his hands shook. Susan liked Constance Garner well enough, she supposed. She had certainly seen enough of Constance on the yearlong journey so far. Now, she wondered, was she supposed to begin to refer to Constance as *Mother*? Susan caught her lower lip under her front teeth. She could never call her *Mother*. Susan's real mother had died only a few months before they left Brandtburg the past year. And Susan did not understand why her father wanted to marry anyone, much less

Constance Garner, so soon.

MaryAnne took Susan's hand into hers. Susan could almost hear MaryAnne's thoughts—*Constance is only three years older than I*—which meant Constance was only four years older than Susan. Surely Constance did not expect to take their mother's place.

Behind her, she was aware of her brother Willy wiggling around as if he had ants in his breeches. She risked a quick look over her shoulder. He had grown so much in the last two years. He used to be able to pat Lucky, his dog, without bending over, but now he had to bend quite a long distance. Only, since this was a wedding, even eleven-year-old Willy was smart enough not to be too obvious about reaching down to scratch Lucky's head. Instead, he had kept his back straight and bent his knees. That brought his over-long arms within reach of the dog's head.

She frowned at him, and he straightened quickly. Following her earlier train of thought, Susan continued to fume. Why this wedding? Why, why, why? She and MaryAnne had done a more than competent job of fulfilling the women's chores of their wagon. They had done all the cooking. Well, that was not truly so, for the Russells had invited them to join in their meals, but Susan and MaryAnne had helped with the preparation of the food for both the families. The two of them had cooked the meals after Mother's death, at home, before they left Brandtburg. They had cared for Father, and for each other, and for Pioneer and Willy. None of the Breeton brothers and sisters needed a new mother. So why did Father feel he needed a new wife?

Her father stepped across the informal aisle formed by the wedding guests—the entire company—and held out his arm. Constance hooked her hand in the crook of Father's elbow, and together they walked to the end of the long wagon and stopped in front of Reverend Russell. Father looked inordinately proud.

Susan knew what to expect, of course. She had witnessed plenty of weddings along the trail. She couldn't help letting her eyes stray across the aisle to where Silas Martin stood, looking casual and handsome and competent. Susan had it all planned out. *Silas and I will marry in two years*, she thought. *Once I am fifteen. Silas Martin and Susan Breeton. SM and SB, just as the design in the platter proclaimed. It was meant to be.* It was right that Susan had rescued the platter last year from Sophrona Brandt's grasping hands.

After the wedding ceremony was completed, the company formed a jubilant circle, with the bride and groom in the center. Alan Fountain struck up a lilting fiddle tune, and Father took the hand of his new bride and began to dance. Gradually other couples joined in. Over the next few hours, they danced cotillions, minuets, Virginia and Scotch reels, and country dances, not stopping until long after dark.

"I am going to join the women in throwing my stocking," Mary-Anne whispered in Susan's ear.

"So am I."

MaryAnne reared back. "You are but thirteen, Susan. Why would you throw your stocking?"

"I might still be the next to marry if my stocking hits Constance."

MaryAnne's incredulous expression was not very flattering, and Susan might have objected except that she was distracted when she saw Willy fastening a boot to the back of their wagon. The boot was a symbol of a long and happy marriage, and Susan did not object to that, but she recognized the boot as one of her own.

Before she could grab his arm and remonstrate, Mistress Russell touched her on the shoulder. "You and MaryAnne will want to sleep with me in our Russell wagon this night."

"Why?" That sounded like a horrible idea. Susan had occasionally, before she fell asleep in her own wagon, heard horrible snores pouring from the Russell wagon. They were always so loud. Early in the trip, Susan had asked her mother to avoid settling next to the Russell wagon when they stopped for a night or for two days, and sometimes for a fortnight.

"Never you mind," Mrs. Russell said. "It would be preferable to leave Mister and Mistress Breeton alone for a night."

"Come," MaryAnne said, bending to roll down one of her stockings. "It is time for the throwing."

Susan bent and removed one of her own, ending up with a small, tidy, rolled-up bundle.

Her father and Constance paused before they entered under the canvas that had been spread on bended staves above their wagon. Mr. Breeton stepped to one corner of the wagon and Constance to the other. When they turned to face the assembled crowd, Susan and MaryAnne—and all the other unmarried women—turned around and threw their stockings backwards over their shoulders, hoping to be the first to strike Constance. At the same time, the unmarried men each turned backwards and each threw a stocking at Willem Breeton.

"Let it be mine that she catches," Susan breathed quickly.

When all who had thrown turned around to face the bride and groom, Susan immediately saw that her stocking had fallen far from the mark, which meant she would not be the next one to be wed.

"Silas," Father called, "'twas your stocking I caught."

There followed a goodly amount of good-natured ribbing of Silas and of Edna Russell, whose stocking had been caught by Constance, but Susan knew there was no chance that Edna and Silas would marry, for Edna would soon be betrothed to Charles Hastings, who stepped forward at that moment to take Edna's arm in a proprietary way.

Good, Susan thought. *There still is hope for me.*

2000

"**HOLD ON, EVERYBODY.**" I pulled a torn and much-weathered envelope from the stack I'd been going through. "Look at this. It's from Pennsylvania. Addressed to Widow Julia Gilman." I looked around the group. "Do any of you know of a Gilman family?" I wasn't surprised when nobody answered. Nobody with that last name had a library card. "It looks like she's part of the Hastings family." More shrugs met this pronouncement.

"Read it to us," Ida instructed.

"First," Dee held up a hand, "who wrote it?"

I looked again at the name and address on the back flap of the envelope. "Caroline Edgerton."

"Doesn't ring a bell," Sadie said and looked at Rebecca Jo, who shook her head.

Ida reached out and touched the ragged envelope gently. "I wonder who tore it like that?"

"Maybe somebody was really angry at the writer and—"

"Cut the drama, Maddy," Ida said. "You don't have to make up an unsubstantiated story about everything we find."

I drew back in my chair. Even for Ida, with her no-nonsense approach to most everything, this seemed a little severe.

Maddy took it in stride, though. "Maybe if Biscuit reads the letter we'll find out." It didn't sound like an apology, but it did seem to smooth Ida's ruffled feathers.

The feather on her hat is not ruffled, and she does not have any other feathers.

Carol laughed. "Go ahead, Biscuit. What does it say?"

It took me a few extra seconds to open the envelope without damaging the letter further. The ripped-out section was right above the salutation. It took out the lower half of the third line of the address, but I could tell from the top of the M and the top of the G that it must have said Martinsville Georgia.

12 May 1773
Wednesday
Healing House
Harrisburg on the Susquehanna
Pennsylvania

Widow Julia Gilman
Robert Hastings Family

My dear Julia,

I hope this letter finds you well and (as I always pray) continuing to thrive in your new home. I cannot thank you enough for having sent a letter so I would know your journey was successful and you are well, and that you are now so firmly established with the Hastings family. I have received only the one packet—I should say the very substantial packet—from you, the first entry of which was dated the 7th of August, 1745. If you wrote other letters, either they have gone astray or will appear when I least expect them. Thank you for explaining that you had to wait to send it to me until there were more settlements farther north in your isolated valley. Otherwise I might have had to accuse you of being a poor correspondent indeed. It was my great delight that your letter was so long – twenty-two years of periodic entries have given my daughter and me many evenings of enjoyment as we read of your adventures along the road and in your new home. Your letter was three years in reaching us, for there has been much disruption of late. I trust this letter of mine will find its way to you.

"Much disruption of late," Carol quoted. "That would be the events leading up to the Revolutionary War, I'd imagine."

I smoothed my gloved hand over the old parchment. "History in the making."

I am very glad your traveling companions turned out to be so amiable, although I am not surprised, for I came to be quite fond of Mister Hubbard Brandt during the time he lodged with you.

"Hubbard?" I looked up from the letter. "Our Hubbard?"

"Of course it's our Hubbard," Maddy snapped. "How many Hubbard Brandts could there possibly be?"

"We can't be sure yet," Carol said carefully, but I could hear the undercurrent of excitement in her voice. "Keep reading. Let's see if she tells us more about him."

I wept with you when I read of the various tragedies you and they endured, and laughed at all the antics, with only five hands between the three of you. Mister Ira Brandt certainly seems from your letter to have mellowed quite a bit since his bout with yellow fever.

"Bingo," Dee hollered. "We found them! Hubbard and Ira!"

Maddy waited until the cheering died down a bit. "I wonder who was missing a hand."

"Missing a hand?"

"Weren't you listening, Easton? She said something about three people and only five hands."

"Oh. Yeah."

"And the yellow fever," Ida said, pointing at the letter. "That was pretty serious, wasn't it?"

"Oh, yes," Carol said. "It was spread by mosquito bite, so it was hard to avoid, particularly in the south. Sometimes it wiped out half the population of a town. But people who survived it were pretty much immune from then on."

"But why," Sadie asked, "would this woman be traveling with the two brothers? Why do you suppose they took her with them?"

"I can't even begin to guess," Rebecca Jo said, "but this letter means Ira and Hubbard both survived."

"Not necessarily," Carol said.

I read back over the first paragraph. "They must have made it here, because she says 'the various tragedies you and they endured.' She was talking about Julia's traveling companions. It sure sounds like our Ira and Hubbard made it this far, unless this Julia left them somewhere along the line and came here by herself."

"She was talking,"—Carol's voice caught a bit—"about my great-great-et cetera uncle and grandfather." She gave a sheepish grin. "I guess I'm more moved than I thought I'd be. It's wonderful to find out Ira turned from a rotten drunk to an amiable traveling companion."

"He was still a murderer," Maddy said, and Carol blanched.

Before the conversation could turn rancorous—any more than it already was—I held up the letter and read on.

You mention Mistress Louetta Tarkington Martin quite often,

"Tarkington," Ida said. "Your ancestor, Melissa."

"I guess so. Through her son Brand and Parley Breeton." She touched her bear claw necklace and then opened her hands wide. "Of course, I don't know that much about all this genealogy stuff. I still feel like I'm guessing about a lot of it. Keep going, Biscuit."

You mention Mistress Louetta Tarkington Martin quite often, so I would surmise that you have developed at least one close friendship, although Mistress Hastings sounds quite pleasant as well. Perhaps, though, despite the fact that you have lodged with her and her husband for all these years, she may not be the sort of woman you want to confide in? I so often find myself wishing there were another such as you here in Harrisburg—although I willingly admit there could never be anyone else quite your equal. My daughter and I carry on your healing work, and so appreciate the gift of your house and extensive gardens. Flower must have been poor recompense in return, although I am glad to hear she carried you safely.

"Flower?" I looked up at the group. "Sounds like a horse?" But I wasn't sure.

"Of course she's a horse," Ida said.

"Who would trade a house for a horse?"

I thought a moment about Pat's question. "It sounds like she needed a horse, and she didn't need the house any more."

"So it was a good trade," Ida said. "Now, can we get on with it?"

"Yes, ma'am," Pat and I said at the same time.

Lucy has kept the herbs flourishing, as she has a special touch with growing things and will be quite capable of carrying on your legacy and now, I suppose, my legacy once I am gone.

I fear that will be sooner, rather than later. You and I may have both been of a certain age when you left here—how can 48 be considered so very old when we have both lived all these many more years beyond that?—but you were ever the more sprightly. Your

I turned the page over. "The next paragraph is where that piece got torn out." I said.

"That's okay," Carol assured me. "Well, it's not okay, but we may be able to figure out what's missing by the context."

Your sense of adventure, which I know is what prompted you to travel on with the Brandt brothers, is far beyond what I would ever dare to admit in myself. In point of fact, I fear I have no adventuresomeness in my spirit whatsoever. I will be content to live the rest of my life here in Harrisburg, with the Susquehanna playing its mighty song nearby.

I am, of course, glad indeed that you survived the attack in February of 1744, but I was grieved to hear of the death o

"Well, phooey," I said. "This is where it's torn. Attack? What kind of attack? What happened? And who died?"

"It can't answer you back," Ida said. "No sense yelling at a letter."

"Maybe it *will* answer her," Amanda said. "Just read further."

... know you were so very skilled with a knife—at least not when used in that way—but I was most distressed as well to read of how difficult it has been for you to forgive yourself for having killed him. ...

"Killed who?"

I looked ahead a few sentences. "I don't know, Dee. It doesn't say."

Carol took a deep breath. "This is part of the trouble with old letters. They were written to someone who knew what the writer was talking about, so there was never any reason for long explanations."

"Makes it darn hard on our end," Maddy grumped.

I pray that your dreams will soon cease to be so disturbing. After all these years, can you not find it in your heart to forgive yourself? He certainly deserved to die. He sounded a most scurrilous fellow indeed.

I find myself wanting to go through your letter page by page and comment about every paragraph, even every sentence, for I so long to have a real conversation with you. Since that is not possible, know that I thoroughly enjoyed reading your epistle, and we plan to re-read it often, especially when winter returns, for although the nights are long then, the fire is warm, and your presence as evoked by your words is most comforting. Lucy has assured me that when I die, she will continue to hold your letter dear to her heart, as it is to mine.

Please know that Lucy and I were grieved indeed to hear of your losses. Would that we had been there to offer you some comfort.

Although I hope to hear from you again, I am fair certain it is most probably a hollow dream. Please know, that whether or not I receive another letter, I will always treasure your friendship. Lucy sends her best wishes, and I send you my undying loyalty.

I remain, your loving friend,
Caroline Edgerton

"Wow," Maddy said. "Sure makes me appreciate telephones."

Dee shifted in her chair to face Carol. "How could anybody spend twenty-two years writing one letter?"

"Well, just think about it. If they came here and settled at the bottom end of a dead-end valley, it sort of makes sense that there wouldn't be any sort of regular travel out of here, at least not until families had spread out more. Then you might get travelers who could pass a letter on from hand to hand."

"More than just a letter," Dee said. "If it had twenty-two years worth of news in it, it must have been a substantial package."

"Unless she wrote really small," Maddy said.

We all gave that remark the attention it deserved, which was absolutely nothing.

Melissa scribbled some figures on the back of what I hoped was a scrap piece of paper. "If this Julia was forty-eight when she left Pennsylvania, and she spent twenty-two years writing the letter to Caroline, that means she must have been seventy when she finally mailed it."

"Or more," Dee said. "We don't know how long she spent traveling with the Brandt brothers from Harrisburg to here."

"Melissa nodded. "Good point. So, seventy-something was a pretty advanced age for those times."

"Usually if people were going to die," Carol said, "they died when they were young. If they made it to twenty, they had a much better chance of living to, say, forty. And if they lived to sixty, then chances were good that they had strong enough constitutions to live another fifteen or twenty years."

"Unless there was an accident." Ira pointed to the torn part of the letter "Or if something else awful happened."

"Looks like another field trip is in store for us," Ida said. "To Harrisburg. Maybe that twenty-two year letter is still up there in a museum or something. Wouldn't that be wonderful? Caroline did say Lucy had promised to keep it."

"It's worth a try," Carol said. "And *Healing House* might have become a landmark of sorts."

"Dee and I could manage a field trip to Harrisburg and do some research on Caroline Edgerton and Lucy and Healing House." Maddy looked at Dee who nodded. "In the meantime, this goes in the top dresser drawer."

"The Foundation could fund your trip," Glaze said. "Since it's for the museum."

Maddy's face lightened. "Great! Now all we have to do is wait for the ice to melt."

Glaze's face took on an impish look. "The Foundation could pay to have Beechnut House remodeled to put in a back entrance to the attic museum."

I stared at her. "Be sure to close the door firmly behind you on your way out."

She is not leaving.

"Is that a *no*?"

"What do you think?"

I think I do not know what you are talking about.

Carol scooped up Marmalade, cuddled her, and muttered something under her breath.

Thank you for explaining, ListenLady.

I waited for Marmalade to quit meowing and then went back to the first part of the letter. "Don't you wonder about the relationship between this Julia, whoever she was, and Louetta Tarkington Martin? And Mistress Hastings? Do you think Julia ever confided in either one of them about the man she killed?" But I knew there was no answer to my questions.

"No wonder the letter took three years to reach Caroline," Rebecca Jo said, returning to our earlier discussion, "if it had to go with somebody up to Braetonburg and then wait for someone else to head toward Garner Creek or Surreytown."

"Not Surreytown," Melissa said. "That's as much a dead end as Martinsville. It would only have to go to Russell Gap to get out of the valley, but we really don't know how many people travelled outside back then."

"That's right," I said. "They'd taken such pains to hide themselves, I'd be willing to bet nobody left the valley as long as Homer Martin was alive."

"You know," Ida said, "I've been wondering how the names managed to get changed so much, if the Surratts really did found Surreytown and the Endicotts really did found Enders."

"And then there's Breeton and Braetonburg," Dee said, emphasizing the BREE of Breeton and the BRAY sound of Braetonburg.

"That one isn't that much of a stretch," Ida said, "but from Surratt to Surreytown? I don't get it."

"It's not so surprising," Carol said. "Language changes. People never used to use contractions, for instance, and now everything's shortened. I imagine the same thing happens with names."

1843

GREAT-GRANDFATHER HERMAN ENDICOTT looked thoroughly dead, Hermione thought, but she still almost expected him to open his eyes and cackle at her through his toothless mouth. He was the oldest person she had ever heard of and had lived with Mother and Father for many, many years, which may have been why Hermione and her twin brother had been named for him.

She listened only half-heartedly to the minister as he droned on and on about the virtues of a long life. "Our dear brother Herman Endicott," he said, "has been a pillar of our community for all of his ninety-seven years."

Yes, yes, yes. Hermione knew all of that. Hadn't she heard her great-grandfather telling her, practically every day of her nine years, that he was the first baby ever born in Enders? He always called it *En-*

dicottville, though, in his voice that sounded like the rattling of dried cornhusks in an autumn wind.

A very long time ago—last year when she was only eight—she had asked him, "Why does everyone else call our town Enders?"

Great-grandfather's rheumy eyes had wandered away from her. "It began when my Uncle Sayrle, the uncle I never met, died in a flood the day before I was born. My grandmother, my father's mother, heard of the death and said"—here he raised his voice to what he probably meant to be an approximation of an old woman's complaining tone—"Well then, that's the ender him." At that, he sighed. "The rest of my uncles thought it was a funny thing to say, and they kept up such a lot of banter about 'ender' it finally turned into the name of the town." Then great-grandfather laughed so hard he made himself hoarse.

Hermione still had not decided whether or not she believed that story.

Mother reached over with a firm hand to still Hermione's jiggling legs. The pew was hard, the service was long, and Hermione would much rather be outside. She pretended to bow her head, but really she was looking under the rim of her Sunday bonnet, just past her mother, to where her twin brother sat between Mother and Father, peeking around Mother and crossing his eyes at Hermione. She crossed her eyes back at him, just in time for Father to look over at her and frown.

Why was she always the one who got caught? Herman was the one who usually started everything. Now she would have to walk back and forth around the living room with a book balanced on her head for an extra quarter hour after the funeral. Half an hour each day was bad enough. Mother insisted, though. *Deportment is important for a lady.* Now Hermione would have to endure it for three quarters of an hour, while Herman would have no punishment at all.

But Mother's strong hand suddenly shot up and grasped the top of Herman's head, turning it back toward the front of the room, toward great-grandfather's coffin, and Hermione saw Father frown. Good. Now Herman would have to gather a bigger pile of kindling than was usually expected of him.

And after her deportment and his chopping, they would take their poles and run off together down to the lake to catch fish for the evening meal.

2000

"LOOK HERE." REBECCA JO held up a yellowed envelope. From where I sat, I couldn't see any details, other than that it appeared to have a huge printed logo where the return address should be. "I haven't thought about this stuff in years," she said.

Dee set down a letter. "More blueing?"

"No, but something just as outdated. More so, really. Sadie," she called over to our table, "do you remember Merchant's Gargling Oil?"

What is a garklingoil?

"The smelly stuff in the blue bottle? I sure do. My mother thought it was the answer to all her prayers."

I like to smell things.

Glaze bent to scratch Marmalade behind the ears. "What is it?"

"Was," Rebecca Jo said. "The company went out of business sometime back in the twenties or thirties."

"And a good thing they did," Sadie said. "That stuff was stinky as could be."

"My mother was so upset when she tried to get some more of it in—oh, probably the thirties. During the Great Depression."

Dee looked more closely at the envelope Rebecca Jo held. "Advertising on an envelope?"

"There used to be a lot of that," Sadie said. "I'm not sure why the practice died away."

"Merchant's Gargling Oil," Dee read. "Was it some sort of mouthwash?"

Sadie guffawed. "Not hardly. It was a liniment. If I remember correctly, they had two versions, one for animals—"

"Packed in a yellow box," Rebecca Jo inserted.

"And one for people."

"In a white box." Rebecca Jo lifted her hands into the air and laughed. "Mama bought the yellow box once by mistake, and it stained my whole chest—and Mama's hand, too—such an awful shade of purplish-brown, we both looked like we had a case of badly healing bruises."

"Your chest?" Dee said. "What happened to you?"

"Oh, some sort of cough. I was only about five. Mothers really believed in that stuff for quite a while. It was considered almost as effective as a mustard plaster." She shivered. "What people used to do to their children in the name of medicine." She handed the envelope to Maddy. "Take a look and pass it on."

"Why did they call it gargling oil if it wasn't supposed to be gargled with?"

"I haven't a clue," Sadie said, "but there were instructions—on the white box for people—that if it was administered internally, the dosage was a few drops—I can't remember how many, maybe three or four. They were supposed to be dropped onto a sugar cube and eaten that way."

"Did the sugar help?"

"No, Dee, it didn't. I think I stayed healthy for the rest of my childhood just so I could avoid being dosed with that ghastly stuff."

"Too bad there wasn't something else just as effective."

"Oh, there was." Sadie dropped her voice to a funereal tone. "Cod liver oil."

Rebecca Jo made a horrible face. So did my mom.

"I heard," Maddy said, "that back in the 1830s, ketchup was sold as medicine. It was in pill form."

"Ketchup?" Pat said. "Did it work?"

"Nope. But whoever sold it made a bunch of money."

"Quacks," Sadie said. "At least Gargling Oil did what it was supposed to do." She got kind of a dreamy look on her face. "It generated a lot of heat where it was applied, and how could that not feel comforting?"

1896

GIDEON HOSKINS TOSSED the yellow cardboard box down onto the straw and peered at the blue bottle in his left hand as he ran his right hand down the leg of Samuel Breeton's bay mare. He had not tried this oil on any of his animal patients, although he *had* used it on himself the night after he was kicked on the thigh the week past by Lemuel Surratt's ill-tempered heifer. The oil had stained his hands and his nose—for he had scratched at an itch, which left his not insubstantial nose sporting a brown stain for three or four days. It had also colored his leg and the lower left portion of his nightshirt. His wife Amelia had not been pleased with the muddy brown stain, but the liniment did seem to have drawn out a good deal of the pain, even though it had left his nightshirt irreparably compromised.

The writing on both the box and the bottle was small enough that he complimented himself on not needing spectacles. He had read it with interest. *Guaranteed to cure everything from human back pain and hemorrhoids to gout and surliness in cows.* "Perhaps I should have used it on Lemuel's surly heifer," he told the horse. "It may be that then she would not have kicked me."

He removed the cork and placed it next to the box, being careful to keep the open bottle away from Young Bay's inquisitive nose. Young Bay still had a good many years left in her. She was not truly young anymore, and the swelling in her joint reminded him somewhat of arthritis in elderly people, but if he could reduce the swelling and clear up the tenderness, she could be back at work in no time.

"You and I are two of a kind," he said. "Your dam was called Bay, and you are Young Bay. My sire was called Gideon." He made a conscious effort not to tighten all his muscles, lest Young Bay sense his tension. "And I am Young Gideon." Luckily, since his father's sudden disappearance and since Young Gideon had taken over the veterinary practice in Martinsville after the death of old Doctor Shaw, most of the town folk had ceased to use the *young* before his name.

Life had been better, much better, once his father was no longer present. If Young Gideon had to answer to Almighty God on Judgement Day, he hoped he would not be condemned for his part in the 'disappearance.' If Mother had not killed him with that flatiron of hers, Young Gideon would have done so himself when Father tried to force his attentions on Amelia. Just the thought made Young Gideon grit his teeth, and Young Bay snorted.

He would have to curb his thoughts, for horses were extraordinarily sensitive to what people were feeling. He tried instead to think of his dear wife. Amelia truly lighted a room with her ready laughter and her gentle hands. She was strong, too, in so many ways that sometimes surprised Young Gideon.

Before he could go further with that thought, Young Bay butted his shoulder gently as if to say *What about me?* "Yes, yes, Young Bay. I will deal with your leg."

He took a step away from her and gave a cautious sniff at the blue bottle. The liniment still smelled as virulent as it had when he had used it on his leg. Iodine and ammonia. He easily identified those two ingredients by their odor and the bilious red color, which was not enhanced by being sold in a bottle of this color. Some soap or soap-like root was in there too, he reasoned, because of the faint lather that appeared when he rubbed it in.

The mare gave a whiffle of irritation, shaking her head.

"You like this smell no more than I do," he said, patting her shoulder and hoping his affable tone and steady hand would calm her. "It is for your own good. Turn your head away if you dislike the odor."

"Do you always talk to your patients, Young Gideon?"

He had not heard Samuel's mother come into the barn. At her advanced age, she was welcome to use his childhood name. "Good even to you, Mistress Breeton." His glance took in the swollen joints of her hands on her knobby cane of gray ash wood. "How do you this day?"

Her face, which had always reminded him of nothing so much as a desiccated apple, took on a rosy hue in the lantern light, and her eyes almost disappeared into the surrounding wrinkles. He loved to listen to her laugh. "How do I, you may well ask." She tapped her cane several times on the hard dirt of the barn floor. "I get along. I get along."

He was not sure, of course, but he had heard that she was well into her late sixties, near the limits of what a body usually endured. He tried, briefly, to envisage what his wife Amelia would look like if she lived that long—another forty years—but the image was beyond his imagination. "I am sure you do, Mistress Breeton, and quite well by the look of you."

She quirked her face in skepticism. "You take after your mother, Young Gideon. Leonora was always ready to say the best about everyone. Even about that father of yours."

Gideon wondered, for just a moment, if that glint in her eye had anything to do with knowledge of what he and his stepmother had done seven years before. Or, more likely, if she suspected that his father had killed his mother—drowned her in the bathtub—when Young Gideon was but a child. He knew the truth of that, but decided not to ask Mistress Breeton for any explanation of her meaning, lest she have an even worse story.

"What is that horrible smell?"

He patted the mare again and held up the bottle. "Merchant's Gargling Oil. Young Bay here needs something for her leg, and I thought to try this."

"Will she put up with the stink of it?"

Gideon smiled. "I doubt she will like it, but it will warm the leg and should help to draw out the pain."

"You go right ahead and put it on her, then. I would like to watch, if you do not mind."

He turned back to his patient and poured a healthy dollop of the liniment onto his palm. It gurgled as it came out of the bottle, and the mare's ears twitched back in response to the sound. He would have to be careful not to wipe his hand on his breeches, unless he wanted brown handprints thereon. "You might want to stay back in case Young Bay objects." He worked quickly, not wanting the fumes to distress the mare too much. She whinnied softly and snorted, but otherwise seemed not to care.

"May I see the bottle?"

He corked it carefully and handed it to her.

"Merchant's Gargling Oil for Man and Beast," she read. "This ape looks most happy." She proceeded to read aloud the poem written just below a picture of a grinning monkey.

If I am Darwin's grandpapa,
It follows, don't you see,
That what is good for man and beast
Is doubly good for me.

Gideon had laughed over it with his wife Amelia, and now he laughed again with Mistress Breeton. She was a merry old woman indeed, but her face turned serious. "Do you think it could help my hands?"

"I … I do not know. It would stain your hands horribly, though the stain does wear off within a week."

She raised her hand—the one that held the bottle. "It would be just one more spot on these already brown-spotted hands of mine." Her eyes crinkled. "Perhaps it will cover up all those spots so my hands look young again."

He laughed with her once more before he turned serious. "I have heard that they sell a different version—for use on people—that does not stain either your hands or your clothing. I could order some for you from Breeton's store."

She raised her hand again, and the rim of the bottle gleamed in the light from the nearby lantern. "Why would I want to wait, when there is possible relief available to me right here?"

He paused for only a moment, then stepped away from the now quiet mare. "If you would allow me?"

She nodded and handed him the bottle.

2000

"**THAT GARGLING OIL** came in a blue bottle, if I remember right," Sadie said.

Rebecca Jo nodded. "Sort of a blue-green. And it had a horrible label."

"How so?"

"You would have loved it, Maddy," Rebecca Jo said. "There was a picture of a monkey on it and a poem about Darwin, something about man and beast."

"Darwin?"

"It wasn't exactly a masterpiece of writing, but it was silly enough for people to remember it."

Sadie shook her head. "I obviously missed something. The bottles we had never had a monkey on them or a poem. Just a flowery-looking girl with long hair and a big smile."

"It must have been the people formula. Your mother was considerably more sedate than mine. I can see how, given a choice, she'd pick the packaging with the girl."

"My mother? Sedate?"

I could see why Sadie sounded so incredulous. I'd heard the stories, from Bob, about how Sadie's mother, Eulalia Russell, had faced down Obadiah Martin when he'd tried to have one of the Old Forest groves in town cut to make room for more houses. Eulalia was a firebrand, nothing sedate about her.

"She probably just never saw the yellow box. I'm sure my mother would have picked the funny monkey any day."

When the envelope reached me, I looked inside. "Did you read the letter?"

"No," Rebecca Jo said. "I was too busy walking down memory lane with the envelope. And the monkey on the yellow box."

Tardy House
Surreytown Georgia
8 April 1860

Miss Eliza Russell
Hornby House
Martinsville Georgia

My dear cousin,

I have just read in your letter of 4 April that you plan to marry Gideon Hoskins.

If this letter of mine is not too late, may I beg you to reconsider? His former wife, Leonora, was well known to my friend Mrs Allenton, who says that Leonora always rued having married Gideon, despite the love she held for her four children by him, particularly Young Gideon, the gentlest of his offspring. She told me too that she wondered when Leonora died how anyone could accidentally drown in such a small bathing tub.

I never knew the cause of Leonora's anguish, nor did Mrs Allenton. I can only speculate, and I know full well that speculation will do my argument no good in your eyes.

Come to visit me, will you not, so I can kidnap you away and keep you safe. My husband is a kind and generous man, and he has assured me that he would be right happy to provide you a home here, and you and I could have such lovely times working together as we did playing together when we were children.

Praying that this letter finds you in time and that you for once in your life will listen to some sense, I remain your ever faithful loving cousin,

Augusta Russell Tardy

I set the letter on the table in front of me and looked up at the surrounding ring of women.

"Oh dear," Amanda said. "That doesn't sound good. Do you suppose the letter reached her in time?"

"Probably not," Maddy said."

"Why do you say that?"

"Because it was here—in the Hoskins' old attic."

"But if she married this Gideon Hoskins," I said, "whoever he was, wouldn't she have destroyed the letter to be sure he didn't get hold of it?"

"It was pretty far down in this trunk," Rebecca Jo said. "And the date is more recent than some of the boxes of letters that were on top of it."

"So, you're saying she buried it," Dee said.

"Probably."

"And it would most likely have been safe there," Ida said. "Can you imagine any of our husbands going through stacks and boxes of old letters like we're doing?"

"No," I said. "But then again, our husbands are all pretty nice guys. Maybe a monster like Gideon Hoskins would have pried into everything she did."

"He obviously didn't," Maddy said. "Otherwise he would have found it and destroyed it."

I touched the letter carefully. "I just hope she was safe."

July 1862

Tardy House
Surreytown Georgia
7 July 1862

Luther Russell, blacksmith
Martinsville Georgia

Augusta put down the quill, inadvertently leaving a splotch of ink on the heavy paper she had spread to protect the surface of the desk. She had been so worried for so long, for none of her letters to her cousin Eliza had been answered. Not truly answered. Oh, she had received plenty of letters, but they were all so … so meaningless. Something was terribly wrong. She knew it.

She stared at the letter. Her brother Luther was the only one she could think of who might be able to help. Gideon Hoskins was thick of arm and neck—and probably thick in his head, as well—but he would be no match for a blacksmith. She toyed idly with the idea that Luther might drag Gideon out behind the smithy, bloody that enormous nose of his, and teach him a lesson, but she was not sure just what that lesson should be. All she had were guesses, and those too nebulous to prove anything was wrong. Still, she knew something was.

She lifted the quill, dipped it in the inkwell, and wrote.

My dear brother,

Most loving greetings to you and your sweet wife. I am so very glad to hear that Suella survived the birth of your second child. I pray the child might thrive.

Have you any other word of our cousin Eliza? How does she? She wrote to me this past week, but that letter, like all her others, was full of airy nothings, as if she had not a care in the world now that her youngest stepson has come through his bout with the fevered croup and appears to be on the mend.

I fear that her husband reads her letters before she posts them and that she is unable to say what is in her heart. Oh that she had never married that man! As you know, I begged her two years ago, before her marriage, to come here to me, but she never answered that particular letter of mine.

Is there a way you can speak with her privately? Or perhaps Suella could call on Eliza to show her the new baby once she is able to be up and about?

Please settle my mind on this most pressing question, for I worry about our cousin almost constantly.

I remain, always, your loving sister,

Augusta Russell Tardy

2000

WE TOOK A LITTLE break for coffee, tea, hot chocolate—and bathrooms, but we didn't let those activities keep us away from the attic for too long. We just took our drinks upstairs with us. "You know," Carol said when we reconvened, "Reebok got me to thinking about something while we were playing outside."

"Let me ... guess. Was it about ... ice?" Ida's coffee mug still seemed to be hot. She blew on it between words.

"Not exactly. He said he'd never known the temps to fall as low as they have this winter."

We all nodded. That was common knowledge here in the well-protected Metoochie River valley.

"There was one stretch of years, though, when it must have gotten this cold or even colder."

Dee snorted. "Why do I think you're going to tell us all about it?"

Pat elbowed her, and a few drops of hot chocolate sloshed out onto Dee's sweatshirt. "Whoops! Sorry," Pat said without a bit of apology in her tone.

"Good thing I'd almost finished." Dee drained the remainder of her mug.

"Good thing that's an old sweatshirt," Pat said.

"So," Dee said, putting her mug on the dresser closest to the stairs, "what's the big story?"

"It all started with a volcano on the other side of the world," Carol said. "In the summer of 1883, Krakatoa exploded violently, literally blowing two-thirds of the island around it out of the water."

"Wow," Dee said. "I've heard the name Krakatoa—I think you mentioned it yesterday—but I never knew any details."

"One of the explosions was so loud, it could be heard three thousand miles away. By the time the eruptions finished—there was a whole series of them—more than 36,000 people had been killed."

"It sounds like an impressive eruption," Ida said, "and I don't mean to make light of that much destruction, but what does it have to do with cold weather?"

"The five-year winter," Sadie said, and Carol nodded, apparently happy to turn the floor over to her. "I learned about it way back in high school."

"Well, I didn't," Dee said. "Tell us more."

"Prevailing winds carried the Krakatoa ashes far and wide," Sadie said. "So far in fact, that they covered almost the whole world, blocking out most of the sunlight."

Maddy cleared her throat. "Sounds ominous."

Carol nodded. "Temperatures dropped drastically because of the lack of sunlight getting through the ash clouds." She looked toward Sadie. "Details?"

"Yes, ma'am." She leaned back in her chair. "Crops failed, starvation was widespread, and people who didn't die from lack of food often froze to death in the winters that followed."

"You said winters, plural." Dee had a question in her voice.

"Five years," Carol said. "The effects lasted all the way until the winter of 1888."

"My parents both lived through it," Sadie told us, "and spoke of it often. It was one of those scary stories that children seem to hate and relish at the same time. The winters were super-cold, and although the seasons still changed to a certain extent there was so much ash in the air and so little sunlight, most of the crops failed. Are you familiar with that painting by the Norwegian artist Edvard Munch called *The Scream*?"

"Yeah," Dee said. "The big-mouthed bald guy on the bridge?"

Sadie raised an eyebrow, but otherwise did not acknowledge Dee's smartass comment. "It's been suggested that the bands of brilliant reddish orange in the sky behind him were caused by the volcanic ash from Krakatoa."

Carol added her two-cents' worth. "Originally, Munch called his painting *The Scream of Nature*."

"So, would people here in Martinsville have seen skies that looked like that?"

"I don't know for sure, Dee," Carol said, "but it certainly would seem so."

"Maybe we should be pleased with just a little bit of an ice storm." Sadie crossed her arms, as if to hug some warmth to herself.

"Although I'll be glad when it's over."

"You just want a chance to go shopping for new clothes," Ida said.

"You betcha." She patted her green sweatshirt. "*I'm So Blue*, *Red a Good Book Lately*, and *Laughender* are tops on my list."

Glaze stepped forward. "Don't forget Reebok's *Come and Get Me Copper.*"

December 1886

CLEUSA BREETON TRACED her fingernail over the frost on the windowpane, spelling out her full name. Her fingerless gloves, fingerless so she could continue to knit without obstruction, caught the little flakes of frost and looked as if a tiny snowstorm had settled on them. Her breath unfurled before her in a cloud of vapor. Behind her, the fireplace put out only enough heat to keep the water from freezing in the jugs that stood as close to the fire as possible. Here, on the other side of the room, the fire had little effect. Her brothers had gone out with Father early that morning to replenish their dwindling stock of firewood, but they had not yet returned. She sighed and returned to her knitting.

Knitting had become almost her full time occupation for the past two years. When the heavy clouds descended more than two years ago, no one had thought they would last long. The sunsets had been magnificent, with broad bands of the brightest orange imaginable. But one could not eat a sunset.

She no longer resented her mother's constant harping over the years about the need to preserve every bit of food their garden grew. The cupboards were still quite full and the root cellar, while no longer full, would keep them for another year, possibly a bit longer if they could keep out the rot. There was no fresh straw for packing around the cabbages and potatoes, though, since the crops had failed last summer. Heaven send that another year such as this last one would not happen.

Sun.

She wanted to see the sun.

Mother was not the only woman in Martinsville to insist on such frugal ways. "Constance Garner Breeton, your great-great-great-grandmother," she told Cleusa, as she had often before, "traveled far to reach this valley, and they might have starved along the way if the women had not saved every bit of food they could raise, glean, or find along the road. It became a habit we have kept to this very day."

"The men must have hunted, too," Cleusa said, as she always did at this point in the tale.

"Oh yes, they did, but constant meals of nothing but venison would have grown difficult to take through the four years of their journey."

And their teeth would have fallen out, Mother always said. Cleusa knew the whole story by heart, having heard it so many times.

"Their teeth would all have fallen out had they eaten naught but meat," Mother finished, dusting her hands on her apron. Hers was an opinion not held by many others in Martinsville, but Cleusa had noticed that her family all retained their teeth, while many of those others did not.

Mother sighed and added more—words that she had never said before. "There is little enough venison to be found now after two years of dying forests."

Cleusa liked the sunshine, and she had always imagined that trees did, as well, although she would never have mentioned that thought to anyone lest they think her a conjure woman. The old spreading trees within the town had survived so far, protected somewhat by the high cliffs surrounding the town, but up above on the cliffs, countless dead branches, brittle in the stabbing cold and intense wind, broke off with every new onslaught of snow or ice. At least the people of Martinsville had plenty of firewood, as long as the men of the town could get through the banks of snow to reach it.

She had just begun to turn the heel of the stocking when she heard raised voices outside. She rose and went back to the window. She did not want to open the door. There was precious little heat inside, and what warmth there was needed to be kept in. She had to wipe away the frost—and her name—in order to see. Father and her brothers had brought a sled filled with wood.

Mother opened the front door. Cleusa dropped her knitting when Mother cried out. Father lifted her youngest brother's limp body from the sled where it had lain atop the load of firewood. She and Mother hurried as fast as they could down the icy steps.

"We had the sled all filled," Father said, "but as we lowered it with ropes down the last steep incline, Warren slipped and fell. He hit his head on a rock."

Cleusa could see the blood staining her brother's cap—the cap she had knitted for him just a few months before.

She looked around her at the stark landscape. There was not a rock in sight. Everything, including the rock wall that bounded their land, was covered with thick ice and heavy snow. How could her brother's head have found a rock in all this whiteness?

They wrapped Warren's body in an old quilt and put him in one of the sheds where they could close the door securely to protect his body from predators. Then they waited until the next chilly summer for the ground to thaw enough so they could bury him.

2000

I HAD TO admit, I was getting ready to have this storm ended, too. While I thoroughly enjoyed tackling the attic—especially with so much ready help—I missed my regular daily routine. "We really are creatures of habit, aren't we?" I hadn't directed the question to anyone in particular, but it must have hit a chord for a number of the women, because I heard murmurs of agreement from all around me.

"Much as I appreciate being able to take refuge here," Ida said with an apologetic look at me, "I keep wondering what we're going to face at the store once the storm is over. The meat should be okay. We moved all of it into the walk-in freezers. We'll have to sell it at a discount, but we shouldn't lose too much money. People always like a bargain. But there's going to be a lot of total loss in other areas like the fresh fruits and vegetables." She lifted her shoulders up close to her ears and let them fall. "I sure hope our generators are still running. If not, we'll have to ditch the canned goods, too. They're not meant to be frozen."

With all the food Ida and Ralph had brought with them, they'd been almost single-handedly feeding the rest of us. Maybe, I thought, we could take up a collection to pay the two of them for all that food. After all, it was food they'd counted on selling in the store.

"Let us know what we can do to help," Rebecca Jo said. "We'll just move the Attic Society down to the IGA and all of us can chip in."

Ida stretched her shoulders back as if they still had a heavy weight on them. "We'll probably just throw it all out—certainly the whole produce aisle."

"I can't blame you for sounding so disgruntled," Maddy said, "but maybe you could sell it by weight—*so much a pound to jumpstart your compost pile!* Can you imagine the flyers you could put up around town?"

"I'd buy some of it," I said. "There's no such thing as too much compost."

I like the compost pile. It is warm. And the worms are wiggly.

Even in the cold days of late autumn and early winter, there always seemed to be trickles of steam rising from my compost pile as it cooked its way into good earth. How lovely to be able, with the help of earthworms and sun and rain, to turn what some people would call garbage into productive soil.

1946

LEON MARTIN LEANED over Obadiah Martin, who lay on the bed without moving. He lowered his ear until it was quite close to his father's face.

"Are you checking … to see if I … have any breath left?"

Leon jumped back at his father's first word. That was precisely what he'd been doing, and had barely felt a trickle of air. "I'm sorry, Father. Mother said she would give us a few minutes alone while she brews some tea to soothe your throat."

"I doubt it will … do any good," Obadiah said, "but it … will make her feel … like she's … helping me. Irmagarde … has been … a good helpmeet … for all these years … as Matilda will be … for … you. … Men in our family … have always … lived long. Except for me, it seems. … I'm sixty-three now, and doubt I'll last … to see my next birthday." He shifted uncomfortably. "I won't even see next week. Can't

… breathe. Lift me higher on the pillow, would you?"

"You'll weather this storm, Father." Leon's father had always been such a substantial man, but now his frail body was light as dandelion fluff, and Leon was distressed at his father's shortness of breath. "You still have some battles to fight in the town council."

"Ever since Bill Fenton died—he was such a thorn in my father's side—and mine, too—I have not had the heart to keep going."

At least, Leon thought, Father seemed to breathe somewhat better now that he was propped up a bit. His words came easier, but Leon had to strain to hear them, for Father's voice was exceedingly faint.

For the past decade, Leon had wanted to sit in the chairman's seat—his father's seat—but he knew the tradition as well as any other resident of Martinsville. All the other council members were elected now, but not the chairmanship. The chairman always had to die before the eldest son would automatically inherit that position. Now that it looked like that time was come, he felt surprisingly unsuited and unwilling to step into his father's shoes.

Father must have read his mind.

"You're old enough to have developed some common sense, my boy. Now that you've made it back from the war without losing a limb—or your head—you should be able to lead this town for a good long time."

"Father," Leon began, but he didn't know what he should say.

"Just remember to chew the grass and sp …" Obadiah was wracked with a deep cough that splattered the sheet with blood, but he didn't need to say any more.

Leon had heard the story of the circus that came to town back in '98 so many times he had it memorized. He finished his father's sentence. "And spit the sticks. Good advice from Mr. Fenton all those years ago."

"That's right. I tried to follow his advice all my life."

"Except for when Eulalia Russell tried to save those trees," Leon said, knowing where this part of the often-rehashed story was headed.

"Durn fool woman. She was a mouthful of sticks if I ever …" Again, the coughing interrupted him.

"Don't worry, Father. I'll be sure the trees are taken down and the sidewalks repaired the way they should be. There'll be lots more room for houses once those trees above the cemetery are removed."

"Good lu—"

This time, the coughing ended abruptly in a gurgle and a moan and an explosive exhalation. Leon's mother rushed into the room with a pot of soothing tea, but she was too late.

2000

IT SEEMED LIKE a long while later—I'd lost all concept of time—when Maddy said, "You know what we haven't found?"

"What?" I could imagine dozens of things, like photograph albums and teapots and recipe books, but Maddy obviously had something specific in mind.

"Everything up here is related to women. There's no male presence in the attic."

Dee jumped on that. "I think I spotted a pocket watch." She looked dubious, though.

"You did," I said. "When we first came up here. I gave it to Bob."

"Okay," Maddy admitted. "But that's only one thing so far."

"How about the rocking horse," Amanda suggested. "It had a boy's name on it."

"And it was a man—and his wife, Arthur and Grace—who prepared the secret room," Glaze said.

I walked over to the table and picked up Hubbard's diary. "This is about as male as you can get." I set it down as soon as I remembered I didn't have the white gloves on.

"Still"—Maddy's voice was firm—"despite those four things, it's mostly female energy up here."

"Suits me just fine," Rebecca Jo said, seating herself back at her card table. "I like all this female stuff."

"Let's find some more," Sadie said. And with that, we set back to work.

My mom, I noticed, was huddled with Esther and Sylvia, Tom's mother, around a stack of cardboard boxes. I kept hearing snatches of giggles coming from them, but figured if it was something they wanted to share, they'd clue us all in.

"We haven't found any china or silverware," Amanda mentioned a little later. "Don't you think people would have stored their extra sets up here?"

"I read somewhere that they ate a lot of their food in hollowed-out bread loaves back in the 1700s," Dee said.

"That's partially right," Carol said. "They were called trenchers. But that was more in the 1600s and before that. By the 1700s people would have had plates and bowls made of pewter or pottery or wood. Even china, although that was pretty much restricted to the wealthier families."

"So," Amanda asked, "why aren't there any dishes up here?"

"It was mostly the Victorians who collected china, wasn't it?"

Carol raised her head at my question, but I had the feeling she was looking right through me. "Yes," she said slowly. "The earlier inhabitants of the town probably had only enough plates and cups and such to feed their immediate families. And people generally carried their own spoons and eating knives with them at all times."

I saw Easton curl her lip—again. "That doesn't sound very sanitary," she grumped.

"Nobody knew a thing about germs back then," Carol said sharply. I think she was getting as fed up as I was with Easton's negativity. Of course, if Ida had made that same comment, I would have just laughed it off. Maybe I needed an attitude adjustment.

What is a nadditudа jusment?

Marmy helped. She jumped, meowing, into my lap, and I just had to smile.

I like it when you smile, but I wish you would answer my questions.

Saturday, 4 June 1768

PARLEY BREETON, THE second of the so-called "barn babies," straightened her shoulders and tightened her hold on the bunch of wildflowers her mother thrust into her hands.

"I am so proud of you, my child," Mother told her. "You will make a fine wife, and I feel certain Brand will be a good provider for you." She sighed. "I can only hope that Brand Tarkington will be as gentle a husband to you as my Willem has been to me all these years."

Father's first wife had died long ago, and Parley knew that Constance Garner Breeton had raised his children, MaryAnne, Pioneer, Susan, and Willy, as if they were her very own. Parley liked having older brothers and sisters, even if none of them had been willing to call Constance Breeton by the name of *Mother*. Parley had always felt safe, secure in the knowledge that those brothers and sisters would always be there for her if she needed them, although Willy did tend to tease her without mercy.

Within moments, it seemed the entire Breeton family congregated around Parley to walk her to the church, where she would wed Brand Tarkington. Willy, beside her, made numerous comments that she did her best to ignore. Instead, she tried as she walked to smooth out the skirts of her new dress—such an extravagance, but one that Mother had insisted upon.

The Breeton house was large, but not large enough to accommodate all the people who would attend the wedding, so the ceremony would be held in the church. Most Martinsville weddings now were held there, and Parley thought the setting leant a certain gravity to what must be this lifelong contract she was making. She and Brand were making together.

She giggled, and Willy preened beside her, thinking he had made her laugh. But she had hardly heard his quips. Instead she was remembering Louise's indignant face the day before when Parley had suggested that perhaps they should wed their husbands in the barn.

There was a small part of her mind that truly wished they could be married there, where Parley and Louise had taken their first breaths. Surely that would be as holy a place as the church.

She blushed at the unconventionality of such a thought, and again Willy misinterpreted. His comment about her upcoming wedding night had been but a jest, but Parley thought it was not in very good taste.

Such a short time later, Parley and Brand—Mister and Mistress Tarkington—turned to face the congregation. Brand placed his arm around Parley's shoulder, an easy thing for him to do since he was so much taller than she was, and grinned down at her. "Shall we go home now, wife?"

"No. That we shall not." She fingered the bear claw she had worn every day since the previous year when Brand had given it to her. "You know the women of the church have put together a meal for everyone to enjoy. We cannot be absent, or there will be speculation."

Brand smiled widely, as if he could imagine just what sort of speculation there would be.

The meal had to wait, of course, because Brand's step-sister Louise Martin's wedding to Frederick Breeton followed immediately after that of Parley and Brand and was, Parley thought, almost as fine a ceremony as her own had been. Almost.

Reverend Anders Russell walked carefully down the three stairs, his ash cane tapping the floor ahead of him, and led the way out of the church, followed by the two newly married pairs and then the rest of the congregation. The day was fine, indeed, with not a hint of rain to mar the noon feast. The two couples formed a line with Reverend Russell just outside the church.

Parley's parents approached them first. Mother embraced Parley while Father grasped the hand of his new son-in-law. "Take you good care of my daughter, Son Tarkington," Willem said with a twinkle in his eye. "And give her many children."

Brand beamed and Parley blushed.

The process was repeated as Brand's mother, Louetta Tarkington Martin, accompanied by his stepfather, Silas Martin, embraced the couple and clasped their hands and shoulders and uttered wishes for "as good a marriage as Mister Silas Martin and I have had all these years."

Parley made a point of thanking Mother Tarkington. What a delight to use those words.

"You know, my dear," Mother Tarkington said with a smile, "I would never let Brand wear that necklace in church. At least, not on the outside of his shirt where it could be seen."

Brand laughed. "You told me it made me look like a wild man."

Parley lifted her chin, but before she could defend her choice of wedding accessory, Mother Tarkington allayed her thoughts. "That claw suits you well, Parley, for I know you have the strength of a dozen bears."

Parley's chin dropped in astonishment. And then she lifted it again. With pride.

Next came all the brothers and sisters. MaryAnne and her husband Thomas Russell, who stuttered out his congratulations while MaryAnne hugged Parley fiercely, Pioneer with Bridgett Hastings, whom he had courted for the past two years, and Willy with Nell Surratt, his intended. Willy, of course, was accompanied by yet another in the string of black and white dogs he had had for as long as Parley could remember. In fact, it was a well-known story in Martin's Village that said Lucky, Willy's first dog, had lain on the quilt beside Parley when she was just a baby and growled at anyone who came near, anyone except the family. Ten years before, Parley had cried almost as much as Willy did when Lucky died after a very long dog life.

Susan, who was still unmarried, hung back until the others had greeted the new couple. She waited to approach Parley and Brand until everyone dispersed to the tables liberally piled with food. "I have a gift for you," she said. "I did not want to give it to you here where there are so many people present. May I come by your house tomorrow?"

"Of course you may, Sister." Susan, of course, was a stepsister, but Parley had never paid much attention to such details.

"Perhaps you will wait until Tuesday," Brand said. "Tomorrow will be filled with church services, and we will take Monday as a day to ourselves."

"Oh! Oh, of course." Susan fluttered her hands in embarrassment.

Parley was equally flustered. She knew that certain things happened on a wedding night, but she was unclear as to the exact details. Only that her mother had said it might be painful at first but that "I hope you will come to enjoy your marital duties as I have enjoyed mine." Mother had looked out the window at Father as he toiled by the barn, and her face had softened, suffused with a glow that Parley thought was absolutely beautiful, even though her mother was so very old—more than forty years of age.

"Yes," Parley said. "Come on the Tuesday and you can help me set up my quilting frame."

Next in line was Mistress Mary Frances Martin, the Widow Martin now for these past six weeks. "May your marriage be blessed, my dear," she told Parley. "May you never be separated."

Parley studied the older woman. What a strange thing to have said. "I am sure we never will."

As if in affirmation, she felt Brand's arm tighten around her shoulders. "She would find it difficult to get rid of me."

Widow Martin nodded and moved away to make room for the others behind her.

WHEN SUSAN BREETON walked through Parley's kitchen door that Tuesday, she was struck by how different Parley looked. It was not anything Susan could point to precisely, but there was an air of suppressed excitement about her stepsister. "I hope you are well," Susan said, setting her fabric-wrapped present on the table so she could embrace Parley.

"Oh, I am very well," Parley said. "Very well indeed."

Susan watched, fascinated, as a tide of red washed up Parley's neck and suffused her face. Susan supposed it had something to do with the enigmatic "happenings" of a wedding night—and possibly, based on the way Brand had postponed Susan's visit, on the happenings of the days immediately after the wedding as well.

But Susan did not know for sure, as she was unmarried and likely to remain so. She did not resent Parley for having married the son—stepson—of Silas Martin, but Susan could never look at another man and not compare him to Silas. She had been but twelve when they left Brandtburg in 1741, but her hopes had been high all along the trail, as she had grown closer to womanhood. Until that awful day in 1744 when Silas married the widow Louetta Tarkington and thus became Brand's stepfather.

Susan could not stop her heart—and sometimes her fists—from tightening each time she saw Louetta and Silas together. She really did love Parley, but now, knowing that Parley would be Silas's beloved daughter-in-law, her mouth tightened, and she had to make a determined effort to unclench her lips.

She turned back to the table by the door, picked up the bundle, and placed it in Parley's arms. "I hope you will like this. I carried it with me all the way from—" She stopped suddenly. All the original settlers of Martinsville had been enjoined by Homer Martin never to mention the name of the town they had left, lest the evil Brandts learn of where they had settled. *If they find us, they will descend on us,* Homer had told everyone repeatedly. *They will descend on us and wreak their vengeance.* Even though Homer Martin had died just a few months before, no member of that original company would ever have considered going against his commands.

"I brought it with me when we journeyed here," she said.

Parley studied her for a moment, and bent to unwrap the parcel.

"Susan, how lovely!" She held up the wooden plate and turned it so the morning light caught the design carved into it. "What an intricate design. Leaves and berries and—are those your initials?"

Susan put out a hand and stroked the entwined monograms. "I had hoped to use it in my own house one day, but I can see that that is unlikely to happen, now that I am almost in my dotage. I would rather have you enjoy the use of it."

"You may marry yet. After all, my husband Brand is only a few years younger than you and he has only now married."

"A man may wait to marry until he is thirty, but we women do not have that luxury."

Parley tilted her head to one side and ran her finger along the carving. "Are these other initials? This looks like it might be an M."

"No." Susan swallowed, hoping the lie would not condemn her eternal soul. "No. It is just a lovely curving design."

As Susan left Parley's house several hours later, having successfully helped to set up Parley's quilting frame, it occurred to her that if she had been fortunate enough to catch the eye of Silas Martin, and to become his wife, she might have had a difficult time explaining just how she had come to own the wooden plate he had carved for Sophrona Blanchard, with his initials twining around hers. In all these years she had never even once thought of that difficulty. Now, she supposed, Silas would see the plate when Parley used it. She very nearly turned around to ask for it back. But then she would have to explain. On the other hand, Silas might ask her about it if Parley said in all innocence, "See the lovely plate Susan gave me."

She could say the plate had been a gift to her from someone in Brandtburg. No. She would say she had found it on her doorstep many years ago. Let him believe that Sophrona had given away the plate after Silas scorned her.

Susan could not admit that she had stolen it from Sophrona when she was but twelve years of age.

She squared her shoulders. She would put it out of her mind. Surely Silas would never say anything to her about the plate.

At least, she hoped he would not. At the same time, she hoped he would. It would give her an excuse to talk with him.

2000

EASTON LIFTED THE top hatbox from the most recent stack. We'd already gone through the two stacks that were on the floor between those two tall dressers. Unfortunately most of those hats had been horribly dated, in sad condition, or just plain ugly.

She opened it and let out her breath in a long *ohhhhhh.*

What is a longoh?

"What did you find dear?"

Sadie was the only person who ever called Easton a dear.

She does not look like a deer. I have seen deer many times in among the trees.

Easton lifted a wide-brimmed confection of black and brown ribbons, feathers, and lace. She whipped off the dull orangey-brown tam she'd been wearing and placed her new find atop her head. "What do you think?"

"I think it's absolutely lovely," Sadie said.

"Marvelous," said Dee.

"Obviously," Rebecca Jo said, "it was made just for you."

I had to admit that with that hat atop the fiery red hair that streamed down her back, Easton looked like something out of a fashion magazine. Too bad she didn't have the beautiful personality to go along with it.

You do not like her at all.

Sadie began singing "In your Easter bonnet," and Easton joined in, "with all the frills upon it." They kept going through the rest of the chorus, and by the time they got to *you'll be the grandest lady in the*

Easter parade, we were all singing along. I was surprised that Amanda and Maddy seemed to know such an old song.

On the other hand, maybe it wasn't so surprising. There were some things—songs, snatches of poetry, sayings—that seemed to infuse the culture. How long, though, would they last?

June 1801

MARY ETTA HASTINGS was beside herself. Her mother would never forgive her if she found out. Oh no, Astaline Shipleigh Hastings was absolutely unyielding about some things—about most things—and for all her eight years Mary Etta had always seemed to be on the wrong side of her mother.

Mother was especially unyielding about dishonesty. About stealing. About lying. "I had enough of lying from my one-legged cousin George," Mother always told Mary Etta. "I will not stand for it in one of my children."

Mary Etta hurried along Fifth Street and ducked onto the path that led through the Old Woods. It was far too late to change her mind now. She had the hat and she could not—she simply could not—leave it. She had wanted a hat exactly like this one ever since she first saw that nose-in-the-air Hannah Russell wearing it in church two months ago on Easter Sunday. And now, it had been like a gift, a gift to her, to Mary Etta. A gift from above.

It *was* a gift. Only a few moments ago, as she headed home after giving Mother's message to Aunt Para Lee, she had heard a shout of dismay from somewhere up on the cliffs, and then the hat had come sailing through the air, right past the branches of the tallest oak tree on Fifth Street, to land in the middle of the lane, almost at Mary Etta's feet. And it was not even damaged, not that she could see. Other than a little dust from the road, but that was easily brushed off. Luckily, the day was not rainy, so there was no mud about. When she bent over to pick up the hat, a searing pain had flashed through her head behind her eyes, but after a moment it abated. She had looked all around her, but nobody was in sight.

Where could she hide the hat? She could never wear it—that was for sure. She paused halfway down the path through the Old Woods. Her head was aching something terrible, but she could not stop to rest. She knew Hannah Russell, or whomever she had been walking with on the path along the top of the cliffs, up above the town, would soon come pelting down the track and along Fifth Street to try to find the wind-blown hat.

Even here in the shade of the Old Woods, the air felt breathless, hot, uncomfortable. She did not understand it. Usually the woods gave a welcome respite from any heat the summer could throw. When she approached the end of the forest path and saw the tall column in the cemetery looming ahead, she slowed and arranged the voluminous folds of her skirt around the hat to hide it from prying eyes.

She sauntered as slowly as she dared—she could not risk her skirts blowing awry and revealing her prize. Several town women bent over various graves, tidying them or tending the flowers planted there. Mary Etta raised her other hand in greeting, but maintained her steady pace. Luckily it was only about two blocks to Beechnut House. If she could just make it upstairs to her room, she could hide the hat under the bed.

But Mother would be sure to find it there, for she poked around incessantly. If not Mother, then Electa, who shared the room with Mary Etta, would find it.

The attic. Mary Etta might not be able ever to admit to having the hat, unless she outlived everyone else alive now in Martinsville, for everyone had seen Hannah wearing the hat on Easter, and the hat was truly distinctive. Everyone would remember it. But this way, Hannah would never be able to wear it again, and that made it worth the trouble Mary Etta was going to, to secrete it away like this. It was Hannah's fault that the hat had blown off her head. She should have secured it better, using a second or even a third hatpin.

Despite a light cloud covering, the afternoon sun felt blinding in Mary Etta's eyes, and her head began to throb again.

Mother, Electa, Rose, and the twins were all five out in the garden, but their backs were bent over the rows of beans. Mary Etta could see Aunt Naomi gathering Muscadine grapes down at the arbor, with her little son beside her. Mother would be upset that Mary Etta had taken so long on her morning's errand. *I will tell her I had a hard time finding*

Aunt Para Lee to deliver the message. After all, that was almost true. Aunt had been out at the back of her garden. Maybe Mother will not even notice that I am late.

Keeping a watchful eye on her mother and younger sisters, Mary Etta sidled up the front steps, careful to avoid the one that squeaked, and into the front room. It took her a long time to walk up the stairs into the dark old attic—she had wanted to run, but found that her legs would not cooperate. She searched until she found a hatbox that looked to be wide enough for Hannah's hat. *For my hat,* she corrected herself. She tossed the contents—a disreputable-looking straw piece with a wilting green ribbon around the crown of it—onto the floor. She could not resist trying on her hat, but without a good mirror, she could not tell just how beautiful it looked. That did not matter, though. She knew how lovely she must appear in it.

She passed a hand across her sweating forehead. The day was not particularly sunny. She could not understand how it could be so unusually hot.

"I will come up here and visit you often," she told the hat as she placed the hatbox in the shadow of an old steamer trunk. "For now, you rest here, for I must go out to the garden and help Mother and my sisters."

Little did Mary Etta know that within a day, she and her closest sister, Electa, would both be burning up with fever.

Little did she know that within a week, she and Electa would both be dead, and the hat would languish for years, unknown and unclaimed, in the attic of Beechnut House.

2000

AS THE EASTER BONNET song was coming to an end, I took a good look at Easton. She and Sadie had linked arms and were swaying in time to the music. I could feel my resentment rising into a slow boil and felt my heart beginning to pound. Easton had been such a thorn in the side of almost every married woman in Martinsville, and probably a good many of the unmarried ones as well, for all I knew. I could still see Glaze spewing venom the day Easton tried to hit on Tom.

With that volcanic hair spilling all the way down her back—that was part of it, I knew. I hated how gorgeous her hair was. But more than that, the way she flirted outrageously with all the men—she'd tried it with Bob, which was probably the main reason I disliked her so much.

Marmalade oozed her way up into my lap …

SoftFoot and I got rid of her that time. I licked her face and she screeched. She does not like cats.

… so I patted her soft back and rubbed her silky ears.

Thank you.

They started on another interminable repeat of the chorus, and despite Marmalade's calming presence, I felt the bile rise in the back of my throat. I couldn't help myself; I glared at Easton. Just then Sadie turned her head and caught what must have been a murderous look before I could erase it.

She held her free hand up to her face and began coughing, slowly at first and then more vehemently. I was getting concerned and rose from my seat to go to her, but Ida and Dee were there ahead of me.

Sadie waved them away. "Easton, dear," she finally gasped, "would you run downstairs and get me a big glass of water?"

As soon as we could no longer hear Easton's footsteps, Sadie slapped her chest a couple of times and heaved a prolonged sigh. "There. I feel better now."

She looked all right, but just to be sure, I asked, "Are you sure you're okay?"

"I'm not ready to croak yet." She gave me a pointed look and then scanned the other faces. "For some reason I just thought about something my mother, Eulalia Martin Russell, used to tell me." Without waiting for our response, she went on. "Holding a grudge is like taking poison and expecting the other person to die."

What does that mean?

Ida gave her a probing examination. "What on earth does that have to do with the price of tea in China?"

What is a prizeatee inch eyena?

We heard Easton pounding up the stairs. "I haven't the slightest idea," Sadie said, pointedly not looking at me. Then she turned to drink from the tall glass Easton held for her.

Okay, Sadie, I thought. You win.

What does she win?
I'll let it go.
Let what go? Mouse droppings! Humans can be so confusing.

Sunday, 7 March 1742

MARY FRANCES GLOWERED after the retreating form of Homer Martin as he stormed out of the wagon in the middle of the night. She was too concerned about her son, though, to say anything. The baby's screams had begun soon before it was time for her to retire for the night. She had not even taken the time to write in her precious journal.

Mister Martin had snored through the first two bouts of the baby's shrieks, but this latest round was too loud and too long-lasting for even Homer to sleep through.

Mary Frances rocked her child, crooned, sang to him, tried to feed him, bounced him lightly—which he usually delighted in—and finally just held him tight against her chest. Nothing would soothe the child, and Mary Frances felt herself grow more and more frantic. Was he sick? What if he died? What had she missed? How could she bear to lose this proof of her love for Hubbard Brandt? Why had her mother chained her to Homer Martin? Why was that man so coldhearted?

She felt the wagon rock to one side and looked up expecting to see Homer Martin returning. She clamped her lips shut to prevent her from speaking the sharp words she felt welling up inside her.

Instead, she saw a woman's shape outlined against what little moonlight came through the opening in the canvas.

"Mistress Martin? May I perhaps be of service?"

Mary Frances almost cried. The mere presence of Louetta Tarkington was so calming, so soothing. "I am sorry we woke you."

"We mothers waken easily when a babe is fractious." Louetta settled herself beside Mary Frances and reached for the baby. Within seconds, young John quieted.

"How did you do that?" Despite the low level of light within the enclosed wagon, Mary Frances could see Louetta Tarkington's face clearly. She was somewhat taken aback at the—what was it?—the pity she saw there.

"A babe is connected in more ways than one to its mother," Mistress Tarkington said slowly. She seemed to measure her words with great care. "When the mother is … is distressed in any way, a young child feels it." She waited for a moment. "Just now, when I entered your wagon, I could see that you clutched your child with … with more fear than his crying might have engendered. And perhaps some anger, too?" Her voice was a gentle question.

Mary Frances raised her hands to her face and massaged her forehead—hard, as if she could erase some of the memories therein.

Mistress Tarkington rearranged young John's blanket about his now drowsy form and then simply waited.

"I … I was forced into this marriage," Mary Frances admitted in a whisper, almost unable to believe she was revealing so private a matter.

Mistress Tarkington nodded. "I thought as much." She laid a gentle kiss on John's forehead. "He is a bonny child, one who does not know how to deal with his mother's feelings of anger."

Mary Frances cried out, somewhat louder than she had intended. "But, what am I to do?"

"Your anger toward your husband is easy for me to understand. I was fortunate because my marriage with my late husband was a happy one. I am sure I would have railed against a forced and unloving marriage." She reached out her hand and touched Mary Frances lightly on the shoulder. "You have your child, though. Can you not concentrate on him alone and let some of your anger slide away? For the sake of young John? And"—she added with a devilish grin—"for the ears of every other mother in this community?" She handed the small bundle back to his mother, and they both smiled as the sleeping baby let out a small damp burp.

"I will try," Mary Frances said. "For my son's sake. Thank you."

From that day forward, Mary Frances did not speak to Homer Martin.

Homer Martin did not seem to notice.

2000
Matthew Olsen's House

CLARA FELT LIKE she'd been slogging through quicksand for the past three months. It wasn't fair. She looked around Matthew's little living room at the other people sitting there as if nothing in the world were wrong, and here was Clara having to be sure Hubbard got to the bathroom often enough. Having to help him into and out of his clothes twice a day. Having to wipe that ridiculous nose of his. He was nothing like his brother Cornelius had been. She'd always hated the way Hubbard looked, and now it was even worse. He was like a robot. He did what she told him to do; he ate when she told him to eat, as long as she fed him. He sat still until she told him to move, and then he went wherever she said to go.

At first, right after he got out of the hospital, everybody was so concerned and so appreciative of how hard she worked to care for her husband. Little did they know how much she was driven by guilt. By what had happened up on the cliffs. By what she had said. By what she had done.

But now, she couldn't help but notice, nobody seemed to care any more. Oh, once in a while somebody would offer to stay and watch him if she had errands to run and things to accomplish, but usually she had to ask them. All those people who used to call her brave and stalwart—yes, that was the word they'd used—now they just seemed to take it for granted that Clara would be there to take care of whatever Hubbard needed.

She poured herself a cup of coffee from the old percolator that sat on the top of Matthew's wood stove. When she sat back down next to Hubbard on the blue couch in the living room, she turned to look at him. Surprising the heck out of her, he turned his head to look at her. It was more than just a quick flick of a glance this time. "Y-y-you." The word, louder than appropriate, staggered out of his mouth like a drunk reeling out of a bar.

"He said something!" Matthew stopped stroking the head of that stupid parakeet of his. "Do you believe it, Mr. Fogarty? Hubbard said something!"

They all gathered around the couch. Nick Foley put his hand on Hubbard's shoulder and squeezed. Anita patted Hubbard's knee.

Matthew—and Mr. Fogarty—leaned close. "Are you okay, Hubbard?"

Hubbard turned once again to look at Clara, his mouth opening and closing, but no sound came forth. Anita Foley intervened. "Nick, Matthew, back up and give him some space to breathe. This is obviously a miracle, but we've got to be patient."

Matthew nodded sagely. "It won't do to tire him." Turning to Clara he asked, "Do you think you should call his doctor?"

Clara had to drag her gaze from Hubbard. A word. Her husband's first and only word since that awful day in September, and what had he said? He'd looked at her and accused her. "No," she said. "We can't drive anywhere anyway. Maybe I should take Hubbard to our room so he can rest."

She had to get him away from everybody. Had to. In case he said something else.

"You're right," Nick said. "That would be best for Hubbard."

Anita twisted her hands together. "Do you think he's going to …?" The words petered out, and Clara didn't even try to help her finish the sentence.

"I don't know," Clara finally said, as she helped Hubbard to his feet.

Matthew took Hubbard's other arm. "C'mon, fella. We'll get you settled down in no time. I'm glad I put the two of you in my room so you don't have to climb any stairs." Once they got Hubbard onto the bed, with a thick comforter pulled up around his chin, Matthew backed up toward the door. "You need anything, Clara?"

She could tell he wanted to be gone, in case Hubbard had to do something disgusting, like go to the bathroom and then he'd have to be wiped. "No," she said. "We're fine. I'll just sit with him."

As soon as the door closed, she turned the lock. Then she was on her knees beside the bed, her voice low, but urgent. "I didn't mean for you to fall off the cliff, Hubbard. You have to believe me. I was just so angry when you threatened to tell the Council you weren't really a Martin. Where would that leave me? Where would that leave us?"

She waited, hoping he'd respond. Hoping he wouldn't. That day she'd followed Charlotte Ellis up to the top of the cliff, she'd hidden behind that tree, planning to confront them for having an affair. She never expected blackmail. She didn't know which would have been preferable, a cheating husband or one who paid hush money or … or what she'd ended up with.

She searched his face, but he seemed to have drawn back into that nebulous nowhere that he'd inhabited for the past three months.

She couldn't count on it, though. He could regain his speech at any time, now that he'd said that one word.

No, please no.

HUBBARD LAY STILL. He was so tired. Clara was there. She hated him. She always had. Hadn't she made that clear enough with what she'd said, what she'd done? It was too much to deal with.

AS LONG AS we were in the attic, we seemed to lose touch with what was happening two floors below our feet. I hadn't heard any complaints about the sleeping places I'd assigned. So far, it looked like we'd all be preparing our own breakfasts—although I was seriously considering suggesting that Bob and I make cheese grits for tomorrow morning. The men made the lunch, so we cleared the tables and washed the dishes. We had to be sure always to keep a couple of kettles of water on the wood stove so we'd always have washing-up water. The generator powered the fridge and the pump, but not the water heater.

Now, though, with the wedding getting ready to happen shortly, our routine was completely disrupted.

"I don't know about all of you," Ida said, "but I'm ready for a potty break, and if we have to wait until after the wedding to eat, I'd like at least to get a little snack before the ceremony. Let's head down to the kitchen."

"I hope the men will agree," Melissa said.

"They'll have to, unless they want to starve." With a grunt, Pat set aside the box she'd been investigating, and it landed on the floor with a heavy clunk and a distinct rattle.

"What on earth's in there?" Melissa asked.

"Mismatched stainless steel flatware." Pat sounded disgusted. "Not worth saving and certainly not worth going in the museum."

Even Maddy didn't object when Pat headed for our reject pile, which was getting taller by the minute.

Sadie stopped her. "Can't those go to Goodwill?" Without missing a step, Pat veered left toward the giveaway pile. "I lived through too many shortages during both the world wars, and the Depression in between them," Sadie explained. "Goes against my grain to waste anything."

I agreed with her, although I hadn't lived through the rationing of the war years, or through the Great Depression. In fact, I was appalled that I hadn't thought earlier about my Reduce, Reuse, Recycle motto. "I'll go back through the rejects," I volunteered. "Later. Once the storm is over. There may be some other things that don't belong in the landfill."

"Not many, I'd imagine," Pat said, as she set the box at the foot of the giveaway pile.

"Here," Easton said. "Sadie, will you help me drape these old sheets over these piles?"

"Certainly, dear, but why?"

"So they'll be somewhat disguised for the wedding."

Glaze's mouth dropped open. "Th … thank you, Easton," she finally said.

I wish I'd thought to do it.

Once the ugly collections were camouflaged, we trooped past the rows of chairs the men had set up and trailed down the stairs. I was last in the line.

No you are not. I am the last one.

Ahead of me I heard Melissa say, "We probably ought to plan a menu for the wedding feast."

I had no idea what form the "wedding feast" would take, and I had to admit that at this point I didn't really care. Sadie was right. I'd been holding a grudge about a number of things for way too long. It was time to let it all go. I remembered something somebody—who on earth had it been?—had taught me. Light a candle. Imagine all the ill feelings gathering inside your breath. When you're ready to release it, blow gently on the candle, just enough to set the flame to flickering, and imagine all the resentment leaving your body and being consumed by the flame. Then blow out the candle and watch the last vestiges of your anger dissipate as the smoke curls upward. I sounded like I was preaching at myself.

You are thinking hard.

My steps lagged as Marmalade meowed behind me. "Snack time," Glaze proclaimed ahead of me as the first of the women made it to the living room.

Rebecca Jo touched my shoulder. "Biscuit? Dee and I are going to move our things now. We'll be down once we're finished."

"Move your things? What are you talking about?"

"Glaze and Tom will need the big bed. The wedding? Remember?"

"Oh. You're right. I almost forgot. I'll need to …" My words trailed off. I'd have to get a clean set of sheets. Before I could race off in the opposite direction, Dee closed in from the other side.

"Stop, Biscuit. Everything's under control. We'll change the sheets and get the room all fixed up for them."

"But—"

"No buts about it. You go on downstairs and relax. Have a snack and stretch your legs a bit. We've already chosen our room."

"From the many available to us." Rebecca Jo sounded as amused as she looked.

"If you're sure."

"Of course we're sure. We'll join you as soon as we can."

By the time I reached the kitchen, everybody else was reaching for pretzels, cutting off slivers of cheese, munching on the last of the grapes Ida and Ralph had brought from the IGA.

I went back into the living room and lit a candle on the coffee table. Marmalade curled up on the couch beside me.

You feel very sad. I will keep you company.

Ida, who must have stopped off at one of the bathrooms on the second floor, came down the last flight of stairs. I could tell she was looking at me, but I went right on staring at the candle flame. I could almost feel her shrug, and her footsteps headed toward the kitchen. I didn't want to explain what I was doing. Thank goodness she didn't ask.

By the time I joined the rest of the group—feeling much lighter, I must admit—everyone was settled into their usual places. Bob looked inquiringly at me, but I just smiled and gave his bearded cheek a quick kiss as I sat beside him. I'm fairly sure everybody else assumed I'd been making a pit stop but I could tell Bob knew something unusual had happened. "I'll tell you tonight," I murmured and he nodded once.

It was so lovely having Mom and Dad here, and Esther and the Parkmans. Twenty-six was just as good a number as twenty-one had been, even better in fact, and the five extra chairs at the table just made everything a bit snuggier. If that was even a word. There was something so completely relaxing about being stranded by the ice storm.

Come see the possums!

Marmalade let out a shriek …

It was not a shriek. It was an invitation.

… and it took me a moment to locate her. She turned out to be on the windowsill in the breakfast nook with her head poked between the curtains and her tail waving like a banner. "What do you think she's looking at?"

"Only one way to find out." Bob scraped his chair back and went to investigate, followed almost immediately by Reebok.

"Oh," Reebok said when Bob drew back the curtain, "come here, everybody. You have to see this."

Rebecca Jo and Dee walked in then, so there was an even larger crowd at the bay window.

Three possums and five raccoons had gathered at the foot of the bird feeder, cleaning up the scattered seeds. Each time one of them tried to move to another position, it slid on the ice.

"This show is better than TV any time," Ralph said.

I saw Ida look at him with some surprise. "Well, then, I guess we'll just unplug our set when we get home and scatter some seeds around on the lawn."

He crossed his arms over his meager chest. "No sense in going that far."

Bob met my eyes and grinned. Thank goodness we both felt the same way about TV. Still grinning, he turned to Ida. "How about one more diary story?"

Thursday, 20 May 1742

MARY FRANCES COULD not decide whether she needed to cry or to laugh. Instead, she stood still with young John clasped to her heart. This marriage, but a week after the one of Constance Garner to Willem Breeton, reminded her far too much of the tragic death of her dear friend Myra Sue in April of 1741. Mistress Black had been widowed that same day, her husband gunned down by an unknown Brandt. Or perhaps, Mary Frances had to admit, perhaps by a Martin bullet gone astray. Here now, just a month after her year of mourning was finished, the widow was marrying old Mister Hastings.

She studied the prospective groom. He looked like he was stunned by the turn events had taken. Mary Frances wondered just who had proposed to whom. Ever since Widow Black's bath last week and her announcement that she would marry Mister Hastings on this day, she had been a regular dervish as she ordered all the details. The wedding feast was already set out upon trestle tables behind the assembled company. The turkey, which Widow Black had insisted someone hunt down and shoot, had been produced in fair time, plucked, prepared, and roasted to perfection, with only a few scorched spots on a wing that had dangled from the spit into the fire. Now it sat ready for consumption in the middle of a gathering of pots and platters of plenteous other foodstuffs.

The Breeton wedding last week had been well enough, she supposed, although Constance was too young truly to take on the mothering of Willem Breeton's brood. Mary Frances imagined that it would turn out to be a good enough match, as Constance and Willem seemed, other than the disparity in their ages, to be well suited to each other. Today's marriage, though, had been the source of much hilarity among the company—among the women, at least, for they had all seen the determination in Widow Black's eyes as soon as she had set her mind to ensnaring the elder Mister Hastings.

As the bridal couple joined arms and paced along the impromptu aisle, Mary Frances could not help but notice that Widow Black appeared to be a step or two ahead, as if she were pulling her quarry after her.

When the last *I will* was spoken, the company turned toward the waiting meal, only to find Lucky, Willy Breeton's black and white dog, standing in the center of the table, gleefully pulling chunks of meat from the hapless turkey.

The Widow Black—for Mary Frances could not think of her in any other way, despite the fact that she was now the senior Mistress Hastings—took after Lucky with a poker she scooped up from a nearby cooking fire. Widow Black was spry on her feet, but Lucky was far more agile than the elderly woman, even though Lucky was encumbered by a turkey leg and a wing—the un-scorched one—drooping from her mouth.

2000

"ONE MORE? FINE with me." Ida pulled the diary and her white gloves out of the capacious front pouch on her sweatshirt. Donning the gloves, she tilted the journal so the light of the window fell directly on it. "Easier than trying to read by candlelight," she said. "I don't know how Abe Lincoln ever managed."

What is a blinkin?

Ida waited until Carol finished her explanation about our sixteenth president.

Thursday 20 May 1742

Willy Breeton's black and white dog, Lucky, was certainly lucky today, for she managed to escape the wrath of Widow Black, who just moments before had become the wife of old Mister Hastings. The bride and groom are both grandparents, but I wish them happiness in their remaining years. The wedding feast centered around a roasted turkey that Daniel Endicott shot yesterday. I must admit the smell of it during the service was enough to take my mind far away from a mere wedding ceremony, no matter how unusual the match. No sooner were the bridal couple pronounced man and wife than we saw Lucky devouring the turkey.

Amid the hilarity bouncing back and forth as we thought about Willy Breeton's dog, Glaze leaned closer to me. "Would you come upstairs and help me get ready?"

I thought about all those pretty bows I'd meant to scatter around the attic. Oh, what the heck. Who needed them?

When Glaze rose, so did Dee and Maddy, my sister's bridesmaids. "Bye for now, folks," Maddy said.

"Where're you going?" Dave asked.

Bob was one step ahead of him. "Looks like it's time for them to get ready for the wedding."

"Too bad we don't have a turkey," Dave said. He pointed to the journal in front of Ida.

Ida stood and walked away from him, taking the journal with her.

"Or a dog."

There are no dogs here.

Maddy ignored him the same way Ida had. "We have to get this bride all gussied up."

Despite what Maddy said, we wouldn't have that much gussying to do. Even in sweatpants, Glaze was always drop-dead gorgeous.

I do not want her to drop dead!

How had her silvery hair stayed so lovely despite hats and at least three days of no washing? A darn good haircut helped, I knew, since her hair always seemed to fall into place. All she had to do was shake her head, and everything looked perfect.

I started out the doorway into the front hall, but Glaze turned aside, leaned down and whispered something to Esther, her soon-to-be grandmother-in-law. Esther looked a query at her, but then smiled and nodded. I wondered what that was about.

"Oh, yuck," Ida said, and I looked over toward where she stood at the window to see what was wrong. Outside, one of the possums had moved to one side away from the feeders and deposited a steamy load of poop.

"This moment of nature," Henry intoned in a truly ministerial voice, "was brought to you by the Sheffield-McKee Foundation."

I do not understand.

That started a round of poop jokes, as Dave and Ralph tried to outdo each other.

We headed for the stairs, but Dee detoured to the end of the living room and picked up a piece of firewood from the rack. "Ooh," she said. "It's deliciously warm—I guess from being stacked so near the wood stove."

"What's it for?" Glaze and I asked at the same time. Dee traded a grin with Maddy. "You'll see."

Marmalade led the way up the stairs and headed straight for the tiny room Glaze had been sharing with Maddy. It looked like she knew where we were going.

Possum poop! Of course I do.

When I reached the landing I turned at the sound of voices and saw the other women exiting the kitchen, no doubt to get away from the poop jokes. I didn't blame them.

Dee closed the door behind us and Glaze opened the small closet.

"This room's going to be lonely tonight with you gone," Maddy said as Glaze pushed aside some coat hangers and rummaged toward the back of the closet. Whatever could she be looking for?

Finally, Glaze emerged holding a dress bag. "I hope it's not too wrinkled," she said.

"You hope what's not too wrinkled?"

Her eyes crinkled at me. "Tom and I figured this storm might last awhile, so we decided to bring our wedding clothes with us."

Maddy gasped. "You brought your wedding dress and didn't tell me? I could have packed that indigo bridesmaid dress I bought. And I'd even have the gorgeous attic hat to wear with it."

"You can't do that, Maddy," I told her. "You don't want to look more spectacular than the bride." Not that I thought she really would—I just didn't want her wearing that dress that should have been mine. I know it was petty of me to think that, but I couldn't help it.

What is peddy?

Maybe I needed to light a candle for Maddy as well.

Why do you need to light a candle? There is plenty of light here.

"You'll be fine wearing just what you have on," Glaze said as Marmalade let out several strings of meows. "Nobody else is going to dress up. Just think about it—Sadie's going to be in her new blue bathrobe. But Tom and I thought we ought to plan ahead, just in case the storm lasted longer than we expected."

"You mean you planned to be married in the attic?" How could she have thought that far ahead?

"No," she admitted. "We were still planning on the church, but we thought we might have to leave directly from here to get there if the ice took a long time to melt."

"All right," Maddy conceded. "You're forgiven. But can I at least wear my hat?"

"Of course you can. I hope Ida will wear hers."

"Maybe I should wear my sunbonnet," Dee said.

Maddy headed toward the door. "I'll be back in a minute."

"Where are you going?"

Maddy grinned at Glaze. "I'm going to tell all the women to go upstairs a little early so they can put on their hats. We might as well make this a spectacular event as long as it's going to be in a historical location." With that, she zipped out the door.

"She won't have to tell Esther," Glaze said. "I already asked her to wear that beautiful hat from London."

"The one that missed going down with the Titanic?"

"Hush, Dee! I just think it's a lovely hat, and Esther ought to wear it to my wedding. After all, she's the grandmother of the groom. If we were getting married in the church, she'd be all dressed up."

"Yeah," Dee said. "Even with Esther wearing a turtleneck, the hat'll look real pretty on her. What are you going to call her once you're married?"

"What do you mean?"

"Esther. Will you call her Grandma the way Tom does?"

Glaze stared at Dee for a few seconds. "I never really thought about it. I guess I'll just keep calling her Esther. Here, trade places with me so I can lay the dress out on the bed."

"Sorry I had to give you such a tiny room," I told her.

"Not a problem. It'll feel like a palace to Maddy this evening once I'm out of the way." The blush that spread up from her neck to her hairline was quite attractive.

"When this house was an inn"—I ran my hand along the antique metal headboard of the twin bed closest to me as Marmalade jumped up onto the comforter—"I wonder how many people they could put up here at one time."

"That could be one of the original beds," Dee said.

"No," I said. "I doubt it. Didn't they always have wide bed frames in the old inns? So people could share the warmth?" I looked at Maddy, who had just reentered, her arms laden with our hats. She nodded.

Tuesday 11 September 1753

ROBERT HASTINGS HAD never lost faith that he would one day have the public house and inn he had dreamed of, but there had been times during the summer as the building was being constructed, that he had despaired of its ever having a right angle anywhere. The men of the town had been willing enough to help with the construction, especially after he and Nehemiah let them sample some of the ale that would, Robert was sure, become the most famous in the entire colony of Georgia—or at least in the valley of the Mee-too-chee River. The problem was that the men all had their own land to cultivate, their own daily chores that could not be ignored. So there had been little or no continuity in the building process.

But now the day had arrived when the first customers would cross the threshold of his new Inn and Public House.

Robert beamed at his wife as their neighbors gathered on the road in front of the tavern. A stretch of dry weather for the past two weeks meant the road was not muddy, a good sign indeed.

Willy Breeton and his dogs ran up and down the lane. Hickory led the pack now that Lucky had gotten old enough to choose lying in the shade over romping in the street. Robert wondered if Willy would ever grow up enough to stop his romping around like that. At twenty-one, he should certainly have begun to act more manly. But then Robert noticed Nell Surratt watching Willy. There was certainly something brewing there. Willy would give up his silliness soon enough once Nell began to exert her influence. Women had a way of bringing men under control. Had not his own wife roped him in so very long ago? And was he not glad indeed that she had done so?

Some of the young girls of the town had already congregated

nearby and were chanting their favorite jump rope song.

We left in 1741,
Our travels then were just begun.
We plodded on in '42,
At times, our leaving did we rue.
We well nigh stopped in '43,
That year was such a misery.
We journeyed on in '44,
Not knowing we had one year more.
We came to rest in '45,
For that was when we did arrive.

The girls—and everyone else in town—might think that forty-five was when the town started, but as far as Robert Hastings was concerned, no town was a true town without a decent tavern. That was why he had asked Silas Martin to carve the *1753* almost as substantial a size as the name. *Beechnut House*, in honor of the enormous tree that had graced the doorway of his previous tavern in Brandtburg. Here, in this fertile valley, he had plenty of oaks and maple and hickory, but none of those names seemed to suit. He had considered *Hickory House*, but his daughter Bridget laughed at the name when he suggested it and said it reminded her of *hickory dickory dock, the mouse ran up the clock*, so of course that name would not have suited. He intended to have as few mice as possible in his inn.

Ultimately it was his wife, the inimitable Jane Elizabeth Benton Hastings, who had, only the day before, thought of *Beechnut House*. "Homer Martin might not want us ever to speak of where we came from," she told him, "but our history is a proud one, and *Beechnut House* will remind the ones who journeyed with us of whence we came."

Mistress Hastings had outdone herself in readying the refreshments that would accompany the opening of the first keg of ale. Charles and Lucius stood beside their father, while Bridget, standing near her mother on the wide front porch, kept the two younger girls in check. Edna, who was married to Charles, held her four-year-old son Alonzo, while Fionella Surratt, to whom Lucius was affianced, stood off to one side of the porch, as if she did not quite know what to do with herself.

Once a substantial crowd had gathered, Robert raised his not inconsiderable voice. "Welcome friends. Welcome neighbors." He looked directly at a young man who had ridden into town just that morning. "And welcome, stranger. It is with great pride that I introduce to you the new Hastings Inn and Public House, otherwise and henceforth to be known as *Beechnut House*."

"That is a mighty fancy name," Willem Breeton called out in his raspy voice.

Breeton's son-in-law, Thomas Russell, asked, "W-w-when will you h h-h-hang out a sh-sh-shingle?"

"It is a mighty fancy name for a mighty fancy establishment," Robert called back, "and the sign is being prepared even now by Silas Martin."

"Give me another few days," Silas said, "and you will have as fine a sign as I can make."

Robert nodded his thanks. "This establishment is one of which every inhabitant of Martinsville can be proud, for many of you—most of you—have helped with the building of it."

He noticed a number of the women nodding. They had certainly kept the menfolk well fed while the building was going on, and even now, most of them held food offerings for the celebration.

"Would you have room in your inn for a stranger to lodge?"

The crowd shifted as everyone turned to inspect the newcomer.

"I do believe we can find a space for you," Robert Hastings said, and many in the crowd hooted. They knew as well as Mister Hastings that the many rooms above the common room would remain empty for years, until the town grew substantially and until folk from outside the valley found the hidden town of Martin's Village.

Up to this point, few strangers had come to town, but the ones who appeared always seemed to be the sort who brought value with them, and most of them had chosen to stay.

Beside him, Robert Hastings felt his wife stir. "You will be most welcome, Sir. Are there any who follow along with you?"

Hastings was well aware of the import of his wife's seemingly innocuous question. Were there, perhaps, Brandts on the trail, even so many years after the unpleasantness of 1741? But the man answered without hesitation.

"Nay, but if I find the town agreeable—which I have no doubt I will," he added quickly in response to a wave of mutterings—"I will return home to gather my family."

Several of the young women in the crowd frowned at that.

"My parents, my seven brothers, and my three sisters long to leave the confines of too crowded a town. We would bring worthy skills."

Hastings raised an eyebrow as he noticed two of the young unmarried women sidle closer to the stranger who had not mentioned a wife, but the young man appeared to think the raised eyebrow betokened a request for more information.

"My eldest brother is a cooper, and the youngest is his apprentice."

Welcome news indeed. Their own cooper, Cyrus Fiske, was far advanced in years, and Nehemiah Garner would have an increasing need for well-made kegs in which to store his magnificent ale as the tavern's custom grew.

Hastings could see questions arising in the eyes of many of the assembled people, but lest this turn into an interview of the newcomer, he raised his voice. "As I have said, you are welcome, Sir, and we can speak later. Perhaps this evening over a flagon of my fine ale."

Once again, the crowd laughed at the ease with which Robert Hastings gathered in a new customer.

"For now, though, I welcome you all to the Beechnut House Tavern. Your first cup of ale will be on the house." Robert felt sure he would have enough cups for everyone. He had the many pewter ones he had brought on the long journey, but there were also the hand-carved wooden ones the other stranger—John Gilman—had created for the Surratt family these many years ago.

Reverend Anders Russell stepped forward and the murmurings of the crowd ceased as the good pastor made his way painfully up the steps, leaning heavily on his cane. At the top he nodded to Mistress Hastings. He never failed to give her good due for having saved his leg—and quite possibly his life—the previous summer. "I will at this time say a prayer of thanksgiving that we now have a second gathering place worthy of our fine community." He must have noticed the curious looks many of the people there gave him. "The first gathering place, of course, is our church. But I acknowledge that there has been need of another, more secular place in which we can congregate. Will you bow your heads." It was a command rather than a question.

Robert was happy to comply, for while he felt sure his business would be a success, he appreciated the implied approval of the minister. He had to restrain himself from laughing outright, though, when Hickory sat at the front of the crowd and bent his head. He was probably just inspecting a bug, but it sure looked as if the big black and white dog was praying along with everyone else.

Once the prayer was completed, Homer Martin mounted the steps. As the leader of the community, he must have thought he was entitled to enter first, but Robert still recalled the fights Homer had instigated at the tavern in Brandtburg, and he was determined not to give Homer Martin that honor.

He beckoned to Reverend Russell to precede him, and Homer Martin had to give way. Then Robert stepped inside the wide front door, motioning to his friends to enter. Everyone waited for Homer Martin, and then pushed their way inside behind him. Robert knew they would be crowded indeed, so he served the first round of ale quickly and sent a number of the people upstairs to look over the multiple rooms. If they kept circulating, he felt sure nobody would feel too constricted. Homer Martin alone showed no curiosity about the rest of the structure. He stayed at the long bar and drank flagon after flagon, never offering to pay for any of it.

The women, as they entered, placed their sharing-food on the tables alongside Jane Elizabeth's contributions, where it was all delved into with great gusto.

Robert fully expected a large number of the men—and that stranger—to gather later in the evening and, hopefully, many evenings henceforward. After all, he had Nehemiah Garner's fine ale in good supply. If Homer Martin did not drink it all this day.

2000

DEE STEPPED BACK and studied Glaze standing there in her softly draped silver dress. It went beautifully with her shiny silver hair. "It's a good thing that dress has long sleeves and a high neckline," Dee said.

"We wouldn't want you freezing during your wedding."

Glaze smoothed the long skirt. "It's not too badly wrinkled, is it?"

"Don't worry, sis," I told her. "You're so lovely nobody will pay attention to a few wrinkles."

"So, you're saying it *is* too wrinkled?"

I think it is beautiful.

Marmalade meowed and rubbed her face against one of the sleeves.

I can reach SmellSweet better when I am up here on the bed.

Glaze laughed. "Looks like it's good enough for Marmalade, so it'll have to be good enough for me." She turned toward the mirror, brushed her hair, then inserted the elaborate hair comb—the one made of horn, the one with a broken prong tip. Had it really been only yesterday that we'd found it? "This is my *something old*," she said.

"Where does that come from?" Dee asked.

"I got it in the attic," Glaze said. "Remember?"

"No. I meant the rhyme about something old, something new."

"Old English." Maddy of course was the one who answered her, since I had no idea where the tradition had begun.

Dee stroked Glaze's soft sleeve. "I think your dress counts as the *something new*, then."

I handed Glaze the handkerchief with the embroidered flowers I'd tucked in my sweatpants pocket that morning. I thought the stain added some historic authenticity to it. The hanky was *not* one I'd used during the day! "Here's your *something borrowed*, Glaze. Now all we need is something blue."

While you are looking, you could play with me.

Marmalade meowed and we looked down to see her holding her favorite chase toy in her mouth. Her fuzzy blue mouse.

"Perfect!" Glaze took the mouse, threw it for Marmy, who pounced on it with delight. Glaze retrieved it.

That is her part of the game.

"May I use it for a little while?"

Why?

She apparently agreed, with such a cute little meow, so Glaze tucked it into her pocket.

You are not going to throw it again?

"Your wedding dress has pockets?" Maddy sounded as astonished as I felt.

"I won't buy a dress that doesn't have them," Glaze said. "You never know when you're going to need them."

"Yeah," Dee said. "You never know when you're going to have a mouse to haul around with you. A blue one."

I could just imagine the laughter as Glaze and Tom readied for bed in a few hours.

Before Maddy could come up with a quip of her own, we heard the tramping of numerous feet on the stairs. "I guess it's time." Glaze reached out her arms to envelope me, her trademark vanilla scent bringing with it—as it always did—the comfortable smell of homemade cookies. "Thanks for letting us have the wedding here."

"I wouldn't have it any other way." Actually, I would have liked it to be in the church, as long as I could have worn the indigo dress, but this was a good compromise. The candle must have done its job because I didn't feel even an ounce of resentment. I looked down at my bulky green sweater and my legs encased in soft gray fabric. "I always wanted to wear long johns and sweatpants to a wedding." I hadn't changed my clothes. Two reasons. First, I didn't want the other guests to feel like they were being shown up. And secondly, that straw colored dress just wouldn't have been warm enough. At least it would have matched my boater hat.

Glaze just laughed. "I don't care what you wear. I just want you to be here with me." She turned and hugged each of her bridesmaids. "Thanks for being my friend, Maddy. Thanks for helping me so much, Dee."

May I have a hug as well?

Marmalade meowed, and Glaze picked her up and kissed the top of her soft head.

Thank you.

"Her purr is so loud, she's actually vibrating." She looked up at me rather impishly. "What good is a wedding dress without a little cat hair on it?"

I will shed some more if you want me to.

"I wish we had some sort of flowers for you to carry," Maddy said. "What good is a wedding without a bouquet?"

"Hmmm," Dee said, and picked up the log, which she had decorated with a big green bow that I recognized as one of the multiple scarves we'd found in the attic. "How about if she carries this?"

Maddy thought about it and nodded.

I thought about it and objected. "A piece of firewood?"

"It's a symbol," Dee said. "The eternal fire of love. What could be better than that?"

"Dee and I had planned to set it on the floor just in front of Tom and Glaze as a sort of surprise, but it would make just as much sense for Glaze to carry it."

"Do I get to voice my opinion?" We all turned to look at Glaze who had set Marmalade on the bed. She held out her hands for the log. "I think it's a grand idea." She tickled the bow. "This is even the same color as the ferns and ivy I'd planned on carrying."

Maddy turned to the bed where she'd placed her indigo hat, Dee's sunbonnet, and my straw boater. Marmalade sat beside the hats, her tail tucked tidily around her feet. "Time for the three of us to don our hats and head upstairs. You *are* going to wear the sunbonnet, aren't you, Dee?"

"Of course."

I wondered whether Easton would choose the ugly brown tam or the gorgeous confection with the black and brown ribbons. The gorgeous one, of course.

"Wait," I said. "One more thing." I ran out to my sewing area and chose a wide bright green ribbon, about the same color as the scarf that Dee had put around the log.

Back in the room, I approached Marmalade. "Would you like to wear a pretty bow?"

Yes, thank you. I do not need it, but everyone seems to be wearing something special, everyone except SmellSweet. But she has my mouse. That is special.

She meowed for several moments and didn't back away as I circled her neck with the wide ribbon, so I tied it in a festive bow and fluffed out the ends so they hung a few inches down on each side of her neck.

"Glaze," Maddy said, "you don't have a hat."

Dee scoffed. "With that hair of hers, she doesn't need one."

I had to agree. Anyway, she had the hair ornament made of buffalo horn.

After the shuffling of footsteps above us had toned down a bit, indicating—I hoped—that all the women had found appropriate hats, we opened the door to find Dad waiting there with his arm extended. Glaze hugged him. "I'm so glad you're here, Dad."

"Wouldn't be anywhere else. Thank the Lord for snowmobiles."

"And firefighters to drive them," Glaze said, laughing.

We all five walked upstairs …

All six.

… to join my dear sister and her gentle, loving fiancé in holy matrimony.

Hole-y matter-mony? What is that? I thought they were getting married the way you and SoftFoot did.

Maddy and Dee led the way down the improvised aisle the men had set up. I waited my turn as they paced slowly along. I scanned the group and marveled at the richness of good friends and family. The hats all the women had donned lent a festive air to the occasion.

Then I paced the aisle myself and only faltered a moment when I saw that Easton had on the subdued brown tam. What on earth had happened to her need always to be the most spectacular woman in the room? Remembering the candle, I smiled at Easton—a real smile for once—and kept walking.

After I joined Dee and Maddy off to the left, Glaze and Dad—and Marmalade—appeared at the top of the stairs. Everyone stood, and someone—Sadie, perhaps?—began humming *Here Comes the Bride.* We all joined in, and I must say it was one of the best wedding intros I'd ever heard, even though it was somewhat off-key, thanks in large part to Dave's insistent tuneless baritone.

Marmalade, her tail waving high above her back, paced beside Glaze, almost as if she, not Dad, were in charge of ushering the bride down the aisle and giving her away.

I will not give her away. She is your sister and my SmellSweet to keep for always.

I saw Glaze glance down at Marmy and clamp her lips together to keep from laughing. I was sure she was remembering how much Marmalade had had to meow about when Bob and I got married.

It occurred to me that Marmalade might have been saying something. Something important.

Of course I was.

Dad had tears in his eyes; I could see them glinting in the candlelight even from this far away. Months ago he had told me that he was planning on playing some dreamy dance music on his tenor saxophone at the reception, but I hadn't seen a bundle that large when he came in from the snowmobile. He must not have wanted to risk damaging it on the frigid, bouncy trip down the valley. Maybe Sadie and Easton would sing something.

I looked over at Mom, who had donned one of her favorite caftans, a bright orange concoction she picked up the last time she and Dad visited the southwestern deserts. That houndstooth hat blended perfectly.

Glaze looked at Mom as she passed by her, and I could almost feel the loving vibrations. She paused and gave Mom a big hug, then turned and kissed Dad …

She loves SunsetLady and DreamMaker.

… but then her eyes shifted to Tom—who had just hugged his parents and his grandmother—and her luminous smile could have lit the attic all by itself, even without the many candles and lanterns someone had set around the perimeter of the chairs.

SmellSweet and Fishgiver are very happy.

As Glaze reached to take Tom's outstretched hand, I was reminded once more of how Marmalade had meowed—well, talked—so much during my wedding to Bob. When I looked at him, I could tell he remembered the same thing, because his smiling eyes dipped to Marmalade and then back up at me. Knowing what I did now about animal communication, I wondered again what Marmalade had been saying throughout our wedding. I supposed, though, that I would never know for sure.

We all had very important things to say that day.

Dee waited until Dad had settled in next to Mom before she pointed to the firewood bouquet. "Maddy and I wanted to include a symbol of some sort in the ceremony."

Glaze bent to place it on the floor and Tom helped by grabbing the other end. Glaze looked at Tom, and we all could see the love and respect oozing out of every pore. "This is a reminder," she said, "for us to keep the love light burning, no matter what may happen in our life together."

"We can burn it on our twenty-fifth wedding anniversary," Tom said.

"Maybe by then you'll have your own wood stove," Dave called out, and I saw Pat poke him with her elbow.

Marmy stepped onto the log, sat beside the green bow, curled her fuzzy striped tail tidily around her feet, and looked up at Henry, as if waiting for him to begin the ceremony.

The wood is warmer than the floor.

"Looks like the cat has the best seat in the house," Dave said.

"And she's wearing the best outfit," Pat said.

Widelap put this bow on me. I let her do it because it made her feel happy.

Henry motioned to everyone to be seated. "Dear friends," he began, "we are gathered here this evening, as you well know, to celebrate the life commitment of Glaze Martelson McKee and Thomas Edison Parkman as they join together in holy matrimony."

There it is again. I do not understand this hole-y matter-mony.

He paused when Marmalade let out a querulous-sounding yowl. He nodded at her and then continued—I love the way you can hear laughter in a voice.

Naturally, I cried.

I couldn't help but wonder how many other Martinsville women had cried at weddings.

Thursday, 27 May 1742

"REALLY," THOUGHT CHARLOTTE ELLIS, "this is most ridiculous, having one wedding after another this spring, one week after another." First there had been Willem Breeton marrying that child, Constance Garner, and then the very next week, the Widow Black had married old Mister Hastings. Now it was to be Juliana Stickney and

Marcus Fountain. And Charlotte was expected to stand here through the interminable ceremony and smile as if this were a happy event. Marcus was the younger brother of Peter Fountain, who had fathered one of the largest broods in the company. It was revolting, all these children running around. Could not the parents keep them under control?

Ever since that first disgusting marriage on the trail, the one between Mary Frances Garner and Homer Martin, Charlotte had hated every wedding she had been forced to observe. Not that she had ever enjoyed weddings, but at least the ones back in Brandtburg had been held inside where there were pews for sitting on. Not that they were particularly comfortable pews, but they were better than standing here on muddy ground, hoping the rain would hold off from falling until after the vows were taken and everyone could disperse to their wagons.

There would not even be any dancing this evening, for Alan Fountain, the brother of the groom, refused to subject his fiddle to the possibility of rain.

Now Mary Frances Garner Martin stood nearby clutching her bastard child—for Charlotte was convinced the boy was a bastard, even if nobody else knew it—and Charlotte once again searched the faces of the men around her, looking for someone who might be paying particular attention to Mary Frances and her infant boy. She still could not rid herself of the thought that her brother Sayrle Endicott might be the father. After all, hadn't the babe had the same shape of forehead as Sayrle?

She studied Sayrle out of the corner of her eye, but he was gazing off into the surrounding forest as if the trees were of great import. Beside him, Joel was digging his elbow into Sanborn's ribs, and Daniel examined his grubby fingernails, as if they held some interest.

Juliana's smile stretched across her whole face. This young bride would be as wrinkled as her mother before many years had passed.

Charlotte had had enough of weddings to last her the rest of her life, thank you, and did not intend to smile for anyone. The only thing that would bring a smile to her lips would be for her to discover for sure who had fathered young John Martin.

How delicious it would be to hold that knowledge over the head of Mary Frances Martin. Charlotte was fair certain Homer Martin had not an ounce of suspicion that the child might not be his, but Charlotte would never be the one to tell him. Just the threat of telling him would, she knew, be enough to bend Mary Frances to her will. If only she could think of something she wanted from that young snip. First, though, she had to discover the boy's true parentage. Sayrle would deny it if she approached him, and it would be better if she did not let him know of her suspicions. Not now, at least. Not until she could decide what she wanted of him as well.

For now, she had the information well recorded in her special papers. The papers she protected from rain and snow and prying eyes.

2000

MY WHOLE JOURNAL entry that night was one great big huge gratitude list. I couldn't get over how everything had worked out so well, especially since Mom and Dad and Tom's family had been here for the ceremony. Well, there wouldn't have been a ceremony if they hadn't been here.

For a long time during the party afterwards, we continued to bring the newcomers up to date on the findings in the attic. They had missed so much in just that short time before they got here. Halfway through the party, I took the green bow off Marmalade, because it had twisted around underneath her chin and was looking rather limp by that point.

I did not need it anyway.

She'd been so cute, with her bow matching the decorated log.

The log was warm to sit on.

I finally laid my journal aside, blew out the candle, and settled into Bob's enveloping arms. "I had kind of an ah-ha moment today."

"Tell me about it."

That was one of the many things I loved about Bob. He was always willing to listen to me without trying to fix me.

So I explained about how Sadie had nailed me over my anger at Easton and how I'd used the candle idea to help me release the anger. "No," I corrected myself, "it wasn't as clean an emotion as anger. It was something festering inside me."

Bob waited a moment, but when I was still groping for the right word, he said, "Resentment?"

"That's it. What a nasty emotion."

"In that case, I'm glad you were able to let it go."

"Bob?"

"Yeah?"

"Thanks for letting me talk about this. I didn't write my usual gratitude list tonight, because I couldn't limit it to only five or six things. Right now I feel like my whole life is a reason for gratitude."

He raised my left hand to his lips, and I felt the gentle scratch of his mustache and now his beard—he hadn't shaved since the power went off. In that soft voice I loved so much, he murmured, "I, Robert, take you Bisque, to be my lawful wedded wife. I promise you my loyalty. I promise—"

Here I joined him in repeating the words we had both memorized and used for our wedding vows. "I promise to laugh with you each day and love you to the best of my ability. I promise that if anything unlike love comes between us, I will seek the Higher Path of greatest good for both of us, the path of compassion and communication. I promise to be worthy of your trust. As a symbol of my vow, I give you this ring, round as the circle of time, and never-ending." Marmalade squiggled down under the comforter between us, purring mightily.

I had already promised to remain true to both of you for my lifetime and to protect you to the best of my ability, and I will repeat what I told you then. I promise to comfort you when you feel pain, to see your goodness when you forget how good you are. I walk the Higher Path at all times, and I promise to remind you where it is if you forget. I promise to be worthy of your trust. I also promise to understand your lack of understanding.

We laughed and hugged her as she continued to purr for quite some time.

"Life can't get much better than this, can it?"

I reared back and looked at him as best I could in the dim light of the bedroom. I could see my breath coming out in little puffs of fog. "Maybe if the power came back on?"

He chortled—there's no other word for it—and hugged me even tighter. "Did you know ahead of time that Glaze and Tom were going to use some of the words from our vows, or was it as much a surprise to you as it was to me?"

"She mentioned it a while ago," I admitted, "shortly after they got engaged, but then she never asked for a copy of them, and I flat forgot about it."

"They obviously have good memories."

"The words must have resonated with them both," I mused, scratching Marmalade idly, "or they wouldn't have recalled so much of what we said."

"I meant every word of it."

"So did I."

So did I.

"Let's make cheese grits tomorrow morning for breakfast," Bob said.

"Cheese grits. Yum." Good old southern specialty. "I've been thinking about them, too. I wonder if Carol's ever had them."

"If she had even one breakfast at Melissa's—and I think she did have just one before the power went out—then I'm sure she's been served them."

"You're right, but that doesn't mean she actually ate them."

"You saw her sliding around out on the ice yesterday," he reminded me. "That sort of adventuresome spirit would certainly at least have *tasted* a new food sensation."

"Okay," I said, "but we'll have to get up extra early so you can get your writing done." I thought about it. "While you're journaling, I'll get pancake batter whipped up. Surely there's enough space on the top of the wood stove to hold the griddle and the grits pot."

"And the coffee pot, too?"

"Well, probably not. So I'll brew the coffee first and pour it into carafes. It's a good thing Melissa brought four of those things along with her to augment the two we already had."

"Augment. I like that word." He pulled me closer to him. "Sounds like we could go into business with our own café."

"Competition for Tom? Not a chance."

To tell the truth, I was—as I'd already mentioned several times in my journal—getting a little tired of all this togetherness, although it had been great fun staying inside and warm while Carol and Reebok and Tom made fools of themselves out on the front yard ice. And we'd really gone through the hot chocolate afterwards, since everybody decided that would be the perfect thing. I should have put that in my journal tonight, but I wasn't about to reach outside the covers. And not only because of the cold. Bob was stroking my hair in that special way he has.

Just like you stroke me? Oof!

Marmalade complained when we inadvertently pushed her aside, but by that point I wasn't particularly worried about the cat.

The cat? You are calling me the cat?

I am thankful for

Widelap and Softfoot, even when they squish me
Smellsweet and Fishgiver
SunsetLady and DreamMaker
LooseLaces and GoodCook
all the other humans who are here
a log to sit on when the floor is drafty
this bed to snuggle into when the room is cold
food to eat when I am hungry
water to drink when I am thirsty
someone to scratch my head and rub my back
and the bird feeders

"I THINK I'M going to keep on my green sweatshirt tonight." Sadie placed one of her other three borrowed sweatshirts, the purple one, under the covers. "So it'll be warmer tomorrow morning," she explained. She was so looking forward to sleep. It had taken her longer than she'd expected to bring Easton up to date about the attic findings—that 1910 account list in particular.

Easton nodded. "Do you think it's ever going to warm up?"

Sadie held back the motherly advice about how the only guarantee was that everything would change. "I daresay it won't last too much longer."

"Sadie? Can I ask you something?"

Sadie had to avoid her first instinct to say *I don't know. Can you?* Like so many of her generation, she had been taught the difference between *can* and *may.* "Yes, dear, of course you may."

"Will you … will you tell me the truth?"

Oh, dear. This sounded serious. "Of course I will." The bed was going to have to wait a bit longer. She breathed a silent prayer that she wasn't getting herself into something she would regret.

"When Biscuit made me stay downstairs, I tried to act like it didn't hurt." She bent to adjust her pillow. "But it did." She fiddled with the pile of clothes she'd set out for the next day.

Sadie sat on the side of the bed. She could tell this was going to take a while.

"I tried to talk to the guys, but they just sort of ignored me. And I knew I wasn't welcome down there, but …" Easton kept her back partially turned toward Sadie, as if afraid to see the older woman's reaction.

"But?" Sadie prodded gently.

"But I wasn't welcome up"— she pointed toward the ceiling— "up there, either." She picked up a pair of heavy socks and put them down again. "Sometimes I feel like there's this wall between me and everybody else."

"Easton?"

"Except you. There's no wall there, but that's not … I mean …"

"Not enough?" Sadie reached for the box of tissues on the broad bedside table and scooted it to within Easton's reach. "I can see how that might be the case."

Easton looked toward the soft sound of the box sliding across the wood. "Nobody likes me." She finally turned and sat on her own bed, inspecting the tufted chenille spread, as if it held the answer she needed. "Why?"

Sadie almost said *Look at me*, but she could tell that might make things worse. Let Easton waken gently to this awful truth.

She thought for another few moments before answering. She didn't want to push Easton away, but she couldn't quite think of phrasing that would soften the bitter truth. "Sometimes," she said slowly, "we come up against the fact that our actions have consequences that last longer than we think they should."

"But …"

Sadie waited for Easton to continue. While she waited, she rubbed her hands, marveling at the way her old dry skin could be pushed into furrows that stayed bunched up until she either smoothed them down or made a fist.

"What did I do that was so awful?"

Sadie cocked an eyebrow at that. "Easton. Look at me."

Hesitantly—Sadie could almost see the reluctance oozing from Easton's pores—she raised her chin. "You tell me," Sadie said. She would not recount the number of times women had come to her practically screaming in frustration as Easton coursed through the town one man at a time. Easton knew. She had to know.

Even women as normally even-tempered as Glaze and Sharon and Margaret, had—what was the term?—gone ballistic while Easton flirted and insinuated, leaving in her wake the husbands or boyfriends who vacillated between being sheepish and being titillated. Sadie didn't think Easton had actually *done* anything with any of those men. But Easton had felt like a threat to the women of Martinsville. For a while there, Sadie had wondered if Easton might try something with Wallace, except that Wallace was well over eighty and slowed down by that stroke and practically unable to walk anymore.

Still, even Wallace had brightened and had tried to sit up straighter when Easton came to visit.

Underneath it all, Sadie saw the little girl who had never truly been loved. The little girl whose father either fawned over her or beat her—and who knew what else he had done? The little girl Sadie had done nothing to protect back then, for it had been a different time, when family concerns were all too often ignored.

Sadie had breathed a sigh of relief when Sam, the older child, finally graduated from high school and took Easton away from their father. Rupert Hastings hadn't been good for either one of them.

And then Easton and Sam had come back to Martinsville all those years later, and look where that had ended up.

Sadie waited. And waited. And waited.

Until Easton began to talk.

IDA MOVED OVER closer to Ralph. She was on the bump, but his legs were a lot warmer than her feet were. Even through her heavy socks she could feel a comforting heat, as if she had her own private thermal blanket. "I think we're going to lose most of what's in the store."

He patted her arm. "We'll weather this storm the same way

we've weathered others."

Ida sighed. That was probably the most romantic thing Ralph had ever said to her.

"HAVE YOU EVER been married?" Melissa probably shouldn't have asked the question. It sounded nosy. "Or engaged?"

Carol didn't seem put out by it, though. "No," she said with only a little hesitation. "I just never found anybody I wanted to spend more than a week with. Four days, in fact. That seemed to be my limit. After that, I got bored."

"I guess people start thinking about such things around weddings."

"Theirs was a great ceremony. I liked their vows."

"They borrowed some from Biscuit and Bob's wedding," Melissa said. "I wrote pretty much the same phrases into my own wedding."

Carol looked at her closely. "I didn't realize …"

"No. I wasn't actually married. My fiancé was murdered before we even announced … anything."

Carol opened her mouth, closed it, opened it. "I'm so sorry. I've … I've never known anyone who was murdered. Is there … anything I can say that wouldn't come across as crass or unfeeling or … or just plain stupid?"

Melissa smiled ruefully. "Don't worry. You already said it. *I'm so sorry* works just fine."

CHARLIE DIDN'T WANT to get undressed. Not in this cold. It wasn't the first time she'd wondered if she should have married somebody. Somebody with warm feet. But this was better. She didn't have to answer to anyone.

She could hear quiet murmurs from the bedroom next door. Sadie and Easton. Nothing from the room on the other side of her. Reebok's room, the rent-a-cop. He was a pathetic shrimp. She clamped her eyes shut. Nothing was going to keep her from sleeping.

She was only halfway aware when she heard Easton get up for the second time that night and head down the hall to the bathroom.

Twice a night at least, maybe even three times, and she took forever in the bathroom. Five, six minutes each time and then she'd tromp back. Irritating to be woken up by something stupid like that. At least old Sadie only got up once a night.

It was only two days, but she felt like she'd been in this house too long. She was beginning to identify people by their footsteps. Come to think of it, though, that might come in handy at some point.

At least the other people along the hall didn't make midnight trips. That scrawny cop with the stupid name in the room on the other side of hers sure was quiet. She never heard him. But he was in a room by himself, same as she was, so there wasn't any reason for him to say anything, but she'd never even heard him unzipping a duffle bag. She knew Ida and what's-his-name were in the room right beyond Sadie and Easton. She'd made sure on the first night to find out where everybody was assigned.

There wasn't anything in the packet about either Sadie or Rebecca. That was too bad. Surely they both had secrets of some sort. Easton was too young to be in the packet. All the entries stopped a bunch of years ago. She was going to have to find another source of income soon. Hubbard was out, of course, after that fall off the cliff. Clara was cooperating so far, but that wouldn't last, not once the word was out about Mary Frances and Hubbard Brandt. It was disgusting that they'd found those journals. Nobody needed to know all that stuff. How had old grandma Charlotte Ellis gotten it wrong, though?

Still, it wasn't over yet. Charlie still knew something nobody else knew.

Clara would do anything, pay anything, to keep Charlotte Ellis from saying anything. She'd been paying for the last two months, hadn't she? And Clara would keep right on shelling it out. Not because of that Hubbard Brandt stuff. Something much worse. Charlotte Ellis knew. She knew Clara had been the last person to see Hubbard. She knew Clara had pushed him off the cliff. One word to the cops and Clara would go to jail.

Charlie hugged that bit of information to herself. Maybe it was worth more. Maybe she could insist on a higher payment each month.

That Sadie person gave her the creeps. Something about the way the woman looked at her, like she could see right through Charlie. Easton took so long in the bathroom—at least she had last night, and it sounded like she was doing the same this time—it wouldn't be hard to step next door, pick up a pillow, and stop nosy old Sadie from ever looking at her again. How hard could it be to smother somebody? She pushed back her covers, but she heard Easton shuffling along the wooden floor. Trying to be quiet.

She'd waited too long, thought about it too long.

That was okay. There was always tomorrow night. This ice storm wasn't anywhere near being over. And tomorrow night she'd be ready the first time Easton got up. Nobody had the right to look at her the way Sadie Masters did.

REEBOK TRIED TO settle in and get to sleep right away, but just when he'd feel himself dropping off, there'd be footsteps overhead. He couldn't identify who was coming from which room, but he sure could tell the destination was the bathroom. Didn't make him a great detective. There was that loud flush afterwards. A dead giveaway.

Finally it sounded like everything and everybody had settled down. He heard a log settle into place in the wood stove, and the light through the glass doors brightened for a moment as the flames rose. He heard the wind moan around the corner of the house. And then he slept.

Matthew Olsen's House

MATTHEW OLSEN FELT so tired he wanted to curl up in a ball on the couch and sleep until noon tomorrow, but the Foleys wouldn't go to bed. Anita kept running around. He had no idea what she was doing, but it sounded like she was searching through his cabinets. In the middle of the night for criminey sakes. He had no idea what she was looking for, but she'd ransacked the kitchen three times over, and he heartily regretted inviting them to stay here.

Almost immediately, though, he felt bad about what he was thinking. Ousting them into the storm might be satisfying for a little while, but come the thaw he'd have to do something with their frozen corpses on his front lawn.

Mr. Fogarty cheeped, and Matthew came back to his senses, listening to the sound of Anita Foley ruining his peace.

Sighing, he got up and went into the kitchen.

"Oh, good, you're still up, Matthew. Where do you keep your sugar?"

He pointed to it.

"In the flour canister? Why on earth?"

"It's bigger than that little bitty sugar holder." That was where he kept a few extra nails, in case he ever needed them. Never knew when you were going to need a nail. More than anything, Matthew believed in practicality.

"Then where's your flour?"

"Never buy the stuff. Don't do any baking, so why would I need it?"

Anita looked at him like she thought he was nuts. Shaking her head, she filled a sugar bowl and set it on the table. Matthew hadn't seen that sugar bowl in years. Not since his wife died.

"How about a nice cup of tea." Without waiting for an answer—it hadn't really been a question anyway—Anita strode into the living room and took the water kettle off the wood stove.

Nick looked at Matthew and spread his hands. "It's easier just to let her do her thing."

CLARA PRESSED HER fingertips into the creases that ran like train tracks across her forehead. It wasn't fair. She had to do so much, and now here she was, in a house with these other people, having to take care of Hubbard without all the conveniences of her own house. Thank goodness she'd brought her glaucoma medicine with her. She hated putting those drops in her eyes four times a day, but the thought of going blind was more than she could bear. She always had the drops with her. Always.

To top it all off, to add to her worry, now she had to deal with the fact that Hubbard might somehow be coming out of whatever you called that vacant space he'd been in, but he'd never be normal again. Never. She knew she couldn't hope for that. She knew she could never depend on him. Not that she'd ever been able to. Not really. He could hardly make a decision without her having to tell him what it should be.

So, what was she going to do if she did lose her sight? Who would take care of her? It wouldn't be Hubbard, that was for sure. If only she'd married Cornelius. If only he hadn't died. He never would have gotten into this mess. Nobody ever would have been able to blackmail Cornelius.

Every time she looked at Hubbard, all afternoon, he'd seemed just a little more … more alive than he had been just minutes before. She kept telling him she was sorry, but whenever she said it, he didn't do anything. He didn't even act like he'd heard her. But then, twenty minutes later, she'd catch him looking at her for just a second or two.

This was driving her crazy.

She had to report to Matthew. It seemed like Anita, that nosy busybody, was knocking on the door every fifteen minutes for the past hour, asking how Hubbard was doing. It was late enough that everyone should have been asleep in their beds, but she could still hear a murmur of conversation through the bedroom door.

She couldn't risk letting Hubbard get out of bed. He'd been so unsteady when Matthew helped her get him back here to the bedroom. She placed both his arms so they lay straight by his sides, and then she tucked in the sheet tight underneath the mattress. She did the same with the blankets, on both sides of the bed. When she was sure he was asleep, she headed for the door.

As she opened it, Anita was just getting ready to knock, juggling a tray in her other hand. "I brought you a little something in case you wanted a late night snack. There's some herbal tea, with lots of sugar. For comfort."

Clara lifted her index finger to her lips. "Thank you." She eased the door shut behind her, wishing she had a key. "Hubbard's resting, and I thought I'd take a few minutes to let everyone know what's going on."

"We're so delighted and, at the same time, so concerned." Anita led the way along the short hall.

Clara followed, mentally trying out several versions of what to say. *He's sleeping peacefully. He's back the way he was.*

But what if he called out loudly enough for the others to hear?

She could say he'd been distraught.

No. Then somebody—probably Anita with her interfering

ways—would insist on calling the ambulance. She didn't dare let that happen. Fortunately, the ambulance wouldn't be able to go anywhere on all this ice and snow, but she couldn't risk even the possibility.

"Has he said anything else?" Anita didn't even wait for Clara to sit down before she bombarded her with questions. "Do you think he's finally waking up?"

"No, no. I don't think it was a word. I think he was just moaning or something—he does that sometimes—and it came out sounding like *boo.*"

"It sure sounded like *you.*" Matthew, a resigned look on his face, sat across the kitchen table from Clara.

"No," Clara said as firmly as she dared. She didn't want anybody to read too much into that one word. "I'm pretty sure it was *boo.* Or maybe it was *who.*"

HUBBARD LAY THERE once Clara left the room. With his eyes closed like this, he felt like one of those … he couldn't remember the word. One of those things in a basket? No. Box? No. Coconut? That was closer. It still wasn't the right word, but he knew what he meant. He thought he knew what he meant. Where you stayed while you waited for wings.

There was something about money. Lots of it.

There was something else. Save? Pave? Wave?

Wrong.

Dave.

He had to tell Clara. Had to.

When Clara came back into the room, Hubbard watched her cross the room to his bed before he closed his eyes. It was too much work to keep them open.

"I'M CALLING DOC." As soon as Clara left the kitchen, Anita Foley moved the tea things aside and crossed her arms on the table in front of her.

"You can't do that," her husband told her, but shrugged when she glared at him.

"I can, too. Somebody who knows what they're doing needs to take a look at Hubbard. Take his pulse or something."

Matthew pulled back the cuff of his sweater to reveal a heavy old-fashioned watch. "It's too late now, Anita. Let Doc get a good night's sleep before he has to walk all this way in the ice and snow."

"He wouldn't have to walk that far," Nick said. "He's staying next door."

"Tomorrow, then." Anita stood, radiating irritation. "But I *am* going to call him." She pulled an already-opened package out of a cabinet next to the useless electric stove. "Pretzels, anyone?"

CLARA SAT THERE for the longest time, just watching Hubbard breathe. *You.* Despite what she'd said to Anita Foley, she knew quite well that Hubbard had said *You.* And he'd been looking straight at her when he'd said it.

She knew it was her fault. She knew it without a doubt. But she couldn't have anyone else in Martinsville aware of that fact. If anyone out there in Matthew's kitchen told what he'd said, put that together with what Charlotte Ellis had threatened her with, she wouldn't have a chance. Everybody would believe she'd pushed Hubbard off the cliff.

In a way, she supposed she had.

What did she even want now? Did she want him to live? Did she want him to die?

But then his eyes opened. So did his mouth.

"Dave."

"Dave? What do you mean?" The only Dave she knew of was Dave Pontiac, Maggie Pontiac's father-in-law. He was a big rich corporate guy of some sort. That was about all she knew about him. Scads of money. "What about Dave?"

"Corn …"

Corn? Was he hungry? That didn't make any sense.

Before she could ask if he wanted something to eat, he said, "Dog."

They'd never had a dog. Why would he be asking about a dog?

"Money."

She'd been hoping he'd talk, dreading that he'd talk, and now she wanted to throttle him. What on earth was he talking about? Why couldn't he speak clearly and say what he meant? "What money?" She kept her voice low, dreading the thought that somebody out there in Matthew's house might hear them and try to come in. "Tell me what money you're talking about."

"Dave."

Oh no, no, no. Please no. Did Dave know about the blackmail money Hubbard had been paying to Charlotte Ellis these past three years?

"Talk."

"Talk about what, Hubbard? What do you mean?"

She shook his shoulder, but he'd passed out or fallen asleep or gone back into that coma state he'd been in for so long. What was she going to do?

HE'D TOLD HER. He could relax now. Hubbard slept.

Friday, December 8, 2000
Day #3

BOB WOKE BEFORE I did, thank goodness. Otherwise I might have slept the morning away. I felt like I could have stayed in our snuggy bed for another twelve or fifteen hours, although once he slipped out from under the comforter, the heat gradually began to dissipate. I eased one arm out and immediately pulled it back in. Even through my long johns and flannel pj's, the cold was devastating. How did people manage before central heat?

He dressed quickly, and I could see a mist of frosty air puffing, dragon-like, out of his nose and mouth. No wonder it felt so cold outside the bed; it *was* cold. Maybe we'd have to leave the bedroom door open from now on. I sure hoped this wasn't going to last much longer.

"Come on, sleepyhead," he said. "We need to get those cheese grits to cooking before the hordes descend."

What are hords?

Marmalade told me to get up too …

I did not.

…or maybe she was just complaining about the frigid air that invaded her space when I lifted the covers. "Aren't you going to write in your journal?"

"Nope. Nothing much happened yesterday."

"What about the liberty hoop? What about the wedding? Surely you wouldn't want that to be forgotten."

He leaned over and kissed the top of my head. "I'm sure you wrote about those, so they'll be saved for posterity."

He was right, I thought, but only if my journal got read by somebody sometime in the future. What if it was relegated to a trunk in a dusty attic somewhere after I died?

I do not want you to die!

Marmalade let out a ferocious growl, for which I saw no reason whatsoever.

If I died before Bob, would he read my journal? Would he keep it? Or would he give it—them—I didn't even know how many booklets I'd gone through so far. Would he give them to one of my daughters? I tried to think back over what I had written over the past few years. Oh dear. Maybe I should put them in an envelope, the way Mary Frances Martin had done with her letter, and direct that it could not be opened until a hundred years from hence. My grandchildren might very likely be dead by then. Would my great-grandchildren care? It was too depressing to think about.

Maybe sometime two hundred years from now, there's be another ice storm and a group of friends would gather in the attic and find my journals and … Oh, get real, Biscuit. This house wouldn't be standing two hundred years from now.

What a horrible thought.

Still, it bothered me somewhat that Bob didn't apparently feel a need to record the daily events of what was going on during this storm. What on earth did he write about? Work, I supposed, although there hadn't been any police calls for two days—which was something of a miracle, now that I thought about it. Maybe because everybody in town was clustered with a whole lot of other people around one of the many wood stoves. If anything happened, they'd just take care of each other. Comforting thought.

On the other hand, when you put a bunch of people together and they were stuck, for want of a better word, would the tensions start to mount? Of course they would. I had to admit we'd been pretty lucky in the mix of people we had here. What if I'd had to endure not only Easton, but Clara and Hubbard Martin as well? A little mayhem, perhaps? Still, I didn't have to put up with them. Thank goodness.

So what was it Bob wrote about in his journal? He was plenty interested in our stories, as the other men were, but none of them volunteered to join us up there in the airy reaches of the third floor. I know some of them had made various treks out to the woodshed to retrieve fuel for the stove, because the huge rack in the living room always seemed to be piled full of wood when I ventured downstairs, but I didn't question it. They'd found their jobs to do just as we had found ours. Maybe that's the sort of thing he wrote about. Boring.

Marmalade left with Bob …

It will be warmer downstairs.

… and I dressed as fast as I could. My clothes were at least warmish from having been in bed all night.

Reebok looked fairly refreshed when I walked down into the living room. His blanket and pillow were tucked out of sight.

"Good morning, ma'am."

"Did you sleep well?"

"I did." He sounded faintly surprised.

"I find I sleep better when I'm physically tired, so maybe it was all that exercise you got outside the past two days tumbling around on the ice."

"Exercise? That wasn't exercise. That was fun!"

The resiliency of youth.

I led the way into the kitchen.

The cheese grits were a big hit, as I'd known they would be, and Carol took two helpings. If the bowl hadn't been completely emptied, I think she might have indulged in another.

She and Reebok took one more turn outside, although they didn't stay as long as they had the first time. The rest of us just sat around the table, nibbling and jawing.

"I had to work off those extra grits," Carol said when she came, rosy-cheeked, inside. "This is the best sabbatical I ever could have had."

Needless to say, Glaze and Tom were a bit late coming downstairs for breakfast. We'd already just about exhausted all the comments about what they'd been doing with their time—"Probably just discussing all the finds in the attic," "Napping, undoubtedly," "Did you put a Monopoly board in their room, Biscuit, so they'd have something to do?" But of course when they walked hand-in-hand down the stairs, all the comments resurfaced.

Glaze had looked radiant last night in the attic, but now her countenance shone even more. Tom looked equally enthralled. Who needed to travel far away on a wedding trip if such a result was possible in the guest room—albeit the nicest one—of an old inn built in the mid-1700s?

I thought back to Bob's and my honeymoon. The fact that he'd ended up in intensive care had not been the most auspicious beginning to a marriage, but we'd weathered the intervening years pretty well. I studied his profile for a moment, and he turned his head and nodded at me. Thinking the same thing as I was, probably.

It certainly hadn't been much of a honeymoon for Tom and

Glaze, either, but at least Tom wasn't in the hospital. I was so grateful to Rebecca Jo and Dee for fixing up the big room they'd started in, the one with the double bed, and who had cheerfully moved to a much narrower room that had barely enough space for the twin beds and a two-drawer dresser.

We shifted around a bit at the table so there was room for Tom and Glaze to sit in their usual places while the rest of us busied ourselves bringing them fresh pancakes, passing the butter, pouring juice, offering the syrup jar, continuing to make jokes about newlyweds.

"Too bad you missed the best culinary offering," Father John said to Tom.

The cheese grits had long since been consumed. In fact, the bowl was scraped clean—almost clean enough for me to just put it right back into the cabinet. Not really.

Tom barely replied. He kept looking at his new wife. They had a whole conversation going on with their eyes. Eventually, though, they came to, enough to field the banter with good grace, and both of them devoured a huge breakfast, which naturally led to more comments about stoking the fires and keeping their strength up.

I do not understand what is so funny.

"I don't know about you," Ida finally said, "but I'm ready to head back up to the attic."

Me, too. I will sit on the warm log.

Marmalade jumped off my lap and bounded onto Glaze's.

Before we go, will you give me back my mouse?

Carol interpreted, and we all watched in amazement as Glaze's face turned a bright pink. So did Tom's.

She pulled the blue mouse out of her pocket and threw it for Marmalade. She studiously did not look at Tom. He studiously did not look at her.

What on earth had that mouse witnessed the night before?

Luckily, Dave was sopping up the last of the syrup with the last of his pancakes, so he missed that fascinating interchange.

Glaze cleared her throat, wiped her mouth and pushed her chair back. "I didn't prepare any of the breakfast. So I guess I have to help with the cleanup."

"Not today," Henry said. "The newly married pair both get a

pass for today."

"In that case," Glaze said, "let's head upstairs."

"You're leaving your brand new husband?" Dave squished his face up until he looked like a dried apple doll.

"Unless he'd like to come along with me." It's a wonder Tom didn't melt from the sultry look Glaze gave him.

Why would he melt?

Tom swallowed audibly. "I'll pass," he managed to say, "as long as you promise to let us know each time you find something interesting."

Ida grunted. "Are you kidding? Everything's interesting. We're on a roll up there."

I like to roll in catnip!

Carol laughed. "We'll have to get you some."

"Yeah," said Maddy, ignoring what was obviously a reply to Marmalade. "We'll find lots of interesting things today. I can feel it in my bones. And there's no telling what we'll learn from Mary Frances."

"And Hubbard," I said.

The phone rang, and we all stopped talking as Bob answered it. He turned his back and lowered his voice, but we all heard him ask, "You're sure?" He turned around. "It's for you, Doc. Why don't you take it back in the office? I'll hold on here until you've picked up."

Korsi slipped off Doc's lap and then hopped right back onto the chair as soon as Doc stepped away from it. He must be used to sudden interruptions like that.

GrayGuy likes to sleep when he is not working.

What sounded like a woman's voice came from the receiver. Bob clapped it back against his ear. "Okay. I'll do that."

He seemed somewhat taken aback when he turned around and we all skewered him with pointed looks. He held up his hands and took his seat again. "She said I could tell you. In fact, she asked me to. It's good news, I think."

Tom leaned forward. "Why do you sound so doubtful then?"

"That was Anita. Foley," he added in case we didn't make the connection, although he knew as well as any of us that she's the only in Anita in town. "She's next door at Matthew's house."

Dave made a rolling motion with his hands.

"Yeah, Dave, I'll get there. She wants Doc to take a look at Hubbard. Apparently he said something last night."

"That's marvelous," Sadie said.

"What did he say?"

Before Bob could answer Charlie—and Dave—they'd both asked the same question—Doc walked into the kitchen, his ubiquitous black bag in hand. I thought back. I'd never seen him without it nearby. If I'd been a doctor, I should think I'd want a light blue bag or a green one. Some color that would be easier to spot, harder to misplace. It wouldn't do to plop it down in a dark corner and then not be able to find it. Of course, with the power out, maybe Doc slept with the bag on his bed.

"I guess you've heard?" He didn't wait for an answer. "I doubt I'll be much help, but Anita thinks it's pretty important that I take a look at Hubbard."

Dave pushed back his chair. "I'll go with you."

"You don't need to—"

"Two people on the ice makes more sense than one person stumbling along." Dave grinned, but it looked a little forced to me. "I'll pick you up when you slip."

Doc shrugged, set down his black medical bag, stroked Korsi's head, and lifted his parka from the coatrack.

ONCE THE TWO of them took off across the treacherous ice field that was our front yard, I led the women upstairs.

No. I am the one who led the way.

First, though, I detoured into my bathroom to brush my teeth, and Marmalade jumped onto the counter next to me. The water from the pitcher was so cold I thought my molars would contract right out of my gums. While I was brushing, I thought about how there seemed to be an unspoken consensus among us women to keep the "attic time" just for us. Not that we didn't welcome the men when they joined us up there, but somehow the attic seemed like it had almost nothing but female energy in it, as Maddy had already noted. Oh sure, there was a man's boater hat—which was now my boater hat—and that old pocket watch, but I'd be willing to bet a woman had deposited them upstairs. Had they belonged to a husband, a brother, a son? Had he died or run away or simply grown tired of possessions he no longer used? And why had she kept them when they were no longer needed or wanted?

I shook myself. Too many questions and not enough answers.

"Hurry up, Biscuit," Ida called from the top of the stairs, "or we'll start without you."

Marmalade jumped off the counter and I followed her out of the bedroom. Who knew what treasures we'd find today?

Upstairs, I leaned over to look into Sadie's and my trunk, while Marmalade located Glaze and Tom's green-beribboned log, which someone had moved off to one side of the circle. She jumped onto it and then right off again. Some new kind of cat game?

The log is not warm anymore, Widelap. Why not?

She must have thought it wasn't much fun, because she came over and calmly hopped onto the card table, depositing her blue mouse on a stack of letters. Maybe I should have sat down so she could have a lap. I love having a furry body keeping my legs warm.

You keep me warm, too.

"Let's get to work," Dee said, rubbing her palms together. "I want to know what we'll find next."

"Me, too." Sadie wore a voluminous purple sweatshirt. I was still faintly surprised to see her in anything other than yellow.

Melissa rubbed her hands together the same way Dee had just done. "Do you think Hubbard's getting well now?" She looked at the journal on the card table behind me. "Not Biscuit's Hubbard, but our Hubbard."

"I'm not sure it's even possible after such a bad injury," Rebecca Jo said.

"Anything is possible," Amanda said, "but from what I've heard, if he does regain his speech, it'll be nothing short of miraculous."

Pat made one of those humming sounds. "I wonder what he said."

"I've been wondering that myself." I thought back to how unenthusiastic Bob had sounded. "If he does start to talk again, I hope he'll be able to tell us what happened."

"Maybe he won't," Patty said. "Maybe just a word or two is all he'll ever be able to say."

“What a horrible thought.” Melissa shuddered. “I’ve heard about something called a locked-in syndrome where somebody’s aware of what’s going on, but they can’t respond in any way, except maybe blinking to indicate yes or no.”

“That sounds absolutely hellish,” my mom said. She turned away. “I’d rather look at attic treasures than try to second-guess what’s happening next door.”

“Great idea, Mom.” I was getting a little tired of going through old letters, though. “I’ll join you.”

Matthew Olsen’s House

IT TOOK EVERY ounce of self-discipline Clara had to keep from shrieking when Matthew ushered Doctor Young and Dave Pontiac into the kitchen. She’d left Hubbard for only a minute or two so she could grab some breakfast—she was going to take it right back to the room of course, so she could feed him and eat a bit herself. The scrambled eggs were noxiously runny, not like the nice crispy brown-around-the-edges eggs she liked, but she’d eat them because she had to keep her strength up.

But this … this intrusion was almost more than she could stomach.

“Thanks for calling me, Anita,” Doctor Young said as he shed his gloves, parka, scarf. “Where’s our patient?”

Anita Foley, that brazen woman, looked like she was ready to lead the doctor back to where Hubbard lay in the bed, but Clara stepped in front of her. “Give me a minute,” she said. She’d deal with Anita later. How dare she call the doctor when Clara had specifically ordered her not to? “Let me be sure he’s cleaned up a bit.” She couldn’t let anybody see how she’d tucked him in so tightly it was almost like prison shackles.

“Don’t worry about that,” the doctor said. “I’ve seen worse.”

And he just stood there and waited for her to show him where Hubbard was.

“Smart,” was all he said when he saw how she’d arranged the sheets. “You wouldn’t want him to fall out of bed while you were out of the room.”

She tried not to let her sigh of relief be audible.

Doc set his bag on the bedside table and pulled out his stethoscope. "Why don't you give me a minute with him, Mrs. Martin? Go finish your breakfast or make yourself a cup of tea. I saw a water kettle steaming on the wood stove. Once I've done a proper exam, I'll call for you."

There was nothing to do but give in. She turned around and almost bumped into Dave Pontiac standing there just inside the door.

Money. Corn. Dave. Talk.

The words kept bouncing around inside her head. *Money. Dave. Talk.*

Obviously that meant Dave knew about the blackmail money Hubbard had been paying Charlotte Ellis. But why did Hubbard want her to talk to Dave about it? She had to make the right decision. What was she going to do?

Dave stepped back and motioned her out the door. Instead of turning right toward the living room, he walked to the end of the short hallway and turned in front of the window. It was cold there, but Clara paid little attention to the condition of her hands. She was more concerned with the condition of her heart.

"We might as well have a little talk," he said. His voice was far too low. Too quiet for this to be a friendly conversation. You couldn't tell it by his words though. As if there were nothing wrong in the world, he said, "I wanted to talk to you as soon as I heard Hubbard was injured …"

Injured? Clara thought. *That was one way to put it.*

"… but I just didn't have the chance. You know I retired a few months ago, so Pat and I have moved back here. We're looking for the right house."

"Yes?" Did he want to buy her house? Hers and Hubbard's?

"This seemed like a good time to talk, what with Doc coming over here like this."

Clara made a non-committal sound.

"With Hubbard as badly hurt as he is, I guess he's not going to be able to say too much about anything."

She eyed him. Where was this leading?

"And if he does ever say anything, what with a head injury and all that, I doubt anybody will ever be able to believe anything he says."

Clara let out her breath, only now realizing she'd been holding it. Nobody had to know about how Mary Frances had a bastard son, no matter what Hubbard said. Nobody would believe him. Nobody ever had to know that Hubbard wasn't a true Martin.

"I think you're right," she said, keeping her voice as low as his.

"So, the money stuff is going to have to stop."

"Money stuff," she breathed. Was he talking about the blackmail money Hubbard had been paying Charlotte these past three years? And now the blackmail Clara was still paying Charlotte. What if it was something else, though? Something to do with the town council? "Money stuff? What do you mean?"

"So you don't know anything about it?"

"Why would I know anything about money?"

"You're sure?"

Why did he sound so surprised? But he'd said the money stuff would stop. He sounded so definite about it. She had to know for sure. "You, you don't mean the black..." She deliberately didn't finish the word. If he knew about it, he'd fill it in.

"The blackmail," he said. "That's what I mean. It's going to stop."

She waved her hand, as if it meant nothing to her, but inside she felt like jumping for joy. She wouldn't have to pay Charlotte Ellis any more. Nobody would believe Clara had pushed her own husband off the cliff. But … but how had Dave Pontiac learned about Charlotte's blackmail scheme? Had Hubbard told him? And why? Of course, they'd both grown up here in Martinsville. Dave was a little older than Hubbard, but Hubbard had always said they'd been friends when he was a kid. Which surprised her. She'd always gotten the impression Hubbard didn't like Dave very much.

Before she could ask even one of her questions, Doctor Young called from behind her. "Mrs. Martin?" She hadn't heard the door open.

"We'll keep all of this quiet," Dave whispered, and all Clara could do was nod. "I'll talk to my bank as soon as the ice storm is over."

"Bank?"

But Doctor Young motioned for her to join him, and she didn't have a chance to ask Dave what on earth he was talking about.

The Attic

CAROL GRAVITATED TO the cheval mirror, again. I'd seen her looking at it yesterday, and the day before, too. "You seem fascinated by that mirror," I called across the attic to her. "Why are you so interested in it?"

"I'm just wondering if this is the one that woman mentioned in her letter. The letter about the hidden room."

"The one from"—I had to search my memory—"Dolly in Brothersville."

"Hephzibah," Glaze corrected me as she stepped closer. "They changed the town name, remember?"

Carol looked from the mirror back toward me. "In that letter, she mentioned a cheval mirror. Something about his having included a sweet thought, or something like that."

"So?" I couldn't see where she was headed with this.

"There's something I felt along the top edge when I was looking at it earlier, before we got interested in the flatirons. Would you help me lift this over closer to a window so I can see what it is?"

"Sure." Naturally, everybody else crowded around.

"This really is like a treasure hunt," Rebecca Jo said.

"I wouldn't expect too much if I were you," Pat said. "It's probably just a rough place where the frame got dinged."

"Or it could be the key to some sort of mystery," Maddy intoned, and Dee directed a raspberry her way.

It might have gotten rowdier, but by that time Carol and I had the mirror in position under one of the eyebrow windows. She released the catch on the side and tilted the mirror downwards—it squeaked a bit as it moved—until we had a clear view of the top edge of the frame.

Once we made out the writing carved into the wood, we were no wiser.

Sunday, 13 January 1856

AS GRACE AND Arthur Hoskins sat through the church service, she was glad she sat on his right, the side away from his pocket, for otherwise she feared his elbow might have poked a hole in her ribs.

All morning long, Arthur had been acting like he had tadpoles in his waistcoat. He kept reaching into it, withdrawing his hand, patting the pocket as if it contained something precious, something that should not be disturbed too much. Grace did not mention it, for Arthur was one who enjoyed having his little secrets. Usually they involved some sort of gift for her, but she was more than usually curious about this one, for today was the anniversary of their marriage twenty-four years ago.

She would wait until they were home in Beechnut House, but if he did not reveal what he was so excited about, she would insist on knowing. Grace enjoyed secrets, too, but not ones that went on for too long.

The service seemed interminable that day, but Grace knew it was only because she was so anxious to learn what Arthur had in store for her. She had a moment's discomfort as it occurred to her that whatever was in his pocket might not be intended for her, but she did not let that thought unsettle her for too very long. She knew Arthur quite well.

Of course, she was right.

She was surprised, though, when he reached in his pocket as soon as they stepped through their front door and presented her with a small brass key, for it was one she recognized as having come from her own ring of keys. "When did you take this, Husband? I was unaware it was missing."

"But yesterday," he said, "after you left to walk up to the meadow."

She fingered the ring and studied the expectant look on her husband's face. "I do not know why I even keep this key close by. You know I never lock that closet."

"I doubt it has been locked ever since my great-grandfather decided no longer to run Beechnut House as an inn and tavern. My grandfather always said that the closet was where Robert Hastings, the original publican, stored the kegs of his finest ales."

"As you have told me often."

Grace knew the story well. Beechnut House had served the town of Martinsville for many years, but, as she knew from having been told countless times by her husband, Robert's grandson Alonzo married the fiery-tempered Margaret DeWitt, whose Irish father had been overly fond of drink and had been, until he died, one of the best customers Beechnut House ever had. Margaret had—so the story went—been unwilling to contribute to further dissipation in the town, and had made it a condition of her acceptance of Alonzo's proposal, that he cease the operation of the tavern upon the death of the innkeeper his father. Apparently Alonzo had not been averse to the idea, for his temperament was not suited to that of publican. He much preferred scholarly endeavors and had determined early in his life that he would become the village schoolteacher.

So, with the death of Charles Hastings, who had been the first-born son of the original Robert Hastings, Beechnut House Tavern had become simply Beechnut House, and Alonzo Hastings moved from the house on the corner, just a little ways uphill from the tavern, into Beechnut House and proceeded to fill the numerous rooms, first with Margaret's remaining family—mother, sisters, and younger brothers, and then with Alonzo and Margaret's own offspring. The first daughter who survived was Lydia, who married Curtis Sheffield. The first surviving son was Arthur's grandfather Reuben, whose love of his wife Astaline Shipleigh was something of a legend in the town, for he had cursed God when she died.

Grace was brought back from her reverie by Arthur, who prodded her arm. "Why do you not open it before our anniversary is over?"

"I suppose I could," she said, delighting in stringing out the moment.

With a laugh, he took her arm and propelled her toward the closet.

There were shelves all the way around the small room, shelves that must have held the ale kegs, but now were used to store linens.

In the middle of the room, though, stood a stunning cheval mirror, its bright surface reflecting the light from the kitchen. In the lovely oval glass, Grace could see Arthur standing slightly behind her, gazing at her reflection.

"Oh! Arthur! It is beautiful!"

"Do you like it then?"

"No," Grace said, but hurried on before his face could fall any farther. "I do not merely like it. I love it."

Arthur lifted it carefully and placed it in the middle of the kitchen. Then he stood behind Grace once more, his hands resting lightly on her shoulders, so they could contemplate the image of the two of them together in the looking glass.

"Wherever did you get it?"

"Sheffield's," he said. " His imprint is on the bottom edge. I happened to be there when he was crafting it some months ago. I asked him to set it aside for me and not mention it to anyone."

"It is a perfect gift, my love." Her mouth bent upwards in a mischievous quirk. "Far more perfect than what we received from Auntie Veronica all those years ago. Do you remember?"

"How could I forget? You almost ignited the steps to the attic in your haste to rid yourself of those two items." He looked around, almost as if they might appear. "Have you seen them since?"

"Never," she said, "and not likely to." She wrapped her arms around his neck. "You were all the gift I needed on my wedding day."

"There is more," he finally said. Stepping forward, he worked the latch at the side and tilted the mirror smoothly so the upper part of the frame came down to her level.

She was not sure what he intended, but she put out her hand to touch the frame reverently, and felt something carved into it. "Bean de Ghrásta, 13 Jan 1856," she read. "Oh, Arthur."

"You have always been my woman of grace," he said simply.

It was several long moments before either of them spoke again.

After they moved the mirror into the large front room and Grace had it positioned exactly the way she wanted it, she stepped aside to her lovely desk and reached for the inkwell. She had to write to Dolly about this, and all her other sisters as well. But first, she gave her husband one more most enthusiastic kiss. The secret room they were creating upstairs was only one of the reasons she loved him. This mirror was another. But, truly, she loved him simply because Arthur was such a good man.

2000

"BEAN DE GHRÁSTA," Melissa read. "What on earth does that mean?"

"What does a mirror have to do with beans?" Pat sounded as confused as the rest of us.

Carol thought a moment. "There's an accent over one of the letters. That probably means this is in some language other than English." She looked around at us, but everyone else was as in the dark as I was. Until Easton stepped forward.

"It's Gaelic."

We all gawked at her.

"I used to be married to a guy who had some Irish blood. His mother's name was Ghrásta. It means Grace." She sure didn't pronounce it the way Melissa had.

"Grace doesn't have anything to do with beans." Maddy lowered her head. Under her breath, I heard her add, "You think you're so smart."

Sadie put a hand on Maddy's arm, and Maddy flinched. Sadie must have squeezed pretty hard for Maddy to feel it through all those sweater layers. I wondered what was going on.

"Beh-ahn," Easton said, stressing the two syllables and glaring at Maddy. I was sure she'd heard the low-voiced comment. "It means woman."

Carol sighed. "Woman of Grace. That certainly is a sweet thought."

"So what's-his-name was Irish?" Maddy walked to the white dresser. "Guess I'll have to put that on the museum display card. The only other Grace we have is the one writing her sister about the secret room." She pulled out the letter and confirmed the names. "Grace and Arthur Hoskins. February of 1856."

"The date here on the mirror," Pat said, "is January 13, 1856. Any idea what it means?"

"Maybe it was her birthday," I guessed.

"This cements it as a mid-nineteenth-century artifact," Maddy said.

Dee threw up her hands in mock despair. "Quit sounding so much like a museum curator."

"But I am one. It's your fault, too. You're the one who nominated me, aren't you?"

"I'd been thinking of replacing the glass and using the mirror," I said, "but that would destroy its value for the museum, wouldn't it?"

Maddy nodded, but Sadie shook her head.

"You go right ahead, dear. Museums are all well and good, but I think these items were meant to be used, and this mirror was certainly intended to be treasured."

"Then why put it in the attic?" Easton's question was a reasonable one—one that I'd thought of myself.

"I doubt it was Grace who consigned it up here," Carol said. "Most probably, once it got cloudy with age, it was someone from another generation altogether who didn't want it downstairs anymore. I'm just glad whoever it was didn't throw the whole thing out."

"No telling what's landed in the county dump," Rebecca Jo said.

"Landfill," Maddy corrected.

"Humph," said Rebecca Jo.

"Well," I said, "as soon as we can get the men up here, I'm going to ask Bob to take it downstairs."

"We can do that ourselves," Melissa said. "It's not like we're weaklings."

I traded a knowing look with Sadie. "I know we can, but Bob likes to help make me happy. And it will definitely make me happy to have this down in the living room, so why not give him something to do?"

"Other than play poker," Ida said. "I'll ask Ralph to help him. That would make me happy."

Glaze made a noise deep in her throat. I couldn't tell if she was laughing or groaning. "I'm going to look for some more goodies. Those boring greeting cards can't be the only things in that trunk."

"Why fill an entire trunk with nothing but paper?" Dee didn't sound like she was expecting an answer, but I gave her one anyway.

"Maybe it started with just a few cards, but then every time anyone was looking for a place to get rid of stuff like that, they thought about the trunk up here. Seems logical, wouldn't you think?"

"I think I would have thrown it all out to begin with," Pat said.

I had to agree with her.

"Leave that alone, Glaze," Ida said. "I miss Mary Frances. Let's read another journal entry."

We all started toward the circle of chairs until Glaze stopped us with a grunt of excitement. "Wait a minute. I've found something."

"Finally?" Dee sounded incredulous.

There were only three sheets of paper written in a hand that was obviously not adult. I could see that the writing, though relatively clear, was large and childish somehow, not anything like the other letters we'd found.

I, Alfred Finlay Hastings, am required by my Schoolmaster to copy six Pages of the <u>Rules of Civility</u>, for I have been less than civil in my Actions. I am to start, he said, with the Rules I have broken. I have found Eight, although there may have been many More.

"Poor kid," Melissa said.

"He got off easy," Sadie said. "I can remember having to write *I will not stand on my chair* a hundred and fifty times."

There was something of a lilt in her voice, so I had to ask, "Did you stop doing it?"

"Of course not. It was the only way I could reach above my coat hook to the shelf where I threw my mittens and hat."

"Poor short Sadie," Melissa said, only this time she was teasing rather than commiserating.

"So," Rebecca Jo said, "what did little Alfred write?"

1 Shew Nothing to your Freind that may affright him.

"I bet he took a big bullfrog to school," Glaze said.

"More likely a snake," Ida suggested.

2 In the Presence of Others Sing not to yourself with a humming Noise, nor Drum with your Fingers or Feet.
3 Sit not when others stand, Speak not when you should hold your Peace, walk not on when others Stop.
4 Shift not yourself in the Sight of others nor Gnaw your nails.

"Boy, would I have been in trouble back then," Glaze said, and I remembered the way she bit her nails almost to the quick the whole time we were growing up, until she finally got the help she needed to combat her depression.

5 Kill no Vermin as Fleas, Lice Ticks in the Sight of Others.

"Ewww," Dee said. "How gross."

"It was a common complaint back then," Carol said. "Just about everybody had to deal with fleas and lice."

"And ticks," Ida said with a shudder.

"I hope the poor kid was allowed to scratch at least." Melissa rubbed her leg, and I felt a bit itchy myself.

6 Keep your Nails clean and short, also your Hands and Teeth clean.

"If he gnawed his nails," Sadie said, "they'd already be short, so I'd imagine this means he always had grubby hands."

"Sort of like yours were when you were a kid," Rebecca Jo said.

"Sometimes," Sadie said, "I look at my hands and wonder how they got like this. I almost expect to see them smooth and supple, the way they were seventy years ago."

Easton reached out and traced one of Sadie's prominent blue

veins. "I think your hands are lovely. They're strong and gentle."

It was a few moments before Glaze continued reading.

7 If You Cough, Sneeze, Sigh, or Yawn, do it not Loud but Privately; and Speak not in your Yawning, but put Your Handkercheif or Hand before your Face and turn aside.
8 Do not laugh too loud or too much at any Publick Spectacle.

"There's some really funny spelling in here. F-r-e-i-n-d and s-h-e-w and c-h-e-i-f on the end of handkerchief."

"Such spellings were common way back when," Carol said. "I think that *Rules of Civility* book he mentioned was written in the middle of the eighteenth century."

"But if this came from the Colonial Era," Maddy said, "wouldn't it have been written on parchment rather than paper?"

Carol thought about it. "They did have paper back then, but it was fairly rare. In fact, most of the school lessons were written on slate so it could be rubbed clean and used again."

"Paper became more plentiful after the civil war," Maddy said, "so maybe that's a good clue."

She sounded dubious though. Why didn't people date everything they wrote?

"Alfred sounds like a great kid," Pat said. "What else is on the list?"

"Nothing," Glaze said. "That's the end of it."

"That's only two pages, not six." I pointed to the other piece of paper she held. "What's on that other sheet?"

She skimmed down it. "Looks like an essay of some sort. Also by Alfred Hastings. Oh my gosh!"

"What?"

"Remember the box with the marbles and the whirligig?" We all nodded. "You said you thought the whirligig was missing a piece, Carol. Here's your answer."

How My Whirligig Got Broken
Written by Alfred Finlay Hastings

The day my Pa died, I was shelling Beans on the Porch with my Mother and my Five Sisters. My Uncle Jonah carried my Pa's body back down from the Upper Feild where he got struck by a Tree that fell on Him, and Ma was so surprised to see them She dropped her Bowl of Beans on my Whirligig, breaking off one of the Vanes. I put it Away in the box my Pa made for Me along with the Marbles he made me because now I have to do So Many more Chores every Day. Pa only had one Arm from the War, which is mayhap why He could not jump out of the Way fast enuogh.

"The war?" Melissa bent to peer at the page. "Does it say which war?"

Maddy stepped over to the white dresser and pulled out the box while Glaze looked over the two pages. "Nope."

"But it must have been the Civil War," Ida said.

Carol cleared her throat.

"Okay, okay. There's a good chance it was the Civil War because of the paper."

"It could just as easily have been the Revolutionary War, for all we know," Carol pointed out.

"Top drawer," Glaze said, and started to hand the pages to Maddy. "Wait a minute. The box. Remember, Carol, you said it was probably made by a child because the rawhide fastener knob was made so crookedly?"

"Yeah, I remember."

"Well, this explains it." She searched through the little essay. "*I put it away in the box my Pa made for me along with the Marbles he made me*," she quoted. "And – here it says *Pa only had one arm from the war*. Could that be why the leather knot was so lopsided?"

"Could be," Carol said. "Could very well be."

"We might be able to find Alfred's name, and maybe his dad's, in some of the old town records," Dee said.

Carol laughed. "You're really getting into this, aren't you?"

It was the same question Bob had asked me.

"In the meantime, I'm ready for another hatbox," Dee said, apparently forgetting Ida's request that we read some more. I wasn't ready to sit down yet, so I didn't remind her.

"Fine," Maddy said. "You can have another hatbox, but I'd rather have another hat."

Dee crossed her eyes at Maddy and lifted the next hatbox from the pile. "Who wants the honor of opening this one?"

"You, of course," Maddy said.

"Okay. You don't have to say it twice." She shook the box gently. "Whatever this hat looks like, it sure is lightweight."

"And it must be packed in there really well," Maddy said. "I don't hear a single swish or rattle."

Dee picked up the accounts book that still sat in the middle of the table where she and Rebecca Jo had left it yesterday. "Why don't you put Nancy Geonette and her milk and egg list in the museum drawer, Maddy?" Then she lifted the lid of the hatbox with calm deliberation.

No wonder it didn't rattle.

No wonder it hardly weighed anything.

It was empty.

1823

"**I DETEST YOU**," ten-year-old Sylvia Martin muttered—not loud enough for Mother to hear her. Only loud enough for her eldest sister's ears.

"You are jealous," Cora said, "but I am fourteen and almost of marriageable age. Therefore I must be the one to have a new chapeau."

Cora disgusted Sylvia when she threw out foreign words like that, but Sylvia had to admit the hat was elegant enough to merit a French name. She fingered the somewhat tattered bonnet strings dangling below her chin. "Why do I always have to get the ones handed down from you to Mary to Annabelle to Cynthia and finally to me?"

"I am too old for such childish clothing as you now wear," Cora said. "If you would but take better care of your clothes, even if they are hand-me-downs, they would not look so … so disreputable."

"You are being super-silly-ent." That new word Sylvia had recently learned did not sound quite right, but she had been looking for a chance to use it. Hopefully Cora, who never paid much attention in the schoolroom, would not know it.

"Supercilious," Cora said, squashing Sylvia's hopes. "And you are being a super silly goose." She patted the bright confection of feathers and ribbons into place and stuck a long, vicious-looking hatpin through it. "Run along now and get yourself ready for church. I will be leaving early."

"Why?"

"Gertie and Susie are going to stop by soon."

Sylvia did not think much of Gertrude Hastings or of Susie Russell. "You just want time to dawdle along and gossip."

Cora ignored her.

"Gossip is a sin," Sylvia said. "Reverend Jonas Russell said so."

Cora's face flushed, but she held herself erect despite her younger sister's disdain.

"You are probably going to burn in—"

"Don't you dare say that sinful word!" Cora wheeled abruptly and slammed the door on her way out.

Sylvia would not have said it. That would have been as much a sin as gossiping.

Sylvia turned over various methods of revenge as she walked behind her parents all the way to the Old Church. She discarded several, such as accidentally dripping candle wax on the hat, for she hoped it would survive its trip through all of her sisters and finally make it to her, to Sylvia. It occurred to her, though, that Cora truly was almost grown. If she married soon, the lovely hat would go with her to her new home and Sylvia would never have a chance to wear it. Instead, it would pass down to Cora's first daughter. Perhaps the candle wax was not such a bad idea.

Outside the Old Church, Sylvia saw Cora and her two friends talking—probably gossiping—underneath the huge elm tree that shaded the church from the morning sun. She slipped away from her parents and sidled up behind the massive trunk, catching just the last part of a pronouncement by her sister.

"… home with you right after the service next Sunday."

"You will stay and eat with us," Gertie whined in that nasal voice that always irritated Sylvia no end.

"I will have to ask Mother, but I am sure she will agree."

Susie said something much along the same line, but Sylvia did not hear the rest of their conversation. She tiptoed away from the tree and then ran to meet Molly, her dearest friend, who was walking with her Uncle Alonzo Hastings and Aunt Margaret along Third Street from their house a block away on Beechnut Lane.

During the sermon—Sylvia hated sermons, particularly since the elderly Reverend Jonas Russell had a dirge-like voice that always sounded as if he were conducting a funeral—she came up with a plan, a very good plan.

The next day, she confided in Molly and swore her to the utmost secrecy. They linked their pinkie fingers and tapped their thumbs together as a pledge that no word of this would ever pass their lips, except to each other, of course. The hardest part of the plan would be to keep Molly's cousin Gertie from suspecting them.

That evening, Sylvia asked her mother, "Could Molly come home with me after church next Sunday?" Meanwhile Molly, whose mother was dead, was asking her aunt and uncle for permission to eat the mid-day meal with Sylvia the following Sunday.

"Now remember," Sylvia said the next Sunday as they circled through the stand of trees toward Molly's front door, "we need to be absolutely silent."

Molly clapped her hand across her lips, her eyes twinkling.

"I will stay out here," Sylvia reiterated, "and wait while you go in and get the hat."

"Of course." Molly dropped her hand and giggled. "I know better than you which porch stairs creak."

"I only hope she has left her hat on the hall tree the way she usually does."

"Your sister is a creature of habit," Molly said. "I do like that term, *a creature of habit.*"

"Where did you hear it?"

Molly looked at her with a decided frown. "Reverend Russell used it in his sermon last week."

“Oh,” Sylvia said. “I was not listening.”

“Obviously not.”

“Enough of this. Remember to listen below the window to be sure everyone is there before you sneak inside.”

Molly laid a reassuring hand on Sylvia’s shoulder. “I know the plan as well as you.”

Sylvia was almost afraid to breathe as she watched her friend approach the house from an angle so she could not be glimpsed from any of the windows.

Molly crouched, as Sylvia had instructed, so her head would not be seen above the flame-colored azaleas that billowed in front of the kitchen window. A few moments later—moments that seemed like a lifetime to Sylvia—Molly crept around the corner of the house to the front porch, and Sylvia lost sight of her.

It took just a few moments to hide the hat under the hawthorn hedge. Then they ran all the way to Sylvia’s house. It would not do to be late for the mid-day dinner, for Mother would have to be able to vouch that Sylvia and her friend Molly had been there all along.

That evening, after both families had endured the explosions that came from Cora at the disappearance of her precious chapeau, Molly crept outside to retrieve the hat. As quietly as possible, she took it up to the attic of her aunt and uncle’s big old house on Beechnut Lane and hid the hat in one of the many hatboxes that had always resided there. She was careful to place it at the bottom of one of the stacks and to note carefully just which stack it was.

Over the next few months, the two friends played as often as they could up in the attic, taking turns wearing the feathered and beribboned hat, until the day Gertie popped up the stairs without any more warning than the sound of her shuffling feet on the last five or six stairs.

Sylvia whipped the hat off her head, dumped it on the floor, and sank down on it, assuming the pose of a dying princess. Molly stuck out her elbow and pretended to be drawing a sword. “I will save you, my beautiful princess,” she declaimed.

“Are you still playing such childish games?” Gertie’s nasal twang sounded only slightly tolerant.

“Yes, and you are interrupting us,” Molly declared. “Why do

you come on our castle unannounced?"

"My mother told me to fetch you and to bring the lantern downstairs." She advanced toward it. "Come down with me now. You do not want to be up here in the dark."

There was very little light coming in through the attic windows, and Sylvia wondered how it had come to be so late. "Can you not give us a few moments to tidy up?"

"Yes," Molly said. "We will bring the lantern down with us shortly."

Gertie eyed them suspiciously, but could not seem to come up with an objection. "All right, but see that you hurry." She turned and disappeared down the stairs.

Molly waited to be sure Gertie was truly gone. "Did you have to sit on it like that?"

Sylvia felt tears come to her eyes when she saw the destruction of her beautiful hat. The stiff ribbons were hopelessly bent, the feathers were broken, and the light basket framework that held it all in place was splintered, wrecked beyond the possibility of repair.

Molly lifted it, crammed it behind a nearby trunk, and picked up the lantern. "I will dispose of it in the back woods tomorrow."

Sylvia placed the empty hatbox back onto the stack it had come from and shuffled down the stairs and all the way home with a heavy heart.

The next Sunday, when Reverend Jonas Russell preached about the wages of sin, Sylvia felt sure he was talking directly to her.

2000

DEE MADE A face. "All of you find fun things, and I get an empty box?"

"Keep looking," Ida said. "You're bound to hit pay dirt at some point."

There is no dirt up here.

"You have the sunbonnet," Maddy said.

Poor Dee looked so irritated, I chimed in. "You're not the only one, Dee. I don't have a hat yet, either. Not a real one. Just the boater."

When she glared at me, I quit trying to make her feel better.

She reached for the stack again and this time brought forth two boxes. “Take your pick.”

“No. I don’t really need a hat. I’ll be happy to take what’s left once we’ve gone through all the boxes.” Off to one side, I heard Ida snort, but I ignored her. She knew I liked my boater hat, the one I’d worn to the wedding. The wheat-colored straw and the perky ribbon were perfect. Who cared that it had been made for a man? Or that the name inside the band was *Loren.*

“If this turns out to be a dud …” Dee left her sentence dangling.

“Then you can keep opening boxes until you find one you like.”

Maddy rolled her hands around each other in a hurry-up motion. “Come on, Dee. Have some faith. It’s bound to get better.”

Dee made another face. “Unless it gets worse.”

She opened the first box. The hat turned out to be a sad-looking beige, shaped like a ragged pancake, with a limp veil. Even Easton wouldn’t have looked good in that one. “Reject,” Dee said and tossed the box to Amanda, who stood closest to the pile of throw-aways.

The lid of the second box took some wrestling before it opened.

“Ooh,” Dee said, and lifted out a lovely little pink cloche with a pouf of cottony fluff decorating the left side. Unfortunately, when she tried to put it on, it perched atop her head like an acorn cap on a watermelon. “Who was this made for, a two-year-old?”

“Guess you’re stuck with the sunbonnet,” Ida said.

“And the sunbonnet looks lovely on Dee,” Sadie insisted.

Dee flashed her a grateful glance and returned the minuscule pink hat to the box.

“I’ll take it for the museum,” Maddy said. “Wish I knew what to put on the placard.”

1824

LORINDA MOON, THE only daughter of Eliza Moon, married Franklin Hastings, the grandson of Curtis and Lydia Sheffield. The mother of the bride closed her shop for that day. Moon’s Fine Furniture was a thriving concern, and the proprietress could well afford to go a day without sales. Although many of the women of the town disliked the idea of attending the wedding, considering who the mother of the bride was, many of them were inordinately proud of the fine furnishings their husbands had bought them. The heavy chandelier, the lion-topped four-poster bed, the gilt-framed mirrors.

Those same women had anxiously checked their mail twice a day to see whether a light pink invitation arrived.

Lorinda, as delicate as a petal, with a waist that looked about the same diameter as a candle and shoulders narrower than a kitchen step stool, was married in a flowing dress, as pink as the peonies that graced the end of each pew. Her matching hat, which clung to her tiny head, sported a delicate puff of white silk.

EVENTUALLY, AFTER SEVERAL generations of Hastings sons had fathered more sons of their own, one of them fathered a boy he named Rupert, who in turn became the father of first Sam and then Easton Hastings. Sam was murdered on a night in the 1990s when the Metoochie River flooded once again, and Easton, everyone said, was the spitting image of that full-length portrait of the fiery-haired owner of Moon's Fine Furniture.

2000

"WAIT!" AMANDA HAD stayed on the periphery of the group for so much of the time, her exclamation surprised me. I think she still didn't feel quite a part of our close-knit group. Maybe it was because she was so much younger than the rest of us, although that shouldn't have made a difference. She'd had her hands on all of us—some of us many times—as she kneaded and poked and muscled and coaxed our tight shoulders and backs into relaxing. We turned, almost as one entity, to see Amanda bent over with her head practically buried in a large wooden crate.

"Sounds like you found a prize," I said.

"I've read about these," Amanda said, withdrawing a box that I could see from here had a glass lid, "but I've never seen an actual one. And here's a whole collection." She brought it closer and laid it on the nearest card table.

"Mourning brooches," Carol breathed with a distinct tone of awe.

"I've never heard that term," Pat said. "What are they?"

"They're made from the hair of a dead person," Carol said. "Sometimes they're braided, sometimes glued—there were lots of different methods."

I sure was glad Easton had taken a bathroom break. I could just see her lip curling.

Why are you thinking so angrily?

I really did need to light another candle. "How sweet," I said, "to want to remember a loved one like that."

"And women had really long hair back then," Amanda said, "which may be why some of these are so large. Look," she pointed, "there's a braided bracelet."

Sadie leaned forward to peer closer. "Is there a date on the box?"

Amanda rotated it, moved it closer to one of the lanterns, and held it up so she could look underneath. "It feels like there's something here, but I can't be sure. The light's not that great."

She was right. The clouds must have thickened outside. I glanced out a window at the sky—the windows were all too high for me to see the ground—and I saw more snow whirling through the air. I turned up the wick on the oil lantern. Bob and I probably should have bought a bunch of high-powered battery lamps instead, but I really liked the idea of our lanterns a whole lot better. They seemed more … authentic somehow.

"Mourning brooches were quite popular during the Victorian era," Carol said. "In fact, some people made necklaces and bracelets"—she nodded at the one in the box—"if the hair was long enough."

"So are you saying my box came from the late 1800s or early 1900s? When did Victoria reign?"

"Eighteen-thirty-seven to nineteen-oh-one," Carol said, without seeming to have to think about it. Was every historian's brain a mass depository of dates? "But mourning brooches have been found that date from the 1600s."

"How on earth can we tell about these?" Amanda opened the lid carefully and set it aside next to Sadie's letters.

"We can inspect each one. Sometimes initials, dates, or even names were incorporated into the designs."

"If I have to be stranded in an ice storm," Melissa said, "I'm glad I have a historian in the attic with me."

I like having you here, too. You listen to me.

Carol laughed and rubbed Marmalade's ears. "Pick one, Amanda, and we'll take a look."

Thank you. That feels good.

Amanda studied the array for a few moments. "This one," she finally said. "It's made of white hair. Someone's grandmother, wouldn't you say?"

"Not necessarily." My sister fingered her own silvery locks. "Mine turned white when I was in my late twenties."

1851

GRACE SURRATT HOSKINS might have been married for twenty-nine long years, but she still took a great deal of delight in studying the angular jaw of her husband. At the moment, that jaw was cradled on Grace's ample bosom. Unfortunately, Arthur's handsome jaw quivered in grief.

"Shush, dear," Grace soothed. "She's gone to her heavenly reward."

Grace had never known a man who could cry the way Arthur Hoskins could. She supposed it was because of his Irish grandmother. She had heard that the Irish were emotional people. She could understand all the tears when their own firstborn had died when she was barely three minutes of age. Heaven only knew that she herself had cried enough for the two of them over that death. And Arthur had cried when his brother Nathaniel died, although he should have been more of a manly example to his nephews. Arthur's other brother, Zenus, certainly never shed tears like this.

And here, in this case, there was not a reason for this much grief. Mother Hoskins had lived far longer than anyone in her immediate family. Seventy-three busy years, constantly giving directions to everyone and everything she came in contact with, dispensing wisdom and comfort in equal measure. She had been hale and more than hearty right up almost until her dying breath. There certainly was not such a call for this much despair, although Grace would miss her dreadfully.

"Shush," she said again as gently as if to a child. Inwardly, she calculated how soon she could become a bit more stern with him. She sighed. Not yet. Let him snuffle at least until they heard his brother Zenus arriving. Then it would be time for Arthur to stand up and make the necessary arrangements. And it would be up to Grace and her sister Melanie, who had married Arthur's brother Zenus, to lay out Mother Rose Hoskins. The third Surratt sister, Delilah, whom they all called Dolly, had emigrated with her husband to the far reaches of the state, living in Brothersville, which nobody from Martinsville had ever visited. Their youngest sister, Elspeth, had moved to Russell Gap after her marriage, so they seldom saw her. And, after all, Dolly and Elspeth were not related by marriage to any of the Hoskins brood the way Grace and Melanie were.

Grace surely hoped Melanie and Zenus would not waste any more time getting here. Mother Hoskins would be hard to handle once death began to stiffen her. And Grace wanted the comfort of her sister, who would understand Grace's grief.

By the time Melanie and the Reverend arrived from Garner Creek, after the neighbor's boy, Stephen Olsen, had ridden his fastest horse to summon them, Arthur had risen, blown his nose repeatedly, and brushed his hair back off his forehead. Before Zenus and Melanie came inside, Arthur turned to his wife and tucked her stray curls back under her cap. "My *ghrásta*," he said, using the Irish nickname he called her only when they were alone. "Thank you for your comfort." *Ghrásta* meant *grace*, and Grace Hoskins always thrilled when her husband used that term of endearment. She smiled up at him, straightened her shoulders, and turned to the sound of footsteps in the entryway.

Melanie went straight to Grace. "I do hope it was peaceful," she said.

Grace nodded.

"You know we would have been here sooner if Zenus had not had to conduct the morning service. He will be in straightaway after he tends the horses."

Again, Grace nodded.

"I will go and see if he needs any help," Arthur said, and adjusted his waistcoat.

The women waited until they were alone. "What is wrong, dear? Other than Mother Hoskins' death, I mean."

Grace took a deep breath. "I have been so busy comforting Arthur, I have not taken time to express my own …" Her words trailed off and she pressed her handkerchief over her mouth. "I loved Mother Hoskins, almost as if she had been my own mother. I shall miss her dreadfully."

Melanie, thank goodness, did not offer any platitudes. "Why do we not each take a lock of her hair and form a brooch for ourselves as a remembrance?"

Grace raised her eyebrows. "Do you think Mother Hoskins would approve such an endeavor? You know how opposed she was to jewelry of any kind."

Melanie raised her eyebrows right back, causing Grace to smile. "Mother Hoskins is no longer in any condition to disapprove of anything."

"Melanie! How can you, a preacher's wife no less, be so irreverent?"

"This is not irreverence. Death is the inevitable end to life." Melanie, Grace noted, was using her *reasonable* voice. "Surely those who have died no longer care what happens here, and"—Melanie leveled a *reasonable* look at her sister—"you know it was not Rose Hoskins who disapproved of jewelry. Not really. It was that husband of hers."

Although Grace had always shared Melanie's dislike of Baxter Hoskins, their late unlamented father-in-law, she was not sure whether Zenus and Arthur would approve of such a comment. It was just as well, then, that the men were out at the stable. She fingered the abundant strands of white hair that spread out across the death pillow. "A brooch might be a good idea. And perhaps a ring for Arthur and one for Zenus as well?"

"And for each of our children, too."

Grace stroked her mother-in-law's hair. "It is long enough, we could make bracelets."

"We will have to be careful not to get so carried away that we render her bald in our quest for enough hair."

Grace touched her sister gently on the arm. "Thank you for helping to brighten this dark time."

"Of course." Melanie laughed quietly. "We will have to get our men to build us boxes to house all our creations, because someday our own hair will join that of Mother Hoskins in mourning brooches our children have made."

Despite Melanie's grim words, Grace gave her sister an affectionate squeeze. "I will go fetch my scissors."

When she returned, she found Melanie gazing out the window.

"I have been thinking."

"Yes?"

"My Zenus is no hand with woodworking, and I would put no faith in any sort of box he made for treasures such as these brooches will be."

Grace had to laugh. "Zenus does indeed seem to have nothing but thumbs on those hands of his."

"Your Arthur is not much of a craftsman, either."

Grace had to agree. For large projects, he could do well enough, but anything that needed a fine finish was better left to someone else. "What about Sheffield's Cabinetry? They do fine work."

"Wonderful. Will you speak to them tomorrow?"

"Not tomorrow. I will wait until after the funeral. There will be enough time, for I doubt not it will take us weeks of working to finish …" She raised the scissors. "Let us begin, at least."

Luckily, Rose Hoskins still had hair as thick as that of a young girl, and the two sisters were able to quickly gather enough of the locks for numerous brooches.

"You cannot even tell there is any missing." Melanie brushed the remaining snowy hair gently back into place. "If it were not so white, anyone would think it was the hair of a young woman." She looked up at her sister. "Your hair is almost whiter than hers."

"And has been since I was eighteen or thereabouts."

"Which is when you caught the eye of Arthur." Melanie laughed, a sound incongruous next to the body of a well-beloved dead woman. "Do you remember your hat?"

"Ahh, the hat. Of course I remember it. I loved those dark blue ribbons."

"To say nothing of the silver tassels."

Grace laughed. "It was a bit ostentatious, was it not?"

"You quite took away the breath of all of us at the cotillion that year, and Arthur most of all."

"I would have married him that night if Mother had not been so set on delaying our wedding. All she wanted was for me to continue to be at her beck and call." She sighed and ran her fingers along the rapidly-cooling arm on the bed before her. "Mother Hoskins was always more of a mother to me than our own mother was."

"She loved you dearly. I know she considered you her daughter of the heart more than simply a daughter-in-law."

Grace cut one more lock and eyed the stork scissors in her hand. "I do believe my daughter-in-law is expecting."

"What ever makes you say that?"

"The scissors reminded me. Leonora seemed much softer, rounder, and there was a bloom on her face when she and my son came to visit Mother Hoskins last week. You know how it is."

"Did she say anything about it?"

Grace scoffed, and Melanie smiled ruefully. "I suppose not."

"She did ask, most quietly, if her family could move back here."

Melanie tightened her lips. "Why? And what did you tell her?"

"I told her that Mister Hoskins and I would be delighted." She rotated the scissors as Melanie made a derisive snort. "Gideon's business concerns have not, apparently gone as well as he had hoped."

Grace reached for the final white lock and laid it reverently across the square of blue gingham they were using to hold the hair. Leonora had lost three babes since the birth of Young Gideon almost five years ago. She prayed that this child might survive.

Grace smiled. Even though her own first child, a sweet daughter, had died, she had had others since then, each one as dear as the one before, although Gideon, her oldest living son, had been something of a problem child for as long as she had had the keeping of him. He still was. She and Arthur were both at a loss as to how to deal with their son's explosive anger. She hoped he never expressed that anger toward his wife. Grace loved Leonora like a daughter.

"Remember how excited we each were to find that we were both with child at the same time?"

Melanie's words brought Grace back, away from the difficulty of Gideon to the joy before her. She stroked the tiny silver bundle molded into the handle of the scissors. "Oh yes. I well remember."

2000

AMANDA SPENT SOME time inspecting the brooch made of silvery hair. "Is this a date?" She pointed to the back of the brooch and passed it around for all of us to see.

"Eighteen-fifty-one, I think." Dee's eyes were in better shape than mine if she could read such tiny markings. "Wow. This thing is almost a hundred and fifty years old. I didn't know hair could last that long."

"As long as it stays dry," Carol said, "which these brooches obviously did. Hair can last hundreds, even thousands of years. They've found Egyptian mummies with their hair intact, although it's usually dried out to a straw-like consistency with all that desert air. I guess there's such a thing as *too* dry."

"Why don't you each pick a brooch," Amanda suggested. "I mean, only if that's okay with you, Biscuit. After all, the attic and everything in it is yours."

"Maybe everything should be kept together just as it was," Maddy said, "for the museum, once we get it started." She looked sideways at the droopy white feather on Ida's hat. "Almost everything," she added with a wry twist to her mouth.

Easton came back from another one of her frequent bathroom breaks just then, and Sadie, in a low voice, brought her up to date.

"Let's not even try to make such a decision yet," I said. "That museum could be a long time in coming. When it's ready, we can spread the word and you can each bring back your brooches and letters and posters and rings." I paused. "And hats," I added, with much the same intonation that Maddy had used, and everyone snickered. "But that's only if you want to. You might be tired of dusting them by then, but then again, you might want to keep them, and that would be fine with me." I looked a question at Maddy.

"Fine with me, too," she said. "The last thing I want to be is the Museum Police." She made air quotes with her fingers.

"Good, then." Once the heavy white brooch had made it around the circle, Amanda fastened it onto her sweater and turned back to the trunk while the rest of us passed the box around and picked our own mourning brooches. Sadie picked a light blond brooch that looked great against her purple sweatshirt. Easton chose a light blond ring for her right index finger. Dee picked a brooch that was a dark brown, almost black. Glaze selected the thick white braided bracelet.

"I could have used this as my *something old*," Glaze said. "If only we'd found these yesterday."

"You had the buffalo horn hair comb," I reminded her. "You probably don't want too many oldies at your wedding."

Sadie looked pointedly at Rebecca Jo. "Does that mean we should have stayed downstairs?"

Before I could retort—not that I could think of what to say—she laughed and pinned her own brooch onto her purple sweatshirt.

The one I chose was made of hair the gray-brown color of the bark on the old maple tree above Bob's beehives. It looked pretty good on my gray sweatshirt.

I replaced the lid so none of the remaining rings or brooches would fall out and turned the box over. Holding it close to the lantern, I could just make out a name carved into the wood. "Look at this, Rebecca Jo," I said. "*Sheffield Cabinetry 1851.*"

Before she could reply, Amanda let out another whoop of joy. Instead of the WAHOOs, I thought, we should call ourselves the Whoop-de-doos.

What does that mean?

"Look! Aren't these the most beautiful scissors you've ever seen?" She stretched out her hands, draped with a square of blue and white-checked gingham cloth. I couldn't see the object that had been wrapped in the gingham until I stood and stepped closer.

"They sure don't make scissors like that anymore," Ida said.

Pat leaned near, wrinkling her brow in concentration. I wondered if she needed glasses. "Is it some kind of bird?"

"A stork, I beieve." Carol shifted the lantern closer to Amanda's outstretched hands. "See the figure halfway down the handle? It's meant to look like a baby tied in a little bundle."

"It *does* look like a baby," Sadie said. "My mother had a pair of scissors similar to these, only she always said hers was a crane rather than a stork, but the baby was much the same."

"What's the difference between a crane and a stork?"

"I don't know, Maddy. I just know my mama always called them her crane scissors."

Ida jerked her neck to one side, apparently trying to get the feather back away from her nose. It must have tickled. "Cranes have thin beaks and storks have thick beaks."

Sadie raised an eyebrow. "Then maybe my mom's scissors were a stork, because the blades were fairly sturdy-looking."

"They'd have to have thick beaks," Pat said, "to carry all those babies."

We ignored her.

"Do you still have them? The scissors," Dee added.

Sadie thought for a moment. "I haven't seen them in quite a while. Of course, I don't do much sewing nowadays." She grinned. "After all, I'm older than mass-produced marbles, so I'm allowed to slow down a bit, aren't I?"

Even though she'd already used that line a couple of times, we all laughed.

Melissa waited for some quiet. "You? Slow down? That'll be the day."

She was right. Sadie might walk a bit slower than the rest of us, and might take longer to climb a flight of stairs, but I was constantly amazed at the amount of work she could turn out when she volunteered at the library. And although Bob helped her with the beehives Wallace had left behind him when he died, Sadie had taken a beekeeping course at the Braetonburg Community College. She harvested almost as much honey from her two remaining hives as Bob did from the ones he'd moved into our yard at Sadie's request when Wallace died.

"I read once that storks don't have any vocal cords," Dee said, "while cranes make a lot of noise."

"Maybe that's why storks deliver the babies," Maddy said. "They won't wake the little tykes while they're—"

"What I'm wondering,"—Melissa interrupted Maddy—"is why anybody would put a perfectly good pair of scissors away in the attic?"

"Maybe she was like me," Sadie said. "Just got past her sewing days and set them aside." She sat back and beamed at Amanda. "You get a gold star for the best discovery of the day."

"Not yet, she doesn't," Ida said. "Let's get busy before we hand out any stars. No telling what else we'll find up here."

Maddy picked up the box, which still had quite a few brooches left in it, and the scissors, and carried them over to the white dresser. "These will fit just fine here in the top drawer."

"Be sure that box doesn't crowd the Mary Frances letter," Carol said. "If the leg gives out and the dresser tilts again, it could do some damage."

I picked up the letter from Caroline Edgerton to Miss Julia Gilman. "Here's something else to add."

Maddy added it and closed the drawer. "I'm being careful." But even as gentle as her closing had been, the dresser wobbled.

"Problem about to be solved," Glaze said. She walked to the front corner of the attic, next to what was left of the row of folding chairs and picked up three or four encyclopedia volumes. "These should work."

While she placed two of them underneath the corner of the dresser, just behind the wobbly leg, Rebecca Jo picked up one of the extra volumes. "Funk and Wagnalls. We used to have a set of these back in the sixties." She fingered the beige volume with a distinct red stripe across the top of the spine and a black stripe where the volume number was indicated. "I can't remember what happened to them."

"They're probably in your laundry room," Dee said, "along with the blueing."

"Or in your attic," Ida said. "I've got a set just like it up in mine."

1966

ELIZABETH HOSKINS SIGNED the order form and studied the salesman as he went over it. He said it was to be sure she'd filled out all the blanks properly, but Elizabeth wondered if he was just making sure he could get her telephone number. She did not trust door-to-door salesmen. Not the ones she'd come in contact with recently.

"Mr. Beene," she said, glad that she had remembered his name

"My husband, Perry, is out of town."

"Huh?" He looked up from the form. "Out of town?"

Elizabeth nodded.

"Then you be sure and keep your doors locked at night," he warned her. "You can't be too careful." He tapped his finger along the edge of the order pad. "I think you'll be really happy with these encyclopedias. Since your son's in high school—tenth grade, didn't you say?—he'll get good use from them. You're getting the very newest edition. They'll be hot off the presses when they arrive."

Elizabeth nodded again. "Lyle is a good boy. He's always such a help to me. He deserves the best."

"That's good because Funk and Wagnalls is the very best encyclopedia, and you can't go wrong with our easy payment plan." He rose to his feet. "Thank you for your order. I'll get it sent in tomorrow. I think you might enjoy them yourself. I see you have beautiful gardens out front. You'll be able to use your new encyclopedias to look up all sorts of information about the flowers and trees you've planted."

She walked with him to the front door.

"That's a fine tree, there." He pointed to a lovely dogwood surrounded by banks of flowers.

"I have extremely good fertilizer," Elizabeth said.

"My wife likes to garden," the man said, his eyes shining. "Oh yes. My Janice Adams Beene is a real gem." He seemed so proud to speak his wife's name like that. "She always wants our house surrounded by flowers."

Elizabeth nodded, and decided not to invite him back to share a glass of wine. She was pretty sure he wouldn't have accepted anyway. Not if he talked about his Janice that way. She liked the way he seemed to relish his wife's full name. A man like that deserved to go home to his wife. Unlike so many of those others.

LYLE USED THE encyclopedias a number of times over the next two years, but he quit high school just three months before graduation. "I won't dig any more holes for you, Momma," is what he said.

"I can't believe I fathered a boy who's afraid of a little hard work," Perry ranted.

Perry didn't know, of course, just what those holes, about six feet long and four feet deep, were used for, and Elizabeth chose not to tell him. Perry wouldn't have understood, even though she knew he would not have approved of those traveling salesmen who had been out to cheat on their wives.

2000

I INVESTIGATED A chest of drawers that was way taller than I was, which might have been a problem for people from the last couple of centuries—I understood that most people were a lot shorter back then, so they wouldn't have been able to look into the top drawers. Only there weren't any top drawers. Instead, the upper two feet consisted of open shelves. Empty shelves. I wondered what people used to store on there. Books? Knickknacks? Folded clothing? Why hadn't someone piled these shelves high like every other flat surface in this attic?

The bottom drawer was empty.

I pulled a brown Western Union telegram from the middle drawer. "I almost hate to read this." I unfolded it. "It's dated October 15, 1918. Addressed to Mrs. Geoffrey Griffin."

"What does the telegram say?" Rebecca Jo's voice sounded like she already guessed the contents.

> DEEPLY REGRET TO INFORM YOU THAT YOUR SON SERGEANT FIRST CLASS ANTHONY BAYARD GRIFFIN SIGNAL CORPS IS OFFICIALLY REPORTED AS KILLED IN ACTION OCTOBER THIRD

I didn't bother reading who signed it. Some general or other.

"The First World War ended in November of that year," Maddy reminded us. "Does this mean her son almost made it?"

"I guess almost isn't good enough where a mother is concerned," Rebecca Jo said.

"Poor woman," Sadie said. "And she was already a widow."

"What makes you think that?" Pat asked.

"Otherwise it would have been addressed to Mr. Griffin or to Mr. and Mrs. Griffin."

I moved the telegram to one side, and Maddy added it to one of the museum drawers.

With some trepidation I opened the top drawer. It held one sheet of paper, headed with two simple lines.

"Okay everybody," I said. "Gather back around. You're going to want to see this, and it's considerably happier than the telegram."

1917

MYRTLE HOSKINS LOVED to rummage around in the attic. For one thing, her big sisters were too old to play in the attic anymore, and her big brother Perry didn't like the attic, so he almost never followed her up here. That meant she had the whole place to herself. At least, until her daddy came home from taking care of the animals in town. He'd come up here and talk to her about all the marvelous things she'd found. And he'd tell her about the cows and horses and dogs and goats he'd helped. Sometimes he'd draw her a funny picture. Myrtle always kept a stash of paper and a pile of pencils handy. The picture last week was of a cow looking over Myrtle's shoulder at the old lamp with the missing dangly things on it.

"I got that lamp a long time ago from one of my patients," he'd said. "Well, the cow was my patient, but the people who owned her gave me the lamp as payment."

"Could we bring a cow up here, Daddy?"

"I don't think the cow would like it very much," he'd told her. "Cows can climb up stairs, but they can't go down them, so she'd be stuck up here without all her cow friends."

"Why can't they go down, Daddy?"

"It's because of the way their legs are put together."

"Then why did you put the cow up here in a drawing?"

Daddy thought about her question for a few seconds. "You can draw or write pretty much anything you want to, but that doesn't make it true."

She studied the drawing. "You draw really good, Daddy."

"Thank you, sweetie. I think you write as well as I draw. I liked the story you wrote for me a couple of weeks ago about the rainbow and the elephant." Myrtle had never seen an elephant, but Daddy had drawn her a picture of one and told her marvelous stories about how big they were, so she'd just had to write a story about it. She added the rainbows because she'd seen lots of those, practically every time it rained.

"Will you write me another story sometime?"

She'd promised him she would, but so far she hadn't thought of anything interesting to write about. That was why she was up in the attic. She was sure to find something good to make a story about.

She chose a trunk and tried to lift the lid, but it was too heavy, so she tried another one. This one had a whole bunch of letters in it! She leaned the lid back against the wall and made sure it wasn't going to fall on her. Daddy had warned her about that. She sneezed. There was a lot of dust up here.

Pretty much at random, she selected an envelope, mostly because it looked kind of old. The writing was funny-looking, but she managed to figure out most of the words. Myrtle couldn't remember a time when she wasn't reading. She was six now. Well almost six in just one more day, but words had always made sense to her. Even these words in old-timey writing. She read the where-it-was-from part and the who-it-was-to part.

The Dakota
New York City
1 January 1816
Monday

Astaline Shipleigh Hastings
Beechnut House
Martinsville, Georgia

And then she read the whole letter.

My dear sister, for so I considered you even before you married my brother,

I have read in the New York papers that 1815 is being referred to as "the year without a summer." It certainly has felt like that.

This woman was telling about a really cold winter a long time ago. That would make a great story. Only it wouldn't be a made-up story. It would be a real one about a real person.

Myrtle had never thought much about the stories she wrote. She just really liked to write, so that's what she did. They were always full of dragons and unicorns and princesses, and the one about the rainbow and the elephant. As she studied the letter in her hands, though, she wondered if it might not be a lot more fun to write about real people. She spread out an old quilt and gathered her paper and pencils. She adjusted her name bracelet on her arm. She liked to do that for good luck, almost like her bracelet was magic. She'd had it for a whole year, since her fifth birthday. She was going to wear it forever and ever.

At the top of the page, she wrote

The Letter I Found in the Attic
by Myrtle Hoskins

This was going to be a really good story.

When Mama called her for bath time, Myrtle had already filled one side of a whole sheet of paper. She put the letter back in the envelope and left it sitting on top of her story. She'd come back and finish it tomorrow.

The next day, though, Myrtle was coughing and sneezing like crazy. Mama put her to bed, smeared some strong-smelling stuff on her throat and all over her back—she called it Vicks—and then wrapped up her neck in a soft flannel cloth. Myrtle loved the smell.

PERRY CLIMBED THE long stairs into the attic to see what his sister Myrtle had been doing before she got sick. He'd asked her once why she spent so much time up there, but all she'd said was that it was interesting.

She didn't know what she was talking about. The place was crammed with a whole bunch of junk, as far as Perry could see.

He almost stepped around an old quilt spread out on the floor, but then he took a closer look at the papers on top of it.

A dumb old letter—he didn't bother opening the envelope. Perry didn't care about such things. He picked it up, along with the paper that was covered with his sister's scrawl. There was an open trunk crammed with letters off to one side, next to a tall dresser. He tossed the letter in the trunk and started to add his sister's writing. Myrtle would probably find it again if he did that, so he opened the top dresser drawer. It was way above her reach. Maybe, if Myrtle didn't bother him too much, he'd tell her where he put it.

But then Perry caught whatever it was Myrtle had, and she tried to give him that stupid name bracelet of hers, like it was going to make some sort of difference. Like he was as much of a baby as she was. *You can find your own letter,* he thought.

Over the next few months, he forgot about what he'd done.

2000

"THAT BEATS ALL," Sadie said. "Myrtle obviously had the writing bug from early on. I wonder if she even remembers having written this."

"That letter she's talking about," Maddy said. "Do you think that's the one we found yesterday?" She scooted over to the dresser and found it. "Yep." She gazed off at nothing in particular. "I wonder why Myrtle didn't keep the letter and her story together."

Of course there was no answer to that, unless we phoned Myrtle about it.

"And I'd like to know why she never finished the story," Esther said. "It was going so well, you'd think she'd have wanted to complete it."

"Finished or not, this story definitely needs to go in the museum," Dee said. "Keep it with the old letter."

"We'd have to ask Myrtle first," Maddy pointed out.

"Knowing Myrtle," Sadie said, "she'll want to finish the story before we put it on display."

"She'll have to say yes," Esther said. "Myrtle's definitely a part of Martinsville history, and we need her in the museum."

"Maybe we should set up a section dedicated to noteworthy

Martinsvillians," Glaze suggested.

"Oh no we don't," Rebecca Jo warned. "Everybody in town will want their ancestors in there. It could generate some ill will."

"That's putting it mildly," Sadie said.

I wondered if she had anyone in particular in mind. Probably Clara. Whoops! There I went being mean again.

You are not mean.

I handed Myrtle's story to Maddy.

Carol ran a hand over one of the shelves on the dresser. "I wonder if there's anything on top of this thing."

"On top? Oh, you mean like the whirligig box you found on top of the armoire?"

"Yep."

I reached up to feel around, not expecting to find anything, but there seemed to be a lip of some sort formed by the decorative edging. Behind it was not the smooth, unfinished wood I'd assumed would be there, but something grainy, rough. "There *is* something, Carol. Here—help me lift it down."

Together we managed to get our thumbs under the edge of it—why hadn't I taken a moment to go get the folding stool?—and lifted it high enough to slide it forward over the edge. The bottom surface, which was all I could see at that point, was plain, although I thought there might be something carved near one end of it. I'd need better light to see it clearly though.

When we lowered it below eye level, I let out a little scream of joy, which brought everyone scurrying over to us. Two words and a date had been carved out of the rough wood and then painted or stained a dark color. The surrounding wood had weathered to a silvery gray.

Beechnut House
1753

Dee blew across the surface, sending a cloud of dust onto the open shelves. "Whoops! Sorry. Guess you haven't dusted up there."

Ida waved her hand to dispel some of the floating motes. "I thought we'd established that Biscuit never dusted anything up here."

"That's because I didn't know there was anything up here worth dusting."

"That's because you never came up here," Glaze said, "except to turn around and leave immediately."

I come up here to eat the spider webs.

"Do they taste good?"

Yes. I already told you that.

I looked a question at Carol. "Marmalade," she said. "She eats the spider webs."

We set the Beechnut House sign down on top of Sadie's and my collection of letters. Ida was already on her way to the top of the stairs to call the men.

DOC AND DAVE came up the stairs right behind Bob. "I didn't know you two were back," I said. "How's Hubbard?"

Doc's face became a little—wary, I guess you'd call it.

"Oh, I'm sorry," I said. "Patient confidentiality and all that. Forget I asked."

"I can give you a bare outline," he said. "After all, Anita started calling people before I was even out the front door."

Some of us laughed, some of us groaned.

"He did apparently speak."

"What did he say?"

I was glad Pat asked. I wanted to know, too, but I figured it wasn't really any of my business.

"Only a few words, but they didn't make much sense. Clara told me he'd said *boo* and something about food and something that sounded like *save* or *wave.*"

Beside him, Dave let out a big whoosh of breath.

Sadie frowned. "That doesn't make any sense at all."

"You know Hubbard," Dave said. "He never made much sense even when he had all his marbles."

"Dave!" Pat elbowed him in the ribs, but this time it wasn't playful at all. "Even for you, that's pretty low."

"Just kidding."

"Well, stop it."

"Sometimes," Doc rotated his shoulders backward as if they were too tight, "words people hear in a situation like Hubbard's are just wishful thinking on their part."

"You're saying he's not really going to get any better?"

Doc studied Dave for a few seconds. "I'm not going to go that far, Dave, but it seems unlikely that Hubbard will ever be back in charge of the town council."

"Thank goodness," Ida said.

Her comment was just enough to shift the mood.

Bob flexed his fingers. "Now, what did you want us to come up here to see?"

We parted, like a swinging door. I watched Bob's face to see the moment he spotted the sign. His delight was manifest.

"Beechnut House? Perfect. We'll have to hang it up by the front door."

"If I were you, I'd put it out by your mailbox," Dave suggested. "That way, more people will see it."

"Or hang it from the overhang," Ralph said. "Right above the front steps and the ramp."

Bob shook his head. "It's already pretty weathered. I'd like to keep it out of the rain—"

"And the snow," Henry said.

"And ice," Father John added.

"I'll take it downstairs for now," Bob said, "if that's okay with all you attic women."

I nodded. "Maybe prop it up beside the front door?"

"On the porch," he said.

"Wait," Carol said. "Let's inspect the back of it first."

"Right! I thought I saw something carved on the back as we were lifting it down."

"Me, too," she said.

Bob turned the wooden plank over and carried it closer to one of the windows. On the lower right corner we saw *Silas Martin - 11 September 1753.*

"We're in luck," Bob said. "Not only the year, but the month and day as well."

Sadie beamed down at the sign. "Do you suppose that's the day the inn officially opened?"

"Makes sense," Doc said.

Reebok sidled through the throng and bent over the letters. "That S in Silas," he said. "It's the same style as the initials on the sketch of the barn in City Hall."

"We have a handwriting expert?" Dave sounded skeptical, but I could see that Reebok was completely serious.

"It's a very distinctive S," Carol said. "Are you sure it matches?"

"Pretty sure. We can check it once the ice has melted."

"Next September eleventh," I looked back at the date and did a quick calculation in my head, "let's have a 248-year anniversary party."

"Count me in," Carol said. "I'll come back here for it."

"Good," Melissa said. "I'll keep your room ready at *Azalea House.*"

"We'll invite the whole town." Pat must have noticed my look of alarm as I thought about all those people tromping through my house. If I didn't want museum traffic in my attic, I certainly didn't want open house through the downstairs. "It'll be like a block party," she said quickly. "We can set up grills out in the middle of the street."

"And a lemonade stand," Maddy said. "Dee and I can do that."

"Hmm," Glaze said. "I wonder if we could rent a cotton candy machine?"

"Cotton candy?" Melissa stared at Glaze with artificially wide eyes. "You just want to recreate a circus."

"What's wrong with that?"

Glaze had something in mind, I could tell. "What are you up to, sis?"

"I don't see why the Martinsville Foundation couldn't fund it. It's historical, after all. It'll take a lot of hot dogs and hamburgers to feed the whole town. Tom, could we hire your restaurant staff to do the cooking and serving?"

"Sounds like a perfect solution. The current class should be ready for catering work by then."

Carol cocked her head at him, so I explained. "Tom runs a vocational school for boys at risk. He teaches them how to operate a restaurant, and they learn every bit about the business from the ground up."

"Sounds like a great idea," Carol said.

"The Foundation can pay the boys for their work," Glaze said.

Dave patted his stomach. It looked a bit rounder to me than the last time he and Pat visited Martinsville. "If we don't all have to chip in on the cost," he said, "why don't we have spare ribs and chicken, too."

"Don't forget Porta-Potties," Ida said. Always the practical one. "Biscuit's not going to want everybody using her composting toilet."

"She's not going to want *anybody* using it," Bob said.

Maddy waved her arms. "We could get one of those popcorn machines on wheels."

"Let's hope," I said, "that September eleventh is bright and sunny next year."

"Too bad we don't still have the original barn to hold everyone in case it rains."

Glaze waved a negligent hand at Rebecca Jo. "We may not have a barn, but we'll figure out a rain date ahead of time."

"Unless you have anything else to show us," Bob said, "I'm going to take this sign downstairs so we can get out of your hair."

You are not in her hair.

Carol laughed and told us what Marmalade had said. I scooped up Marmy and gave her a big hug.

Thank you. I like your hugs.

Once the sound of male footsteps faded away, Maddy spread her arms wide. "There's been so much change just in a couple of days up here."

"What do you mean?" Pat bent down to touch her toes. "Oh, that stretch feels good after all the sitting we've been doing. We all ought to do this every half hour or so."

"If I tried that," Rebecca Jo said, "I'd get a hitch in my gitalong."

What is a giddalong?

"Amanda could fix it for you," Sadie said. "She's good at getting rid of hitches."

What are hitches?

"That means her back is sore," Carol told Marmalade.

Maddy ignored the phys ed lesson and the cat communication. "Just think about it. When we came up here originally, we didn't know the house had a name, we didn't know there was a secret room, we didn't know hardly anything about the families that lived here."

"We still don't," Easton muttered, but I thought her voice held more wishing than complaining.

"Speaking of change," Sadie said, "why did you dye your lovely red hair, Charlie?"

"Huh? It's not … Oh, I don't know. My roommate and I did it when we were seniors, and I guess I just got used to it."

"You've mentioned your roommate several times," Sadie said. "Were the two of you close? Did you keep in touch?"

Charlie's eyebrows creased. "Not really. She went one way and I went another."

I began to laugh, somewhat ruefully. "I dyed my hair once. Only once."

"Sounds like there's a story behind this," Pat said. "What happened?"

"I followed the timing directions on the package, but my hair turned out the exact same color as the middle line of a highway — that bright ugly yellowy-orange."

"Did you leave it on too long?" Amanda's hair looked like she'd never colored it in her life.

"She probably didn't leave it on long enough," Pat said, with the air of somebody who knew what she was talking about. "I'm the same way. My hair has extra dense color, or something, so the color stripping takes longer. Until that's done properly, any dye you add won't do a bit of good."

"I guess that's good to know," I said, "but I never tried to change my hair color again."

"I like your hair the way it is."

Gosh, I love my sister!

Ida, obviously tired of the hair talk, picked up the Mary Frances journal. "Let's read some more." She opened to the short length of ribbon she'd been using as a place marker. "My next entry is June eighteenth. What about yours?"

"Same day," I said after a quick check. "I wonder if they often wrote at the same time?"

"Not that I've noticed," Ida said. "Let's watch for it from here on." She gestured at me. "You go first."

Friday 18 June 1742. I believe finally that my brother may live after watching him lie close to death for several weeks. Would that we had braved a night spent on the trail in the rain rather than come to what has befallen us.

"That sounds ominous," Rebecca Jo said.

"I'm almost afraid to read more."

"No you're not," Maddy said. "Don't keep us waiting.

Nigh on four weeks ago, we rode along the banks of the Susquehanna River and came upon a heavily stockaded town. When Ira insisted because of the threatening rain clouds that we spend one night in their inn, I agreed, despite my desire to speed farther along the road. The inn was cheap, but the price we paid was high indeed, for Harrisburg was barricaded that night by determined men from the next town south. Ira has the yellow fever now—indeed, the men of the town are hard-pressed to dig graves fast enough, and many bodies have been interred in a common pit, onto which lime is poured.

"Yellow fever? That was pretty serious stuff." Glaze looked toward Carol for confirmation, but it was Maddy who answered her.

"Sure was. Wiped out half the population of a town sometimes."

"What caused it?" I was glad Dee asked, because I didn't have a clue.

"Mosquitos," Maddy said. "It started with a high fever and got progressively worse from there."

"It was almost always fatal," Carol said, and I turned back to Hubbard's diary with a fair amount of dread.

We board with Miss Julia Gilman and her sister

"Miss Julia," Maddy said. "She's the one in that letter, the one who wrote for twenty-two years before she sent it to—what was her name?"

"Caroline Edgerton," Carol said. "In Harrisburg."

... with Miss Julia Gilman and her sister, Mistress Anna Lazdell. Two such different women I never have met, one tall and energetic, the other stooped with a back so bent that I can seldom see her face unless I kneel before her. Miss Julia is a rare healer, for Ira still clings to life despite the number of deaths around us. Miss Julia doses him regularly and feeds the two of us naught but greens from her garden.

"Greens?" Pat sounded dubious. "Is that a cure for yellow fever?"

Carol shook her head. "Not that I've ever heard of. I don't think many people were vegetarians back then. But that dosing might have helped. Maybe if she caught it in time …?"

Her voice trailed away, and I figured I'd be reading about Ira's death in the next page or two.

Early June 1742
Somewhere in Pennsylvania, along the Susquehanna

HUBBARD WANTED TO keep traveling, but Ira was insistent. "Your wife will not be that much farther ahead if we stop but one night." Ira swatted at a swarm of mosquitos that surrounded him, and Hubbard wondered as he often did why those pesky insects always left him alone but seemed to love biting his brother.

Evening was not the best time to approach a town, but the sun still had another hour before it would set. They had been long upon the road and Ira claimed he was weary enough to need a dry bed under a sheltering roof rather than a makeshift tent of wet canvas and pine boughs.

"Let us simply eat a decent meal and then be on our way." Hubbard looked up at the darkening sky. "We could be seven or eight miles farther down the road before nightfall."

"And have to sleep once again in the rain? Look at those storm clouds! No, I say. Let us rest here this night, break our fast slowly tomorrow, and then leave."

Hubbard did not like the idea, but he gave way. "Let us not linger long tomorrow morning, though. I wish to be on our way at first light."

Two men guarded a gate that formed the entrance to the town through a stout stockade fence. The wood was newly cut and reeked of that smell of pine sap that always reminded Hubbard of cold winters beside a fireplace with a stack of cut logs off to one side. He preferred oak or hickory or maple, but pine burned fast and hot and was always a good way to start a fire.

Neither one of the two guards sought to stop them, but Hubbard was curious about the fence. He pulled his hat farther down to shade the ruined side of his face from the meager rays of the late afternoon sun and the lanterns already lit and swinging above the guards, and eased Star to a halt. "Indian trouble?"

"Something like that," one of the men said, before the other one made a quelling motion.

"What brings you here?" the second man asked, none too friendly.

"We seek lodging for the night."

The first man gestured over his shoulder and went back to pacing to and fro across the road. Ira nodded in acknowledgment, but the sentry ignored him.

"We have seen no sign of disquiet along our road," Hubbard said to the second man out of the working corner of his mouth. "Need we be worried as we travel on toward the south?"

The man scratched idly at his armpit, coughed explosively, and spit in the general direction of a nearby ditch. When he had his voice back he admitted, "One of our womenfolk has been gone since a fortnight ago. We fear she was carried off in the night by savages."

Hubbard thought of how easily Mary Frances had climbed out the window of her friend Myra Sue Russell's bedchamber fourteen months previously. He privately questioned the assumption that Indians were responsible. It was just as likely the woman had found some amiable young man to spirit her away. "Have you found no trace of her?"

"We still have men out looking." He swatted at the swarm of mosquitoes surrounding him. "As you can see, we have enclosed the entire town so no one will be able to creep upon us unawares again."

From what Hubbard knew of the Abenaki Indians who hunted

near Brandtburg, a simple stockade fence would not keep them out if they wanted to get in. He imagined the Indians from hereabout had equal skills, but he did admit that someone abducting an unwilling woman might have trouble heaving her over the eight-foot poles, which had been sharpened to points on the top end.

"May we enter?" The question seemed to be moot, since Ira had already ridden Blaze a good five yards inside the palisades, where he waited impatiently.

"Of course. There is no look of the savage about you." The man shifted his Brown Bess from one shoulder to the other and used a none-too-clean kerchief to wipe the sweat from his forehead. "You have come just in time. Another hour and we will bar the gate and open it for no man until dawn."

Hubbard touched his hat in recognition of their good fortune, clucked to Star, and trotted ahead to where Ira slapped at the cloud of mosquitos that still surrounded him but ignored Hubbard. There was an old joke that Ira recounted frequently every summer—*mosquitos only like the taste of a real man.* Only Ira thought it was funny, though.

Ahead of them they saw the hanging shingle of a two-story inn. *Dabbill's Tavern,* the sign proclaimed, with a line of smaller letters beneath—*Horatio Dabbill, Prop.* "Like as not there will be rooms above," said Ira.

Hubbard studied the ramshackle building. "Like as not there will be fleas aplenty." Fleas, unlike mosquitoes, did not seem to care whom they feasted on.

They entered a low-ceilinged room with a meager fire at the far end and a cloud of cigar smoke that filled the room. There were few patrons, normally the mark of a less than salubrious establishment, but Hubbard guessed that most of the town's men would be at their own fireside eating the evening meal, so he was not alarmed at the lack of patronage. No doubt there would be a crowd later in the evening, but by then he hoped to be sound asleep. As long as he had a dry bed at hand, he planned to make full use of it. He nodded his head at the proprietor as Ira asked for ale for the two of them.

Hubbard paid, knowing Mister Dabbill would not draw their drinks until he saw their money.

"Would you have a room for the night and stabling for our horses?"

Dabbill studied Ira before answering him. He turned and looked closely at Hubbard. Hubbard was not surprised. A one-armed man and one who looked more like a monster than a man. He turned his head so the unburned side of his face showed.

Dabbill expelled an enormous cloud of smoke from his mouth and then took another draw on the fat cigar he held between his teeth. "Have you come far?"

"Far enough," Ira said. "Far enough to be weary of sleeping in the rain."

"Which direction?"

Hubbard could feel Ira bristle at the question. He stepped forward before Ira could complain. "We come from the north. We follow a group of around ninety people who may have passed through here within the last number of months. Know you aught of them?"

The man seemed to relax fractionally. "Oh, them. Yes, there was a group that large who were here in—when was it?—April perhaps?"

"We are close, Brother." Hubbard could hardly bear the thought that he might see Mary Frances sooner than he had hoped. Might see her and then, because of his face, would have to leave her. He turned back to the publican. "Did they take the road south from here?"

Dabbill puffed on his cigar for a few seconds. "After they buried their dead, they did."

"Their dead?" Hubbard felt his throat close in fear.

"They asked to bury one of their women in the churchyard, and the parson said yes."

"Where is the church?" Hubbard's voice was insistent, his heart striving to beat its way out of his chest.

Horatio Dabbill waved a negligent hand. "Down the road a piece toward the center of town. Not far."

Hubbard left his ale, left his brother, left the innkeeper puzzling. He had to know. As soon as he ran outside, he encountered swarming mosquitoes. His immediate concern was to find the graveyard, but a small part of his brain registered the lack of mosquitoes inside the tavern. The heavy pall of cigar smoke, perhaps?

It took him no time at all to find the churchyard. Finding the grave was a bit more of a problem. There were many fresh mounds. If this town was having Indian problems, it looked as though there had been a massacre, and not too long ago. He inspected the crosses at the top of each grave and finally found what he sought off in the far corner. *Anthina Shipleigh 5 January 1742.*

January. Not April, as the innkeeper had said. Hubbard clenched his fist. Mary Frances was farther ahead of him than he would wish, but he knew he would find her soon. At least he had not—he turned away from Mistress Shipleigh's grave—had not found her here. He found he had to rest for a moment before he returned to the tavern. He had been used to run without stopping, but of late, especially since the … the accident, his heart pounded at the slightest exertion. He leaned against one of the older stone markers and waited for his heart to resume its slow steady beat.

Eventually, he rejoined his brother in the smoky tavern. "It was the old Mistress Shipleigh who died." He did not want to rejoice in another family's bad fortune, but he could not help his smile.

"Not that wife of yours? So you are determined to go on?"

Hubbard did not even bother to respond. The answer should have been obvious, even to Ira.

Halfway through the night, Hubbard was awakened by a mighty disturbance, with voices raised in anger. He went to the window only long enough to assure himself that the inn was not afire, nor did he see the light of any flames anywhere else, other than torches carried by a number of men as they passed by on their way toward the tall fence. In the distance he heard thunder.

"Is this an Indian attack?" he called to one of the passing men.

"No!" The answer was short and surly, but reassuring enough that Hubbard climbed back onto the bed, turned over, and was soon snoring almost as loudly as his brother. Even the shot of a single gun did not disturb his slumber.

The next morning, they ate their breakfast early, then stood, gathering up their bedrolls and saddlebags, which they had placed beside them on the long table.

"You might want to return those to your room," the innkeeper said.

"No," Ira said. "We told you we wanted the room for only the one night."

"That may be, but you will find it hard to leave."

"Why would we not leave? Were our horses stolen during the night? Even if so, we still could walk." Ira's voice had taken on that purr of threat that Hubbard had learned long ago to be wary of. Ira could rage or Ira could simmer. The simmer seldom died without having broken into fury first.

The man stepped behind his counter. Hubbard thought Mister Dabbill was wise to want something sturdy in front of himself before he answered Ira's question.

"You"—he pointed at Hubbard—"you visited the graveyard yesterday. Did you notice all the fresh graves?"

Hubbard nodded, not liking the sound of this.

"We built the fence to stave off Indian attacks," the man said, "but last night men from the next village south of here came and barred our gate from the outside."

"Why?" Even as he asked it, Hubbard was afraid he knew the answer.

"The yellow fever. It starts with a cough, and then the person almost burns up and most often dies. We have lost fifteen men, women, and children in the past week, and the folk from the next town south who were our neighbors"—he filled that word with scorn—"fear to let any of us leave the town lest we carry the fever to them."

"We have to leave," Ira insisted. "We do not ail."

"Come, my brother." Hubbard hoped to forestall any unwise actions on his brother's part. Anger at the tavern keeper would not further their cause. "We will ride out and tell them our errand is urgent."

"You can tell them all you want," the innkeeper said as he polished the none-too-clean counter with a gray and fraying cloth, "but they will shoot you before they will let you leave here."

"They would not—"

"They already did, last night. There's one more grave to be dug today. Cornus Longbottom tried to slip over the fence. Did you not hear the shot? Even now, folk are out there arguing." He indicated the direction of the gate with a nod of his head and Hubbard became aware of an undercurrent of angry voices, like the buzzing of a hundred hornets.

Ira grabbed his belongings and stormed out of the room. He turned right, toward the fence, rather than left, toward the stable. Hubbard left his saddlebag and ran after his brother, glad that the mornings were still cool. As the innkeeper had said, there was a large group of men milling about just inside the barred gate, and there was plenty of shouting, for all the men of the town were as angry as Ira at being forcibly confined. Despite all the clamor, there was nothing to be done about it.

Eventually most of the crowd dissipated, and Hubbard and Ira headed back toward the inn in the company of a number of men who had chosen to wet their whistles before they had to inform their wives that they were indeed prisoners in their own town.

"I was against the fence from the start," one man proclaimed.

"Is that so?" another rejoined. "Then why did you help build it?"

Before they entered the inn, Hubbard turned on Ira, who was swatting away yet another cloud of mosquitoes. "If we had but left yester eve, we could have been far down the road."

"You fret so about nothing. This will not delay us long."

The man walking beside Ira pulled the kerchief from around his neck and wiped it across his forehead. "Blasted hot out here," he complained.

IRA BEGAN HIS own sweating four evenings later. The next morning he shook with chills so much he could not walk down the stairs to break his fast. When Hubbard entered the common room, intending to buy food for his brother and take it upstairs, Horatio Dabbill pulled him aside. "You have to leave. I cannot afford to have the fever here in my tavern. I have to think of my other customers."

Hubbard understood the man's reasoning, but it was blasted inconvenient. "Know you of a house where we can lodge?"

"There's a widow woman who might be willing to care for your brother. She seems not to be afeared of the fever for herself."

"Tell me how to find her. I will make the arrangements and return for my brother when I am sure there will be a place to take him."

"No." Dabbill turned casually and retrieved a wicked-looking rifle from under the counter. He did not aim it. He simply held it at the ready. "You will take him with you now." He proceeded with clear instructions on how to locate the house of Widow Gilman.

Hubbard did not argue. He helped Ira down the stairs and steered him to a handy water trough outside to perch him on. "Wait here, brother. I will be back for you as soon as I can. Mister Dabbill said we could leave the horses and their saddles here for now, since Star and Blaze are not like to have the fever." He could not help the cynicism in his voice. He understood the innkeeper's concerns, but thought it hard indeed on himself and his ailing brother.

Ira was wracked with a fit of shivering as Hubbard turned to leave, which gave Hubbard second thoughts. He eased his brother down onto the ground and propped him with his back against the trough. "This way you will not fall in and drown yourself."

"Not funny," Ira said through clenched teeth.

THE WIDOW'S HOUSE was small and neat, but showed a lack of upkeep that Hubbard thought sad. Had she no children to maintain the property for her?

The woman who answered his knock was bent so low over her cane, he saw first the back of her head, where sparse white hairs barely covered the pink scalp. His first thought, of which he was instantly ashamed, was that he had almost more hair than she.

She leaned to one side and tilted her head so she could look at him from the side of her eyes. He instantly dropped to one knee to make it easier for her to see him. "Good morrow, madam. Am I fortunate enough to be speaking with Mistress Gilman?"

"You are a stranger here, I see. I am Mistress Anna Lazdell, but no doubt you wish to see my older sister, Mistress Julia Gilman. She is known as the healer here, although it is God's strength she calls upon."

Oh, no, Hubbard thought. This old woman's sister was like to be too infirm to help anyone.

"Come in and set yourself down while I fetch her." She waved vaguely in the direction of four ladder-backed chairs near the fireplace and toddled out of the room, her cane making a slow but rhythmic tap-tap-tap as she went.

Hubbard inhaled deeply. There was a freshness to the air. No mosquitoes, either, although it was certainly not cigar smoke that had dispelled them from this house.

He heard another door open. "Julia! A man to see you. Can you come?" He heard a reply of some sort, but he could not make out any words.

The woman tapped her way back into the room and settled into one of the chairs. "Sit, sit. She will be but a moment. She needs must gather up her basket of herbs from the far side of the garden." As he lowered himself into the chair farthest from her, the old woman studied him from under her grizzled eyebrows. "You look well enough. Why need you my sister's healing skills?"

"It is my brother," he began, but jumped to his feet as an exceptionally tall, straight-backed woman with an amazing abundance of white hair—not even halfway covered by a faded sunbonnet—strode into the room and set her overflowing basket on a table beside the doorway. A whiff of green herbs accompanied her.

"Good morrow, Sir." She pushed a stray lock of hair under the rim of the bonnet, but it promptly sprang forward again. "You wanted to see me?"

Hubbard tried to see behind her. This was most likely the old woman's daughter. Perhaps the old woman's sister was lagging behind. "I wished to see Mistress Julia Gilman, the healer. Mister Horatio Dabbill, the proprietor of the—"

"Oh, cut the fancy chatter, my boy. I am called Miss Julia by most who know me. You have already met my sister, Miss Anna. Who are you?"

The shock must have registered in his eyes as he looked from the bent old woman in the chair to this astonishingly healthy-looking woman. The laugh lines around her eyes crinkled, and Hubbard could not help but smile in reply.

He introduced himself and explained his need, at which point some of the twinkle went out of Miss Julia's eyes.

"How long has he been fevered?"

"Just this morning. But how did you know?"

"That is how it begins." She drummed her fingers against the tabletop. "We may have caught it in time. Bring your brother here."

"Then you will care for him?"

"I will look at him first and will decide then."

Her tone left no room for him to argue the point. It took but moments to return to Ira, but much longer to make their way back to the Gilman house, with Ira stumbling along beside him as Hubbard struggled with the saddlebags and bedrolls. No one paused to offer help. Passersby skirted them warily, and mothers pulled their children to the other side of the wide street. Hubbard could not blame them.

MISS JULIA ENLISTED Hubbard's help in stripping Ira of most of his clothing. "It will have to be boiled," she said, and although Hubbard could not imagine why, he did not question her authority. "My late husband had a nightshirt big enough to fit your brother. Keep him from falling over if you can until I can fetch it. If he lies down we will have a hard time getting the shirt onto him."

Once they had him settled in a bed that was clean, with a thick blanket that Ira promptly thrust aside, Miss Julia sponged Ira's forehead with an herbal-scented water and spooned some evil-smelling tea into him. When Ira would have objected, she pinioned him with a gimlet gaze. "If you plan to die, you will ignore what I tell you to do. If you plan to live, you will open your mouth."

He opened his mouth.

"I have cared successfully for plenty of ill folk in my time, and I do not intend to have you blot my record."

Hubbard thought of all those graves in the churchyard.

"The ones we had to bury were the ones who did not come to me," she said with finality.

While he did not want to call her a witch, her unerring response to his thoughts unnerved Hubbard. Still, if he had to have a desperately ill brother, he might as well have a completely competent healer. "My brother cared for me when I was recovering from …" He gestured to his face.

"Fell in the fire, did you?"

"I was—" He stopped. He did not want to say that the man she was caring for was the one who had pushed him into it, lest she refuse to serve him.

"Drunk?"

"Something like that."

"Serves you right then. I hope you learned your lesson. I will have no hard liquor in my house."

"We have none with us." That, he thought, is because Ira had already drunk it all.

"See that it stays that way."

FOR MORE THAN a fortnight, there was little change in Ira's condition, except that he seemed to grow more wraith-like with every bout of vomiting. The teas and broths Miss Julia fed him may have had healing properties, but they were not putting meat on his bones. Hubbard had little time to worry about his brother, though, for Miss Julia kept him busy throughout the day, shoring up the sagging front stoop, splitting firewood, helping her to tend her extensive garden, and carving a new spindle for Miss Anna's spinning wheel.

One muggy morning in late July, Miss Julia asked him to find where the roof was leaking, for there had been a persistent drip near her bed the night before. He propped the ladder against the eaves, gathered the supplies he would need—nails, a few spare shingles, and a sturdy hammer—and climbed onto the roof, crouching low to keep from overbalancing. It would not do to plunge to the ground. He did not need to guess where the rain was seeping inside, for he easily saw the curled shingles. The repair went quickly, but as he slid around to make his way back to the ladder, the heat and the very wetness of the air made him stop for a moment. He leaned forward, as if he could curl himself around a growing pain he felt inside his chest. Sweat dripped from his forehead. It is like working under a waterfall up here, he thought. After a few long moments, though, the discomfort eased, and he made his way down the ladder, more slowly than he was wont to do.

That evening it rained again, and Miss Julia reported success. She laid her hand on his arm when she thanked him, and that simple touch reminded him of his mother.

After they had eaten and had fed what they could to Ira, they sat, as they generally did of an evening, in companionable silence while Miss Anna spun and Miss Julia either knitted one stocking after another or wove long woolen blankets on her large loom. "What the two of you need," she said one such evening, "is warm stockings to replace those threadbare ones you have chosen to travel in." She held up her knitting as if for inspection.

"We had little choice, Mistress. We have been on the road for more than a year."

"Be that as it may, when you leave here, your feet will be well-provisioned."

Hubbard could not help himself. He turned his head and looked across the room to where Ira lay, limp with exhaustion, as if lying abed all day took energy.

"If God wills it, your brother will recover," Miss Anna said. "My sister tells me he has a strong heart."

"Are my thoughts that easy to read?" He had not thought she could have seen his glance, since her head was bowed so painfully close to her chest.

Miss Julia set her knitting down for a moment and pointed toward her brow. "Your thoughts are so loud my sister and I can both practically hear them."

"And," Miss Anna said with some asperity, "I do not need to see you to hear your chair creak when you turn to look at your brother."

He could hear the underlying laughter in their voices. Mayhap they were not witches after all, but even if they had been, he was glad they appeared to have his and Ira's best interests at heart.

"You would need to use your ears," he said, "for you most likely could not tell even if you were looking straight at me. My face has not much movement to it." He seldom referred to his scarred face, but he felt so comfortable with these two old women, he found himself speaking words he would never have said to anyone else.

Miss Julia rocked for several minutes before she spoke. "I lost my husband and all three of my young children to a house fire nigh on twenty years ago. I would have been in the house as well, except that I was off tending the Clandis family through that night."

And Miss Anna? Hubbard thought. *Where was she?*

As if she had read his mind—again—she said, "My sister lived at the time with her husband two streets over. My son and his two sisters had been the only ones who made it through their infancy—five others, babes every one of them, were buried in the churchyard. After the fire, there were nine of my immediate family buried there."

Before Hubbard could think of what to say in the face of that tragedy, she continued. "When we were children, my sister and I both had the yellow fever, just like your brother, and they say that if one survives it, they can never again be affected. That certainly seems to be the case with us. I am surprised you have not been ill yourself, but perhaps you are one of the lucky ones." She knitted another few stitches, and Hubbard was lulled by the click-click of the swiftly-moving needles. "Lucky or blessed. I am not sure there is a difference."

"We are all blessed," Miss Anna said, and Hubbard sighed quietly. Miss Anna always seemed to bring the topic of any conversation around to church matters. Still, listening to her preach was a small price to pay for his brother's life. "I was certainly blessed," she continued, "to have my sister here when my back began to bend so."

"And I, too, am fortunate," Miss Julia said, "for I have both my sister and my dear friend Mistress Caroline Edgerton. You have not met her yet, but I will let her know as soon as your brother is over the worst, and she will be by to meet you. She and her daughter are herb women whom I have taught over the years. After I am gone, they will carry on my work."

She said it so matter-of-factly that it took Hubbard a moment to register what she had said. "I'm sure that will be many years yet," he finally managed to say. She looked so young, but Miss Anna, her younger sister, looked so very old, he wondered who would be the first to go.

"We shall see. We shall see." Her knitting needles sang for several more minutes.

"If my brother survives …" Hubbard did not know how to complete what he had been about to say. He was not even sure he knew what he had been about to say.

"If your brother survives—and he will—it will take him a long time, perhaps as much as a year, to regain his strength, but, as long as you continue to help us with our chores, I will be happy to care for him and to feed the both of you."

"You …" He did not know quite how to put his question. "You do not mind the … the look of my face?"

She glowered at him from under her heavy, still-dark eyebrows. "You hush that mouth of yours, young man. Do you know how much I would give to see my dear children, who would not have been much older than you are now if they had lived? I care not about scars." She gestured toward Ira's stump that lay almost lifeless on the coverlet. "Nor disfigurements. Be glad you are alive, and go fetch another bucket of water from the well. We will need it in the middle of the night when your brother wakes, raving with the fever."

2000

"THAT'S IT? THIS woman doses Ira regularly? That's all he says?"

I couldn't blame Dee for her indignation. I felt the same way. There were precious few details for us to go on. "Ira obviously survived," I said, "based on that letter from Caroline Edgerton."

"And Miss Julia obviously traveled with them," Maddy said, "because she made it all the way to Martinsville."

"But what happened in the meantime!"

Carol made a quelling motion toward Dee. "This is a big part of the frustration of being a historian. All we get are these glimpses—"

"Not very big glimpses," Dee grumped.

"… into people's lives."

"It makes me want to write a whole lot more each evening in my journal," I said. "Put down all those details to enlighten the next century."

"You really think anybody's going to read it a hundred years from now?"

I stared at Easton.

Before I could answer—not that I could think of a thing to say—Sadie put out her hand. "Isn't it lovely that we don't know what's going to happen a hundred years from now? I think it's wonderful that you're going to expand your memoirs, Biscuit."

"Memoirs? They're not memoirs. It's just a daily journal."

Sadie nodded. "And that's exactly what memoirs are. The memories of what's happened to you."

That shut me up. Of course, it shut up Easton too, which was just as well.

Ida picked up the Mary Frances journal.

Friday, 18 June 1742

The elder Mister Hastings died in the early hours of this

morning under unusual circumstances. The Endicott brothers find great reason for hilarity, and while I rue their insensitive guffaws, I cannot help but smile a bit myself. The Widow Black has apparently had three happy weeks since her marriage to her elderly bridegroom, for he died in the middle of the night while they were engaged in—oh, I cannot write it.

Friday, 18 June 1742

IT HAD NOT been a month since the wedding of the Widow Black to old Mister Hastings, when Mary Frances and the entire camp were awakened shortly after midnight by blood curdling screams emanating from the tent that the two elderly newlyweds inhabited. Mary Frances checked quickly to be sure young John slept on in his basket beside her, and then she scrambled from the wagon, grabbing a shawl and pulling it tightly around her shoulders. Homer Martin crawled more slowly from underneath the wagon, where he was wont to sleep most nights.

Across the circle, Mary Frances saw the Widow Black emerge from the tent where she and her new husband slept. "He's dead," the woman wailed. "Dead!"

Someone stoked up one of the campfires in the middle of the circle, as people materialized in ones and twos from their various sleeping arrangements. Louetta Tarkington reached the old woman first and placed an arm around her shoulders. "Are you sure? Shall I check to be certain?"

Carolina Black Hastings nodded dumbly, and Mistress Tarkington ducked her head and disappeared, only to reappear a moment later. She had a strange look on her face, one that Mary Frances could not interpret.

"How did it happen?" Reverend Russell spoke in a kindly tone, and Mary Frances saw Louetta Tarkington shake her head as if she wanted that question not to have been asked.

"He just died," the Widow Black said as everyone gathered closer around the tent. "One moment we were … that is to say, he was … I mean …"

Her voice wound down to a mere whisper, and even in the uncertain light of a nearby fire, which by this time was blazing merrily, it was easy to see the rosy hue of a blush that infused her leathery neck and mottled cheeks.

One of the Endicott brothers hooted. “Too much activity for his old heart, eh?” The rest of the Endicott men cackled. “Taking his pleasure, was he?” Mary Frances couldn’t tell which brother it was who had asked, but all of them were far too bawdy for her taste, so it could have been any one of them. They were interchangeable fools as far as Mary Frances was concerned, except perhaps for Sayrle. He was marginally better than the rest. At least he could read.

The Widow Black, now the Widow Hastings, nodded dumbly, and the rest of the company stood in quiet astonishment. To think that two such elderly people still engaged in … well, it was just too surprising to even think of. Mary Frances noted that Carolina’s daughter, Geonette Black Surratt, looked even more embarrassed than her old mother. Geonette’s daughter Presila for once was not bouncing around on her toes. Instead, she placed an arm around her mother’s shoulders. The girl obviously had no idea what had happened.

Presila raised her head then and looked at Mary Frances, the beginning of a smile quirking her lips up on the sides. Perhaps, Mary Frances thought, the girl was more knowledgable than anyone guessed.

Mary Frances returned to her wagon in silence. Let the others deal with the body and all the arrangements that accompanied any death. She lay there for hours remembering the delight of her wedding night—her real wedding night—and wondering yet again why her husband had not followed her, for the trail they left behind them was broad and the ruts deep from the passage of so many wagons.

Just before dawn, she was startled awake by the thought that perhaps Hubbard had followed her, and had spied on the camp enough to see her with a child or, worse yet, to see her climbing into Homer Martin’s wagon of a night. Would he then have left? *Dear God,* she prayed, *let that not be so.*

2000

“YOU THINK THEY were having sex?” Maddy sounded scandalized.

Sadie laughed. "That's what married people do, Maddy. At least, those of us that were happy together." She rubbed the back of one of her brown-spotted hands. "Even when we got to the point where we couldn't quite manage it anymore, Wallace and I still cuddled together every night." Her face was radiant. "And sometimes during the day, too."

I like to cuddle.

All I could do was hope that Bob and I would always stay connected like that.

I will stay connected to you and SoftFoot, even when you squish me.

Carol grinned and ruffled Marmalade's head, but she wouldn't tell us what Marmy had said.

"Who has the next diary entry?" Melissa looked from Ida to me and back again.

We compared dates, and I began to read.

Thursday 22 July 1742. I have not taken up this book of late, for I find myself short of breath so often, and when night falls I wish nothing more than to sink into my bed, even if that means missing the easy companionship of my genial hostesses. I try not to rub at my chest, for I have seen Miss Julia study me when I do so. At times, though, rubbing it is the only thing that allows me to relax.

"That doesn't sound good," Amanda said. "He's too young to be sickly."

"He must have gotten well." I lifted the journal, like a talisman. "There're a lot more entries."

"What do you think it was?" Rebecca Jo waved her hand as if to erase any thought of Hubbard's ill health. "I know it's just guessing, but I'm worried about him."

"Heart," Amanda said.

"Lungs?" That was from Sadie.

"It could be his gall bladder for all we know," Pat said. "Or his liver. Let's just keep reading. We're bound to find out eventually.

Monday 11 October 1742. Winter will soon be upon us, and Miss Julia keeps me working from dawn to dusk and sometimes into the evening hours. Ira is barely able to sit by himself, but that was enough for Miss Anna to put him to work. He sits knee to knee with her and holds his hand and his stump forward within her easy reach so she can wind her yarn around and around. Only a few months ago he would have scorned to do such 'women's work,' but now there is so much of a change in him. I would almost say it is miraculous.

"Miss Anna was amazing." Ida shook her head and smirked. "Imagine her talking Ira into serving as her yarn holder."

Melissa nodded. "Miss Julia, too. It sounds like she kept Hubbard too busy to worry about his face. I wonder what all he was doing for her?"

"There was a great deal of upkeep on those old houses," Maddy said. "Wooden shingles to be replaced after wind storms, decaying porch supports, and then there was her garden."

"Gardens," Mom said.

"I hope he takes care of himself," I said before I went on reading.

I have been wont to read to these two gracious women in the evenings. They are much taken by the books I was fortunate enough to find along the trail, and we have had many brisk discussions about Mister Pope's epigrams. Tomorrow I plan to begin reading that drama, The Miser. It looks to be most entertaining.

"The Miser?" I said. "Moliere? I wonder why Hubbard's journal is here, but the book isn't?"

"Maybe it is," Melissa said, "and we just haven't found it yet."

"If you find any old books," Carol said, "be sure to pick them up carefully. Better yet, don't pick them up until Biscuit's taken a camera shot in situ."

"In situ," Pat said. "What's that?"

"It's Latin," Carol explained. "It means *in place.* Right where you find it."

"And then, gloves," Maddy warned.

"Do you think it'd be worth a lot?" Pat asked.

I held up a restraining hand. "Let's not hook up the horses if we don't even have the wagon yet."

Horses? Where?

It took Carol quite a while to explain to Marmalade.

I still do not understand how a wagon can be a book.

While Carol was talking to Marmalade, Pat scanned the attic with what looked to me like a mercenary glint in her eye. Was I being too trusting here? I shook my head to clear those awful thoughts and went on reading.

Last evening after Miss Anna retired, I pegged together a low, wide, sturdy stool that will make it easier for her to climb into her bed. As short as the legs of her bed are, she has always needed her sister's help when she retires for the night. I have easily heard their low-voiced comments. I am sure Miss Julia is not aware of the thinness of the veil that separates her words from my hearing. This morning I managed to slip away from Miss Anna's notice and to place the stool beside the bed while Miss Julia was out in her garden. What a delight it was to hear their exclamations of surprise when the time for bed was upon them. Miss Julia surprised me exceedingly when she came out to my chair and planted a firm motherly kiss on my forehead. The last person whose lips rested there was my dear wife, although her kiss was not motherly in the least!

I take great joy in being able to contribute more than just the strength of my arms to these fine women. The chores I am happy to do, but such small gifts as this stool or the wooden cups I carved and decorated for them bring me a welcome sense of satisfaction. Miss Anna's cup has a whimsical knitted scarf carved as if it winds around the bottom, while for Miss Julia I carved a leafy vine. She asked if I might carve two more cups, for Caroline and Lucy Edgerton, and I was happy to do so.

"Golly day," I said. "He is so sweet."

"Was," Easton said. "He's dead."

I wanted to slug her.

Why?

Ida pressed her lower teeth against her upper lip. I was pretty sure she felt the same as I did.

About what?

Sadie reached forward and placed a restraining hand on Easton's arm. "The beauty of the written word is that someone long dead can seem very much alive. I certainly feel like I've gotten to know Hubbard—and Mary Frances, too."

"Speaking of which," Ida said after she waited for a particularly loud blast of wind to settle a bit, "Mary Frances is up to Christmas now for her next entry. Unless you've got something else, Biscuit?"

"Nope. Not till next April. Seventeen-forty-three." I pulled my fleecy vest tighter around me. The attic felt colder today.

That is why I am curled on your lap.

All that wind. Brrr. Maybe I'd get one of the men to widen the damper on the Defiant so we could get a bit more heat up here. We'd go through more wood, but I was pretty sure it'd be worth it. In the meantime, I zipped up my vest, careful not to catch the mourning brooch in the zipper, and settled in to listen to Mary Frances. To Ida, that is.

Before she started reading, she straightened her back, and I remembered how women back then were always taught from an early age to maintain an erect posture. It was almost like Ida subconsciously took on that persona.

Christmas Day 1742

I have written so little over the past twelve months, for I have been much occupied with caring for my precious child. He is hale, thanks be to God, but I so often find myself choosing to watch him sleep rather than taking up my quill. Today marks the birth of another who must have seemed equally miraculous to his mother when he was born. It is a good thing that no person here can read this backward writing of mine, for I would surely be condemned for daring to compare myself to such a Mother as she, but I cannot believe that there is not a loving mother alive who has not at one time or another wondered what greatness might be in store for her child.

Ida kept reading, as if there had been nothing remarkable about those last few words. But then again, I supposed there hadn't—at least not to Ida, who had never borne a child. I looked across the circle to my mom, who was looking back at me.

I am safe, though, for no one except my sister Constance even knows that I write this way, for I am always careful to write in private, as she has repeatedly warned me. Homer Martin, of course, would not recognize the usual way of writing even were he to pay any attention to me as I scribble what he thinks are notes about the household. Or should I say wagonhold?

I must write about this, though. Over the course of our months on the trail, Call and Geonette Surratt have lost many of their household items. Neither of them has the faintest idea how to pack a wagon. We never let them be the last wagon in the train, for when something falls, there must always be someone behind them to pick it up or to warn them of what has happened. Their losses occur when something breaks upon falling such a long distance, for Call insists upon piling everything so high, the entire stack teeters with every step of his long-patient horses, who must stop repeatedly while items are either retrieved or cast aside as irredeemably damaged.

Ida sounded more and more judgmental as she read. "You'd think they would have learned better by now."

"Litterbugs," Melissa said. "That's what they were if they were just throwing things out like that."

"That's always been what people do," Carol said.

"Some people," I said. "Not everybody."

Amanda, the peacemaker, spoke up. "I'm not sure I'd know how to pack a wagon."

"Maybe not at first," Ida said, "but this far into the journey, why couldn't they have figured it out?"

I wondered how I would have coped. "They obviously knew the trip would be long, lasting over a number of seasons, so they would have had to plan for all kinds of weather."

"Imagine a sudden rainstorm," Glaze said, "and no idea where you'd packed the raincoats."

"Did they have raincoats back then?"

Carol didn't answer Dee directly. "They probably would have known that a lot of their basic everyday needs, like bedding and cooking utensils, would have to be easily reachable, but you're right about the changing weather. That would have been a challenge, especially since they couldn't count on being able to readily replenish supplies along the way."

"Lordy," Pat said, "I can't pack for a week's vacation without having five suitcases."

Dee nudged her with an elbow. "Are you sure you're not related to the Surratts?"

I thought back to when Pat and Dave had shown up with Melissa. All those bags and suitcases and boxes filled with food. I wondered how much of it had been Pat's clothing. Come to think of it, I'd been wearing the same sweatpants for three days, but Pat had worn a different outfit each day. Usually cashmere.

Yesterday, it was not a skillet or a stack of quilts that fell off, but young Edward. He is eight, certainly old enough to know better than to try to balance atop an unwieldy pile. It is a wonder he did not break his leg—or his pate—when he tumbled, but he picked himself up and brushed aside the concerned comments of the Stickneys, whose wagon was directly behind. Edward's mother did not even rein in the horses, but took a quick look at her boy back over her shoulder and said, 'It is a good thing he bounces.'

"I think I like Geonette Surratt," Pat said.

"Good," Ida said, "because she's probably Dave's great-great-great-grandmother."

Geonette spoke quietly enough that only a few heard her, but those few spread the word very quickly, and we all had a good laugh about it as we worked to prepare the evening meal. Edward is unflappable, even at his young age, and he grinned cheekily at the ribbing of the company. Until, that is, Daniel Endicott scooped him up and threw him across the fire to Joel, who caught the boy and looked ready to toss him back across the fire. He might have succeeded in finding out indeed whether the boy always bounced, but that Silas Martin stepped in—never a safe thing to do where the fractious Endicotts are concerned—and suggested most strongly that Joel set the boy on his feet. Male humans being what they are, I was certain that a fight would erupt and thought perhaps that Edward himself might object to being rescued, even though he quite obviously had not enjoyed his journey across the leaping flames. It is a wonder his clothing was not set afire. Silas Martin is such a diplomat, though, he said in the most dry tone of voice imaginable, 'What would you do for your evening meal if you dropped the boy in the stewpot?' It set exactly the right tone, allowing all parties concerned to laugh it off without loss of prestige, but I did not like the way Joel's lip curled as he watched Silas turn and walk away from the Endicott's fire.

Ida shuddered, and I couldn't blame her.

"You mentioned the Endicotts back at Azalea House," Melissa said, "but I'm still unclear about them, except that they're probably the ones who founded Enders."

"I don't know that much about them," Carol admitted. "Except for their names."

"It's a good thing they left the train," I said.

"It sounds like they might have killed somebody if they'd stuck around." Maddy sounded hopeful. "Or maybe they did, and that's why they had to leave. That comment about Joel's curled lip sounded ominous. Read some more, Ida."

"I sure hope Silas was okay," Rebecca Jo said. "He sounds like quite a guy."

"This entry was Christmas 1742," Ida said. "The next one is"—she counted on her fingers—"three and a half months later. April eighteenth."

"Mine, too," I said. "Same day."
"You go first."

April 1743

IT HAD BEEN ten long months since June of 1742 when Ira and Hubbard were first detained in Harrisburg on the Susquehanna. From June through August, the town had struggled under the enforced quarantine, until the fever seemed to wear itself out. It was hard for Hubbard to believe that the men from the neighboring town could have guarded the fence so unstintingly for those three months, but numerous shots had been fired whenever men from Harrisburg tried to sneak over the wooden boundary. No one had been killed, but two men had sustained broken arms when they fell from the top of the eight-foot stockade fence, and one man had been shot through the shoulder.

It was good the gate was finally unbarred after three months, for near starvation had come upon the town. Hubbard and Ira had suffered far less than the others, for Miss Julia's garden provided ample food, even if most of it was green. So many of the other inhabitants of Harrisburg had wasted away for want of meat, while Miss Julia swore—rightly it seemed—that her gardens could not only keep them alive but would allow Ira to gain back some of the weight he had lost through his time of illness.

His recovery, as Miss Julia had predicted, had been slow, and Hubbard often despaired, for he felt he might never find Mary Frances after all this time, especially if his brother was unable to travel far in a single day. He set himself to help his brother build up his strength, urging him to walk somewhat farther each day, eat a little more, wake a few minutes earlier, stretch his arms and legs a bit more strenuously.

Miss Julia and Miss Anna both complimented Ira every chance they had, praising his returning strength despite the fact that the strides he made were small indeed from one month to the next. And of course, Miss Julia fed him greens, greens, and more greens.

It was early in their stay with the Widow Gilman that Hubbard brought forth the container of green liquid the Indian healer had given him, now less than half-full. When he explained the use of it, Miss Julia took it in hand and examined it with wonder, sniffing the contents and touching her finger to the lip of the container. "This is truly marvelous," she said.

Thereafter it became her goal to determine the ingredients of the liquid, and Hubbard often heard her muttering to herself, "Onion perhaps? No. It is garlic. The oily consistency, what plant does that come from?" She mixed dozens of concoctions, always without quite duplicating the miraculous liquid. Over the months, her dozens of experiments turned into hundreds, but she refused to admit defeat. "There is no rosemary," she grumbled. "Could it be …" And off she would go to wander through her garden, alternately sniffing the vial and bending to finger a plant.

"I am forty-eight years of age," Miss Julia declared one evening in late April as the two men sat down to platters of boiled kale, stewed cabbages, red potatoes, baked beans, yellow squash, and green onions, as well as several other foods that Hubbard could not readily identify. "I have lived," Miss Julia continued, "in robust health all these years eating this way."

Ira grumbled under his breath, but Miss Julia did not acknowledge him.

Miss Anna's nose almost touched her plate. "I do not understand why I have not your health even though I am two years younger than you."

Hubbard was gratified finally to know the ages of the two women, but he could not believe that Miss Anna, who looked as if she were in her seventies, could possibly be but forty-six.

"You have health," Miss Julia told her younger sister. "It is only your back that is bent, not your constitution."

"Still …"

Hubbard thought Miss Anna sounded uncharacteristically sad.

"I find this harder to deal with as each month passes." Miss Anna pushed an untouched wedge of green cabbage to the other side of her plate. "I know not why my Heavenly Father chose to burden me in this way. Promise me that you will not grieve once I am gone."

Miss Julia stared in consternation at her sister.

That very night, Miss Anna took to her bed and did not rise the next morning nor the one after that. Miss Julia plied her with every known remedy to strengthen her body as well as her spirit, including water containing the Indian remedy, but the life seemed to have gone out of Miss Anna.

When it was finally over, less than a week later, Hubbard grieved deeply, for he had come to love the old woman. Over her grave, he wished silently that he had told her of his affection.

As soon as the last shovelful of dirt was thrown onto Miss Anna's coffin, Ira turned away and strode out of the churchyard. Hubbard was sure his brother was not unfeeling, for he had come to respect Miss Anna as much as Hubbard did. Ira's pride would not let him show his anguish.

Miss Julia watched Ira's back for a moment and then turned to Hubbard. "It is nigh time for you to leave. Your brother has regained much of his strength, and I know you wish to be on your road again, particularly since you will have to travel slowly at first until he is able to ride for long stretches."

"That is true," Hubbard said. "But I will miss you. I have taken great pleasure in our conversations of an evening."

"You need not miss me," Miss Julia said, "for I propose to travel along with you."

The lane was perfectly smooth, packed down hard over the years by the tread of thousands of feet, but Hubbard stumbled as if there had been boulders blocking his path. "With us? What do you mean?"

"You do speak the King's English, do you not? What do I have left for me here, now that my sister is gone?" She turned in a circle, surveying the surrounding houses. "Your journey sounds far more exciting than waiting here in Harrisburg until the end of my life. I always wanted an adventure."

"What about your house? Your gardens? Your …" He ran out of words.

"The only people here that I will truly miss are Caroline Edgerton and her daughter Lucy, but I have already spoken with them."

"You already …"

"Yes. It is all arranged."

"But …"

"They will move into my house. Lucy loves the garden and will care for it even as I have done. She is a fine weaver, too, and I will be most happy to leave my large loom for her use. The small loom as well, for she delights in making warm scarves to distribute through the community as the weather turns colder each year. Best of all, they are both exceptional healers, and they will carry on my work here."

"We have no extra horse, and you would not find it comfortable to ride double."

"Caroline has no need for Flower, her late husband's mare, so she has assured me that I may take it to ride, in part payment for the use of my house. I will not slow you down too much, for I have re-sewn my skirts so they are divided, and I will be able to ride astride with no more difficulty than a man. Furthermore," she said before he could object to such an outrageous idea, "I have knitted ample scarves and stockings for the two of you, and for myself of course, and have enough felted blankets that we will be well-protected on the journey, both from cold and rain."

He thought back to all the evenings she had woven and felted and knitted. "You have been planning this for some time, have you not?"

For answer, she simply smiled.

Hubbard tried one more time. "How will it look, though, if you …"

"I am certainly old enough to be your mother. If you like, if it will soothe your sensibility, you are welcome to introduce me as such to any other travelers we might meet. I would not mind having you for a son." She gazed up the road in the direction Ira had gone, with a thoughtful expression on her face. "Perhaps you should introduce me as your mother-in-law."

She wants me *for a son, but not Ira,* Hubbard thought, and felt momentarily guilty for the pleasure that thought brought him. He lifted his hand to his scarred face—he had forgiven his brother. He had, had he not? He rubbed the scars, which no longer hurt him, for the salves Miss Julia had anointed him with for the past many months had worked wonders, continuing the healing the Indian woman's green ointment had begun.

After a few more steps, he gave in. "Very well, Mother Julia, let us go inform my brother."

2000

Monday 18 April 1743. Two years ago I was wed. Today I leave Harrisburg with my brother and with Miss Julia. I fear that neither of them will be able to ride as quickly as I would like to go, but this appears to be my lot in life now, to nurse my brother and to care for the woman who saved his life.

"Their anniversary." Maddy sighed. "Sad, sad, sad."

Why are you unhappy, CurlUp?

"It is sad that Mary Frances and Hubbard had to be separated." Carol was obviously explaining things to Marmalade.

Monday 18 April 1743

I fail to see how one element can be both so productive and so destructive as is a flame. When I am beside the fire cooking, knitting, feeding my child, reading, listening to the singing or the fiddle or the stories of an evening, I am convinced that the warmth and companionship that a fire provides is a boon indeed, one might almost say a gift. The myth of how Prometheus must have loved humans to have stolen fire from Mount Olympus to give it to us poor people, must indeed be true.

"Ormsby sure was a good teacher," Rebecca Jo observed.

"Mary Frances was sure a good student," Sadie countered. "I doubt Ira or the Endicotts or any of that crew learned nearly as much."

Ida ignored them.

I believe that myth, though, only until I see the double-edged sword. I am mixing up my analogies here, but I still feel somewhat rattled by the events of this afternoon. We are in yet another enforced camp. This stop was indeed enforced upon us, for if Homer Martin had listened to his advisors, we would have stopped two months ago to replenish our supply of smoked meats. The process of preparing the meats, building a smoking shed, and completing the smoking process is time-consuming, and we have all known that as our supplies dwindled, we needed to plan ahead. But Homer Martin had it in mind that we should have been farther along in our journey and has pushed us mercilessly to put miles beneath our wagon wheels.

"He's such a louse," Pat complained.

"I wouldn't say that." Carol for once seemed to want to defend Homer, although I couldn't guess why. "If he hadn't pushed so hard, they might not have made it here."

Each mile we go is one more mile away from my Hubbard. We were married two years ago this night. I cannot lose hope that he will some day find me, although I know not whether he will believe that John is his own son and not that of Homer Martin. Surely his eyes will not deceive him. I marvel every day that no one in this company sees the likeness of Hubbard in the face of my dear boy.

"I sure wish we had portraits of the two of them." I fingered the silver pendant with its delicate miniatures inside.

Rebecca Jo turned to look back over her shoulder at the expanse of the old attic. "Somewhere up here," she said, and let the delicious possibilities dangle.

But I digress. I have little good to say about the Endicott brothers except that they are well-accomplished hunters. Sayrle burst into camp several afternoons ago to requisition extra horses. He led them out in a string and the four brothers—Worthy had not accompanied them on their hunting expedition—returned with eight good-sized deer. There was, of course, much whooping and hollering—when is there not where the Endicotts are concerned? The meat was much appreciated, though. It was far more than we could consume with-

out its going bad, so Homer Martin was forced to agree to stop long enough for us to prepare the meat and smoke it.

All would have gone well, except that the fire built under the smoking shed grew out of control and burned the shed to the ground. The meat was dreadfully scorched before our bucket brigade extinguished the blaze, but we have been able to render some of it usable by scraping off the char and soaking the meat in brine. No doubt there will be much complaining of the taste when we serve the meat, but not every day yields fresh game, and we must not waste what we have. We needs must find a town soon that has salt to sell, for we are scraping the bottoms of the salt barrels.

"Barrels?" Pat sounded confused. "Their salt was in barrels?"

"That's right," Carol said. "There were two kinds of barrels back then. Dry ones for flour and such, and the so-called wet barrels that held anything liquid."

We learned from a fellow traveler on this road that three months behind us was a town called Saltville, where we could have replenished our supplies easily. He journeys there once each three years to fill his wagon for all the members of his home community, and was even now headed that way, but his information did nothing to help us and did much to discourage us, for he knew of no other salt sources on the road ahead of us.

This year will surely go down in whatever annals are recorded as the most distressing of our time upon the trail. We have lost infants, livestock, wagon wheels, and stores of our precious seeds. We were so careful to divide the seeds among the families so that no one mishap could destroy the entire stock, but why we entrusted any of the priceless seeds to Call and Geonette Surratt is beyond my ken. Our only guess is that their seed box bounced out during one of the recent river crossings and no one spied it as it drifted away. It is a grievous loss, even more distressing than the two goats we lost to a painter last month. The herd boys—all of them—have been upbraided for their failure to keep the herd together, although with goats, one can never be sure of their compliance. And now, with the burning of the smoking shed, we are a glum company indeed.

"IT SURE WOULD have been easier if they'd had grocery stores," Easton said.

"You're right, dear," Sadie said, "but then we wouldn't have been nearly so entertained by the diary entries."

"And they might not have kept traveling," Pat said.

"Why do you say that?"

"Well, look at it this way, Biscuit. If there had been all the conveniences along the way, don't you think they might have stopped somewhere long before they got here?"

We all thought about it for a moment.

"Nope," said Maddy. "Homer wanted to find a secret place, a hiding place. If they'd settled for the conveniences of grocery stores and hardware stores, they'd have risked having the Brandts find them, and I don't think Homer would have allowed that."

"But the Brandts weren't following them," Glaze objected. "At least not a big posse of them. Just Ira and Hubbard."

"Homer Martin didn't know that, though," Maddy said.

"Homer certainly did seem to be single-minded about it." Carol stretched her arms out to the sides, like she'd tightened up considerably just sitting here.

Ida waved the diary in the air. "Aren't you forgetting what Mary Frances says? The only thing Homer was single-minded about was his drinking."

"It looks like we're almost finished with this first volume," Melissa said. "I don't want them to end."

"Don't worry." Ida waved the diary one more time. "There are three or four more entries in here, and then three more volumes to go."

"I'm glad we found this on the very first day," Maddy said. "How awful it would be if we'd missed seeing that package."

"If the ice melts before we finish reading them," Amanda said, "can we come back?"

"It'll be a while before we can come back," Rebecca Jo said. "We're all going to be faced with fridges full of spoiled food, probably some structural damage with the weight of all this ice on the roofs, and who knows what else."

Amanda dipped her head. "I guess I forgot about all that."

"Let's just keep the possibility in mind," I said. "After all, I'm still going to want to get all this stuff sorted."

"And there's the museum to plan," Maddy said.

"And," Dee said, "all those field trips you've lined up for us."

"Hubbard has another April entry," I said, and Ida waved her hand at me in a *go-ahead* gesture.

Saturday 30 April 1743. Miss Julia is proving to be a staunch traveling companion. We have been more than a fortnight upon the trail, and she has enlivened the journey with tales of the medicinal qualities of plants I have failed to notice in years gone by, not ever guessing that they might have miraculous properties. She has, too, an endless store of amusing tales that seem to take Ira's mind off his troubles and, since I prefer to be frank here in this private journal, they relieve my mind as well. Not that I do not long to hurry ahead the faster to see my wife, but I find myself riding content or sitting beside our nightly fire relaxed and well satisfied. My brother gains strength daily. In rereading what I have just written I find it sounds as if Miss Julia babbles constantly, but that is not the case. We often ride for long stretches in companionable silence. I look forward to the day when Miss Julia will meet my wife. She is certainly old enough to be my mother, but I cannot think of her as elderly. I wish her a long life indeed.

"I sure wish I could have met that woman," Glaze said. "She sounds a lot like Biscuit."

I gaped at my sister. "Like me?"

Glaze just smiled.

I had to think about it for a minute. It was true that I did enjoy silence, which was one reason I was beginning to feel a little frayed with all these people here round the clock.

You and Softfoot are often silent at night. But sometimes you are not. That is when I go under the bed.

Marmalade meowed for a long time and nuzzled her head against my tummy. I rubbed her ears gently. I looked at Carol for a translation, but she just shook her head and burst into laughter.

Maybe I didn't, after all, want to know what my cat was saying.

"I wish my mother had lived that long," Ida said, but then she seemed to pull herself up short. "Or maybe not. If she'd lived, she would have had to endure what happened to Diane Marie."

I saw Carol look a question at Melissa, but Melissa shook her head. This wasn't the time to go into all that.

"No parent should have to lose a child," Rebecca Jo said.

Sadie turned to Charlie. I thought it was lovely the way she always tried to include Charlie in our discussions. "When did your mother die, Charlie?"

"A long …" Charlie shook her head. "It seems like a long time ago now, but really it was only a year before I moved back here."

Sadie nodded. "So it's been four years? A lot can happen in that length of time."

June 1996

"**WHY DIDN'T YOU** call me, Mom?" Charlie dumped her backpack on Mom's bedroom floor. "I could have come home a lot sooner."

"And interrupt your junior year? Never." Mom patted the hospital bed just beside her. "I knew I could last."

Charlie felt so much anger well up inside her, it was hard to keep it from overflowing. She took a very deep breath, something that usually calmed her. But this time it didn't. "We could have had a few more months together at least."

"It's been so gradual, honey, I was hardly even aware. Not until my doctor mentioned hospice."

"Are you hurting?" Charlie spread her arms to indicate the rented hospital bed, the small table overflowing with tissues and medicines, a carafe of water, and a stack of folded washcloths.

"Not … not really. Not too much. Everything just seems to have gotten a lot slower since New Year's, sort of like a watch winding down." Her eyes went out of focus for a moment, almost as if she'd stepped away from her body. "I suppose I'm showing my age. Nowadays with batteries, watches don't gradually slow down, do they? They just stop." She smiled up at her next door neighbor. "The Palmers have been a wonderful help. I don't know what I would have done without Marie."

Charlie glared at Mrs. Palmer. "You should have called me." She tried not to sound too judgmental, but it was a losing battle.

"Let's not go into that," Mom said. "I asked her not to call you. Between Marie here and my home healthcare nurse, it's not like I've been neglected. And you and I have talked a lot by phone, so we've stayed in touch."

"But you didn't tell me the truth."

"The truth?"

"About what's been happening."

"Charlie, Charlie, Charlie." Her voice got softer with each iteration of Charlie's name. "I never lied to you." When Charlie opened her mouth, Mom raised a finger, which seemed to be all she could manage. "Okay. Maybe it was a lie of omission. But what I did tell you—how much I love you, how proud I am of you, how Marie and I have been having a lot of good talks—was true. I told you what mattered the most."

Charlie picked up her mother's hand as gently as she could from where it lay on the chenille bedspread. It was so thin, so frail. "But you didn't tell me about …" she waved her free hand around the room, "about all this." She didn't want to use the word *metastasize.*

Marie Palmer eased over to the door. "I'll leave you two alone to talk. I'll be back before supper time. Call if you need me sooner than that." Without waiting for an answer, she left. Charlie heard the front door open and close.

"I didn't want you to worry." Mom reached up her other hand and stroked Charlie's red hair back off her forehead. "Next June, you'll be the first Ellis Girl to graduate from college. I would never risk your losing that."

"But, Mom, that doesn't matter. Not if … if …"

Mom sounded suddenly fierce. "It *does* matter. Do it for me, Charlie. My mother always held me back. I would never do that to you." Just as quickly, the fight seemed to drain out of her. "I just wish I could be there when you graduate."

Charlie's tears mingled with her mom's. "You will be there, Mom. In one way or another, you will be there."

"It won't be long now," Mom said, "but I have great faith in you. You are all I ever … could … have … asked … for." She separated her words, as if each had a weight of its own. "You'll be fine, Charlie. I know you'll be fine."

2000

WE WERE SILENT for a while, not quite knowing what to say about Charlie's mom dying. Not that anything I said could have helped. I looked at my mom, wondering how I would ever cope when she or Dad died. Inconceivable. Thank goodness I'd have Bob to help me through it.

And me. I will help you.

I set aside Hubbard's journal and gathered Marmalade into a tight hug.

"Okay," Ida said. "We're up to June thirteenth."

Monday 13 June 1743

I write huddled beneath the canvas cover of our wagon. To-night is the first time in more than a seven-night when it has not rained, although the skies are too threatening for us to spread our goods to dry. My quilts are sodden, as is my dress, the blankets, and every crate that was not treated with beeswax before we left ~~Br~~ our former home. I have scarce been able to keep my young son from toddling through every puddle he finds. He was early to walk—to run indeed—and he delights in all things he encounters, even the soggy trundle on which he must lie at night. The sky, both day and night, is clouded over. I long to see the stars, but fear they have been swallowed up by the all-pervasive rain.

Tuesday 14 June 1743

Praise be! This morning we met with another small group of wagons traveling to the north, and there was much to-do as the drivers and horses tried to sort themselves out to pass each other on a trail that is almost too narrow for one set of wagons, much less two.

Amidst all the shuffling, someone—most likely Silas Martin—

thought to ask if there were a ready supply of salt available ahead of us on the road. Although the answer was no, they agreed to sell us two casks of this vital element. The price must have been exorbitant, for I saw Robert Hastings hand over a goodly amount of coin. We have been in such need for so very long, I feel safer, somehow, knowing that we will have enough to maintain us for a long while, although we will have to be thrifty with the use of it. This journey feels endless. Will we ever find a safe haven? If we find one, will my Hubbard be able to follow me there? He must, or I will surely go mad.

"Hubbard wrote just a few days after Mary Frances," I said. "Looks like he was far enough behind her not to catch all that rain."

Saturday 18 June 1743. Our path lies between verdant fields, and it is all Miss Julia can do to refrain from begging the inhabitants of the houses we pass for seeds or cuttings. We have no way to store much more, as our patient horses are already laden with all we carry, and I can almost feel their relief when I unsaddle them each evening. I find it hard to believe that the bags they carry are so much heavier now than when we started. When I found those precious books along the trail, I thought nothing of adding that weight to my pack, but since we left Harrisburg we have bartered along the way for many necessaries. I was surprised our first night on the road when Miss Julia pulled out the vine-covered cup I carved for her so many months ago in Harrisburg. When I asked why she would take extra room in her small pack for such an item, she replied that the Edgerton women had their own and she wished to keep hers and Miss Anna's with her. To think that these meant so very much to her. We have, too, the extra blankets and stockings and scarves Miss Julia and Mistress Anna provided for us, and welcome they are when the nights turn chilly. The stars shed almost enough light to cast shadows. I feel certain my wife looks up at the same stars in wonder.

"Oh," Maddy said, "that's so sad."

Dee cocked her head to one side. "What's sad?"

"She's complaining about not being able to see the stars, and he's hoping she's looking at the same stars he is."

"He's not just hoping," Glaze pointed out. "He's sure she is."

"That's the trouble with being miles apart like that." Pat waved her hand at both journals. "I wish he'd catch up with her soon."

Ida looked at me. "Does Hubbard write anything before September?"

I checked his journal. "Nope. September twenty-ninth."

"I'll go next then."

Thursday 22 September 1743

Funerals are becoming such a constant occurrence that I dread the dawning of each day. Four infants have died a-birthing in the last three weeks. I could not write about those deaths when they occurred, for each death pained me exceedingly.

"She doesn't say who they were," Ida said.

"This is one of the reasons the average life expectancy was so short back then," Carol said. "If children lived past the age of five or six, they had a good chance of making it into adulthood, but an awful lot of them didn't survive even to their first birthday. That lowered the average for everybody."

After Mister Homer Martin leaves me at night, I lift my John onto the pallet beside me and curl my body around his as if I could somehow thus protect him. I wonder if he is surprised to open his eyes in the morning and find himself beside me. If so, he does not complain. Mama has become my favorite word in the English language. He has not yet learned to say papa, and I do not encourage him to do so. He has been slow to speak, but his eyes are always alert, except of course when he drowses. Knowing that, I will not be concerned despite what Mistress Russell says. I love the way he winds his arms about my neck and babbles at me.

"I hope he stays so sweet," Maddy screwed up her mouth.

"I don't think I was that sweet when I was little," Dee said. "My mom said the first word I said was *dog*. She never thought I'd call her mama."

"My first word was *cuckoo*," Amanda said. When we gaped at her, she shrugged. "We had a cuckoo clock and I loved watching the little bird pop out every half-hour. Every time it sounded, my mom would say *cuckoo, cuckoo*. Is it any wonder that was what I picked up on?" She turned to Sadie. "What about you? What was your first word?"

Sadie blushed. "My mother swore in later years that I was trying to say *food*, but what came out was *poo*."

I had no idea what my first word was. I looked over at my mom.

"Mama." She smiled.

Thursday 29 September 1743 Michaelmas Day and we have no ...

"Michaelmas?" Dee interrupted. "What's that?"

"September twenty-ninth," Ida said. "The day St. Michael threw Lucifer out of heaven."

"September twenty-ninth?" Pat sounded incredulous. "They kept a calendar back then?"

"Michaelmas Day," I repeated. I had no wish to get into a theological discussion.

and we have no goose.

"No goose?"

I wasn't surprised when Dee interrupted me again.

I lowered Hubbard's journal. This was probably going to take a while. "I have no idea what that means."

"You're supposed to eat goose on Michaelmas," Ida said with exaggerated courtesy, as if that were something everyone should know, just as she obviously thought we all should have known about Michaelmas.

Dee leaned back and held up her hands in mock surrender. "Just asking." She looked at me with an obvious appeal to be rescued. I obliged.

As I use more of these pages I begin to fear that I shall run out of them. If that happens, I suppose I will simply go back to the beginning and crosswrite,

This time it was Ida doing the interrupting. "Crosswrite?" She looked over at Carol. "What's that?"

"Paper was so precious, people often would write on both sides of a sheet of paper, and then they'd turn the paper sideways and continue to write on top of what they'd already written. It was easier to figure out if they wrote large to begin with, but if they wanted to save paper in the first place, they usually compressed their writing."

"How did they ever read it?"

She furrowed her brow. "It takes some getting used to it, Ida, sort of like the way you've gotten used to reading that backwards writing. If you try it sometime you'll see what I mean."

"Crosswrite," I repeated.

... but I am loath to cover up the dear name of my wife in any way, for she appears so frequently in these pages as she is always in my thoughts. I had hoped to share my journal with her and I so often imagined sitting beside her in the evening as the two of us wrote together and then read to each other from what we had written. Now, of course, with my face the way it is, that can never happen. I wonder, though, if I should arrange to have this journal delivered to her—perhaps by Miss Julia?—so that she will know the depth of my love.

"He makes me so mad I want to spit," Glaze said.

I'd seldom seen my sister so angry. "Why?"

"Doesn't he trust her to love him? You think I'd give up on Tom if he got injured like that? What would you do if Bob got … got hurt somehow? Would you divorce him?"

"Of course not."

"Then what makes him think Mary Frances is so shallow?"

Mom leaned forward in her chair. "Honey? Try to look at it a different way. If you were as disfigured as Hubbard is, missing an ear and one of his eyes, with heavy immovable burn scars over much of his face, would you want to subject Tom to that sight every day?"

"But Tom would love me anyway!"

"Of course he would. Just as Mary Frances would surely have loved Hubbard. But he could barely stand to feel all that scar tissue. He doesn't for a moment doubt her love. He doubts his lovability."

"Oh."

Monday 14 November 1743

I will be so happy to see the end of this year, for it seems we have had nothing but troubles. Last evening, thinking to lighten everyone's mood, Alan Fountain hauled out his fiddle and began a merry tune, only to have one of the strings break. He improvised as best he could, but the few couples who had begun to dance a reel soon gave up. I should not complain about an imperfect fiddle, but it seems to be only one more in a string of ill-omened events that have plagued us throughout this year.

There are numerous small disagreements among the company. Perhaps this is not too surprising when so many people are constrained to travel cheek by jowl day after day, and I suppose I should be grateful that few actual fights break forth, but the constant bickering begins to fray my nerves. Charlotte Ellis and her sister barely speak to each other for days on end. I believe Sarah Russell to have the constitution of a saint to have put up with Charlotte's company for so many years. Adah Stickney is like to explode with her anger at the Endicott brothers. And poor Eunice Endicott is ever caught in the middle, for her husband never seems to notice the discord all around him.

Young John has been plagued with a nasty cough, and I feared for some time that this ague might weaken him beyond his ability to recover, but the Widow Tarkington brewed him a tea of something she calls licorice root. I have tasted it and found it exceed-

ingly sweet and it does appear to lessen John's cough.

"I'll be darned," Amanda said. "Licorice root tea."

"Annie sold it to me in the herb shop," I said, "and Pumpkin still carries it. I love the stuff, but Annie told me I shouldn't drink more than a cup of it in a day."

"Why not?" Maddy asked.

"Something about blood pressure."

"Widow Tarkington wasn't dumb," Ida said. "Listen to this."

She warned me against giving him too much of the tea, so I dole it out sparingly, just enough to soothe his throat. Please let this year end soon.

"That's it," Ida said, "until next, uh, March tenth."

I took a look at the dates in Hubbard's diary. "I've got two more to read then."

Wednesday 28 December 1743. Between the three of us we have somehow managed to keep track of the dates, but sometimes I feel we will be slogging through cold mud for eternity and I care not what day of the week it is or even what year. Miss Julia insists upon dosing us with vile-tasting teas and administering poultices to calm our coughs, but both Ira and I are exceedingly tired of her doctoring. I would never tell her that, of course, for she is unfailing in her tending of us, but this very moment, if I could curl in a ball like a hibernating bear and slumber away the rest of the winter, I would do so without a qualm. Only the thought that my wife draws ever farther from me with each passing day makes me willing to clamber into the saddle each morning. Our horses no longer even twitch when we cough so explosively close behind their ears.

"Makes you wonder how they ever made it so far," Glaze said. "Between the Martin's troubles and Hubbard's woes—sounds like a song title, doesn't it?"

I didn't think so, but I kept my mouth shut.

March 1744
Somewhere in the Shaconage

CHARLOTTE ENDICOTT ELLIS would have been perfectly happy if she never had to lay her eyes on another Endicott as long as she lived. Even though they were her brothers, she thought the lot of them to be as useless as a bunch of squirrels. She supposed Worthy was not too objectionable. He provided well enough for his wife and children, although she knew from personal experience that he had a mean streak down his back as wide as a skunk's stripes. But the other four would try anyone's patience. No wonder none of them had ever found a woman who would accept them. Sayrle was the best of the lot, but Charlotte had seen him mooning after Mary Frances Martin too often to think he would ever consider courting another.

Joel, the third oldest of the brothers still insisted on carving those ridiculously useless little birds—or what he called birds, although they did not look like any bird Charlotte had ever seen—to bestow on the young unmarried women of the company. Just this evening she had seen him thrust a handful of the excrescences on Nell Surratt, who was finally old enough, just barely, to be considered marriageable. Charlotte almost laughed aloud when she remembered the look of pained disgust that covered Nell's face as she stood there with a handful of wooden lumps, watching Joel's retreating back incredulously. She doubted not that Nell would dispose of them as soon as possible.

No doubt it was Nell's indifference to him that brought on Joel's surly attitude. Or more likely, the fact that Daniel had seen the interplay and taunted him about it. No wonder Joel had instigated a quarrel with his brothers.

This time it had taken seven men to break up the fight among the devil's quartet, which is how she thought of them, although she had never spoken those words aloud. That would not have been seemly. If it had been her decision, she might just as soon have let them kill each other, but they'd knocked over two tents already, bumped into Arinda

Everest hard enough to bang her against the side of her wagon, and almost trampled one of Adah Stickney's sons, which was why the other men had stepped in to stop the fighting.

As soon as order reigned once more, Charlotte's brother-in-law, the Reverend Anders Russell, ushered the four brothers behind his wagon and proceeded to give them a good tongue lashing, but she could hear their raised voices arguing with him. Arguing with a minister of God's word. It was a scandal.

Anders was not as forceful as Charlotte thought he should be. Perhaps that is why they felt they could contradict him. *He said ... No he said ... You hit me first ... It was not my fault ... I could not help it if* ... If they had been older than the minister, she might have understood, but they were young enough they should have had some respect. At the same time, they were grown men who should have known better. The excuses went on and on, the way they always did. Why did Anders not simply threaten them all with hellfire and be rid of the entire matter?

It was usually Daniel, the second youngest, who was the instigator, although he was seldom involved in the actual fighting the way he had been just now. A sly word here, an insinuation there, and pretty soon two or three of them would have black eyes and bruised ribs. That young man had more of Lucifer in him than any dozen other men she'd ever known. No wonder his hair was so red. A clear reflection of hellfire, that was what it was. Tonight, though, he had gotten what was coming to him. His eye would be blacker than funeral garb come morning, and Charlotte was fairly certain, from the way he'd held himself when Reverend Russell intervened, that at least one rib was broken.

She toyed with the idea of stirring up a certain concoction that would lay him low, which is what he deserved, the young hellion, although she was not sure how to administer it. He was not likely to trust her if she offered him food or drink. None of her brothers had trusted her ever since she had been widowed. She did wonder if they were a bit suspicious. Rupell, her husband—her late husband—had shoveled in food so fast, it was a wonder he ever tasted anything, which is what had made it so easy to …

"Silas says the Cherokee call these mountains *the place of blue smoke*." Charlotte's sister, Sarah Endicott Russell, lifted a pewter plate from the wash water and handed it to Charlotte.

"I suppose so," Charlotte said, surprised that her sister had begun speaking to her again after their last difference of opinion. She did not care what the mountains were called. This everlasting mountain mist was more than she wanted to deal with. Her clothes clung to her as damp as the linen towel she was using to sop the water off the plates. She could not rightly call it *drying them*, as they ended up hardly drier than they had been straight out of the wash water.

Sarah raised her eyes toward a nearby ridge where the setting sun illuminated the tips of towering fir trees. Down here, the valley was filled with the blue haze that had permeated the very air they breathed every moment since they entered this stretch of wilderness. "Shah-coh-nahg-ee." Sarah pronounced each syllable carefully.

"Sha-what?"

"That is what the Cherokee word is. Shaconage. Place of Blue Smoke."

"Blue smoke?" Charlotte harrumphed. "It is far too smoky for me. I should have stayed in Brandtburg."

Sarah looked at her with surprise. "You never said you wanted to stay."

"How could I?" Charlotte's voice was bitter with long-standing resentment. "You and Anders made the decision for me." Maybe, Charlotte thought, when I fed my husband his last meal, I should have given a bit to Anders as well.

But then there would have been no one to take her and her daughters in.

Sarah's lips thinned until she seemed to revise her thoughts. "I am sure you were sorry you had to leave your beloved Rupell's grave behind you," she commiserated.

Ha! If only she knew.

2000

"MARY FRANCES WOULD have helped us a lot if she'd given more details about those arguments," Pat complained. "Don't you wonder what stopped Sarah Russell from talking to Charlotte Ellis?"

"And that awful-tasting tea Miss Julia made Hubbard and Ira

drink," Maddy suggested. "I sure would like to know what she put in it."

"Probably just whatever was available along the trail," Carol said. "At this point they'd been traveling—what?—a year or so? I imagine her medicinal supplies would have run out by now."

"Mary Frances keeps making snide comments about the Endicotts," Amanda said. "Could they really have been that awful?"

Sadie looked at Carol. Rebecca Jo looked at Dee. I looked at Glaze. "Yes," we all said at the same time.

I picked up Hubbard's journal again, but my thoughts were still on Mary Frances and her problems.

Saturday, 3 March 1745

ADAH KELLOGG STICKNEY had had enough. The tinker who stopped with them the evening before had been a pleasant-enough man, full of entertaining tales of his travels, but the scuffle that had broken out between those loathsome Endicott brothers had not only interrupted his stories, it had nearly ended in tragedy. This was the second time in as many days that her youngest son had been near trampled by Joel and Sanford Endicott, and Adah felt ready to go on the warpath.

If the tinker resumed his tales after she took the boy to their wagon, she had no idea, for her heart had been pounding so, from fright and anger—no, make that rage—that the Endicotts' childish, stupid behavior had endangered her child.

If those Endicotts were going to settle in the new town Homer Martin was leading them to, she wanted nothing to do with it.

The tinker had just come from a small town to the southwest of where they now were. All she knew was that they were in the colony of North Carolina. The town was called Cullowhee. Rather a charming name, Adah thought.

"Aye," the tinker had told them. "I was born and bred in Cullowhee, and leave it the seventeenth of every February to wander throughout the spring and summer. Come autumn, though, I always turn my steps toward home, for it is a fine place to overwinter."

Why the seventeenth, Adah had wanted to ask, but before she could speak up, the man answered her unspoken question.

"February seventeenth is the day my wife—she died these many years ago—'twas the day she always decreed that it was time for me to be on my journeys, and it does not feel right for me to remain in town past that day."

"You were a traveling tinker when your wife lived?" asked Silas Martin.

"That I was," the man replied. "She was ever happy to see me return home before the winter snows." He paused just long enough before he added, with a showman's perfect timing, "And she was ever happy to see me leave four months later." He laughed heartily, along with the rest of the company.

Adah exchanged a glance with Arinda Everest. They knew how the wife must have felt. It was one thing to love the man you were married to. It was another to have him underfoot for months at a time if he had no regular work to keep him busy. She felt certain this journey was considerably harder on the women than on the men.

"The winters are not as cold here as they are farther north," the tinker said. "Our children have no trouble reaching the schoolhouse each day, for the snows are never too deep." There seemed to be a question in his voice, as if to ask from how far north they had traveled, but no one answered him. He also sounded to Adah as if he were trying to sell them on the advantages of Cullowhee.

Still, the town did sound as if it might be a good place to raise children. And if it turned out not to be, surely the roads went farther. They had traveled for so long, what would another few months matter?

The weather was mild enough now and the trail in that direction was, according to the tinker, as good a one as the path they now followed. "You cannot miss it," he had told them. "A fair wide road branches off to the west directly toward Cullowhee just a week's journey from here."

"We cannot travel as fast as you do," Silas Martin had said.

"A fortnight, then," the tinker said. "Not far at all. Which reminds me of the time I stumbled entirely unexpectedly between two bear cubs and the mama. I lived to tell of it, but I found out the hard way that …"

But then the brawl had erupted between Joel and Sanborn, and she had retreated with her badly frightened son to her tent, seething. His bruised face was smeared with soot from the ring of firestones where he had rolled to a stop. Adah shivered, thinking how easily he might have rolled into the fire itself had not the soot-blackened stones stopped his path. Just to be sure, she dosed the boy with a large spoonful of the cod liver oil she had bought the previous month from a different tinker. Judging by the boy's objections, Adah decided the oil must be efficacious indeed. She wished she had bought two bottles rather than just the one.

A fortnight was too long for her to wait. Those Endicotts had gotten between this mama bear and her cub once too often. Getting away from them had become a priority for her, but she knew she would have to curb her impatience.

She spent the whole night long fuming and planning. Now, with no sleep to sustain her and perhaps soften her attitude, she waited until after she had cleaned up the remains of the morning meal before she approached the Everest wagon.

Arinda's oldest daughter had taken the younger ones aside to clean their faces and delegate the morning's chores. Arinda was stowing a kettle in the back of the wagon where it would be easy to reach when they stopped for the evening meal and where the caked soot from its sides and bottom would not rub off on anything important.

Adah Kellogg had never been one to take three sentences to say what could be said in two. Or better still, in one. She had known Arinda Surratt Everest for all her life. Arinda would not think her too abrupt.

"I want to leave this company, Arinda, just as soon as I can talk Timothy into going. Would you be willing to speak to Joseph and go with us?"

Arinda rubbed her left shoulder. "Good morrow to you as well, neighbor."

Adah tossed her head, like a filly avoiding a bridle. "If I have to endure another day in the company of those Endicotts, it will be one day too many."

Arinda went straight to the heart of the matter, as Adah had known she would. "How does your boy?"

"Some bruising on his ribs, where one of those wildcats must have kicked him and a dark bruise on his cheek. It was sheer luck they did not topple him into the fire." She glared across the clearing to the place where the five Endicott men not only wolfed their bread but ignored the woman who fed them. "How Eunice bears them, I have no idea. The woman is a saint."

"I am not sure I agree, Adah. Eunice had no other suitor but Worthy Endicott. With only the one choice, what was she to do? It is not sainthood that keeps her there, but necessity."

Adah sighed. "I have never heard a single word of complaint from her. I can not suppose she actually likes her brothers-in-law."

"Perhaps she does."

"I said she was saintly, but I doubt she is stupid." Adah turned her back on the central area. "What say you? You heard the tinker. There is a small town but a few weeks' travel from here that has ample water, ample land. There is even a schoolhouse, for he mentioned the schoolmaster, so our sons could learn to read and write better than you and I can teach them. We could make an end to this journey in Cullowhee." She stopped, sensing that her friend would need time to think about the proposal. Turning away from the Everest wagon, she said over her shoulder, "Just a fortnight down this trail and then two or three days easy travel to the west would take us there." She was not sure the trail would be easy, but once they were embarked on it, they would take what came and would deal with it.

"Have you spoken to Joseph yet?"

Adah turned back, stepped closer to her friend, and lowered her voice. "Not yet. I would like to know that we would have another family with us when we undertake the journey. Then I could suggest that he ask your Joseph. And, of course, you would already have plowed that ground."

Arinda smiled, looking something like a conspirator, which, indeed, she was. "You think of everything, Adah dear."

"How does your shoulder this morning?"

Arinda shrugged off the question. "It will mend. Particularly once we no longer have those Endicotts running into us."

2000

"I HOPE WE FIND out more about Miss Julia," I said as I opened

Hubbard's journal. "She sounds like a real winner, although those teas she served the men must have been awful for Hubbard to have complained about them like that."

"He didn't just complain about them." Maddy made a face. "He called them vile."

"Sometimes," Mom said, "I think all the medicines that taste so good are a real mistake. Why bother to get well if you can get sugary cough syrup whenever you want it?"

I groaned when I thought of some of the awful-tasting things I'd had to down when I was a kid. On the other hand, I'd been exceptionally healthy. "Maybe there's something in what you say."

Sadie had only one comment. "Cod liver oil."

Rebecca Jo groaned, but she had a bit of an upturn to her lip. I wondered if there was a story here. I doubted she'd ever fed any of that stuff to Bob, but I made a mental note to ask him about it later.

Saturday 3 March 1744. Surely we must be getting closer to my wife. There seems to be a curse on me, though, for as soon as I begin to think that way, something happens to stop our progress. Ira's stump is paining him more than usual. Miss Julia has examined it and says that we must seek respite at the next public house we pass. 'He needs to sleep in a bed,' she says, 'for the constant damp of this rainy springtime has affected him wrongly.' I must say it has affected me wrongly as well. I can see nothing but flat expanses of fields and forest in the distance ahead, and I long for mountains. When I lived in Brandtburg, I fear I did not fully appreciate the beauties that surrounded me on all sides. The mountains were ever stalwart sentinels. Bah! I grow maudlin. Enough of this.

"Well," I said, "talk about a lousy journey. What do you suppose was really wrong with Ira?"

"Sheer orneriness," Maddy said.

"You still haven't forgiven him for Myra Sue's murder and for what he did to Hubbard, have you?"

She didn't answer me, but her eyes narrowed. Maybe I should tell her about lighting a candle?

It helped you a lot.

"You don't have to like him," Rebecca Jo said, "but I think it took quite a change of heart for him to admit he'd been wrong."

Maddy snorted. "Didn't do much good for Hubbard, with his face ruined like that."

"He's made peace with it," Sadie said.

"I don't think he has," I said. "If he were truly at peace about it, wouldn't he have realized that Mary Frances would love him anyway?"

The women were silent for a few moments, and I could see that my question had touched something deep inside all of us.

Rebecca Jo finally answered. "I think the problem is that he"—she nodded at Sadie—"he may have made peace with the injury, but he's not … he doesn't … I don't know how to say this. I think he doesn't like himself the way he looks. Does that make sense?"

"Do you mean," I asked, "that if he can't love himself, he couldn't possibly believe anybody else could love him?"

"I agree," Amanda said. "I saw countless people in my practice down in Atlanta who didn't believe in themselves. It was almost like they didn't really want to recover from their aches and pains, because then they wouldn't have an excuse for whatever they were complaining about—coworkers they couldn't get along with or spouses who didn't understand them. It's easier to blame it on a physical ailment than to face up to whatever needed to be fixed. And no matter how many exercises or stretches I suggested, they just didn't do them."

I stared at her. So did everybody else.

Her face reddened. "Sorry. I guess I got a little carried away there."

"Just a little?" Ida scoffed. "Ha!"

"Maybe you need a candle," I said, and proceeded to explain the process—although I left out the details of how and why I'd lit my own candle so recently.

Sadie gave me a wise and extremely knowing look. It might have felt disconcerting, but it really just felt like a deep connection between us.

"So"—Maddy pointed at Hubbard's journal—"What's he going to do when he gets to Martinsville?"

"We'll have to keep reading," I said, lifting Hubbard's journal again. "March twelfth."

"No you don't," Ida said. "It's my turn."

Saturday 10 March 1744

My wish to see the end of 1743 was fulfilled, and now this year has been much more promising. We travel apace with not a single death so far, nor a broken wheel, nor any lost goats. Adah Stickney might well have throttled the Endicott brothers during this last week, for yet another fight erupted between the three younger ones and they trampled Adah's youngest who had been happily playing next to the Stickney's tent. The boy needed minor patching, the tent required extensive work to repair the tears, which the Endicotts were required to do, but of course they foisted the job onto Eunice. That woman is either a saint or a fool, I cannot decide which. Arinda Kellogg sports a sore shoulder where they plowed into her, pushing her against the rim of a wagon wheel. My John has passed his second year, and just yesterday was proclaimed hale and hearty by Mistress Tarkington—soon to be Mistress Martin. I would to God she were the only one who will be called by that name in this company, for I despise being called Mistress Martin. Silas is such a good man, so unlike his brother. I am sure Louetta will be as proud to be Mistress Martin as I am repelled by that name for myself.

Ida's feather had begun to droop lower onto her cheek, almost as if it mirrored her thoughts, which I was sure were as gloomy as mine.

"You're on next, Biscuit." She eased the Mary Frances journal onto the small table beside her. "I need some water."

"I'll get it for you." Easton took off for the stairs.

I watched her go, hardly able to believe she was being helpful. I glanced at Sadie, and saw her nodding. There was something about that nod—I wondered if she'd given Easton a talking-to. If so, maybe Easton was getting the message.

"Looks like we'll have a happy wedding coming up," Dee said, "with Silas marrying Louetta Tarkington. I hope she writes about it."

"Can't imagine she wouldn't," Ida said. "That had to be a really big event for the group."

"I hope Homer didn't ruin it," Melissa said.

"Did they have marriage licenses back then?" Pat shifted on her chair. "I mean, they never mention them, but how did people know they were married legally?"

Maddy, of course, was the one who answered her. "It was all done through the church. They proclaimed the banns—that means they announced in a church service that these two people were going to get married a couple of weeks later. That gave people time to object or—I guess—talk the couple out of it. Then, after the wedding, the event would be recorded in the family Bible."

"What about Mary Frances and Hubbard?"

I wondered why Pat was so adamant about this.

"They never had anything announced in church," she went on. "And it couldn't have been recorded in a Bible. Does that mean they weren't really married?"

"I'm sure they were," Carol said. "The ceremony was performed by a minister, and the minister's wife served as a witness."

Pat curled her lip. "Doesn't sound very official to me."

"So, I wonder," Sadie mused, "whether they had some sort of signed document from the minister." She smiled her sweet smile. "Wallace and I framed our wedding certificate."

"Ralph and I put ours in our safe deposit box," Ida said. "What are you going to do with yours, Glaze?"

"We haven't talked about it. I like the idea of having something framed, but maybe we'll make a copy to put on the wall and put the original in a deposit box." She nodded at Ida. "That does sound like a good idea."

Pat let out an extremely undignified snort. "Don't you wonder what all ends up in safe deposit boxes? I don't mean stuff like marriage certificates and mortgage papers and car titles. I mean the really good stuff."

"Or the bad stuff," Dee intoned, and I briefly wondered about that embezzling former husband of hers.

"Those boxes can be really handy," Charlie muttered. I think I was the only one who heard her.

September 1996

AT THE START of their senior year, Charlie and Tricia unloaded, unpacked, and put everything away, everything except one sturdy cardboard box that Charlie laid in the center of her bed. "I wish you could have been there for my mom's funeral," she said.

"I had to work."

"I know, I know. It's just that I …" Charlie turned away from Tricia. "It was okay. Mr. and Mrs. Barker were there and all their kids, and the Palmers. All the neighbors, in fact, and people from the office and, well, the church was packed. Mom—and Dad—were really well-liked. The Palmers sat with me on the front row since there isn't any other family now."

"What's going to happen to your house?"

"I can't sell it, not until the will is finished going through probate, and heaven only knows how long that will take. Once I graduate, I guess I'll go back and live there, at least for a while until I can get it ready to sell." She stretched her arms high above her head and rotated her neck. "In the meantime, I've rented it to the Palmer's oldest son just for this year. That's why I didn't feel comfortable leaving this"—she lowered her arms and indicated the box on her bed—"lying around. I trust Joey, but my dad always said there was an eleventh commandment."

She expected Tricia to ask her what it was, but Tricia just stared at the box.

"Thou shalt not tempt," Charlie finally said. "I didn't want Joey to get curious."

"What's in it?"

"It's … it's something my mom showed me. A couple of years ago." She lifted a fabric-wrapped parcel from the box, but didn't untie the string that held it together.

It took Charlie quite a while to explain about the Ellis Girls. Not that Tricia didn't know a lot about them already. Charlie felt sometimes like she'd spilled her whole entire life history to Tricia. Tricia was such a good listener. But Tricia didn't know this part. What Charlie's grandmother had done, grandmother and all the Ellis Girls before her.

Tricia huffed out a loud breath once Charlie was through. "So all your family were blackmailers?"

"Well, uh, yes. But my mom wasn't. She stopped the cycle."

"Why on earth would anybody care about a bastard son after all these years?"

It took Charlie some effort to convince Tricia just how stiff-lipped the Martins were about their antecedents. "Mom didn't even want me to mention the town name to anybody once we moved away to Atlanta."

"Why not?"

"I guess she just didn't want anybody to connect us to—well, to such a shameful part of our family's life."

"Did you?"

"Did I what?"

"Tell anybody."

"Of course not!"

"You told me."

Charlie didn't have an answer to that. "The trouble is," she finally said, patting the packet beside her, "I brought this here to keep it safe from prying eyes, but"—she looked around their small dorm room—"somehow this doesn't seem much better. Mom didn't want me to destroy it because it's history."

"Maybe you should get a safe deposit box," Tricia said.

"It would have to be a big one."

"Don't you think it would be worth it? So you don't lose it. What if the dorm catches on fire?"

Charlie shivered. "I never thought of that."

"You ought to have somebody else who could sign for it, too. That's just common sense. You know, in case you break a leg or something or need somebody to pick it up for you."

On Saturday, Charlie talked Tricia into going with her to the bank and signing the paperwork along with her. "I want somebody else to have a key, in case I lose mine," she explained. She certainly wasn't planning on breaking a leg, like Tricia had mentioned, but she'd lost enough things in her life already. She didn't want to risk losing this.

Once the packet was stowed in the bank vault, Charlie felt a lot safer. Someday she'd have a daughter of her own, and then the two of them would decide how to dispose of the Ellis papers.

2000

EASTON RETURNED SOON with two full pitchers, as well as a bag of plastic cups tucked beneath one arm. "I'm sorry, Biscuit," she said when she saw my frown. "I know you don't like plastic, but I figured we were all parched, and I couldn't carry glasses."

Would wonders never cease? Easton being thoughtful? "Don't worry," I said. "We'll wash them out and re-use them for lunch."

"And supper," Melissa said with a grin.

"And breakfast, probably," Pat added.

"And—"

But I held up a hand before Dee could add to the litany. "I get the idea."

"Just give us a marker," Rebecca Jo said, "and we'll label our own so we don't get them mixed up."

Once we were all thoroughly hydrated, I donned the gloves again and picked up Hubbard.

Monday 12 March 1744. We have wasted six days here while Miss Julia fusses about my brother almost day and night. He was feverish by the time we reached this town, and a dismal place it is, but the rains have been pounding down for all six of these days, and I must admit that Miss Julia knew whereof she spoke. The publican keeps a roaring fire going all the day long, and my bones feel better for being able to warm myself. I have been reading Isaac Watt, and was struck by the lines 'Time, like an ever-rolling stream, bears all its sons away; They fly forgotten, as a dream dies at the opening day.' I am sorry indeed that Master Ormsby is without his prized books, but glad I am to have the use of them until such time as I can return them to him.

I am of little use in the sickroom, and Miss Julia seems glad to have me out from underfoot, like a wayward child. If my wife and I were still in Brandtburg, we would most likely have a child or two of our own by now, and I would not care if our babes were noisy or fractious, for I would see my dear wife's face reflected in theirs. It is an idle hope now, of course, but I cannot help dreaming.

I set the journal down, took off the gloves, and reached for my hanky.

I wasn't the only one.

Friday, 16 March 1744
somewhere in western North Carolina

DESPITE SILAS MARTIN'S reservations, Homer insisted. "I swore four years ago that I would buy you your last drink as an unmarried man, just as you did for me before I was married."

It was but three years, Silas thought, but did not contradict his brother. Silas felt settled, with a hot cup of tea from the kettle warming his hands and the pleasant after-meal smell of roast fowl wafting around the fire circle. Even the rock on which he sat was not uncomfortable, for it was still warm from the day's bright sun. "I would just as soon spend the evening here, brother."

"No, no. The town is but a scant mile from here. And from what the Endicotts tell me, it has a fine tavern."

"They would certainly know."

"You speak true." Homer headed toward his horse.

They had been here in this narrow dell for two nights, a necessary stop to allow time to re-shoe horses and repair several of the wagons whose traces were in dire condition, but the Endicott brothers had disappeared the previous evening before full dark to backtrack to the town they had passed most recently.

"I suppose he will need me to guide him back," Silas muttered as he set his cup aside. It was almost empty anyway, and Louetta had been in the Shipleigh wagon for some time now, tending a sickly child. He doubted he would have a chance to see her before the morrow. He walked over to Devil and apologized for the need to re-saddle him. He imagined Devil would have preferred to stay within the confines of the camp as well, but Homer had already left the ring behind and urged his horse into a trot.

The public house was little more than a shack, but from the

sound of it, it was already filled with men whose voices assailed the ears even before the tavern itself came into view. "Let us hope their ale is as powerful as their singing," Homer called back over his shoulder.

"I would be reluctant to call that music." Silas knew his brother had no ear for a tune. He should fit right in here in that case. Silas just hoped he would be able to drag Homer away in time for the ceremony tomorrow. Louetta would be sore at him indeed if Silas came late. If it came to a head, Silas decided he would leave his brother here rather than risk falling asleep at his own wedding.

He also hoped that Homer would this evening keep his opinions to himself for once. There was no need to incite another fight.

"Ale," Homer called as they entered, and the singing ceased. "A final ale for my brother who will give away his freedom by marrying tomorrow."

"Willingly," Silas said as the men hooted their condolences.

Homer rooted about his pockets but was unable to find aught but lint. The publican, nothing at all like Robert Hastings, was a surly sort. He waited to draw the ale until Silas tossed a coin onto the long counter. "Come far, have you?"

"Far enough," Homer answered. "Far enough to give me a powerful thirst." He raised his cup in a toast. "To my brother. May the lord have pity on him."

Silas had all along suspected that his brother's marriage to Mary Frances Garner had not been a joyful union, but he was surprised even so at the level of bitterness in his brother's voice.

"To happily-married men and their lovely ladies," Silas countered, raising his own cup. Even though he had to pay for his own drink, he thought it was exceedingly well worth it to be able to praise his intended with this toast.

He was glad beyond measure that Louetta Tarkington had finally agreed to be his wife. *It will be a good marriage,* he told himself, *and I will have a ready-made son in Brand, although I cannot help but hope that between us, Louetta and I might beget another child.*

Ready money was in such short supply, Silas had gone to Robert Hastings the last time they approached a good-sized town and had begged the loan of enough cash money to buy his own wagon. He would not take Louetta Tarkington into the wagon that Homer Martin shared with Mary Frances. The wagon Silas had been sleeping underneath ever since his brother's marriage. The wagon Homer slept underneath as often as not.

SEVERAL HOURS LATER Silas had to drag Homer to the hitching post, but luckily did not have to boost him onto his horse, for Homer still had enough sensibility left to mount the animal by himself. Silas considered tying his brother to the saddle, but decided Homer might just as easily fall off and strangle himself in the reins, which would not be an auspicious sign. *Why do they follow him*, he wondered yet again, marveling at the magic of the Martin name, and at the ability of his brother who, he knew, would be able to walk in a straight line on the morrow despite the numerous flagons he had imbibed this night. Silas had refused to pay for more than one drink apiece, but Homer had found enough small coins in other pockets to keep himself well lubricated.

Silas had stretched out his first and only flagon of ale to last the entire time they were in the tavern. He would be clear-headed on the morrow. His brother's head would ache something fierce, though. Of that, Silas was certain.

Saturday, 17 March 1744

BRAND TARKINGTON STILL missed his pa, and he was bound and determined not to start calling himself Brand Martin just because Ma was marrying with Mister Silas, even though he liked Silas plenty. But he could still remember the day the bear killed Pa. The way his ma walked up behind that bear and shot it. He had been just a child that day, but now, almost three years later, he had grown strong, working with the other men—well, the men and the other boys—as they traveled so far to the south.

He looked down at his left arm, bare to the elbow, and flexed the sinews by clenching his fist and twisting his forearm. He left his sleeves rolled up most days, for his arms were getting too long. Ma would probably insist on making him a new shirt, but with summer coming on, he preferred to stay in this one. It was soft. A new one would be scratchy for a while.

May of 1741, that was when the bear killed Pa. Three years ago almost. The wildflowers had been blooming back then. And now, they'd come so much farther south, there were wildflowers all around this clearing, too. Ma had stuck some of them in her hair this morning. She looked right pretty.

He studied Mister Silas standing beside Ma in front of the gathering. Brand could remember how a long time ago he had to raise his eyes way up to look at Mister Silas when Mister Silas first appeared in their dooryard. Now, though, he hardly had to look up at all. That was one way he knew he had grown taller during the three years he and his mother had been traveling with these people. A lot taller.

He fingered the bear claw that hung around his neck. Ma always insisted that church was no place to display a claw as big as that one, so he had tucked it inside his shirt, but he could feel the bulk of it through the thin fabric. "It makes you look like a wild man," Ma always said with a little bit of a twinkle in her eye, "too wild to be in church." The trouble was, this wasn't really a church. Just Reverend Anders standing at the back of his wagon with his prayer book in his hand and everyone gathered around in the shade of an enormous oak. One of the horses whinnied nearby, and another nickered in answer, almost like an echo to the amens of the congregation.

Mister Martin—Homer Martin, not Silas Martin—stood nearby, and Brand wondered what was wrong with him. His eyes were red-rimmed, and he kept reaching up to touch the side of his forehead, like it hurt something fierce, but Brand could not see any sort of bruise there.

Afterwards, once they had recorded the event in Ma's Bible, everybody called her *Mistress Martin*, and then they all just went back to doing what they would have done if this had been like any other Saturday on the trail. Only Brand knew, from seeing other weddings along the way, that there would be dancing once they finished all their daily work, and his ma would be sleeping inside the new wagon with Mister Silas now, instead of with the other women in the Russell wagon. Brand guessed he was going to have to decide where to sleep himself. Under the Russell wagon the way he had been doing ever since he and Ma had joined the group? Or under the new wagon Mister Silas used?

Once the evening meal was finished and it was dark, and after everyone was through with the dancing and the men had finished with their drinking, Brand picked up his blanket and spread it close to the big central fire, where most of the other young men slept unless it was raining. He was almost as big as they were. He wondered if his ma would notice.

If she did, she didn't say anything.

2000

"THIS IS IT," Ida said. "The last entry in volume one."

"Hope it's a good one," Pat said.

Ida squinted at the page. "Looks like she wrote this one in a hurry. It's even harder to read than the other ones."

"You've gotten so good at reading backwards," I said. "I'm still amazed at how easily it seems to come to you."

"Ralph has been known to tell me my head's on backwards," Ida said. "Maybe that explains it."

Saturday, 17 March 1744

I have but a few moments in which to write. Mister Homer Martin is carousing with the rest of the wedding party, but soon, I fear, he will come into our wagon. How I wish he would pass out from the drink, but he is surprisingly resistant to its effects.

"I guess that explains the hurried writing," Ida said.

"It's eerie," Maddy said, "the way you can almost read that woman's mind."

"Makes sense." Rebecca Jo leaned back in her chair. "A journal like this is so personal, it's like she's invited us right into her brain."

"Except she didn't invite us in," Melissa pointed out. "I wonder if she ever showed her journals to anyone while she was alive."

Ida stared at the book. "I doubt it."

Louetta Tarkington married Silas Martin this morning.

I was in awe of her radiant face. The clean lines of her cheekbones looked almost as if they had been carved from beech wood, and they were somehow at odds with the smile that seemed to keep getting wider with every word Reverend Russell spoke. I must wonder if I looked that happy the night I married Hubbard Brandt. There was no one to see me, of course, except Reverend and Mistress Atherton, but I can remember feeling that my smile could have lit up an entire clearing that night. I was never afraid, never doubtful. Not even when we retired to the hayloft of Reverend Atherton's barn where Mistress Atherton had spread a large quilt. Where my young precious John had his beginning. It was an entirely new experience, and only a bit painful at the first—I blush to write about this, even though I know that no one will read these words—but I have never, never regretted a moment of it.

"Do you think," Amanda said, "I mean you don't suppose she minds us reading it, do you?"

Charlie let out a huff. "It's been two hundred years. She's—"

But Sadie cut her off before she could say it. "I think she'd be delighted to know that we're all on her side. After all," and here she gave Carol a long look, "sometimes people just want to be heard." She smoothed the arms of her purple sweatshirt and smiled to herself.

Almost fifty years it had taken us to hear Sadie. Of course, that was how long it had taken her to speak, so maybe there was no need to assign blame.

That first wedding was so very different from my second supposed wedding, when the tears coursing down my face were ones of absolute despair. Why did I not cry out when those fateful words were spoken?

'If anyone knows of any reason why this man and this woman,' Reverend Russell intoned this morning, and of course nobody stepped forward to stop the joining of Silas Martin and Louetta Tarkington, as no one had stepped forward at either of my own marriage ceremonies, although everything within me screamed silently

that my second wedding was a sin.

I do wonder if Louetta's first marriage was a happy one. She and that long-dead husband of hers certainly created a fine son. Brand stood behind his mother so proudly, moving his shoulders back as if to emphasize how much he had grown in the time they have been with us on the road. His father must have been a tall man, as tall as the boy's new stepfather is.

"Brand," Ida said, looking at Melissa. "Your ancestor."

"Probably." She fingered the necklace she still wore. I wondered if she slept with the thing around her neck.

"Definitely," Pat said. "He was the one with that bear claw."

Easton interrupted. "What about Brand? Keep reading, Ida."

Sadie and I exchanged a satisfied glance. Easton really did seem to be mellowing.

My own son, mine and Hubbard's, slept inside the wagon throughout the wedding. He grows so fast, he seems to tire himself out with the way his little body stretches to fill out the lengthening of his still-small bones. He will one day be as tall as Louetta's son is now, and then will eventually be as tall as his real father, as tall as Hubbard, far taller than the man all these people think is his father. I pray silently every day for the safety of Hubbard, but I cannot help but wonder why he has not followed me—why has he not come for me?

Reverend Russell was only halfway through the short ceremony when I began to cry, as silently as I could. Silas took Louetta's hand, and I was startled to feel my own hand grasped by Homer Martin. I looked at him in some confusion for he has never before done such a thing, not even in private, much less where everyone could see him.

"Yuck," Pat said. "That man gives me the creeps."

"You and Mary Frances both," Ida said.

Rebecca Jo nodded. "All of us, I think."

'Remind you of our own wedding, does it?' he asked me. The smell of his fetid breath spilled over me, and I tried my best not to recoil.

What could I do but nod, wondering what on earth he might be thinking? His eyes were red-rimmed from excessive drink the night before. I imagine that as soon as everyone retires for the night, I will find out precisely what he has been thinking. The thought of it chills me to the bone.

I am reluctant to end this first precious volume on such a despairing note, but this is the last page, and I have no room left to tell of the sweetness of my little son.

We were silent for quite some time after Ida stopped reading and closed this first volume. That phrase of hers—*the thought of it chills me to the bone*—seemed to echo around the rafters above us, and I found myself shivering.

Are you cold? I will warm you.

Marmalade jumped into my lap, and I wrapped my arms around her. A welcome diversion.

I am not a divershun. I am a cat.

Saturday, 17 March 1744

CHARLOTTE ENDICOTT STOOD behind Homer and Mary Frances Martin, wondering, not for the first time, just what went on between the two of them. Surely she had been right. John Martin was not the son of Homer, but Charlotte could not think how to use that knowledge to her own advantage. If only she could tell which of the men in the company were the father, but as far as she had been able to see, no particular man had ever favored Mary Frances in any special way, except perhaps Charlotte's second-oldest brother Sayrle, who had a tendency to follow Mary Frances with his eyes whenever he thought no one was looking.

But of course, Charlotte was always looking, and she had seen the lust he tried to hide.

Could he have forced himself on Mary Frances? Charlotte would not put it past him. Perhaps that was why Mary Frances seemed to avoid him pointedly, except for that one time Charlotte had seen the two of them talking together, but Charlotte was not sure whether Mary Frances treated Sayrle differently than anyone else. She had certainly never seemed to look at him, but she did not interact with any other man, either. She did not even look at her own husband very often. Charlotte, thinking back to her own loveless marriage, could understand the desire to make the man disappear by simply never acknowledging his presence.

The more she thought about it, the more certain she was that Sayrle was the father of the child. She would find a time later this evening to write about it in her special papers. There would be a time, sometime, when she could make use of the knowledge, and it would not do to forget any details. Had not the baby John had a high forehead when he was born? Did not Sayrle have that same feature?

She was surprised when Homer Martin reached out and took the hand of his wife into his grasp. Charlotte was happy to see that Mary Frances looked thoroughly startled. Charlotte leaned forward, but was unable to hear what Homer whispered. She was close enough, though, to see the tears run down the woman's cheek.

Charlotte never cried at weddings. She had never yet seen a wedding she did not think was ill advised.

2000

"I KNOW YOU'VE said a lot about the problems the Martin clan probably had on the trip here," Melissa said to Carol, "and Mary Frances has said so as well, but don't you think they must have had some good times, too?"

"Undoubtedly. That was a time when pleasures were simpler in many ways."

"Like what?"

Carol looked at Dee, seeming to marshal her thoughts before answering her. "In times before electricity, people went to bed a lot earlier, although I'm sure there was a fair amount of just sitting around a fire in the evening, talking, maybe singing or listening to someone tell a story or play a fiddle."

"Or a penny whistle," Maddy said with a laugh, and I remembered the cute little tune she'd tootled our first day up here.

"Penny whistles weren't invented until the 1800s," Carol said, "but still, there would have been a fair amount of music in the camp most evenings."

"Sounds like when I was a kid," Rebecca Jo said.

"I doubt they stayed up too late, though, since everyone, even the children, worked hard. There were always chores, and often people's lives depended on getting those tasks accomplished."

Dee shuddered. "That sounds ominous."

"Well," Carol said, "just think about it. The animals had to be tended. Cooking was not a quick and easy task. Unless they passed through a large town, there wouldn't have been any food stores or taverns along the way, as we've already mentioned. If the wagons weren't kept in good repair, a breakdown would stop the whole caravan."

"I see what you mean." Dee shivered as much as I had.

Why is everyone cold?

Finally, I picked up Hubbard's journal. "March seventeenth. Here's another case where he wrote the same day she did."

"I hope it's a happier entry than hers was," Pat said.

Saturday 17 March 1744. This evening Miss Julia saved my life. She killed a man.

"Uh … um … did I just read what I think I did?" I double-checked the words. His handwriting was small but clear. "She really did. She killed somebody."

"Keep going," Easton said. "Keep reading."

I will write no more about it, for she seems to be shaken indeed, and I take these few moments to write while I wait for the water to boil. She has directed me to a particular packet in her large medicinal pouch and instructed me that tea made with just a spoonful of it will help both of us. Ira is asleep, insensible to how much Miss Julia and I shiver.

I felt a quiver of indignation across my chest. How could he have not explained it? I have to admit I was startled, though, by the vehemence of everybody's comments.

"What? No details?"

"He can't leave us hanging like that!"

"No fair."

"Phooey on him."

And so on, for several minutes as we debated the possible scenarios. I looked ahead in the journal, but he didn't say another word about it.

Phooey on him, indeed.

"At least," Carol said when we'd all toned down a bit, "this explains that comment in Caroline Edgerton's letter about how Miss Julia killed somebody and then had trouble forgiving herself for having done it. This must have been what she was talking about."

Maddy uncurled herself from her pile of pillows and retrieved the letter. "This is the letter that was torn, remember? That's why we're missing the start of this sentence."

She looked around and we all nodded.

... know you were so very skilled with a knife—at least not when used in that way——but I was most distressed as well to read of how difficult it has been for you to forgive yourself for having killed him. I pray that your dreams will soon cease to be so disturbing. After all these years, can you not find it in your heart to forgive yourself? He certainly deserved to die.

"I guess that tea she had Hubbard brew didn't help all that much," Rebecca Jo said.

"And we still don't have any answers," Pat grumped.

Saturday, 14 March 1744

MORE AND MORE spring flowers dotted the roadsides as Hubbard, Miss Julia, and Ira headed farther south. Hubbard longed to press on at a rapid pace, as fast as Star could carry him, but Ira had still, almost a year after having left Harrisburg on the Susquehanna, not regained his full stamina. The yellow fever that ravaged his body had, despite Miss Julia's careful tending, left him a mere shadow of the man he had been before. Hubbard sometimes imagined he could see all of Ira's bones beneath the skin that hung slack and grayish after a day's ride, even at their moderate rate of speed.

Hubbard heard a "whoa" from behind him and turned in his saddle. Miss Julia was already dismounting by the time he reached her.

"Something is wrong. Flower has begun to limp badly." She ran her hand down the mare's near hind leg. "I noticed her gait seemed to be off a bit just after we forded that creek several miles back, but now it has become much worse."

Ira, who dismounted as seldom as possible, since remounting was still difficult for him, peered down at the mare. "Her hock seems to be swollen."

Hubbard could feel the heat in the joint the moment he touched it and went immediately to remove the saddle. "Poor girl. You don't need to carry this excess weight."

Neither Hubbard nor Ira, nor Miss Julia for that matter, could diagnose the reason for the problem, for there appeared to be no stone caught in her hoof, but they dared not press Flower to continue lest she go completely lame.

"The weather is fine, and this seems a pleasant enough place to stop for a day or two," Hubbard said after he and Star checked out the surrounding area. A small clear stream skittered nearby, and there was ample grazing in the small woodland meadow beside the creek, as well as a convenient thick stand of pines from which they could gather branches to soften their beds.

"This will be perfect," Miss Julia said.

Hubbard wondered how Miss Julia's elderly bones managed sleeping rough every night as they most often did, but she was never one to complain.

"I see some promising woodland plants." She lifted her gathering bag and walked away from the two men.

"Do not stray too far," Ira warned.

In answer, she hoisted her gathering knife from the sling she had fashioned for it at her waist, waved it in the air above her—the keen edge glittered in the sunlight—and disappeared behind a stand of close-growing saplings.

Hubbard smiled to himself. That knife of hers was so sharp, no wonder it gleamed. She had honed it herself just the evening before. It would take her little time to gather her plants. Unless she wandered too far afield searching them out. He checked himself. Miss Julia was far too canny to lose herself in the forest.

He started a fire, gathered water from the stream, and set the kettle on to boil, while Ira spread out a length of canvas, readying Miss Julia's tent for the night. The nights had been mild enough of late that Hubbard and Ira both had been content to sleep under the stars near the fire, but neither one of them felt it was quite proper for Miss Julia not to be covered by her own tent.

Flower discovered the stream on her own, and stood for a time in the middle of it, letting the cold water soothe her weary legs. Eventually Hubbard led her and the other horses to the far side of the meadow where they would be shaded from the unseasonably warm afternoon sun. He hated the thought of hobbling them, but he could not risk losing the horses.

After their evening meal, Hubbard spent some time finishing his carving of yet another small animal, this time a minuscule fox, for Miss Julia. She insisted on keeping every one of his carved offerings. "They take up almost no room in my pack, and they are light enough that Flower will never notice the weight of them."

Flower's leg improved slowly over the next few days, no doubt due to the poultices Miss Julia applied "to draw out the heat."

"I dare say we might be able to leave tomorrow," Ira said after inspecting the mare just as the sun was setting on the fourth day.

"We shall see," Miss Julia said, and stepped into the woods to relieve herself as she did each nighttime before crawling into her tent. Ira disappeared into the woods in the opposite direction. He had finally learned to undo his laces with but one hand and to pull his breeches down and back up again without his brother's help, although it did take him a powerful long time to accomplish the re-lacing.

Flower and Star were in the deep shadows of the trees at the far edge of the meadow, barely visible in the fast-fading light. Blaze, munching contentedly near Miss Julia's tent, raised his head toward the road and neighed softly.

Hubbard tensed. Within moments he heard a horse approaching. They had seen few signs of other travelers for the past few days, and though most of the people who passed them by were pleasant and generally happy to stop a bit to share the warmth of a fire or merely to talk of the condition of the wide rutted path they followed, there had been occasional surly sorts, who rode past them with nary an acknowledgment.

The man who now approached the fire was stocky, unhealthy-looking, and, as Hubbard soon learned, a man of few words. He stopped his horse when Hubbard rose, rifle in hand.

"Not much of a welcome."

Hubbard nodded. "Ride you alone?"

The man flicked his eyes from side to side. "As you see."

"You may share the fire to warm yourself a bit before you ride on." There was something about the man Hubbard did not like, but the responsibility of common courtesy determined his invitation. There was no need to extend the courtesy too far, however. The night was mild enough and the man could build his own fire farther along the road. Hubbard hoped Miss Julia would remain out of sight for a bit. "My evening meal is finished, and I have nothing to share."

Again, the man glanced quickly to one side, this time toward the tent. He nodded, more to himself, Hubbard thought, than as an acknowledgment of Hubbard's lukewarm invitation. Once he had dismounted, he tied the rein carelessly around a branch on a sturdy sapling.

The attack was so sudden, Hubbard had not a chance to defend himself. The man seemed to be settling down onto the ground, across the fire from Hubbard, but as Hubbard set down his weapon and sank to his own seat, the man launched himself straight across the fire and had Hubbard on his back and by the throat before Hubbard could react. Within seconds, Hubbard's vision blurred and seemed to grow dim, but not so dim he could not see the man draw a wicked blade and raise it overhead.

When the man's body collapsed, it took a moment for Hubbard's eye to focus, to see, just past the stranger's head, the avenging white-haired angel with her hands recoiling from the gathering knife she had plunged into the man's back.

2000

"WE'LL HAVE TO find something," Maddy said. "Somewhere, there's going to be a letter—"

"We already have a letter," Pat said, "and it was no help at all."

Maddy shot a quelling look at Pat. "A letter or another diary entry or something." She swiveled her head around, scanning the attic. "There still are a lot of trunks to finish."

"But we'd have to stop reading the diaries if we did that." Glaze turned back to me. "I bet Hubbard says something about it later. Maybe he just couldn't write about it while it was still so … so raw."

"It must have been awful." I looked back at what he had written. "I can see Miss Julia being upset, but Hubbard says he's still shivering about it."

"Of course he is." Maddy's voice rose. "He almost got killed in the process." She glared at us, as if we'd objected, although nobody had. "She saved his life. That meant he was in danger. Real danger."

Sadie laid a hand on her arm. "You needn't worry, dear. He survived to write about it."

"Maybe the tea helped them both," Amanda said.

"Maybe Maddy could use some," Rebecca Jo said.

Autumn 1744

EUNICE SURRATT ENDICOTT stared at Worthy for five or six heartbeats. "Surely you jest, my husband. You cannot think to leave the safety of this group." At the corner of her eye she saw Ellen, the youngest of her four living children, born sixteen months before on the trail, scrabbling too near the fire, but for once Eunice did not turn to the child. "Isabelle," she said from the side of her mouth, addressing her eight-year-old, "tend to your sister." She turned her attention back to her husband. "How can you hope we will survive without the protection of the group? We know nothing of this land."

Around them, the early morning mists of the Blue Mountains floated on errant breezes, looking like nothing so much as tormented souls writhing in the dark before dawn. Eunice shivered and pulled her shawl more tightly about her bony shoulders. They had been far too long in these mountains where the going was rough and the dampness invaded her bones.

"There will be enough of us," Worthy Endicott said. "Do you doubt that my brothers and I can defend ourselves? And you," he added as an afterthought.

Eunice kept her face carefully blank. Her husband's brothers were masters at the art of hunting. She did have to admit that. And they were equally good at eating. They displayed an inordinate amount of glee anytime they hauled fresh meat back into the camp. She was not afraid of starving. She was afraid, though, of what might become of her and the children should anything happen to Worthy.

Around her, she was acutely aware of the sounds of her children. She had been so terrified when that painter chased Willie Breeton several years ago. What if something like that happened to one of her children? She could not depend on another dead tree to fall. She could not depend on Worthy's brothers. Nor could she depend on Worthy's father, who had left the Russell wagon and joined the Endicotts soon after Worthy threw out the belongings of his four unruly brothers.

She would especially not enjoy being the only woman to feed and care for six grown men. Worthy's mother did not really count, for she had been addle-brained for years. No wonder, with the five of those boys to deal with through their years of growing up.

At least here in the midst of the large Martin clan, there were always other women for conversation, for borrowing small bits of herbs, for counseling and discussions when there was a sickness beyond Eunice's ability to deal with. If they left the group, she would be alone. Alone with six men, four children, and one old woman, yes, but that amounted to being alone indeed. Did her husband not understand that women needed other women?

Of course he did not.

Worthy turned away, the discussion ended as far as he was concerned. "I will tell Homer my decision when we stop for the evening."

"Husband," she laid a tentative hand on his massive arm, "I beg you to reconsider. Can you not wait five or six months until winter is over and we come closer to the land where we will finally settle?"

Underneath her fingers, she felt the muscles bunch. When he did not strike out immediately, she relaxed fractionally and lifted her hand slowly. As if unseen beings hiding in the mist decided to intervene on her behalf, a sudden squall of cold autumnal rain pelted through the clouds.

He pulled his jacket more tightly about him. "I will think on what you have said, Wife. It may be that this is not yet the time to leave. But leave we will, at some point."

Eunice knew better than to heave a prolonged sigh of relief. She was well aware that an unseemly show of victory would most likely make him change his mind again to what it had been before. "I am sure you know the best," she said, and scooped up Rufus, the younger of her two living sons who, at four, looked set to follow the tradition of his uncles in foolhardiness. "You must not go that close to the fire, my youngling." Her thoughts were not completely on her child, though. Her thoughts were on the man who carried her safety and that of her four children in an uncertain hand.

She needed to speak to her sisters-in-law. A lifetime of being responsible for young ones, however, had formed a strong habit in her. She thought quickly over the disposition of her children. Ellen was safe with Isabelle. Her oldest son, Jonathan, had run off somewhere, which left Rufus untended. Unwilling to trust the child this near a fire, she carried the squirming boy with her across the circle to the Russell wagon where her husband's two sisters bustled about, readying their possessions for the day's journey. "Good morrow to you, Sarah," she said to her favorite of the two. "And Charlotte. Might I have a word with both of you?"

"Only a quick one," Charlotte said. "Can you not see we need to be about our work?"

Eunice stifled the quick retort she would have liked to give. "Of course. I have work of my own, but I have something of great import to ask of you."

Sarah set her half-filled basket in the back of the Russell wagon. "What is it, Eunice?"

"Worthy has decided that he and his brothers, and I and the children, must leave and set off on our own."

Eunice saw Sarah's hands clench in response, but Sarah said nothing.

"As you know, that would leave me alone, without the company of any other women."

Charlotte cleared her throat. "You have Sarah's and my mother with you. Is she not company enough?"

"No, Good-sister. She is not enough, as you would well know should you bother to think about it. I spend my time caring for her, not conversing with her."

"When will you leave?" Sarah sounded as if she might be sorry to see Eunice go, and for that Eunice was grateful.

"Although I do not know when my husband plans to leave, I am fair certain it will be soon."

"Surely he would not leave with winter coming on," Sarah said.

Eunice considered this. "Most likely it will be in the spring. But no matter when it is, I wish to ask if you would bring your families along with us. I know, Sarah, that you would need to ask the Reverend. But you, Charlotte, could decide for yourself—and your daughters." Even Charlotte would be better than no other women in her household.

"I will talk with my husband," Sarah said carefully, "but I cannot agree that leaving is a good idea."

"Of course it is not a good idea," Charlotte said with some heat. "Worthy ever was hare-brained."

Eunice supposed she should defend her husband, but truly she agreed—for once—with Charlotte. If ever an idea was without merit, it was this one. She had not expected instant agreement from these two women. In truth, she had not expected agreement at all, but her disappointment was greater than she had anticipated.

As she returned to her own wagon to set about packing up the remains of the morning meal, she passed by the Surratt wagon. Geonette was nowhere to be seen. Of all the women except Sarah, Geonette was the one to whom Eunice felt the closest. She wondered briefly why she had not thought to ask Call and Geonette to break away from the group and accompany Worthy wherever he might be planning to go. But Eunice knew that Call and Worthy never saw the same side of any question. If Worthy said the day was bright, Call would find a storm cloud on the horizon. If Call said a man could be trusted, Worthy would attempt to lock up the wagon. Even the nine children—Geonette's children Nell and Edward and the other three, and Eunice's four—never spent time in each other's company if they could avoid it, even though their wagons frequently traveled one behind the other.

Eunice set her jaw. If she had to be alone, so be it. But she knew she would not enjoy the experience, whenever it might come.

2000

IDA HANDED VOLUME one to Maddy. "Top drawer, of course." She picked up the next book in the small stack. "Time to move on."

"No," Dee groaned. "Maddy needs some calming tea"—she grinned—"and my tummy's growling so hard I sound like a lion."

Another lion?

"Unh-uh," Pat said. "You sound like a tugboat."

What is a tukboat?

"Or a freight train," Maddy said.

What is a fraytrayn?

"Marmalade's hungry, too," I said without thinking, and then looked at Carol who shook her head.

She took a moment to explain to Marmalade about noisy things, before we all headed downstairs.

It was so warm down there I peeled off my fleece vest and draped it over the back of the wingback chair. In the kitchen, I slid my arms around Bob's waist and nuzzled my ear against his back. He turned and wrapped his arms around me. I could feel his four-day-old beard rasping gently against my hair. "We got hungry," I said.

"You aren't the only ones," Dave said. "We were just getting ready to pull out the food."

I looked at the remains of cookies, chips, and pretzels spread around the table. "Getting ready to? Looks like you've been eating all morning." Of course, they could have been using the pretzels as their poker chips.

"Those were just snacks," Ralph said from the other side of the table. "It's time for the main course."

"Sandwiches?" Ida inquired sweetly.

Her ever-lovin' husband grinned at her. "What else?"

"I'd better help." Bob unwrapped his arms. "What's that?"

"This?" I patted the mourning brooch of gray hair. "Something we found—well, Maddy found—upstairs."

Dave looked around Bob's shoulder. "Downright purty," he said. "Is it plastic?"

Pat shouldered him aside. "It's hair, silly. There's no plastic in the attic."

"Hair?"

"Don't sound so incredulous," I told him. "It's a mourning brooch."

Glaze held out her arm to show the white bracelet. Tom, I noticed, wasn't looking at the bracelet. He was looking at Glaze's face. *Ah,* I thought, *young love.* Or at least younger than some of us.

The men weren't too interested, so we didn't even offer to let them choose some of the men's rings that were upstairs in the box. I'd show them to Bob later. After everyone left. Whenever that was going to be. Once we were back on schedule—once the storm was gone and everybody had left—I was going to hustle Bob up to the attic and share all the wonderful things we hadn't told the men about.

"I know it's toasty warm down here, guys," I said, "but the attic's gotten kind of chilly."

Bob walked over to the bay window and looked through the curtain. "Maybe it's all this wind. Look." He pulled the curtain open all the way so we could see the trees swaying. "Must be just pulling the heat right out of there."

"I could open the damper a little bit more," Reebok offered. "That gets more heat going." His face brightened. "The fan would spin faster, too, so it'll push more heat your way."

"We can always take off some layers down here," Father John said.

Luckily, Dave's mouth was full of chips. Otherwise, I'm sure he would have given us some sort of one-liner.

"You're right," Doc said. "We don't need all these sweaters." Reebok headed into the living room, and everybody took off at least one sweater or sweatshirt or vest. Within moments, the kitchen looked like a consignment store during a super sale, with discarded clothes draped over every chair.

Dave spent most of lunch cracking jokes. Rather lame ones. He acted almost effervescent, as if a big weight had lifted off his shoulders. I noticed Pat look at him a couple of times as if she, too, wondered what was going on. Oh well, if it was something important, I was sure we'd find out about it eventually.

Or maybe not. No harm in asking, I thought. "What's going on, Dave? You seem awfully happy."

He paused, his sandwich halfway to his mouth. "Uh … nothing much. Just … just enjoying lunch."

Pat gave him another one of those looks, but he either didn't see it or else he ignored it.

"We finished the first volume of the Mary Frances diary," I said as I downed the last of my sandwich.

"If there'd been anything good," Dave said, "you would have told us about it, right?"

He didn't sound like he expected that would ever happen, and after his comment about the plastic, I was ready to shoo him out into the storm. Couldn't do that, though, since I liked Pat well enough.

"It rained a lot," Sadie said.

"And a bunch of people died," Rebecca Jo commented.

Reebok asked a few good questions. So did Henry and Doc, but the mood around the table was down somehow, except for Dave. I looked a query at Bob, who shrugged.

When we finally left the men after we'd finished our cleanup chores, I retrieved my fleece vest. Bob waylaid me at the foot of the stairs and whispered in my ear. "I think this inactivity is getting on everybody's nerves."

"So, go out and play in the yard. It was like a funeral around the table, and I sure don't want to go through that again this evening."

He tweaked my nose with the tip of his index finger. "Good idea.

Neither do I."

We women took a bathroom break and gathered once more in our circle.

Ida zipped up her hooded sweatshirt before she started reading. I felt fairly certain Reebok's damper-opening scheme would work eventually, but in the meantime we needed to protect ourselves.

Friday, 15 March 1745

In looking back over the first volume of this journal of mine, I find that I have been most lax about writing, for my last entry in that volume was a year in the past. I have not even recorded the wonderful growth of my son. John is now more than three years of age. I see my Hubbard in his face every time I look at the boy, although he must not look so much like his father to eyes other than my own loving ones, for no one has said aught.

I long for an end to this seemingly endless journey, and yet, now, while there is much that occupies Homer Martin with the details of traveling—although he truly seems to leave most of the decisions to his brother—I am left alone most of the time save late at night. When we have come to the end of our travels, what awaits me? When he and I and my son are confined to one small cabin, just the three of us, what will become of me?

Ida looked up, distress etched into the lines around her eyes, but she didn't say anything. What, after all, was there to say in the face of such despair?

Dee didn't hold back, though. "I cringe to think what she's going to have to go through when they get here to Martinsville."

"Most of the families back then were large—and several generations tended to live together." Maddy was in her educating mode, and I saw Ida roll her eyes. "The adults took care of the children until it was time for the youngsters to take care of their elderly parents."

"But Mary Frances didn't have anybody," Dee said. "Her mother was out of the picture, her dad was dead—"

"Her husband was missing," Pat said.

"And Homer was a total loss," Maddy added.

"The Stickneys are leaving," Ida said.

"No fair," Dee said. "You're looking ahead."

Ida looked like she was going to make some sort of smart aleck comeback, but instead she just went on reading.

This morning, as soon as we broke our fast, both the Stickney and the Everest families left our company, as they had warned us a week ago that they intended to do. They headed west along a trail that branched away from the one we follow. They have determined to go to Cullowhee, which is a settlement here in the colony of North Carolina. We learned of that small town from a tinker who bided with us a fortnight ago. He assured us that the people there are welcoming to newcomers, for there is much land available nearby. Arinda and Adah had both told me separately that there is a school, which was of great importance to the two of them.

There was much discussion at the time about whether or not we as an entire company should turn aside from this southerly route, but Homer Martin said he would never settle where the Brandts might so easily find us, particularly since the tinker seemed to serve as a town crier for Cullowhee, from whence he comes, and would be like to tell everyone he meets on his journeys about the large company that settled there at his invitation.

"Well," Carol said, "that answers our question about why the names of the Stickneys and the Everests never showed up in census records here in Georgia."

"Maybe we need to have a field trip to Cullowhee, North Carolina," Maddy said. "Isn't that a great name?"

"Don't we already have enough field trips to keep us busy?"

Maddy looked at Dee like she was crazy. "There's no such thing as too many field trips."

"The only one you've talked about is Brothersville," Sadie pointed out.

"Hephzibah," Dee corrected. "And all those trips to the Keagan

County records offices."

"And that town on the Susquehanna River," Pat reminded us. "To find the letter with twenty-two years worth of news."

"How could I have forgotten that one?" Sadie said.

Maddy pulled out a notebook from her pocket. "I think I ought to start making a list. All the places we need to go and all the things we need to research."

"Good idea," Dee told her. "Be sure you include this new trip to Cullowhee."

"I wonder if the town still exists," Glaze said.

I ran downstairs for my atlas. "Yep," I said a few minutes later. "There's even a university there."

"I wonder if it evolved from the school Arinda and Adah mentioned." Pat wasn't serious, I knew, but stranger things had happened.

I know not what Homer Martin seeks—only that the place must be secretive. I do know that he has no trace of knowledge about such a place, so we travel as blindly as if we were newborn kittens. Our path at the moment is still on fairly defined trails. Sometimes the men must clear fallen trees or cut ones that have grown between the wheel ruts, but there is clear evidence of others having travelled this way. Eventually, though, if what he seeks is to be truly hidden, we will have to embark across the wilderness and hide our steps.

This morning we passed with a great deal of difficulty through a narrow opening between large boulders and I saw that a tree had grown up through one of the cracks in the largest of the rocks. Its trunk, as it filled the opening, had grown twisted and bent, but the leaves at the top were the bright green of early springtime. I feel my life is as twisted as that tree trunk, and the only greenness to my life is that my son is here by my side.

How will my dear Hubbard ever find me? Why do I even continue to hope? If he does follow, it will be the graves of those we have lost that will mark our forward path.

"Graves," Maddy said. "Worse than breadcrumbs."

"They last longer," Charlie said.

It didn't sound like she was trying to be funny, which was a good thing, because I didn't think it was funny at all.

I am not surprised that the Stickneys left, for I saw the look of rage on Adah Stickney's face when Joel and Sanborn Endicott came perilously close to knocking young Uriah Stickney into the fire the night the tinker was here. I knew then without a doubt that she would talk her husband into leaving. Timothy Stickney was ever willing to bend to Adah's will, although Adah is, I have noticed, always careful to make it appear to be her husband who makes the choices, in rather the same way that Silas Martin is always sure to appear to defer to Homer Martin's proclamations.

Nor was I surprised to learn that Joseph and Arinda Everest would accompany the Stickneys. Adah and Arinda have long been fast friends, and their husbands seem to work well together. Throughout this journey the two wagons have always traveled close to each other.

I was surprised, however, that they took no other families with them. Had I the means to escape from Homer Martin, I would have gone with them willingly, if only I could have left some token to tell my husband that we had turned aside from the southerly trail.

The roughshod ways of the four young Endicott brothers grate on my nerves—and of everyone else in this company. I particularly detest Joel Endicott. He is ever upon my heels, and I feel his eyes upon me most evenings as we sit around the fire. I am careful always to stay within earshot of others in the company.

"Creepy." Dee ran her hands up and down along her arms. "It sounds like he was stalking her."

We all indulged in a collective shudder. "At least she's being careful," I said.

Ida studied the diary for a moment, turning it over in her hands, but keeping one gloved finger stuck inside to mark her place. "I sure hope we don't come across anything … any …"

I couldn't blame her for not wanting to name the dread. I felt it too.

"I wouldn't worry, Ida," Rebecca Jo said. "Mary Frances is smart. She'll stick close to the others."

"If anything like that happened," Glaze said, "I wonder if she'd even write about it."

"Of course she …" But then Rebecca Jo seemed to rethink what she'd been about to say. "I imagine she'd write around it, but we know her well enough to figure out what she was hinting at."

Like Ida, I hoped we never had to do any such interpreting.

I thought Sayrle was the problem one, but after I rejected his proposal, he has avoided me. Joel seems to have taken up the reins in that matter, even though he openly tries to court young Nell Surratt. I wish he had followed his brother's example of removing himself quickly from my path, but Joel has never approached me directly, so I have had no excuse to scorn his advances, yet he watches me constantly, and when he looks at me, my skin seems to crawl.

I wish the Endicotts had been the ones to leave rather than the Stickneys and the Everests, for I truly have enjoyed the company of Adah and Arinda through the years I have known them. Our quilting bees in Brandtburg were always a source of vast amusement, and I have spent many hours laughing in their company, in ways I have not laughed since I was forced to leave my husband. I wonder if I shall ever see those two women again. I wonder if I shall ever see my Hubbard. I wonder, shall I ever laugh again?

"I can't imagine the depths of that woman's despair," Carol said.

"I can."

We all looked at Sadie, but nobody seemed to know quite what to say. Losing her child. How did that compare to Mary Frances losing her husband? I wondered how long it had taken Sadie before she could laugh again, but I wasn't about to ask.

"Surely the Endicotts have to leave the company soon," my mom said. "If what you said is true, that they never made it here to Martinsville. And now it's just a couple of months before the Martins find this place, right?"

"Right," Sadie said. "But a lot can happen in a couple of months."

We heard a whoop from downstairs, followed by the slam of the front door. "Playtime," I explained.

"It's about time," Ida said. "They were getting on my nerves." She stood suddenly and rubbed her posterior. "Time for a diversion."

Esther found the next treasure—it was way happier than her Titanic hat.

1765

MARGARET DeWITT HAD already set her sights on Alonzo Hastings. He was the only man in the village who could keep her interest for any length of time. She knew there were more important considerations to the choosing of a husband besides just being interesting. Could he provide for her and the children they would have? Was he respected in the community? Alonzo was the oldest son, destined to inherit the Beechnut House Tavern, but Margaret was fair sure she could convince him otherwise. The house, yes. The business, no. But they would have to be married first. And before that he would have to discover another way to support a family. That could be a problem.

She fingered the letter that had been left on her doorstep that morning. Nicholas Foley, of course. She recognized the way he formed his letters. She felt disturbed by how much he mooned over her. Mother thought he would be a fine match, for he was not a drinker. But then, neither was Alonzo.

Both Margaret and her mother had had more than enough dealings with strong spirits and the devastation they caused. Had Father not sold most of their household treasures, and had not those proceeds all gone directly into the Beechnut House coffers in exchange for nightly doses of spiritous liquids?

No more. Mister Charles Hastings, Alonzo's father, could not live forever. Margaret could see the future, almost as if she had been a conjurer. Once Margaret was married to Alonzo, and as soon as the elder Mister Hastings died, Beechnut House would close its doors. She would not wish an early death on Alonzo's father, for he was a kind man, as well-lettered as his son, but neither would she grieve too much when his appointed time came.

All this, though, had nothing to do with the letter she held.

She broke the seal and noticed that once more there was no salutation, for he seemed unable to refer to her yet as 'dear.' That, at least, was a stroke of luck. She read the short note aloud to her mother. There were no secrets between the two of them.

I pray that this Note finds you well, Miss Margaret, and that your Mother continues in good Health. I leave early tomorrow Morn to journey up the Valley to offer my Help to Lucius and his Sons for another Barn raising.

May I hope that when I return we might enjoy a Walk together?

With fondest Hope, I remain,

Nicholas Foley

She toyed with the idea of throwing the letter away, as she had done with all the previous ones he had left for her, but this one—most likely because that walk he asked for might indicate that he was ready to ask her if he might expect a positive answer to his expectations—seemed portentous enough that she should not dispose of it. If he asked her directly, she could give him a definite—and most negative—answer. Keeping the note was a whim, and Margaret was not usually disposed toward whimsy, but this case seemed different somehow. She hid the letter with the muff her grandmother had given her for her sixteenth birthday.

2000

"NICHOLAS FOLEY," DEE mused as Esther passed the note around the circle. "Must be a forebear of our current Nick, but the Foleys never lived here in Beechnut House, did they?"

"Not that I know of," Sadie said. "But you know how things up here must have gotten shuffled around over the years."

"You can say that again."

Why would she do that, Widelap?

"Nick's going to want to be connected to this guy," I went on after Marmalade quieted down.

"Why so?" The question came from several women at once.

"Just a feeling. You know how he's got all those awards all over his office? I can see him framing this note as proof that his family comes from original Martinsville stock."

"But there's no date on here," Easton pointed out.

"Yeah," Maddy said, "but the paper looks really old. Maybe somebody died and one of the Hastings inherited all that person's papers."

"I have a simpler explanation," Rebecca Jo said.

"By all means, keep it simple, unlike what happens with some other people I know." Dee screwed up her face and ogled Maddy.

"Maybe this Margaret he mentions is the Margaret Hastings who lived here way back when. She was married to—Alonzo, wasn't it?" She referred her question to Sadie, who raised her palms along with her eyebrows. "I wonder why she kept it?"

"Oh come on, Rebecca Jo," Pat said. "Don't tell me you never kept any old love letters."

Rebecca Jo looked nonplussed for a moment. "The only love letter I ever got was from the man I married."

That shut Pat up.

"We'll have to show this to Nick," Dee continued, "and to Anita. He can frame it if he wants to, for all I care. It's not like it would be of any value to the museum."

Glaze looked up toward the windows. "He'll have to wait for the framing till the ice melts."

"I imagine it'll be a few days after that," Ida—always the practical one—said. "We're all going to be digging our way out of the spoiled food in our fridges."

"Yuck!" Easton sounded as disgusted at the thought as I felt.

"No need to worry about that right now," Sadie said. "We'll just deal with whatever comes when it gets here."

What is coming?

"Meanwhile, I'm ready to get back to Mary Frances. Ida, can you do the honors?"

What are onners, LooseLaces?

Carol bent to talk to Marmalade, while Ida slipped on gloves and picked up the journal, but before she could begin reading, Maddy interrupted. “Lucius and the barn raising.”

“Yeah,” said Dee, “what about it?”

“He said he was traveling up the valley. Does this mean for sure that Lucius is the one who founded Hastings?”

Carol wiggled her hands in that maybe-maybe-not gesture. “There was a Lucius Hastings who left Brandtburg in 1741. He was just a child at the time. I was surprised to see someone so young listed by name. We can’t be sure of this, though. Not unless Mary Frances will be kind enough to mention it in her diary.”

“We still have a ways to go,” Ida said. “We’re only at 1745, and Lucius couldn’t have founded Hastings until he was grown.”

She had a good point.

Thursday 18 April 1745

Three years ago this day I was married to my beloved Hubbard. Three years. Three long years without any indication that he still cares for me or for our marriage. I look at his son lying here asleep beside me and cannot—can not*—believe that the boy’s father is indifferent. Or worse. Surely I would feel somehow in the depths of my being if he had been killed. I cannot think of any other reason, though, why he might not have followed me. I refuse to think that his love for me has faltered. It would be better for me to think him dead.*

Ida coughed and reached for her handkerchief. No wonder she looked so distraught. I felt horrible enough about it—and I knew why Hubbard left her like that—but I couldn’t even begin to imagine how awful poor Mary Frances must have felt, not knowing about Ira’s missing arm or Hubbard’s injury or Ira’s bout with the yellow fever. “I think I would have gone nuts if I’d been in her place,” I said. “How did she ever keep her sanity?”

“You’ll see,” Ida said.

If it were not for my son, I would almost wish myself dead. I know that is a grievous sin, but life without my Hubbard—and with the man I am now bound to—is almost more than I can bear.

I didn't want to hear that. It's one thing to say *I think I'd die—*

Do not die!

Sorry Marmalade, I thought when she meowed ferociously, *I didn't mean that.* Even though I didn't understand what she was saying in cat language, this was proof that she reacted to stray thoughts of mine.

Thinking about death was one thing, but it was altogether different to act on such a thought. Still, could I have kept going if I'd been stuck with Homer Martin? I felt the bile rise in my throat, and swallowed hard.

Saturday 20 April 1745

If only the Stickneys and Everests had waited another five weeks, they could have continued with us and been shut of the Endicotts forever, and our company would not have been decreased by so many. Admittedly, most of those were but children, yet children grow and become ever more useful to the community as they do so. Worthy and Eunice Endicott left this morning with their entire family. Almost the entire family. His two sisters of course remain with us, Sarah Russell with her husband, and Charlotte and her daughters, who are dependent on Reverend Russell. Those reprehensible Endicott brothers are gone, though, for which I thank the Good Lord. I will never again have to endure Joel Endicott and his prying eyes or feel uncomfortable when Sayrle skirts around me.

"Well, good," Sadie said. "Joel's out of the picture."

What picture?

Carol explained while Ida took a final slug of her coffee. It must have been awfully cold by that point, but she didn't seem to mind.

I fear Robert Hastings is mightily disappointed, for Worthy Endicott took his father with him. Old Mister Chauncey Endicott has always brewed the best ale in the colonies, and Mister Hastings counted upon him to supply his public house, whenever and wherever it may be established. Mister Hastings even offered Mister Chauncey Endicott a place in the Hastings wagon, but Worthy Endicott forbade it—and seemed to enjoy the sense of power it must have given him to do so. There has ever been hard feelings between those two men.

Still, while I am sorry for Mister Hastings, I cannot bring myself to rue the departure of those disgraceful young men. And surely Mister Hastings will find another source for the spirits he needs.

I pity Eunice Endicott, for she will have no one, no woman, with her save her mother-in-law, who is I fear more of a burden than the sort of company a woman needs.

I find myself thinking often of Adah Stickney and Arinda Everest, wondering how they fare in Cullowhee. I hope they were welcomed there with open arms.

Friday, 19 April 1745

CHARLOTTE ELLIS REMAINED adamant. "I tell you again I will not go with you, Eunice. I am very well provisioned for, here with my sister Sarah and her husband. My daughters and I, and my four granddaughters." Charlotte noticed how Eunice tightened her lips at that, but she ignored her good-sister's expression. "We would not be best served by leaving." Charlotte would not blame her two daughters for not marrying, although she did occasionally wonder why at least one of them seemed to insist on breeding every year. She had tried moving her sleeping pallet in front of the opening to their wagon, but knew that she slept too soundly herself ever to feel the girls creeping out in the middle of the night.

Sarah looked up from the cauldron of stew that hung over the fire. "You know my family and I cannot leave, Eunice. The Reverend would not abandon his large flock to follow along with only the twelve of you."

Eunice pulled her shawl more tightly around her shoulders, nodded, and turned to leave. She stopped and, after a moment during which Charlotte wondered what Eunice was going to do—throw a fit? scream? cry?—she turned back. "I wish you well, my good-sisters, even though your hearts are hard." With that, she whisked around the far end of the Russell wagon.

"How dare she accuse us of being hard-hearted? Our brother should not even be thinking of leaving the company. Worthy is the one who is hard-hearted."

"Hush, Charlotte. I daresay she is frightened at the thought of leaving. Eunice faces an uncertain road ahead. Think of how hard we all worked together to survive the bitter hailstorm three years ago. Or the day the painter almost caught young Willy Breeton. She must remember such times as well and wonder how just those few men will be able to protect her and the children."

Charlotte looked around to be sure no other person was nearby. Just to be safe, she lowered her voice. "If the truth be known, I will be happy to see the last of those brothers of ours. A useless lot."

Sarah looked horrified, but did not disagree.

Charlotte studied the well-laid-out camp with some degree of satisfaction. Two days previously, Homer Martin had instructed that they would stay in this one place for at least a fortnight so that harnesses could be mended, horses could be tended to, and a supply of meat could be obtained and smoked. There had been a number of such intervals during the journey south, and Charlotte had been pleased to note that as each year folded into the next, the travelers became more and more adept at quickly setting up the most efficient way of grouping the wagons, placing the livestock, and arranging the cooking fires.

Sarah took a moment as if to recall what she had been about to say. "I would not be surprised if the Endicotts are back within a dozen days, before we leave here."

Charlotte scoffed. "You know full well that our brother Worthy would never admit to having made a mistake. He would not return even should they near starve."

"There are many signs that springtime is fully here. If they must leave," and Sarah shook her head sadly, "then this is perhaps the best time, for there will be time for them to plant and harvest before the next winter."

"Only if they settle nearby here," Charlotte said. "What if they continue traveling on through the summer?"

"They will not."

"Why seem you so sure of that?"

"I overheard Daniel and Joel talking some evenings back, after they returned from their last hunting trip. They said they had found a lake just three days ride from here."

Charlotte peered across the circle of wagons to where the Endicott wagon squatted. "A lake? Think you that is where they will go?"

"I cannot imagine that even our five pig-headed brothers would leave the safety of this group unless they had a destination in mind."

"Perhaps they will tell Homer Martin of their discovery," Charlotte mused. "We must needs find a lake or at least a river to settle near."

Sarah looked at her with disbelief writ large across her face. "If you think Worthy would give over his secret lake to Homer Martin, you have gone daft in the head, sister."

"Then perhaps we should mention it. If there is a lake nearby, would you not rather we had it for ourselves? Let Worthy and the others be the ones to go farther. I am ready to end this desolate journey. It has lasted far too long."

"I would not like to stand in your shoes if Worthy finds out you revealed his plans."

LATER THAT EVENING Charlotte approached Homer Martin's wagon, only to see him lying insensible beneath it, an empty ale flagon clutched to his breast as he snored loudly. She would have to wait until the morrow.

But that night Charlotte's newest granddaughter developed a nasty cough, and Charlotte was awake long enough that all thought of Worthy's nearby lake left her head.

Eunice sat upright on the first of the Endicott wagons as they left the next morning, refusing even to look at the companions she left behind.

Charlotte took no time to wish her brothers or Eunice well on the road ahead of them. She did glance out from under the covering of her wagon just in time to see Nell Surratt toss Joel's carved birds—or whatever they were meant to be—off into the grasses beyond the campfire as soon as the Endicott wagons disappeared from sight.

2000

"POOR EUNICE ENDICOTT," Melissa said. "Sounds like she had a hard row to hoe."

What is a rowtoohoh?

"It meant she had a tough time," Carol said, "like a farmer whose field is stony or full of weeds."

Thank you.

"I know that." Melissa sounded a bit querulous.

Carol pointed to Marmalade.

"Oh."

"So," Sadie said, "we've accounted for all the families except …" She looked a question at Carol.

She thought for a few seconds. "I guess the Fountains are the only other ones."

"And they seem to be lost forever." Maddy said.

"Maybe not." Rebecca Jo spread her arms wide. "Think of it! They could be hiding anywhere up here."

There is nobody hiding in the attic.

Ida held up the Mary Frances journal. "That's what this is for."

"Don't you wish we could find another one," Rebecca Jo said, "so we could get somebody else's point of view? But it might take a miracle to find one."

Pat looked around the attic. "That may be asking for too much."

"No such thing as too many field trips or too many journals," Maddy said.

"Or too many miracles," Sadie said, running her hands down the front of her bright purple sweatshirt. I wondered which of us had loaned it to her. Or, more likely, given it to her.

Wednesday, 1 May 1745

There has been little of interest to write about, which may account for the fact that this journal of mine has lain forgotten in the bottom of my clothing trunk for almost a fortnight. We all grow tired of this seemingly endless journey. We have settled into such a routine that we take the ordinary—and frequent—mishaps in stride. Even our evenings seem to be the same from one day to the next. There is always a story to be had from the elder members of the company, occasionally some brief games, and generally some music, for Alan Fountain found a replacement for his broken fiddle string in the last town through which we traveled.

Despite the evening's varied entertainments, I find myself wanting nothing so much as to curl myself around John's small body and sleep as soon as the sun sets. I find that if I am sound asleep well before Mister Martin comes into our wagon after his evening drinking, he tends to leave me thus—a blessed relief indeed—and as often as not crawls beneath the wagon to sleep there.

We are camped tonight near a promontory overlooking the wide river valley that Homer Martin tells us is to be our new home.

There was an audible gasp from everyone around the circle.

"They found it," Maddy said.

Found what?

"Well of course they did." Ida sounded grumpy. "How else would we have gotten Martinsville?"

Carol looked from one to the other and didn't say a word.

It is hard for me to imagine that we are almost at the end of our journey, yet I know that there will be much work ahead of us before we can build a town with all the necessary components so that our life in this new settlement may be one of peace and contentment. High rocky cliffs surround the valley. Mister Silas Martin assures us that the cliff far to the south of here is pierced by a gorge through which the river passes, but it is so narrow, no person could approach us from that direction. I can spy that river only occasionally, for there are few gaps in the multitude of trees. Although the land from the base of this cliff down to the river is steep, it seems to even out to the north, providing ample room for farming. Indeed the land here where we now rest for the night in a wide clearing is flat. If we fell the surrounding trees, this area could provide even more room for crops, so long as there is a convenient break in the cliff through which our men could reach the upper field. Silas assures us there is such a cleft to the south, near where the river leaves this valley. It is too steep and too narrow for our wagons, however, so tomorrow we must travel far to the north to find the pass. He says we should reach it within three days of travel, and Reverend Russell has stated that it would be right for us to stay at that gap for the Sabbath so we might enter into our new home valley at the beginning of a week. I do hope that Mister Russell's gap will be wide enough for a comfortable camping spot.

"Russell's Gap." Melissa's voice was filled with wonder. "There's where the name came from."

"As soon as I knew there was a Russell family in the group," Ida said, "I figured they were responsible for Russell's Gap—the town I mean. But it's so much fun to find it written here in her diary."

I enjoyed seeing the puzzle pieces fall into place, but even more so, seeing the animation on Ida's usually solemn face. She was like a totally different woman.

Next evening, 2 May

My youngest brother Able brought a good deal of merriment into the camp this afternoon as we forded a small but swift creek that Silas tells us runs off the cliff within half a mile of here and plunges straight into the valley toward which we journey. I still remember well the grumbling Able always does before the spring bath, but also know it is his voice I have heard rising merrily from down the stream while we women bathe out of sight. I find it hard to believe that in these four years on the trail, Able has grown so very tall. His voice has already dropped to a most impressive deep tone.

As we crossed this particular stream, he suddenly jumped into the water and began splashing about. He may be almost growing whiskers, but he does enjoy larking about. Rifle, Willy Breeton's gray dog, jumped in after him, and grabbed the tail of his shirt. That poor shirt was well tattered to begin with, and Able yelled—how did his voice ever get so loud?—as Rifle's teeth pulled off a large chunk of the shirt. When Rifle let go of the fabric and pounced again upon Able, apparently intending to pull him from the water, the loose half-shirt was swept downstream and out of sight.

Able looked forlorn for only a moment before his usual gleeful attitude reasserted itself. "I hereby christen this stream Garner Creek" he called in that powerful bellow of his, discernible even above the laughter of the men and women and the snorting of the horses as they pulled the wagons up the gentle slope on the far side.

When asked why he had jumped into the water, he replied that the river had given him enough of a scrubbing, so perhaps now he wouldn't have to endure another bath next spring. My sister Constance disabused him of that notion fast enough. She has ever been a believer in frequent bathing.

"Able sounds like a real corker," Sadie said.

"Able Garner. Garner Creek." Melissa looked at Carol. "What would you like to bet he was one of the ones who left Martinsville after he grew up to found the town of Garner Creek?"

Carol thought for a moment. "That could very well be. Wilbur, one of the two older brothers, wasn't in the running."

"What do you mean?" Melissa asked.

"He was the one Mary Frances described as being childlike, remember?"

"Now that you mention it, I do. Sort of."

"The oldest brother," Carol went on, "Nehemiah, would have been the one to inherit the family land, and of course Mary Frances and Constance, Able's two older sisters, were already married. Is there really a creek by that name, or is it just the name of the town?"

"Oh, there's a creek all right," Rebecca Jo said. "It still runs swift and true off the upper level and into the valley, just the way Silas described it. There's a magnificent waterfall."

"We've picnicked there," I said. "My kids loved to try to get through the pounding water to the cave etched out behind the waterfall."

"It's a great cave," Sadie said, "even though it's small. I've been in it." She looked up at our surprised faces. "About seventy years ago."

"I'll bet there's something in the Garner Creek town records that would tell us for sure," Maddy said, "but it definitely sounds like Able must have been the founder of the town."

"I know," Dee said with fake resignation, "one more field trip and one more research project for you and me in the dusty old archives."

"We'll have a blast, and you know it," Maddy said. "Keep going, Ida. What's next?"

We were visited this evening by a group of seven Indians who came with hawk feathers stuck in their long hair and game in their pouches. Mister Silas Martin has a facility for understanding them and for speaking in such a way, with many hand motions and facial expressions, that they apparently were able to understand him. Naturally, we offered them the hospitality of our evening meal, and there was much hilarity over some of our dishes that appeared to be totally unknown to them.

Silas has assured us that they offer no objection to our settling in the valley of the Mee-too-chee, which seems to be their name for the river. He was unable to discern the meaning of the word, but I think it is a lovely name indeed. There was a fine mist over the river this evening just before sunset, and a rainbow appeared as the sun sank below the forest canopy in back of us. This valley reminds me somewhat of the beauty of the Shaconage, the Land of Blue Smoke, which we journeyed through so many months ago.

Four of our women are heavy with child, and there is much speculation about whether the births will wait until we are settled.

Ida's voice faded away. Sadie broke the silence. "I wonder if those were the barn babies?"

"There were only three barn babies, though," Rebecca Jo said.

"Or so the town stories say."

"That means either one of the babies was born before they got here, or …" I didn't want to finish the sentence.

"Or one of them died," Ida said, and continued on the next page.

My sister Constance Breeton had to leave the fire circle well before it was time to retire, for the first of her birth pangs seemed to come upon her, although now she has settled and there is no more appearance of eminent birth. Her waters have not come forth, which is a good sign. I do hope the babe will wait until we have at least one shelter built, for I love my sister immensely and would not see her suffer as I did in a jouncing wagon.

Just a moment ago, the candle flame flickered, as if a gentle wind had entered the wagon, but I felt no breath of air. It is one of the Bay Berry candles Mister Breeton acquired several months ago in the small village of Rufus. Made from the waxy berries of a sturdy shrub, they give off the loveliest smell when they are extinguished, or as in this case, when the flame is disturbed by a wafting of the air. As I watched the tiny sweet-smelling wisp of smoke it released, I wondered whether my dear Hubbard is reading by candlelight at this very moment, safe and warm in his house in Brandtburg. Or might he be behind us on the trail, delayed by some unknown circumstance, but still true?

I fear that if he does follow, he may lose our tracks, for Mister Homer Martin has insisted that men trail behind the final wagon, erasing as much as possible any indication of our passing.

"Surely," Dee said, "you can't erase the marks of that many wagons and livestock so easily."

"What a shame," Rebecca Jo said. "Homer was downright fanatical about the Brandts, wasn't he?"

"I sure wish Hubbard and Ira would hurry up and get here," Maddy said to the room in general.

Pat shook her head. "They never made it here. Mary Frances wouldn't have stayed with Homer Martin, as much as she detested him.

Not if Hubbard had shown up to carry her away."

"You're forgetting she had a child," Sadie said. "Maybe she stayed because of her boy."

Thursday 2 May 1745 It has been more than four years since I saw my wife. I despair at times of ever seeing her, yet I somehow know that I will, even though I must hide myself from her sight. This rainy night we sleep in a wayside barn, abandoned some time ago. There was little hay, but the smell of it was enough to bring back a memory of my wedding night. How I wish I could send my love to Mary Frances on a sunbeam to light her way or a wisp of smoke to touch her cheek, a hummingbird to hover joyously in front of her or a rainbow to dance for her. I wish I could have stood with her months ago, when we passed through the mountains of blue smoke, the place the Indians we met called the Sha-co-na-gee. I think I have the word right. Did my wife love those same mountains when she traveled this way? Did they remind her—as they did me—of the northern mountains of our home, our former home, which the Abenaki call the Wabanahkik, the Dawn Land?

2 May 1745

HUBBARD MADE UP the softest bed of straw he could manage for Mother Julia and overlaid it with as deep a layer of softer hay as he could gather. Before he deposited one particular handful of hay on the makeshift bed, he raised it to his nose, instantly transporting himself back to Reverend Atherton's hayloft and the wonder of his wedding night. Hay would always reopen that memory for him. He was glad indeed that it had been only an ear and an eye he had lost, rather than his nose, for he would not give up this small pleasure.

It had taken him some time to collect every last wisp, for there had been but a sparse deposit of either on the floor of this abandoned barn they had found after slogging through a drizzling rain for most of the day. The rain had finally abated an hour or two before sunset, and soon after that, they had come upon this abandoned farmyard. The house was in poor repair, for a corner of the roof had caved in, but the back corner of the barn was still snug.

Their wool blankets, the ones Mother Julia had insisted they bring with them from Harrisburg, had been welcome indeed, not only today, but through most of their journey. Though they absorbed the rain, they seemed to maintain the body's heat within their folds.

The hard-packed dirt floor was a safe place to build a fire once all the straw and hay was swept up to make the bed, and the ample cracks at the roofline gave the smoke—and the hundreds of bats whom their entrance had disturbed—an easy exit.

Even on this warm early May evening, the fire was welcome indeed, not only for heating water and cooking a meal, but for drying both blankets and clothing. It gave, too, enough light so that Hubbard could read a bit to Miss Julia from the works of Alexander Pope, a practice that he had begun in the long months in Harrisburg when Miss Anna still lived and while Ira was recovering from the yellow fever. Now, Ira chose not to listen overmuch to the readings, but Hubbard could hear him on occasion chuckling from his bedroll.

Once the reading was dispensed with, Miss Julia turned to sleep, but Hubbard continued to sit beside the fire. The smoke rose straight to the roof, for there seemed not to be a breath of air stirring through the barn. On an impulse, he leaned forward and blew into the low flames, sending them dancing about merrily and causing the smoke to swirl upward. For an instant, he imagined that the small burst of extra light might wend its way to his wife, to his Mary Frances. He thought of her almost constantly, even after these four years of separation, but there were times, like now, when he felt an extra closeness to her that he could not explain, but could only treasure.

2000

"HE REALLY WAS something of a poet, wasn't he?" I laid Hubbard's journal on the cardboard table. "His next entry isn't until August."

"Wait," my mom said. "He just wrote that he wanted to send his love on a wisp of smoke. And what was it Mary Frances said? Something about the bayberry candle flickering?"

"You're right." Ida looked back at her last entry. "And they were both written on the same evening."

"They were connected, and they didn't even know it," Maddy said with a sigh.

"It could have been just a coincidence."

Leave it to Charlie to throw cold water on all our hopes.

"But I hope not," Easton said, and my opinion of her rose a fraction. A tiny fraction.

Wednesday, 15 May 1745

It always amuses me to see the way men absent themselves from any birth, which is just as well, as the women in our company would be scandalized should a man wish to remain nearby during a birthing. I must admit, in the pages of this private journal, that I longed to have my Hubbard with me when our John was born that first winter on the trail. I cannot believe he would have left me at such a time. Although I appreciated the way Sarah Russell laved my forehead with cool water, I would rather have had those cloths held by my Hubbard.

We now have three fine new babes in this community, two born within minutes of each other, and the third born a day later. They all look robust enough to survive. Louetta Tarkington Martin was delivered of a girl, whom she and Silas have named Louise.

Ida looked up, startled. "Louise Martin was Silas and Louetta's child? That's my ancestor, but I always thought she was the daughter of Homer and Mary Frances."

"Logical assumption, I suppose," Rebecca Jo said. "Most everybody here seems to have discounted Silas Martin."

Ida shook her head back and forth several times, and I had the feeling she was having a hard time assimilating this new information. "This is good news," she finally said. "I'd hate to think I was descended from Homer."

My sister and Willem chose to name their daughter Parley, since the first birth pang—false though it turned out to be—struck during our parley with the Indians a fortnight ago. It is as well that almost half our men rode ahead of the wagons, and began to clear the land for the barn that is now sheltering us. The rough-hewn walls were almost complete by the time our first wagon arrived, and the roof barely in place before Louetta's time came upon her. I was amused to see men scatter all up and down the hillside to sit on the various stumps they have not yet had time to remove.

The third child is a boy, born to Call and Geonette Black Surratt the day after the birth of the two girls. I do wonder at Geonette's sense of humor, for she insisted on calling the boy Barnard. I fear he is doomed to a lifetime of droll remarks about his name and his birthplace, but even now he has meaty fists and long thick legs. He was so large when born, that Geonette has sworn she will never be able to carry another child for he 'broke the walls of the tunnel coming through,' which is how she managed to describe the birth. How anyone can laugh like that so soon after such agony is beyond me, but Geonette was ever a strong woman.

There has been much laughter, and some consternation, caused by Willy Breeton's black and white dog, Lucky, who has for the last few days seemed to adopt little Parley as one of her own pups. She lies beside Parley's basket and will let no one except the immediate family approach the child.

"Lucky," Rebecca Jo said. "Wasn't that the dog that absconded with the turkey leg at the wedding?"

I loved the way these stories were all twining together.

Ida set the book down in her lap. She had a far-away look on her face that I couldn't identify. "We had a dog when I was a baby," she said. "Piney, her name was. She used to guard me like that."

"I imagine there've been a lot of dogs over the centuries in this town who've done the same thing," Rebecca Jo said.

"And probably a lot who couldn't care less," Pat said. "We had a dog for a while who would've let anybody pick up Norm when he was a baby. Could have been a kidnapper, and Fido wouldn't have cared."

"You named your dog Fido?" Dee shook her head.

"Believe me, we never came across another dog with that name.

Only ones in cartoons."

"You mean it was so trite it was unusual?" Maddy was obviously laughing at her, but luckily Pat didn't seem to take offense.

"Parley and Barnard," Carol said, shaking her head and getting back to the journal entry. "I'm not sure I believed you, Melissa, when you told me about those names while we were at *Azalea House*."

"I've always liked the name Parley," Melissa said, "but I sure do feel sorry for anyone named Barnard."

"Maybe with his … what did she say? His big fists?"

"Meaty fists," Maddy told Carol.

"Maybe he didn't need to be worried about his name. I can just see him fighting every other kid in town until he earned their respect."

Maddy made a derisive sound. "Or their fear."

"Do you know what this means?" There was something in Ida's voice that made all of us turn to look at her. "Since John Martin was the son of Hubbard Brandt—not of Homer Martin—and Louise was the daughter of Silas Martin and Louetta Tarkington, then that means …" She paused dramatically. "It means I'm the direct descendant—the only descendent—of the original Martin family." She paused again and spaced her words portentously. "Which means … I'm the one … who should be … the chair … of the town council."

The charged silence lasted only a few heartbeats before we erupted in cheers. I expected the men to join us momentarily, but there was no sound from down below.

Rebecca Jo rubbed her palm across the bottom half of her face. "Who's going to be brave enough to tell Clara?" Then she and Esther and Sadie—and I—began to laugh.

What is funny?

It wasn't really funny. I knew none of us wanted to be the one to tell her, but we—all of us—couldn't wait to break the news.

Carol just shook her head at us, obviously at a loss to understand.

We didn't try to explain.

When we finally settled down, I heard sounds coming from the front of the house, outside. We took turns standing on the footstool and looking out the high windows at the men, cavorting on what would have been a lawn and a bunch of flower beds if there hadn't been two feet of snow and ice covering everything. It was a bit of a challenge looking through the wavery leaded glass panes, but I warned everyone to pick just one of the panes and "get your eye really close to it."

Somewhere the men had found a football, but it was like watching an old-time movie, the jerky action as they slipped and slid around, sometimes staying on top of the ice, sometimes breaking through it with one leg while the other leg splayed to the side.

"They're going to want a boatload of hot chocolate," Pat said.

"Let Tom fix it for them," Glaze said. "He knows where everything is."

"And Reebok can help him," I said.

"What they're really going to need is a bunch of that Merchant's Gargling Oil," Rebecca Jo said. "Too bad there isn't any."

"Doc's there," Amanda pointed out. "He'll think of something."

"If not," Pat said, "your services might be needed."

"Nope." Amanda splayed out her hands, palms forward. "I'm on vacation."

June 1997

"THIS FEELS ALMOST like summer vacation." Charlie Ellis crammed her favorite pajamas into her suitcase on top of her flannel sheets. It was a good thing she'd decided to leave the packet of blackmail papers in the safe deposit box until she could decide what to do with them. That big a packet wouldn't have fit in either of her suitcases, stuffed as they were. Even the cardboard boxes she'd wheedled from the grocery store down the street were packed full. "No more classes, no more exams, no more studying ever again."

"Until we get jobs," Tricia said. "Then we'll have to buckle down."

"I wish …" Charlie sank down onto her bare mattress. Everything in the dorm room looked so bleak now. "I wish Mom and Dad could have been here for graduation."

"You said you weren't going to dwell on that," Tricia reminded her.

"You're right, but they would have been here for you, too, if …"

"If they hadn't died." Tricia's voice was flat.

Charlie gulped. She halfway appreciated Tricia for being so matter-of-fact. *I don't need to get all crybaby about this*, she thought. After all, she'd graduated, just like Mom and Dad had wanted for her. Still, sometimes she wished Tricia had been the kind of person Charlie could cry with. Tricia was an orphan, just like Charlie. Surely Tricia understood. Maybe, though, since Tricia's parents had died such a long time ago, maybe she didn't remember what it was like. Was that even possible?

Charlie shook her shoulders to shrug off her mood. Tricia had lived through it, and so would Charlie. "You never did tell me what your plans are from here on."

Tricia's lips thinned. "Don't have any, except to look for a job."

"I know. Me too. I floated a few resumés, but I haven't heard anything. Or, not anything positive. Right now, all I'm planning is to go home and check on the house. Joey moved out last week, but Mrs. Palmer said she and Mrs. Barker were going to go in and clean it for me. Joey was offered a job in Cincinnati, did I tell you that?"

"Several times."

"Sorry." Charlie leapt up from the bare bed and—careful to use her strong arm—hauled one of her suitcases over close to the door to join her pile of boxes. "I've been thinking. I'd like to go back to Martinsville. Maybe just for a visit, but I have some good memories from there. Maybe I could even find a job. It would be nice to live in a small town again." She paused. "I think. The house … my house"—she couldn't think of how to phrase it—"the Atlanta house is really way too big for me."

"Maybe you could rent it to me for a few months," Tricia said, fastening her second suitcase. "You know, until I can get a job. Then I can get a place near where I'll be working. I'd hate to move into an apartment downtown and find out I have to commute to Alpharetta or Sandy Springs or Doraville every day."

"What a great idea! That way I won't have to put it on the market right away. I really dread the thought of selling it." She grabbed a stray piece of paper from the trash can and scribbled a quick map and directions. Well, it wasn't quick. Finding Martinsville was not easy. It had taken Mom a long time to tell Charlie how to get there. "Here. If I move to Martinsville, you can come visit me."

"Not if I'm working every day. You don't get a lot of vacation time when you're new."

"I know that, but weekends? Martinsville isn't that far, just a few hours."

Tricia made a noncommittal sound.

"Don't worry, Tricia. We'll keep in touch. That's what friends do." She locked this suitcase and pocketed the key. "I won't let you slip away."

2000

"GOOD IDEA," IDA told Amanda. "No sense in letting anybody impose on your time."

"It's not just that," Amanda said. "When I do therapeutic massage, it really helps people relax if they're on my table. Here," she looked around her, "I'd have to have them stretch out on the living room floor, and that wouldn't be relaxing at all."

"You could let them lie on one of the beds," Easton suggested.

"No!" Amanda's response was immediate and vehement. "First of all, it's really hard on my back bending over that low. Second, it can give the wrong idea."

I had to agree. Not that I didn't trust any of the men here—well, Dave was a possible exception to that—but it made sense for Amanda to protect herself from innuendo as well.

"Makes sense," Ida said. "Now, I'd like to read some more."

"You just want to find out more about your ancestors," Dee said.

"Yeah? So?"

Dee spread her hands in apparent surrender. "Okay by me."

1 June 1745

The fields are, of necessity, small this first year, for the men have had to clear the land, dig out stumps, and plow before any sowing of seeds could be accomplished. The land is fertile indeed, so the clearing of persistent weeds will most likely be a constant struggle throughout the summer months, and it will require the effort of every member of the community. Some days it seems like a Sisyphean task, but I try to remember that we are slowly gaining ground rather than losing it.

"Sisyphean," Pat began.

Before she could continue, Maddy said, "Sisyphus was that Greek guy who was punished by the gods. He had to push a big boulder up a hill every day, and just when he got near the top, it would roll back down to the bottom."

"I know that," Pat said with a great deal of heat. "If you hadn't interrupted me, I was about to say their never-ending weeding was sort of like cleaning up this attic."

Maddy held up her hands in mock terror. "Sorry, sorry. I go into instructor-mode every once in a while."

"I know," Pat grumped.

Trying to defuse the situation, I said, "I wonder if she ever used such words around Homer."

"Of course not," Glaze said. "Homer wouldn't stand for having his ignorance highlighted."

"Maybe he knew what it meant," Amanda suggested.

Ida let out one of those explosive puffs of air. "Are you kidding? The man couldn't write. Why on earth would he try to improve his vocabulary?" Without waiting for an answer, she read on.

As soon as children can be trusted to tell the difference between a weed and a new stalk of barley, they will be set loose to tear out the weeds by their roots. We have determined that the children will be best suited for this, as they can rid a field of weeds without damaging the barley grains with their small, slight footprints. My John is still too young, which is perhaps just as well, for he would gleefully rip up every green shoot he could get his small fingers on. I pray he will grow more sense as he ages, yet I treasure his spirit.

"He sounds like quite a handful," Rebecca Jo said. "Sort of reminds me of Bob when he was a boy."

I laughed and threatened to tell Bob what she'd said.

"Oh, that wouldn't matter. He knows darn well he drove me crazy at times." She paused, and a smile spread across her face. "He turned out pretty well though, wouldn't you say?"

I would indeed, but before I could say so, Ida kept on with that entry.

We women have contributed all our gathering baskets to the endeavour, Jane Elizabeth more than most. While some prefer to knit of an evening, Jane Elizabeth knits only when she must. She is a basket-maker at heart. She has turned out a number of smaller-than-usual baskets for the younger children, who seem to delight in filling their containers with numerous weeds. Work that is done with a good heart—and one's very own basket—appears to take less time than work that is powered by resentment. My sister has written the child's name on each basket, making sure they understand the letters so they will recognize their own basket when it is in a pile. We do so need a schoolhouse here, but the food supply must come before we search for a schoolmaster. Who among our group, other than Constance, might be qualified? More of that later.

There has been a prodigious effort on the part of all the community, for we know our survival may be dependent on the success of these first fields. None of us wants to return to the leanness of the past two years. While we still will be thrifty with our foodstuffs, it will be a relief to see edibles growing both for us and for our livestock. Barley, oats, and corn are sown in the largest fields, with ample pulse already beginning to entwine the young cornstalks.

Ida lowered the book. "Pulse? What's pulse?"

"It means beans," Maddy explained. "You know, chickpeas, lentils, green beans. Any edible plant that will twine around a tall stalk-y crop like corn and help to keep the weeds down."

Ida studied Maddy for a few seconds. "Even for a writer, you're fairly helpful."

Maddy just laughed at her. "Happy to be of service."

The beans will grow strong here, I know, and I look forward to learning more about the possibilities of the cowpeas, with their pale outsides and black 'eyes,' for the ones we tasted when we were near to Roanoke in Virginia, were delicious, especially when cooked with a hock of ham, and we were assured they would grow well, supported by the corn.

"Do you think she's talking about black-eyed peas?"

I didn't even have to think about Dee's question. "Of course she is. What else could they be? It's nice to know they have a long heritage here."

Our precious flax seeds made a poor showing this year. Little wonder, for we brought them with us over the four-year trek, and despite our most careful wrapping of them, some were subjected to rain, which rotted the seeds. The harvesting and preparing of flax requires such intensive labour, I fear it is not the favorite activity of any of us, but we have great need of the fibers for the spinning of thread. Most of us wear clothing that is more patches than prime linen!

Fortunately, we are all in the same circumstance, so we none of us seem to notice it too much. I fear, though, that a traveler happening upon Martin's Village, as our small settlement is oft referred to, would think us poor indeed. The likelihood of a passing stranger is improbable, howsoever, so we need not fear.

"Martin's Village," Sadie said. "I think I like the sound of Martinsville better than separating it into two words."

"I agree," I said. "It flows better."

Yesterday evening Mister Silas Martin came to speak with

Homer Martin about building a schoolhouse. I was amused by the proposal, for I knew he was beginning early to try to persuade his brother of the need for a school, only because Silas now has a daughter who will be in need of one within the next five or six years. I hid my smiles, though, lest Homer Martin think I was mocking him. His inability to read is ever a sore point. He never refers to it, but I do believe he does not like anyone to know of his lack of knowledge. As if he could conceal it. Every woman in town is well aware, although the men seem not to be so concerned that their leader has such a deficiency.

I was fascinated to see how Silas made his brother think it was <u>his</u> idea to set aside a portion of land behind our cabin for the school. Now we must only attract a schoolmaster. That may take the entire span of the five years before young Louise is ready to benefit. If I know Louetta Tarkington Martin, though, she will not wait. She will have taught her girl the alphabet and numbers well before then.

"Okay." Ida put her ribbon bookmark in place and closed the book. "Time for another little break."

"Already?" Maddy sounded horrified.

"I'm not going to let my butt go to sleep just to satisfy your curiosity, Madeleine Ames. Anyway, this'll build suspense." She thumbed through the rest of the journal. "We want it to last, don't we?"

"There're two more volumes beyond this one," I reminded her.

"At least the last one is full, right to the last page," she said. "I looked through it while the rest of you were slogging through old letters."

A number of us asked the same question. "Did you read it?"

"That last entry is from 1800, eighteen years before she died, and no I didn't read it and wouldn't tell you what it said even if I had." She set the journal, the second volume, down on the packing crate table beside her chair. "You rest here awhile, Mary Frances, and we'll be back soon."

Amanda gawked. "You're talking to the journal?"

"Why not? It's been talking to us."

She was right.

I have been talking to you, too, but only ListenLady understands me.

Carol told us what Marmy had just said, and everybody laughed. Everybody except me. I felt sorry for my ignorance. How many times over the years we'd been together had Marmalade tried to tell me something? I picked her up and hugged her. "I'm sorry, Marmy. I'll take a class as soon as I can find one."

All you need to do is listen better.

Sadie stood and rubbed her posterior. "I've been wondering about that brass lamp over there, the one with the green shade." She headed in its direction just as a stray shaft of late afternoon sun peeked in through one of the wavery eyebrow windows. It set the glass dangles around the bottom of the shade to sparkling. Sadie shook the lamp gently and rainbows danced across the old desk it sat on. "Poor thing," she said. "It looks gap-toothed, doesn't it?"

Sure enough, I could see that a few of the dangles were missing. "That's probably why it's up here and not downstairs."

"It looks Victorian," Maddy said.

Pat humphed. She sounded a lot like Ida. "It looks ugly."

"That was the style back then," Maddy said.

"It's still as ugly as warmed-over sin."

"Not if you like that sort of thing."

"Do you?"

"Well," Maddy admitted, "not exactly." She gestured over her shoulder toward the ponderous armoire against the far wall. "You have to admit, though, these things have a certain charm to them."

"I don't have to admit any such thing," Pat said, as if the subject was closed.

Melissa stepped up to Sadie's side. "Has anybody looked in the desk?"

There was a general chorus of *nope*, *no,* and *not me.*

"I guess it's up to you," Rebecca Jo said.

Melissa opened the top drawer and drew out a thick leather-bound book. She opened it to the first page.

Veterinary Records
of Gideon Hoskins
1890 to 1919

"Look at this," she said. "You can tell the first two lines and the 1890 were written by the same hand, but 'to 1919' is in a different style of writing." She turned to the back of the book. "The last few pages are blank, but here's one final listing for 23 August 1919."

"I bet he died in 1919," Pat said. "And somebody filled in the date for him, maybe his wife."

"Or a son," Ida suggested.

"Or daughter," Sadie said.

"And then put the book back in the desk," Maddy said, "and never looked at it again. How sad."

"I wonder if he didn't have any children," Sadie mused, "or if he did and they just weren't interested in veterinary work."

"Why would you think that?"

"Think about it, Easton. Most sons back then went into the family business, following in their father's footsteps."

"Like that blacksmith and his sons," Maddy said.

"Or the Breeton's general store," Dee suggested.

"Wait a minute," I said. "If this man died in 1919, then he was probably Perry's father." I started to explain to Carol who Perry Hoskins was, but she remembered.

"His widow's the one you bought this house from."

"Right. And Perry certainly wasn't a veterinarian."

Melissa thumbed to a random page. "Looks like Gideon got paid with a lot of chickens and eggs, at least at first."

"There wasn't necessarily a lot of cash money—coins—back in the eighteen hundreds," Carol said.

"But remember the accounts list," Rebecca Jo said, "the one where Nancy whoever bought the organ for thirty-seven dollars? That was in 1910."

Melissa turned to another page, farther back. "It looks like everything was bartering at first, but then he started getting money, a dollar here"—she pointed—"and three dollars here, around the turn of the century." She flipped to the next page. "Ewww!"

Naturally, we all wanted to see. "Looks like his case notes as well," I said, marveling at the detail of the drawings that outlined precisely what his equine patient and its insides had looked like before and after surgery.

"Easton, dear," Sadie said, "run downstairs and ask Doc to come upstairs. I'm sure he'll be interested."

Tuesday, 12 March 1895

AMELIA STOCKWELL HOSKINS surveyed the pleasant front room of Beechnut House. She knew, as did everyone in town, that she and Young Gideon lived in a house that had originally been an inn and public house. She wished she knew the history of the place. Someone, somewhere along the line had decided the public house was no longer to be maintained. But who had that been? And why? She wondered occasionally if there might be old records of some sort in the attic, but the thought of wading through all that furniture and those innumerable trunks was almost more than she could bear. Amelia had more than enough chores to deal with on a daily basis without taking on such an impossible task.

She lifted the thick ledger book from the long drawer of the desk and opened it to her latest entries. Young Gideon had tended three foalings and two calvings over the past week, as well as treating a colicky mare, a cow's inflamed leg, and the swollen joints of a goat, for which he had been paid a total of seven dozens of eggs, nine bales of hay, two bushels of turnips—obviously left over from last autumn—and a hodgepodge of other vegetables, as well as two knives and one iron cook pot. Young Gideon could never say nay to whatever he was offered for his services, even the parched turnips. Perhaps if she soaked them long enough in salted water. She had no idea what she was going to do with yet another cook pot, either. Put it in the attic, she supposed. Surely someone, someday, would need an extra.

From the kitchen she heard Mother Eliza set one of the flatirons back onto the cast iron stove with a clang. She had a sudden, unbidden vision of scorched shirt, bloodied scissors, and a hidden grave, but quickly put those thoughts out of her mind.

From above her, she heard her three daughters singing some sort of nonsense song as they went about their simple morning chores. She laid a gentle hand on her stomach. She knew without a doubt that she was breeding again, although she had not yet told her husband, and she knew as well that this would be yet another girl. The three older girls would be a help to her in raising this one, but she hoped that the following child would be a boy, someone to follow in his father's footsteps.

She picked up the scribbled notes Gideon had left for her and entered yesterday's tallies, then pushed the ledger to the back of the desk top. Gideon would want to record his latest notes and drawings. She had, when they were first married, been appalled by his detailed sketches of torn muscles and swollen abdomens, of calves born deformed and foals born dead, but she had gradually, over the course of their marriage, gotten used to the depictions that he said were so important. "Some day," he told her, "our son will read through this and learn from it."

She cleaned her pen carefully, corked the inkwell, and rearranged it so the ink would not be tipped over accidentally when the girls ran through. They were always running, and she did not want any more damage to the desk than what it had already endured. The desk had been her father's, and she treasured it, even though, as it had passed down through the generations from her great-grandfather, it had borne the brunt of the years. She felt along the numerous scratches and gouges, imagining the rambunctiousness of the boys—and undoubtedly some girls as well—who had created such markings. Some day it would belong to her son, Gideon's son, if only the boy would be born. She already had a name chosen for him. Perry. Her great-grandfather's name and the name of her late brother, the only son of her father. Had he lived, this would have been his desk.

BEING THE ONLY veterinarian in Martinsville had its rewards and its problems, Gideon Hoskins thought, not for the first time. He trudged up the hill toward the Breeton's barn, where Clover, according to the youngest Breeton boy who had pounded on his front door just moments before, was having trouble with dropping a calf. The Breeton's cows, and horses too, kept Gideon in business, and young Dickie had made numerous runs to Beechnut House to summon the vet.

Ahead of him, the boy ran back toward his father, proud to have delivered the message so quickly. Gideon longed for a son to train, but he would not trade his three daughters. Rather, he hoped the next child would be a boy. Although Amelia had not said a word, Gideon recognized the signs. Her skin had a healthy flush to it, almost a bloom. And she felt more … he groped for the right word … more substantial in his arms. He would bide his time, though, for he knew she feared to announce the good news too early, lest she lose the child as she had lost two since the birth of their first daughter.

Grandfather Arthur Hoskins, Great-Grandfather Baxter Hoskins, Reuben Hastings, Alonzo Hastings. He thought back over the generations of men who had lived in Beechnut House, deliberately skipping his own father, whose name was better left unsaid, unthought-of. Alonzo's father had been Charles, who had come here to the valley with his father, Robert Hastings, the original innkeeper, and with Homer Martin, the town's revered founder.

He wondered idly as he approached the Breeton barn whether the well-respected Homer Martin might have been like Gideon's own father—seemingly respectable on the outside but hiding a rotten core. Before he could follow that train of thought, though, he heard an indignant bellow from Clover in the barn ahead of him, and hurried his footsteps.

"IT IS ONE of the new electric lamps," Mistress Breeton said several hours later as she pushed the ungainly contraption into Gideon's hands. "Well worth the price of saving our cow and delivering such a fine new calf. Samuel ordered it special through the store, and it came all the way from Savannah."

Gideon inspected it as best he could, which was not well at all, considering how Mistress Breeton had pressed it practically against his nose. The glass dangles tinkled. "I thank you. I am sure my wife will find great use of it."

He had heard of electricity, but it sounded to him like an idea that would never catch the fancy of anyone with a lick of sense. What could possibly be more dependable than lantern light? Or lovelier than candlelight?

AMELIA TURNED IT around and around on the desk, poking her finger into the gaps produced by several missing glass dangles. "What are we to do with this, Gideon?"

"It is an electric lamp."

"I know that. You already said so, but what is this wire supposed to attach to? And these prongs on the end of the wire—what are they for?"

"That, I know not," Gideon admitted. "But you must admit it is a lovely … uh … ornament?"

"I suppose Samuel Breeton never considered that there was no way to make it work since Martinsville has no such thing as e-lec-tri-city." The numerous syllables in the unusual word felt awkward in her mouth.

"You know Samuel. He always must have the latest invention."

She laughed and leaned her head against Gideon's shoulder. "Up to the attic with it. I do not need one more useless gewgaw to collect dust." Before he made it to the stairs, she added, "And take that iron cook pot with you, too."

2000

OF COURSE, DOC wasn't the only one who hotfooted it up to the attic. All the men poured into the space to see the veterinarian's journal. It had taken them awhile to get out of their playing-in-the-yard jackets and boots, but eventually they all made it up the stairs.

"He was quite an artist," Doc observed after paging through the journal for several minutes, "even early on, but he gets even better as the years go by. He sure does manage to get the details right."

Bob peered over his shoulder. "I didn't know you were an expert on cow guts, Nathan."

Doc waved a hand in dismissal. "Intestines are intestines. But a cow has a lot more of them than we do."

I glanced past Bob's arm and turned away. "A lot more."

"To say nothing of those extra stomachs," Henry put in.

"It's too bad he didn't have colored inks," Doc said. "But look how he's used shading to indicate this area."

"Gangrene, probably," Maddy said. When Doc looked surprised, she added, "Book research."

"Poisons, rotting bodies, shattered limbs," Ida said. "What else have you researched, Maddy?"

Maddy laughed. "Believe me, you don't want to know."

"Now that we're in the mood," Ralph said, "is anybody ready for a snack?"

We all groaned. "Just a suggestion," he said, and headed for the stairs. "I need some fuel after all that exercise."

"I'd love to take this with me," Doc said.

"Fine with me." I was almost sad to see the beautiful old book go, but he'd certainly appreciate it better than anyone else.

"We'll need it back for the museum someday," Maddy said, "so take good care of it."

"Of course."

ONCE THE MEN were all gone, Easton pulled the pair of ice skates from behind the cheval mirror—the ones I'd stuck back there to get them out of the way. "How do you think these got here?"

"The only ice skates I've ever seen are on TV," Ida said.

I'd seen them in Boston when I worked there right after college, but couldn't imagine why there'd be a pair here in Martinsville. "These are obviously really old," I said. "Look at how the leather's all cracked."

"Maybe that spell of cold years after the volcano went off," Pat suggested. "When was it, Carol? Surely everything would have frozen and people could have skated then."

"Krakatoa erupted in 1883," Carol told her, "and Tambora in 1816—the year without a summer. These skates could easily have come from either of those times."

"But there's hardly a flat place in this whole town," Rebecca Jo said. "Can you see people trying to ice skate down Beechnut Lane? As steep as it is, they'd end up in the river for sure."

"Then maybe they skated on the river," Carol said.

1816

LYDIA HASTINGS SHEFFIELD shivered uncontrollably. There was precious little fuel available, and the management of The Dakota had moved guests into the smallest rooms available in order to conserve what little heat there was.

Who could ever have predicted snow in July?

Still, she had to write a letter to accompany the skates she and Curtis had so delighted in purchasing. She ran her quivering fingers over the elegant heading on the creamy hotel stationery. *The Dakota, New York City*. So far, all she had written was the date, centered under the hotel name. She thought for a moment, added a few words below the date, and continued writing. The sooner she finished this, the sooner she could walk downstairs to the hotel dining room and request a pot of tea, not so much to drink as to wrap her fingers around the cup. Perhaps she could hug the teapot to her chest?

She had spent a great deal of time in the dining room lately.

Tuesday, 2 July 1816
(our year without a summer)

Mr Reuben Hastings
Beechnut House
Martinsville, Georgia

My dear brother,

The irrepressibility of youth! As I sit here at the window of the Dakota, wearing layers and layers of clothing despite the warmth of the blazing fire in the coal stove—in July no less!—I look out through the fogged pane and see scores of children skating in Central Park. Despite the bitter cold, their laughter is most infectious. They are so bundled up against the frigid temperatures, they appear to be nothing more than round parcels of gaily-colored wool, yet they skate with glorious abandon.

Curtis had come back to the Dakota an hour earlier than expected the previous Friday, so they had taken the time to step across the frozen streets into Central Park, where the laughter of the children drowned out the clatter of horse hooves and the rattle of the sleighs.

Astaline, had she lived, would have delighted in this gift.

Lydia sat for a moment and massaged her stiff fingers. Praying on the one hand that she could see Reuben's children cavorting in their new skates on the frozen Metoochie River when she and Curtis returned home—and on the other hand that this unearthly weather would abate by then and the skates would no longer be of use—she tried to clear her mind of freezing thoughts. That would have been easier to do if she had not been able to see a tiny cloud of mist huffing out of her mouth with each breath.

It is for this reason that I send these nine pairs of skates, which we purchased on Saturday when I went down to Fifth Avenue with my dear Curtis. I feel certain Rose and the twins will enjoy learning to navigate on them—and I know Franklin and his brothers will delight in it—although it may take them all the experience of a few tumbles before they learn how to stay on their feet. Tell them not to lose heart, for it is great fun when one is upright and flying over the ice. Rose's two boys must have grown immeasurably since last I saw them, so we chose larger skates than we thought they might have need of. I cannot wait to see Arthur and Zenus when we return home. Curtis and I have our own pairs of skates, which we tried last night for the first time (which is why you may have noted that my writing is a bit shaky today, as I sprained my wrist slightly upon falling for the third—or was it the fourth?—time). The largest pair is for you, of course, for I cannot imagine you would refuse to join your children and grandchildren in their fun. Do be careful, brother. You are so tall, you have much farther to fall than the young ones have.

I remain as always,

your loving sister,
Lydia Hastings Sheffield

Post script: I bought all the skates two sizes too large, as I am sure you have noticed. You will each need to wear extra socks to keep your toes from freezing. The clerk who served us is the one who suggested the larger sizes, and indeed a woman who came in just after us to purchase skates for her own children verified that such precaution is necessary.

Lydia blotted the ink, realizing as she did so that there was hardly any need, for the ink seemed to have already frozen onto the paper.

She tucked the letter into the package of skates and tied it closed, imagining all the while the delight of her nephews and nieces when the parcel arrived. If only their mother had not died ten years before. She took a breath. Had it really been that long? Lydia thought of Astaline so often and with so much affection. The world was a darker place without Astaline's bright smile.

2000

"SHOULD THESE GO in the museum?" Easton sounded doubtful.

"Of course they should," Maddy said at the same time Ida snorted, "No way. Just toss them."

The two women looked at each other, each of them registering disbelief.

"How can you possibly want those old things in our museum, Maddy?"

"Because they're old," Maddy said. "Isn't that the idea?" She held out her hands toward Easton, took the skates, and bundled them into the deep bottom drawer of the dresser. "The whole reason for a museum is to preserve the old stuff, so keep your mitts off these. We can always weed things out later, but once we throw something away, it'll be gone forever."

Sadie began to giggle. "Wouldn't it be wonderful if those belonged to the first"—she squiggled her fingers in air quotes—"Mrs. Martin."

"Or the horrible Charlotte Ellis." Pat looked at Charlie. "Sorry, but she was."

Charlie raised her hands. "I didn't say a thing."

"The only way to find out," Ida said, ignoring the byplay, "is to find some documentation." She headed toward one of the trunks we hadn't opened yet, lifted the lid, and began pawing around.

"Careful there," Carol said. "No telling what you'll find."

"I'm not going to waste my time on all this modern stuff." She shifted a stack of notebooks to the floor on one side of the trunk—they looked like grade school memorabilia. "I'm looking for something really old."

Easton scoffed. "You think you're just going to ask for something and it'll show up?"

"Won't find it unless I'm looking for it," Ida said. "Like this!" She held up an envelope that did look quite weathered.

It looks old to me.

"Weathered means old and worn out." Carol pointed at Marmy when I raised questioning eyebrows.

"That doesn't look like it was ever mailed," Rebecca Jo said.

Ida turned the envelope over several times. "I think you're right. No stamp, no postal marks—what were they called? Franks?"

Maddy handed her a pair of gloves, and she pulled out several pages covered in a dense script.

Thursday, 13 February 1812
North House
Martinsville Georgia

The Hoskins Brothers
Widow Parson's Boarding House
New Madrid

My dear brothers,

I write this with no hope of ever being able to send it to you. Three days ago my last monthly letter to you was returned by the post office with a note that the letter was "undeliverable." I had no idea what that meant, and when I questioned it, was told only that the letter had been sent back from what Miss Slocum called an intermediary office. I was unsure what that meant as well, but she said she had no other information for me. She is the new postmistress, someone who came to this town only recently, so you would not know her.

Yesterday when I read the newspaper, I learned why that letter was returned.

Your search for adventure, your trip to the West, has ended, for

I now know that the town of New Madrid no longer exists. All those lives lost. When the earthquake struck, did you have moments of terror, or was the end so swift you barely had time to comprehend what was going on? I pray that it was the latter. Although I have berated you both many times for having left Martinsville, you know I bear a sisterly devotion to each of you.

Ida looked at Carol. "Do you know anything about this?"

"I do," Maddy said when Carol shook her head.

Dee laughed. "Of course you do."

"There's a huge fault line that runs sort of under the Mississippi River. In 1812, there were three huge earthquakes and a lot of after-shocks. The first earthquake, not the one she mentions"—she tilted her head toward Ida's letter—"really messed up Memphis. That town of New Madrid was completely destroyed in the third one."

"Is—was—New Madrid near Memphis?" I was glad Glaze asked. I wondered about it, too.

"No. New Madrid was in Missouri, way north of Memphis. At that time it wasn't a state, though, which I guess is why her brothers' trip to *The West* was considered such an adventure. From all I've read, that area was still pretty rowdy."

We felt the tremors here, you know. I mentioned them in my previous letters—which you did not take the time to reply to. I wish you had told me of the earlier earthquakes, although perhaps it is as well you did not for I would have worried needlessly. There was naught I could have done, other than urge you to come home. I feel certain you would not have heeded my sisterly warnings. The first tremor struck on the night before my wedding to Baxter Hoskins, so I cannot forget that date. For the next two, I might not have recalled the dates precisely, but I did save the newspapers that reported on them, for I knew they had happened in the area where you were last known to reside.

The first, long before dawn on the morning of 16 December caused the church bell to ring and the walls of Beechnut House to tremble most violently. It was frightening enough to waken all the household.

We felt the second, in late January on the 23rd, and the third, the one last week on the 7th that completely destroyed your town.

I have little hope of your survival, dear brothers, and Baxter tells me that I am foolish even to entertain such a notion, but how I wish you might show up on my doorstep, appearing as precipitously as you left.

This is the last letter I shall write to you.

As always, I remain
Your loving sister,
Rose Hastings Hoskins

Dee let out a sigh that seemed to emanate from her toes. "Do you think there's any chance they survived?"

I hated to be pessimistic. "It sure doesn't sound like it. Otherwise, they would have found a way to contact Rose."

Glaze ran her hand through her hair. "Was the other letter in there, Ida?"

"What other letter?"

"The one she mentions, the one that was returned by the post office."

That, of course, set us all to sorting through the remainder of the trunk's numerous papers, but nothing from that time period showed up.

"You'd think she would have kept it," Pat grumped.

"Maybe she did," Maddy said as she ferried the letter to the white museum dresser, "but somebody else in the past almost two hundred years decided to clean house."

"I wonder if Mary Frances wrote about the earthquakes in her diary," Amanda sad. "She was still alive then, wasn't she?"

"She sure was," Ida said. "She died in 1818, remember? When she was ninety-three."

"I wonder if she wrote anything about the volcanoes or about Easton's ice skates," Sadie said.

"No," Ida said with finality. We gaped at her. "Remember? I told you her last journal entry was 1800, when she ran out of pages."

"Well," my mom said, "she may not have written about skating, but I bet she tried doing it."

"Could be," Ida said. "From everything I've heard, she was active right up almost until the end."

I could hear the admiration in her tone, but I had to add, "Somehow I doubt she would have been ice skating in her nineties."

"You never can tell," Sadie said. "Fred Astaire went skateboarding when he was seventy-eight."

"Yeah," said Ida, "and he broke his wrist doing it."

"So what? I bet he had fun! I'm well into my eighties and I'm still tap-dancing."

That was true. Our Tuesday night tap dance groups had been together for a number of years now. I lagged at the back of the class, and when we put on our little shows, I always made sure to be at the rear of the high school stage. Sadie was usually on the front row—not only because she was short, but because she could dance rings around the rest of us. As long as everybody in the audience had their eyes glued on her, I didn't have to worry about taking a wrong step.

A couple of years ago, Sadie had to have a minor operation on her foot and had to use a walker for a while. She'd shown up at dance class anyway. When we asked her how she was going to manage, she'd said, "So what if I have a walker? It has wheels."

Melissa sidled up close to Sadie. "Are you going to get some blue tap shoes now? Or maybe pink?"

Ida looked back at the diary, which she'd placed on the packing crate table. "We can deal with Sadie's shoe choices later. Time to keep reading."

"That's the shortest break in history," Glaze said.

"Yeah," Pat said. "I thought you didn't want your butt to go to sleep."

Ida shrugged and rubbed that portion of her anatomy. "You can keep rummaging if you want to, but I'm going to read some more."

But she didn't get to read. Doc came flying up the stairs. "Look what I found!"

Reebok was right behind him, and the rest of the men trailed upstairs in their wake.

They are very excited.

I guess their endless poker games didn't offer much excitement any more. It was a good thing Korsi had remained below. He might have gotten trampled if he'd been in the herd.

GrayGuy is smart enough to stay away from moving feet. And everyone is well, so he does not need to be here.

We all gathered in the central section, next to our circle of chairs, mainly because it was the only place in the attic with enough empty floor space, and Doc lifted the vet's ledger. His index finger, I could see, was stuck between a couple of pages near the back of the book. "I was glancing through this and I found something stuck between a stomach ulcer and a set of triplet calves."

Only a doctor would describe a book location that way.

"Do calves come in triplets?" Maddy sounded dubious.

"They're not very common, but it does happen. I'm not sure what their survival rate would have been a hundred years ago, but Gideon Hoskins' notes indicated that all three of these survived."

"Before we get into a lesson on animal husbandry," Ida said, as dry as ever, "are you going to show us what you found?"

"Oh, yeah, sure." He slid his hand farther into the book and extracted a photograph. "It's your porch swing, when it was brand new!"

I could see why he was so excited. I loved our swing. Bob and I sat there a lot in the evenings, especially in the spring and autumn.

"Is it dated?" Carol asked.

"Sure is. On the back. And the women in the picture are named. Will you do the honors, Bob?" He handed the picture to my husband, who grinned with delight. He loved the swing as much as I did.

My mother Eliza Russell Hoskins
and my new wife Amelia Stockwell Hoskins
trying the New Swing on 5 June 1890

"New Swing is capitalized and underlined," Bob added, handing the picture off to his mom, who stood on his left. "The whole thing's written in pencil."

"That's a good thing," Carol said. "Ink might have bled through and ruined the photo."

"Eighteen-ninety," I mused. "Could our swing possibly still be the original one?"

"I doubt it," Rebecca Jo said and handed the picture to Sadie. "It's been—what?—a hundred and ten years? I should think it would have worn out by now."

I thought about it. "The wood's really smooth, and there aren't too many scratches, but maybe you're right. Ours could be a replacement."

"Either that," Sadie said, "or all the rough spots got worn off by a hundred years of rear ends sitting there."

"Ours is a replacement," Bob said. I wondered why he sounded so sure. "Look at how it's suspended. The picture shows rope, but our swing is attached with chains."

Sadie studied the photo. "You're probably right, but the rope could have just worn out and they used chain to replace it." She passed the picture on to Dee, who turned it over and re-read the back.

"Amelia?" Dee's voice went up about an octave in her excitement. "Wasn't Amelia the name of the woman in that other photo? The one where she was looking back over her shoulder?"

Maddy rummaged a bit through the museum dresser and extracted the photo in question. "Does this look like the same handwriting?"

"A better question," Ida said, "would be, does it look like the same person?"

Dee compared the two and answered both questions at once. "Yep."

5 June 1890

YOUNG GIDEON HASTINGS felt thoroughly ill at ease facing the camera. The Breeton's Guernsey was bound to calve at any moment, and he hoped no one would come for him until after the photography session was completed. He knew the Breetons would summon him, for old Doctor Shaw's hands were becoming too infirm to deal with the difficult births, and Bess the Guernsey was not one to pop out any of her calves easily. He shifted his feet, and the swing beneath him jiggled.

"No, no, no," Morgan Martin said. "You will ruin the photograph if you move at all." Grumbling under his breath, Morgan muttered about the stupidity of posing on a swing, such a moveable swing.

Young Gideon knew the pride Morgan Martin felt over his new camera and his growing expertise with it. Had Young Gideon himself not felt the same sort of pride just last week when he had saved the leg of Lem Surratt's best goat after she became entwined in barbed wire? It made Young Gideon's blood fairly boil. Barbed wire might be cheaper by far than wooden fencing, but at least the animals were safe around wood. Young Gideon shifted again, and rubbed at his nose. Like all the Hoskins men, his was prodigious, and when it itched, he had to scratch it.

Amelia reached out and touched his arm. "We must be still, Husband," she said, and Young Gideon could hear the pride in her voice at being able to use that term when she spoke to him.

He hoped she would always feel such pride. He hoped he could be a good husband to her. His—he paused before even thinking of the man—his father, had never been good at showing Young Gideon what it was to be a good husband, other than to give a perfect example of how a man should not treat his wife. Thank goodness Father was up the valley this day on business. He would never have approved of the use of a camera at any rate. Such dire thoughts caused Young Gideon to straighten his shoulders in defiance, just as Morgan, whose head was muffled below the black cloth of the camera, pressed the relevant button.

"No, no, no," Morgan shouted, emerging so quickly from under the cloth that the camera wobbled dangerously on its tripod legs. "You moved! The photo will be ruined!" The heavy scar that covered most of his lower jaw had turned livid.

"Doctor Hoskins, come quick!" Dickie Breeton pounded up the path to the porch. "Bessie is in trouble! Papa says come fast or it might be too late."

Young Gideon sprang up from the swing and headed inside to retrieve his bag of supplies. Over his shoulder, as he ran along the path, he hollered, "I'd like a photograph of my mother and my wife on the new swing."

Before Morgan could complain yet again about the unsuitability of the seating, Eliza and Amelia settled themselves into place, grasped hands, and held extremely still, determined that this photograph would not be ruined by untimely movement.

2000

ONCE THE MEN left, and once Maddy had stowed the two photographs in the museum drawer, we settled ourselves again, and Ida went back to reading.

Monday, 24 June 1745

This day dawned bright and clear, a welcome relief from the dark clouds of the past four days. John is well over the sniveling nose and deep cough, for which I am glad indeed. He is the reason I have not written for a number of days, but now the worst is past, I am of much better cheer. There was a good omen this morning, for when we were fetching water from the river Louetta and I saw a fawn. It seemed a fair token that we may have a good harvest this year.

"This is where we came in," Ida said with wonder in her voice. "That was the first sentence I read."

"I sure am glad you recognized how Mary Frances did her writing," Pat said. "Otherwise we wouldn't know any of this backstory."

What is a bax torry?

I added my two cents' worth as Carol explained something to Marmalade. "I'm still amazed at how much easier you seem to be able to read it after all this practice."

Ida twisted her mouth. "I think a person can get used to pretty much anything if they just keep doing it."

This valley is replete with herbs aplenty. Louetta is far more versed in the usage of many of the plants than I, and I feel a regular dullard at times when she points out the leaves or flowers of some plant that has never before piqued my particular interest. This morning it was a plant she called heart's-ease. I told her she must jest, for I had always known it as 'tickle-my-fancy' but she said heart's ease was its name in the colony where she was raised. 'It does nothing, though, to ease the heart,' she told me. We spent a pleasant time discussing the colors of dye that could be extracted from it.

Ida held the diary at arm's length. "What on earth were they talking about?"

I spread my hands. "I never heard of anything called *tickle my fancy*."

Maddy, of course, was the one who clued us in. "It's a viola, what we usually call a Johnny-jump-up."

"You've got to be kidding," Melissa said. "Why ever did they call it *heart's ease* or, even worse, *tickle my fancy*?"

"I don't know about the tickle thing, but heart's ease goes back to the Middle Ages. People had some amazingly effective herbal remedies back then, but"—she grimaced—"they also used a lot of things that could kill you."

"I'd rather go to Doc Nathan," Rebecca Jo said. "When he prescribes something herbal, I know I can depend on it."

I couldn't help giggling. "And when you go to Doc's office, you get the comfort of Korsi. As long as you're sick."

Carol looked confused.

"We told you Korsi was Doc's office cat," I explained, "but what you'd have no way of knowing is that Korsi won't have anything to do with people who are healthy. If somebody with a problem walks in, though, he's right there leaning against their leg or putting a paw on their knee."

"I guess I'm glad he ignored me, then." She thought for a moment. "Korsi. That's an unusual name. Any story behind it?"

I grinned. "Oh yeah. He likes classical music, so his official name is Rimsky-Korsakov."

Ida waved her hand in dismissal. She wasn't much of a cat person.

I am in great curiosity about the dark cave openings on the far side of the Mee-too-chee. Several of the men have waded across upstream where the river is slightly wider and more shallow, and they tell us the caves seem to go forever back into the cliffs, although none of them was brave enough to venture far inside. Being men, they said the floor was too uneven for safety, which is why they did not go in. I imagine, however, that it was the sound of the bats that deterred them. Those flying creatures pour out each evening from the caves to my great delight, for they consume hundreds—thousands?—of the pesky mosquitoes which seem to have been born only to afflict us poor humans.

"Some things never change," Melissa said.

"Oh? You still have bats there?"

"That's right," Melissa said. "When you come back next summer you can see them."

"I hope the bats are okay through this weather," Amanda said. "Do they hibernate in the cold?"

Nobody seemed to know the answer to that, not even Maddy. "They must be hibernating," I said. "There aren't any bugs out for them to eat."

"One more thing for us to research," Dee said, and Maddy grinned, obviously in her element.

Tuesday 13 July 1745. I know we draw closer to my wife each day, despite how slowly we travel. I can not blame my brother or Mother Julia for our lack of speed, for I seem to grow weary each day and I find myself suggesting we stop well before dark. It leaves us more than ample time to prepare a sleeping site, and I often doze as my companions prepare the evening meal. I welcome my bedroll soon after we have eaten and find it almost a chore to stay awake long enough to write herein. Mother Julia plies me with teas, but I feel little improvement after her dosings.

"Something's wrong with him," Amanda said. "He's way too young. He shouldn't be running out of steam like that."

Today we saw more remnants left behind, ones that were identifiable as belonging to the Endicotts. I cannot imagine anyone whittling so poorly as Joel Endicott—his initials were on what I assume was meant to be the bottom of each figure. He seems not to have improved at all in the past years. Three small carvings of what were most likely intended to be birds lay beside our trail mid-morning, near where a rutted path headed toward the west, the ruts not nearly so deep as those that continued more directly to the south. I feel certain some two or three families left the Martin group. It could not have been my Mary Frances, for Calvin Garner her father has ever been a staunch follower of the Martin name. Despite the fact that he was buried long ago by the trail, I cannot see his wife—my mother-in-law—deviating from her husband's wishes.

"That must have been when the Endicotts headed toward Enders," Pat said.

"Which wasn't Enders until after they founded a town there," Glaze reminded her.

"This is all supposition," Carol insisted. "We don't have any kind of proof."

Maddy blew out a breath between tight lips. "It's proof enough for me."

"Why," Rebecca Jo asked, "do you suppose Joel Endicott left his carvings behind?"

"Because they were so awful," I said. "Isn't that obvious?"

"Take care," Carol warned me. "Few things about history are truly straightforward."

I looked again at Hubbard's words. Seemed pretty obvious to me.

"Isn't it funny that both these diaries," Glaze said, "are about looking for a home."

"Hubbard isn't looking for a home," Pat said. "He's looking for Mary Frances, and she's just getting hauled along for the ride by that … that monster, Homer Martin."

Glaze jutted out her chin.

She seldom argued with anything, and I was surprised to see her so adamant about this. "Don't you think Hubbard and Mary Frances each would have considered any place home if they'd been there together?"

We all looked around at each other, quieted by the forceful words of a newly-married woman. I hoped she'd still feel the same way six or seven years from now. Of course, looking at her right fingers caressing her wedding ring, I felt fairly sure she would. She and Tom were so well suited to each other.

Smellsweet and FishGiver like each other very much.

I know I'd feel at home anywhere with Bob.

And with me!

And with Marmalade.

Sadie had the house she'd shared with Wallace. Ida and Ralph had been married gosh only knows how long—thirty or forty years? But what about the younger ones? Maddy, I knew, had left her home in Atlanta to move here, and in doing so had gotten away from an overbearing mother. She seemed pretty happy to me, and I know she was close to Father John, her brother. Dee had fled Atlanta after a nasty divorce and was doing beautifully living with Rebecca Jo. Carol—well, Carol was only here temporarily, but she certainly seemed to be well-settled in Vermont. Charlie? Hmm. Martinsville had been her birthplace, but since she'd spent almost all of her school years elsewhere, did this really feel like home to her?

Saturday, June 7, 1997

"SINCE YOU'RE GOING to be renting my house," Charlie said, inspecting the bare dorm room to be sure she hadn't left anything behind, "why don't you follow me home now? Unless you have somewhere else to go first?"

Tricia shook her head. "I don't have anywhere in particular to go. Just as long as I end up in Atlanta."

"Great! So, you can go home with me, help me put the house in order, and I can wait until you're settled in, and then you'll be comfortable while I drive up to check out Martinsville."

"Fine with me."

"Once you get a job and find another place to live, I can put the house on the market. Sounds like perfect timing to me." She headed for the door. "Be right back. I want to call Mrs. Palmer and let her know we're both coming."

"You have to check in with your neighbor?"

"That way, if you pass me and show up first, she won't be startled."

Less than an hour later, Charlie felt relieved to finish loading her car and head out to what, she realized, was really the start of her new life. She looked at the scads of boxes and wondered how she'd managed to fit everything in. Just before she slipped behind the wheel, she gave Tricia a thumbs-up. "Can we stop for an early lunch? You know that place where we stopped last year when we went home for Thanksgiving?"

"It's a lot closer to here than to Atlanta. You just ate breakfast. How can you think about food already?"

Charlie widened her eyes comically. "I like to plan ahead."

"Fine with me," Tricia said, in an exact echo of her earlier comment.

"Anyway, then we can have a second lunch when we get home."

Tricia raised an eyebrow, but Charlie ignored her.

When she approached the diner, Charlie waved her hand out the window and pointed right, toward the parking lot. Her turn signal hadn't worked for the past month. One more thing to fix. She sighed. Maybe Mr. Palmer could help her with it when she got home.

Over meatloaf and mashed potatoes—cooked in a good old Southern style—Charlie chattered, the way she usually did. Tricia listened, the way she usually did.

"Maybe I should just drive directly to Martinsville," Charlie said.

"Why?"

"Why not? We're not that far from it." Charlie's eyes took on that unfocused look that always means somebody's remembering something. "Fishing in the Metoochie River with Mr. Masters was so much fun. I haven't thought much about him and Grandma Masters in years, but now that there's the possibility of seeing them again …" She didn't finish her sentence. "I'll only be gone a day or so, just long enough to take a look at some job possibilities, and then I could join you. Or you could come with me."

"No. I already told you I want to get started looking for a job as soon as I can."

Charlie sighed. "Okay." She mashed her potatoes into her meatloaf, stirred them around, and lifted a big forkful. "I'm really looking forward to seeing Martinsville again. I have some memories of it, but they're pretty hazy, except for the fishing. I remember the cliffs, too, and the hills—did I tell you it's a really hilly town?"

"Quite often."

Charlie munched on a mouthful, nodding her head. "Yeah," she finally said. "Going there is a good idea. I think that deep down I might be more of a small-town sort of person. I know there are a couple of bed and breakfast places around that area where I can stay. I doubt they're full up this time of year. I can scout out the job possibilities, in case I decide to move there permanently. Here." She rummaged around and took her house key off her key ring. "You take this. Tell Mrs. Palmer what we've arranged—I'm sure she'll ask you, and if she doesn't, then Mrs. Barker will."

"You'll need a key," Tricia said. "If I get an interview I don't want to have to stay in the house waiting for you to come home."

"Don't worry about that. We always hide a key under a planter on the back porch."

Tricia raised an eyebrow.

"The Palmers and Barkers keep an eye out. Not that anybody strange has ever shown up there."

When they were ready to leave, Charlie wanted to hug Tricia, but she knew Tricia wasn't the hugging kind. "I'll be turning off to head to Martinsville a few miles down the road. I guess I'll see you in a couple of days. You know how to get home from here?"

"Of course."

As they pulled out of the parking lot for the final leg of the trip, though, Charlie's engine gave a tremendous bellow, and something smashed into the underneath side of her hood. Steam or something—Charlie hoped it wasn't smoke—billowed. She piled out of her car.

Half the men in the diner came out to take a look.

"That engine's shot for good," one of them said.

"Yep. Blew a piston," said another.

"Cost a lot to rebuild it. Take a long time, too."

Charlie got more and more depressed listening to these horror stories as the men puttered dolefully beneath the dented hood. She did wonder if they knew what they were talking about. "I can't afford the time," she finally said. "What am I going to do?"

Eventually, the man who owned the diner took pity on her. He'd seen enough of Charlie in the past four years to feel like he knew her. He shooed the crowd away, slammed the hood, and told her, "There's Larry's Used Cars in the next town, just a couple of miles farther on. Honest enough chap. You can get a good deal. Tell him George sent you, and he'll cut you an even better one. For twenty dollars, I'll haul your car there so you can at least get some trade-in."

"But, it's not worth anything."

"He'll sell it for scrap."

Charlie looked at Tricia. "What do you think?"

"Sounds good to me. I'll drive you there. I have plenty of room, so we can move all your stuff into my car."

"Wish I could buy a bigger car." Charlie could feel her face lighten. "You're a great friend, Tricia."

"I can't leave the diner until after closing time," George said, "but I'll call Larry and tell him the make and model of what I'm bringing in. He'll give you the credit for it, and you can be on your way as soon as you sign the papers for the new car."

"I'm going to need a cheap one," Charlie said. "Can you warn him I'm on a tight budget?"

"Will do. Don't worry. He'll play fair with you." He and Charlie shook hands on the deal, and Charlie gave him a ten and two fives. Before he walked back inside, he asked, "What's your name, anyway?"

"Charlie. Charlie Ellis."

"Good enough. I'll tell Larry when I call him."

As the man disappeared into the diner, Tricia turned to Charlie. "Is that really the way people do business around here?"

"Sure. Why not?"

Tricia shrugged as she opened her trunk and they began to load everything from Charlie's dead car into Tricia's live one. "Fine with me."

2000
Matthew Olsen's House

THIS WAS SO much worse than before. After Hubbard fell off the cliff, and after he got out of the hospital, he'd been a handful. There had been a never-ending list of care-taking chores to be done every day, and every night, too.

At least she'd managed to get some sleep, though.

And during the days, knowing he would never speak again, she'd felt comfortable—well, relatively comfortable—leaving him with somebody like Ellen or Anita to be there just in case anything happened.

But here? Now? With Matthew and the Foleys breathing down her neck? Clara had gotten Anita's husband to move a twin bed downstairs into the room where Hubbard slept away most of the day and night. "I don't want to risk jostling him," she'd said, even though the truth was that she couldn't bear to be in the same bed with him. But she did need to hear him if something went wrong, didn't she? So she needed to be in the same room. In a separate bed.

Clara couldn't possibly relax. What if he woke up completely? What if he started to talk? What if he told somebody what he'd threatened to tell? What if he told somebody what she'd done?

What was she going to do?

Dave had said it didn't matter any more. "No more money stuff," he'd said. The payments to Charlotte Ellis were going to stop. She wasn't sure how he'd make that happen, but she had to trust Dave to straighten everything up. But Hubbard could still tell the town that he wasn't a Martin.

Wait! That didn't matter anymore. Dave said nobody would believe him.

But here she was, stuck, not knowing when anything was going to change.

She stared at Hubbard, as if her thoughts alone could somehow make something change. Maybe he would die. That would be the best thing.

Doctor Young had been no help whatsoever. He hadn't said

much of anything. *Maybe he'll regain a few words. Maybe he'll regain all his speech. But I wouldn't hold my breath waiting for it to happen. These things take time.*

What a load of blather. Hubbard was going to wake up, and he was going to say something about Mary Frances Martin, and everybody would hear about it.

And there was always the chance that people, even if it was only a few people, would believe him. Clara would never be able to hold her head up in Martinsville again. Especially not if he told anyone about what Clara had done up on the cliff.

The Attic

"MARY FRANCES WRITES just a couple of days later," Ida said, "on the sixteenth." Without waiting for any comments, she straightened her back and read.

Friday, 16 July 1745

Willy Breeton and Able Garner entertained us all around the communal fire in the central square last night as they regaled us with their exploits—somewhat exaggerated I would imagine—during their overnight sojourn as they were lost in the caves across the river.

"Bob and Tom were lost in the caves once when they were kids," I said, "but they didn't manage to get out on their own. Their friend Sam had to go in and lead them out." I looked at Easton. She was Sam's sister, and Sam had been murdered on Halloween night just a few years ago.

"Sam was the only one who's ever had the caves memorized." Easton raised her chin, as if daring us to contradict her.

Carol started to ask, "Was he—", but I shook my head slightly and she apparently took the hint and changed her question to "What else does Mary Frances say?"

Each of their mothers assumed yesterday that her son had lodged out of the sudden downpour of rain at his friend's house. Constance and Geonette are both gracious women who would have welcomed a stray to take shelter. It was only when the boys returned in the middle of the morning that anyone was even aware they had been gone. They had to wait until the sun came out and then followed the slight light toward the opening. There are, they said, deep and dangerous holes in the floors throughout the caves. When the heavy rainclouds darkened the cave, they dared not try to traverse it. I do hope my John will not be so fool-hardy as to try to emulate the older boys.

"Ha," Ida said. "Of course he would."

"It's a good thing for Martinsville that John didn't fall into any of those holes," Pat said.

"It's good thing for Mary Frances," I corrected her. "I can't imagine what she would have done if she'd lost her son."

"The town would have recovered from his loss," Ida said. "After all, there were plenty of men who could have led the the town council. It didn't have to be a Martin. It might have turned out a lot better that way, without any Martins around."

Pat blew a raspberry. "It could have turned out worse."

A Martinsville without Martins? I'd have to think about that. Of course, that would mean we wouldn't have Hubbard—and Clara—at the helm now. Hmmm. Maybe not such a bad idea after all. "It still would have been horrible for Mary Frances. Maybe the town would recover, but I'm not sure she would."

Homer Martin has long been set against the drawing up of a town charter, but Silas Martin finally convinced him that it was necessary. The decision balanced on whether or not to require a provision for 'an officer of the peace.' Homer Martin insisted that such a requirement was necessary. He proposed to fill the role himself, but was for once voted down by the other town leaders, who convinced him that he had more important roles to play. I do believe they are learning from Silas Martin how to maneuver that man.

"How about those beans," Ida said as she set the journal aside. "There's where Bob got his job."

Thursday, 1 August 1745

IRA BRANDT REINED in his horse well before they reached the edge of the precipice. He could see easily how the land dropped away, and the creek they had been following made a considerable roar as the water plunged over the edge. The resulting mist blew gently back into his face and felt refreshing after the heat of this day's ride.

They had lost the Martin trail some miles back, but Hubbard had said he was sure they would cross it soon. He was the one who had insisted that they veer slightly to the east.

Ira held up his stump and waited until Miss Julia rode up on one side of him and Hubbard on the other. Ira was concerned about Miss Julia. She looked pale and sat hunched over, her hands slack on the reins, her eyes downcast.

He turned and raised an inquisitive eyebrow at Hubbard, who seemed to read his mind.

"Miss Julia?" Hubbard leaned forward to look around Ira. "Would you be willing to stop here for the rest of the day?"

"If you think I am about to die on you, you can disabuse yourself of that notion, young man. I seem to have twisted my back the wrong way when I mounted after our midday meal, and it pains me some."

Ira studied her wan face. He imagined she was in dire distress to have admitted even this much.

Hubbard had already turned Star. "We can return to that small clearing we came through just a few minutes ago."

Ira could see the sense of that. This area was too open, and there might be strong evening breezes sweeping up from the tree-filled valley before them. Even now in midsummer, the nights were occasionally chilled. He waited for Miss Julia to trail behind Hubbard, and then he let Blaze follow at the rear.

Hubbard lifted Miss Julia down from Flower while Ira took her bedroll from behind the saddle and spread it out on a bed of soft moss beneath a wide-leaved tree, for which none of them had any name. They had seen many trees like it as they traveled south from Pennsylvania. Hubbard eased her onto the blanket, where she promptly curled onto her side, groaning softly. "I will be better after I rest a bit," she told them. "If I can get myself to relax, I will be able to stretch out my back a bit, and then we can be on our way."

"There is no hurry," Ira said, contradicting the feelings he had inside him. There was something about that valley … He met Hubbard's eyes and thought perhaps his brother felt the same way. The marks of the trail had been much fresher of late, as if the three of them were gradually overtaking the Martin party. Surely they could not be so far behind the Martins now as when they left Brandtburg four years ago.

The fact that they had lost the trail a short time ago surely indicated that the Martins had taken care to erase their tracks. They would have had no reason to do so unless they had been near their destination.

"I will get a fire started," Hubbard said, and Ira was glad his brother seemed to have the well-being of this motherly woman at heart, even more than his desire to find Mary Frances Garner. Mary Frances Garner Brandt, he amended. He took a moment to study his brother. With his face so disfigured, was Hubbard perhaps reluctant to find his wife, knowing that he would then have to turn around and search out another place to build a house for the three of them—Ira, Hubbard, and Miss Julia? Ira could not see how Mary Frances could possibly accept Hubbard looking as he did.

His thoughts surprised him. He had merely assumed that the three of them, he and Hubbard and Mother Julia, would stay in this southern land after they found the Martins. He had long given up the idea of returning to Brandtburg, but he could not say just when that decision had been made. He had, for some time—months, years perhaps—ceased to think about the children he had left behind. Four boys and … was it three girls? Yes. Three. They had been Felinda's children more than his.

Even when Hubbard informed him, after the amputation, of the death of little Samuel, Ira had been more concerned about his own missing arm than about his missing—dead—son.

He gazed at the surrounding trees, but did not see a single one of them. Although he had been oblivious to the death of one of his own children, why should he believe that Homer Martin would let him live—the man who had murdered Homer's wife? Surely Homer Martin still mourned his young bride.

Myra Sue Martin's death, Ira's indifference to his own child, Hubbard's face. Did Ira perhaps deserve to die?

His death, though, would pain both his brother and Miss Julia.

Perhaps it would be best if he saw the two of them safely into the Martin camp, wherever and whenever they found it, while he stayed hidden. It would not do to provoke another fight merely by his presence when the two of them, his brother and this woman Ira loved as a mother, were both innocent. Surely Homer Martin would not blame the two of them?

Yet, he felt a strong urge to see Homer Martin face to face. To beg his forgiveness.

"Brother," he called softly, so as not to disturb Miss Julia, "I would like to take a closer look at the valley yonder before the sun sets."

Hubbard nodded, intent on coaxing a spark from the leaves and kindling he had already arranged. "Will you return before dark?"

"Of course."

From her blanket, Miss Julia's voice admonished him. "Take some food with you just in case."

"In case of what?" Ira felt happy to hear her strong enough to boss him around, but her next words were so weak he could barely catch them.

"Just … in … case."

He knelt beside her and touched the side of her face softly. It seemed on the one hand a terrible presumption, but he could not resist. "Rest well. My brother will care for you."

She reached out one hand and laid it softly on the stump of his arm. "You are a good man at heart, Ira Brandt. I am glad you agreed to have me along with you on this adventure."

Ira felt himself blush like a beardless boy. "You have always been welcome, Mother Julia." As soon as he called her that, he regretted this further impertinence, but she did seem like a mother to him in so many ways.

She was obviously not offended. In fact, she smiled. He stroked her hair softly until she fell asleep. Hubbard had the fire well started by the time Ira stepped away from her.

"Why are you so set to explore like this, Ira?"

"When I saw that valley ahead of us, I felt that if I were journeying, looking for a new home, that valley might be what I would choose."

"I, too, feel that way," Hubbard said, "but do you think Homer Martin has as much sense as you and I have?"

"Mayhap not," Ira admitted, "but his brother Silas could probably talk him into it."

Hubbard was silent for a moment. "Silas is indeed a better man than Homer."

Ira touched Hubbard's shoulder softly. He had not slapped or punched Hubbard since that fateful day beside the fireplace in the small pine-roofed cabin. This was the first time since then that he had even touched his brother when Hubbard was anywhere close to a fire.

Hubbard must have felt his thoughts, for he looked up at Ira, the moveable side of his mouth turned up slightly. "Go safely, brother," Hubbard said. "Head north. I feel sure that is where a way into the valley will appear."

Ira slung his travel pouch back over his shoulder and mounted Blaze. "Nightfall. I will return before then."

Mindful of the trail that had veered to the right so many miles before, Ira ignored Hubbard's recommendation and turned to the south as soon as he was out of sight of the clearing and had passed through the ring of trees that bordered the valley.

He came across some rutted tracks, possibly from the Martin wagons, but they turned north. Surely Homer Martin, as stubborn as anyone Ira had ever known, would have maintained his insistence on traveling to the south. The Martin tracks would have to show up soon. Or he and Hubbard—and Miss Julia—could backtrack to the last place they had seen the tracks and search more carefully from there.

For now, though, Ira wanted to see more of this valley. Perhaps this would be a place where he and Hubbard could build a house, well away from the Martins. A house for the two of them and for Mother Julia.

He stayed well back from the edge of the cliff. One never knew when an edge might have been undercut by the wind or by water from the many small streams they forded. Blaze was a heavy-barreled horse, and Ira did not choose to risk placing that amount of weight on ground that might be unstable.

He saw the smoke long before he was close enough to see the village. Three, four, six streams of wispy smoke curled up from the valley ahead and to his left. He dismounted and dropped the reins so they dangled to the ground, knowing full well that Blaze would not stray. He removed his rifle from the loop that held it and stepped quietly toward the edge of the cliff. Before he could be seen by the people below, he dropped to his belly and inched his way forward until he could peer into the valley through tufts of summer grasses. There were a number of cleared fields—small but well tended—beginning to turn golden with crops of grain. To his left, beyond a large barn-like structure, he could glimpse a trail through the forest. So, the Martins had indeed come into this valley from the north.

He supposed it could have been some other group besides the Martins, but he could see foundations and half-built houses. There were areas to the north of the fields where trees had been cut, but the stumps had yet to be removed. This was a new village for certain. The timing of this settlement was too much of a coincidence to have involved two separate groups of travelers.

He was too far above the town to recognize any of the people he saw scurrying about, but near the barn-like structure was a building that seemed to be a church, with several grave mounds beside it, and a number of houses, as well as those foundations for more buildings. Near each house was a privy, a shed of some sort, and in most cases, a stable. It looked about the right size to accommodate the Martin clan, and he was reluctant to let himself be seen. Even if this were not the Martins, people in such a secluded valley might be wary of a stranger—a stranger with a rifle—suddenly appearing above them.

A slight breeze sprang up and carried the smell of smoke and of cooking food, causing his stomach to contract and complain. He wished now he had paid attention to Miss Julia's instruction. A bite of dried meat would go down well at the moment. The westerly sun behind him was already low enough for the cliff before him to have strewn a deep shadow into the valley. He would need to return soon to honor his promise to his brother and to Miss Julia. Mother Julia. There would be food waiting when he got there.

He slid himself back out of sight, glanced back to be sure Blaze was staying put. With his nose down in a patch of sweet tufted grass, Blaze was not likely to go anywhere. Ira headed farther south. There was ample time for him to explore a bit more. Perhaps he would find a place where he could descend the cliff safely. Then the three of them could come this way again on the morrow and approach the houses slowly.

They would need to advance carefully indeed. For four years, Ira had rued the anger with which he had attacked Homer Martin on the steps of Reverend Russell's church, and had rued even more that his shot had gone astray. How could he have killed an innocent woman, even if she was a Martin? He wondered now if the loss of his hand had been divine retribution. Still, it did not seem enough. Did not the Bible say an eye for an eye? How could the loss of half his arm compare to the loss of that woman's life?

Would the Martins see his sufferings—his life with only half an arm—as a kind of atonement? Would they let him live? Pray God there would be no explosion of anger when two Brandts came into the Martin valley. Pray God, too, that Miss Julia would be safe.

He shifted his canvas bag more comfortably over his shoulder and then decided to secure it over his head so he could dangle it at his back without the risk of dropping it. He made sure his rifle was primed and ready, just in case. He had not gone far when he saw that, perhaps a hundred yards ahead of him, the valley ended abruptly at another cliff that adjoined this one. He could see a break in that cliff far off where the river must pass through. If Homer—Silas—had chosen this place, he had chosen it well. Ira had a clear sight of the ground ahead of him. There was no break in the cliff. No way to approach the village from here. Hubbard had been right. The Martins must have come into the valley from the north.

Twilight was well advanced by now. It was time to retrieve Blaze, go back for an evening meal and a good night's rest—no sign of rain, fortunately. He found he was excited at the thought of telling his traveling companions that the end was in sight. In the morning they would proceed north to find their way into the valley. He sent up another brief prayer that Miss Julia—Mother Julia—might be well recovered by then. Perhaps he should insist she ride Blaze, whose gait was considerably steadier than that of Flower, Miss Julia's frisky little mare. Flower had a tendency to prance to one side at the slightest provocation, which must have pained Mother Julia each time it happened. Why had the woman not told them earlier that she had hurt her back?

He risked a peek over the edge but could see no people out and about now. He wondered why no one had begun to build a house in the large meadow below him, but then thought that a good precaution, since falling rocks from the cliff might endanger anyone directly below.

He imagined everyone gathered around their hearth fires, eating together, praying together, and then retiring for the night. With less concern over being seen, he hurried back toward Blaze.

When the edge of the cliff collapsed beneath his feet, he did not have time even to cry out. His rifle had already fallen from his hand long before his broken body lay quiet, surrounded by clods of dirt and tumbled boulders, one of which had come to rest on Ira's head.

HUBBARD LOOKED THROUGH the canopy of trees at the bright stars. Ira should have been back long ago, but knowing Ira, he had pushed himself to go just a bit farther. The valley had looked as though it stretched miles in each direction. Still, Hubbard had known at some deep level, almost in his very bones, even though they had lost the Martin's trail, that Mary Frances had traveled north. Perhaps Ira had found them?

He hoped his brother would have the sense not to approach any encampment so long after dark, or at least to call out well before getting close to any habitation.

Miss Julia, whose head rested on a mossy root that rose from the ground, called to him. "There is a horse coming. I hear its racing feet through the vibrations of the ground."

Hubbard craned his good ear forward, as if he might hear the rider sooner that way. Within moments, Blaze burst into the clearing and skidded to a halt beside the other two horses. The saddle was empty, the reins hanging loose. Ira's bedroll was still attached behind the saddle, but his rifle was gone from the loop that usually held it when he rode.

"Good boy," Hubbard soothed. "Where did you leave my brother?"

"He must have fallen off," Miss Julia said from her blanket behind him.

"I had already deduced the same," Hubbard said, "but it is good to have the confirmation of another set of eyes. Still," he tried to keep the worry out of his voice, "Ira is too good a horseman to fall unless there was some grave mishap."

She tried to raise herself up onto one elbow, but the effort was too much for her, and she sank back in abject misery. "You must go and try to find him. We heard no gunshot. Blaze must have been spooked by something to have run so fast for here."

At that moment a painter screamed in the distance, and all three horses shuffled nervously. "I will not leave you at the mercy of that creature." Hubbard could tell the painter was far away, and was behind them, in the direction from which they had come this morning, so Ira was likely not in danger from the big cat, even if he was lying injured somewhere, but painters could travel swiftly, and Miss Julia could not even stand, much less mount her horse in order to flee should the painter come closer. He added two more logs to the fire, knowing that a blazing fire would repel most predators.

"We will look for him in the morning. No doubt we will find him walking back toward us, cursing his ill fortune to have fallen from his horse." But within his heart, just as he knew Mary Frances had traveled north from here, he was certain his brother had not fallen from his horse. Blaze was too steady a mount to have allowed that to happen, and even one-armed, Ira was a fine horseman.

Hubbard's chest felt tight. He was torn between a need to protect Miss Julia, a need to find his brother, and a need simply to sit and rest. This was not like him. He felt as weak as a newborn kitten.

THE NEXT MORNING, Miss Julia still could not stand on her own. Hubbard helped her hobble away from the campsite and he turned his back while she struggled to relieve herself. Then he helped her limp back to her mossy pallet. "Ira will show up soon enough," he assured her, and sat beside her until she sank back into pain-ridden sleep. That evening when she woke, Hubbard stoked up the fire enough so that he could see to read to her from Master Ormsby's books. She and Miss Anna had enjoyed hearing him read in Harrisburg as they whiled away the evenings there. Now it was more a matter of trying to take her mind away from the spasms of pain that wrenched through her body.

Each day she urged him to leave her to search for Ira, but each day they heard the cry of the painter and Hubbard would not leave her unprotected.

It was another four days days before she recovered enough to mount a horse. Hubbard insisted that she ride upon Blaze, since the gelding had a gentle gait that would be easier on Miss Julia's back than the prancing that Flower tended to do.

"I cannot take his horse," Miss Julia objected.

"You may borrow it, though, until we find him."

They searched northward slowly along the rim of the valley without finding any trace of Ira. They came across the remnants of a wide trail, forged, Hubbard knew, by the wagons of the Martin train. He longed to race ahead, but knew that Miss Julia was in no condition to bear even a trot, much less a heavy gallop, so he held Star back to an easy walk. They camped at last one evening amongst the charred remains of a number of old campfires at the western end of a gap in the cliffs.

Surely this was the trail of the Martins and the Garners and the Breetons and all the others, but there still was no sign of Ira.

Hubbard built a small fire that evening and helped Miss Julia cook a simple meal. After they ate, he brewed a bit of tea they had bartered for weeks ago at the last town they passed through.

"Are you ready to tell me, truly, what you seek?"

Her words startled him, and some of the tea sloshed out of his carved wooden cup. He seated himself on the log beside her and gazed at the stars just beginning to show in the nearly-night sky. "You know we follow the trail of the Martin family."

She did not even dignify his statement with a response, only waited for him to go on.

Finally, as he had done two years before, he told Miss Julia, as he had told his brother, of all that had led to his marriage to Mary Frances Garner and all that had happened afterwards, up until the time he and Ira reached her house in Harrisburg on the Susquehanna. He left out nothing. When he spoke of how Ira had pushed him into the fire—"It was an accident," he assured her—she gasped slightly, but otherwise made no sound and hardly moved at all through the long hours of the story.

After he finished the tale, they sat without speaking for many minutes, the only sound the flitter of bat wings above their heads, the soft susurration of the fire as it died down into a heavy bed of coals, and the distant hooting of owls in the forest. "Thank you," she said, pushing herself up with only a little difficulty. "I like to know what I am getting into."

2000

AFTER WE COMPARED dates, and found that they had once again written on the same date, we did a sort of eenie meenie thing, and I started with Hubbard's entry. I really did like reading the two diaries in chronological sequence like this, although I couldn't help but wish they'd written more often.

Friday 2 August 1745. I am deeply concerned. Blaze returned to camp last night without my brother. I fear he may lie injured somewhere, but I cannot leave Miss Julia, for there is a painter close enough by to be a danger to her should she be left alone. She may be fierce, but with her back awry, she would be helpless.

"I wonder what happened to Miss Julia," I said.

"It sounds like she threw her back out of joint," Amanda said. "Too bad they didn't have a massage therapist or chiropractor along for the ride."

"What I wonder," Carol said, "is what happened to Ira."

"I'm afraid I have the answer," Ida said. "I looked ahead. You're not going to like this, Carol."

Carol pursed her lips. "Is he dead?"

"Of course he's dead," Easton said. "This was more than two

hundred years ago."

Sadie put a quelling hand on Easton's arm. "We know that." I thought Sadie sounded rather put out with Easton. "All these people are dead, but somehow, I can't help but feel that they're alive for us right now, here in the attic."

I do not see them.

"Knowing logically somebody died a long time ago," Carol said, "is different than finding out how it happened."

"And this man's daughter was Carol's ancestor," Dee added, sounding just as perturbed as Sadie.

Easton just leaned back and crossed her legs, but then I saw her look at Sadie, and she dropped her head, almost like a dog that's been reprimanded.

There are no dogs here.

Carol looked at Marmalade and cocked her head. She looked confused, but didn't say anything.

Friday, 2 August 1745

I am reluctant even to write this evening. There has been a great deal of death lately. Three had been long anticipated, for the people were elderly and each had been infirm for some time, but one of the deaths was completely unexpected.

This morning, Louetta Tarkington went foraging for herbs halfway down the meadow at the bottom of the cliff. She came upon the crushed body of a one-armed man who had apparently fallen yesterday or in the early hours of this morning.

"I'm so sorry, Carol," Ida said. "For Ira to have come so far and then not to make it."

"Sort of like Moses overlooking the promised land," Rebecca Jo said, "and not being allowed to enter it."

Easton opened her mouth, but Sadie gave her a look, and she shut it without speaking.

"I hope he didn't suffer." Carol had a catch in her voice.

There was a newly made rift in the cliff, and it was obvious from the boulders and rocks strewn around the man that he trod too close to the cliff edge and it collapsed beneath his weight. At least he seems to have died quickly,

"I guess he didn't." Carol sounded relieved. I could understand why.

... died quickly, Ida repeated, *for his head had been crushed beneath a large boulder. Willy Breeton told us the man was not there yesterday shortly after the noon meal, for Willy and Lucky had gone walking through the meadow then. Willy would certainly have noticed a body such as this one. Even if he missed seeing it, Lucky, his ever-inquisitive dog, would have nosed out something as obvious as a corps.*

"That's funny," Ida said. "She spells it c-o-r-p-s. I assume she means corpse, with an e?"

"That's the way it used to be spelled," Carol said. I could hear the impatience in her voice. "What else does she say?"

There was nothing in the canvas sack slung over the man's shoulder to indicate who he might be, nor did he have even a bit of food with him. There was no identifying mark on the rifle found some yards away from the poor man's body. Although several of the men climbed up to the top of the cliff, along the slanted path the fallen boulders had gouged out, they found evidence of where a horse had cropped the grass and deposited its manure, but no other people and alas, no horse either. I fear the poor beast will perish, for painters and wolves are abundant in this wild land.

"At least we know Blaze made it out safely," Maddy said.

"Huh?" I had no idea what she was talking about.

"You just read it a minute ago, Biscuit. Hubbard said Blaze returned to camp without Ira."

"Oh." I'd been so worried about the dead man, I hadn't thought about the horse.

I have never seen a horse.

Then again, I'd never known a horse personally.

I pray the painters in this valley will not take advantage of the cover afforded by so many lovely trees. I wonder sometimes about the wisdom of the town leaders to grant the appeal of Willy and MaryAnne Breeton to save large swaths of trees within the limits of the settlement, but I fully understand how children such as they can be so adamant, considering it was a tree that saved Willy's life when he was chased by that painter. Has it truly been almost four years ago? Mister Silas Martin was a well-spoken advocate for the children's plea.

We buried the man in the churchyard, close by the church. There are already too many graves there. A simple wooden cross marks his resting place. Upon it, Silas Martin carved the words "May this Unknown Man rest in Eternal Peace" and the date of his fall from the cliff.

Ida set the book aside on the small table next to her. "I hate reading things like this."

"I wonder if we could find his grave," Maddy said.

"Probably not," Dee said, "unless they replaced the wooden cross with some sort of headstone."

Maddy grimaced. "Yuck. Why does this all have to be so … so unfinished?"

"The good news," Sadie said, "is that now we know who saved the stands of old growth forest."

"I'm surprised anyone listened to them," Rebecca Jo said. "They were children."

"You're right," Maddy said. "That was a time when children

were supposed to be seen and not heard."

"Silas Martin stuck up for them," Sadie pointed out.

"The tree must have seemed like divine providence at the time." Dee sounded like she wasn't completely sure. "Maybe the townspeople had some superstitious belief that trees were instruments of God, or something like that?"

Ida snorted. "Well, they sure did cut down enough of God's instruments to build all their houses and barns and the church."

"Don't forget the outhouses," Maddy said. "I wonder how they justified that?"

Saturday, 3 August 1745

"IT IS FOR the glory of God," Homer intoned.

Silas eyed his brother skeptically. "You have never done anything in your life for the glory of God. What is your real reason?"

Homer stuck his lower jaw forward, and Silas recognized the all-too-familiar pugnacious glint in Homer's eyes. It would be well nigh impossible now to talk him out of anything.

Homer became somewhat less disagreeable as soon as Silas gave in to the idea of hand-carved doors on the church. "All you have to do," Homer told him, "is show our arrival, with the valley spread out below us."

"That is too poetic for you to have thought of it yourself, Brother."

Homer ignored him. "Like Moses and the parting of the Red Sea, the trees parted before me, leading me here, so I could bring our people into our own Promised Land.."

Silas thought of his own solitary journey, following the flight of that hummingbird, and of how long he had argued with Homer before he could convince him to take the northerly path he suggested. How could Homer possibly think of himself as a modern Moses?

"It should not take you long to complete them." Homer turned his back on his brother and walked away, confident that his word, as unchallenged leader of the Martin clan, would be obeyed, and the church doors would show the story of the founding of Martinsville. Or, at least,

Homer Martin's version of that story.

Silas wondered what Homer would say if Silas pointed out that it had been Joshua who did the leading back then. Moses himself had never set foot in the Promised Land.

2000

"I CAN'T STOP thinking about Ira dying like that," Carol said. "Do you think they ever figured out who he was?"

"How could they?" Rebecca Jo leaned forward in her chair. "He had no papers with him, at least not according to Mary Frances. Nothing but a knapsack and a rifle."

"And remember," I said, "the last time any of these people saw Ira Brandt, he had both his hands. They wouldn't have had any reason to connect this faceless, one-armed man with the Ira Brandt they'd known."

Glaze leaned back in her chair. "I wonder how he found this place to begin with."

"What do you mean?" Carol asked.

"Well, wouldn't you think that after four years, the trail the Martins left would have been grown over or covered up at least? And this valley's not easy to find under the best of conditions."

"You can say that again. If it hadn't been for Melissa's meticulous directions, I'd still be lost between here and Atlanta."

"And yet," Glaze went on, "there have been a lot of people who've found us over the years. Most of them … it seems like they were just meant to be here."

That was so true. Over the years, the ones who came to Martinsville, to all the towns in Keagan County, had been people who needed the refuge the valley offered. The peace.

Several of the more grisly murders that had occurred over the past few years came to mind, but I deliberately squashed those thoughts. The rest of the people here were good.

But then I thought of Hubbard Martin, lying next door unable to communicate, barely able to shuffle along. I couldn't believe he'd just fallen off the cliff. The man was an idiot, but he wasn't stupid. Surely somebody had pushed him—why was I not surprised about that? I detested the man, but I certainly wouldn't have wished this on anyone. Bob was, I knew, as frustrated as I. He and Reebok had interviewed practically everybody in town. I was fairly sure that even through the protracted idleness of this ice storm, their brain cells were still working away, sifting facts, reexamining who had said what.

"Biscuit?"

I jerked my head up, and everyone laughed. "I wasn't asleep," I said. "I was thinking."

Glaze said something that sounded like 'comatose'.

Toes? What are komah toes?

"You'd better be awake," Ida said. "It's your turn."

Friday 9 August 1745. Night overtook us before we could reach the settlement where my wife surely lives. We see smoke rising from a number of hearth fires well ahead of us. Had I been alone, I would have spurred Star into the village without thought for my own safety, but it is fortunate that Mother Julia's presence keeps me from such impetuous action. Nightfall is not the best time to approach if one is unknown. I pray that somehow my brother has found shelter in the town and that we will find him not only well, but reconciled with the Martins.

Although that is what I pray for, that is not what I expect. I fear my brother perished in the woods above us the night he did not return to our camp, and even now his body lies mouldering. Because I do not know for certain, I am unable to mourn him.

Tomorrow morning we will break our fast here—Miss Julia has found ample green stuffs along this meandering river. It is as well we have reached our goal, for our dried foods are nearly exhausted. I do not know what I will do when I enter the settlement on the morrow. I only know that I must keep the good side of my face averted lest my beloved wife recognize me.

Before I could commiserate with Hubbard Brandt, Charlie spoke up.

"Speaking of night overtaking us, is anybody else ready for supper?"

"Yes," Glaze said with a great deal of enthusiasm.

I wondered how much of it was due to hunger and how much to wanting to see that new husband of hers. Her next words left me with no doubt.

"Tom's going to want—I mean, all the men are going to want to hear about what all we've discovered."

Naturally, we razzed her a bit.

"Bring your gloves and the Hubbard journal," Ida told me. "Looks like the two of us are going to have to work through the meal."

The men were ready enough to eat—their outside playtime seemed to have helped ramp up their appetites. They'd lost the football. Somebody—Dave, probably—had thrown it out into Beechnut Lane, where it skittered down the steep incline. Maybe we'd find it someday. Unless it ended up out in the middle of the ice on the Metoochie.

"Why didn't you go after it?" Pat's question seemed a logical one to me.

"Too steep," her husband said. "We never would have made it back up the grade."

It sounded like a lame excuse to me. Then again, I wasn't the one outside slipping and sliding on that treacherous surface.

It didn't take us women long to get food ready and served. Once again, the table rang with conversation, made somehow more intimate by the candlelight. Once this storm was over, I planned to make candles a regular part of Bob's and my evening meal routine.

"Okay, women," Bob intoned from the end of the table, once we'd all taken a few bites, "we're all listening. What's been going on up there?"

I could tell we all wanted to talk at once, but Ida took the lead. "We finished the first volume, like we told you at lunch, and started on number two. We've lost three families. The Stickneys and the Everests left to settle in some town called Cullowhee."

"I know Cullowhee," Henry said. "A friend of mine from seminary teaches at Western Carolina University."

"Maybe we should send you on a field trip," Maddy said, "to see if you can find any of the Everests or Stickneys."

Henry gave one of those portentous pauses—you know, the kind where somebody takes a deep breath and you just know something big is going to come out? "My friend married a Marcia Everest. I was best man at their wedding."

I heard *small world* from about a dozen people, including me.

Bob cut through the ensuing chatter. "You said three families, Ida. Who were the other ones besides the Stickneys and the Everests?"

"The Endicotts, of course. We knew they hadn't ended up here in Martinsville—or at least we were fairly sure. Mary Frances said she missed Adah Stickney and Arinda Everest, but she seemed relieved to see the Endicotts go."

"That's when the Endicotts turned southwest and founded Enders." Dee looked around the table and a number of us agreed.

Naturally, Carol the historian had to mitigate Dee's bold statement. "It's certainly possible."

"And then," Ida said, and Dee started one of her usual drum rolls on the table, "they met up with a group of Indians who told them the name of this river—the Mee-too-chee. Within a week, they'd made it through Russell's Gap and all the way here."

"Good summary," Bob said, "but I want to hear it from the horse's mouth."

A horse? Where?

"You can hear it later," Carol said after she murmured something to Marmalade. "We don't dare get food spills on the diaries."

The men cleared the food away, but they just rinsed the dishes and stacked them in the sink. "We'll wash them later," Bob said. "I want to hear the rest of this story."

Ida and I took out our white gloves so we wouldn't risk damaging the fragile journals, and we brought the men completely up to date, straight from—as Bob said—the horse's mouth. It wasn't too late then, so we kept going.

Saturday 10 August 1745

I can barely suppress my excitement and my despair. My dear husband is alive. He is here in Martinsville. I am apparently the only one who recognized him when he rode into town this morning, he and a white-haired woman. I glimpsed him through a sur-

rounding crowd of men as he lifted the woman from her horse, and I took young John aside so that we would be within hearing range but not so close that he would see me. His face—according to the stories he told the men—was badly disfigured in a fire, the details of which I will not take the time or space to write, for I am sure that story was, if not false, then not completely true. Only suffice it to say that I know he has not told the entire story of how the accident happened. It is not like my Hubbard to stumble headfirst into a bed of coals. Had there not been all those people around, I would have run to him the moment he appeared. My husband, my husband!

How can anyone else not know him? I have wondered that all this day, but I see that no one seems to want to look directly at him, not surprising considering the extent of damage to his dear face. His voice does not sound at all the same, coming as it does from such a restricted opening. Many of the sounds of the words are distorted, his f's and his s's in particular. But I watched him as he went to the Hastings house, and he still walks with that distinctive slightly lop-sided gait that I would know and love anywhere. His hands still have the graceful lines I could never forget. His shoulders. His waist. My husband. Our son sleeps beside me as I write.

"It's probably your turn." Ida's eyes looked suspiciously bright, and I had to reach for my hankie before I could start reading.

"Same day," I said.

Saturday 10 August 1745. I saw her the moment we rode into the village. She was walking away from me, holding the hand of a small boy. A nephew perhaps? Her sister would be old enough now to be wed. Within moments we were approached by a number of the men of the town, and I was ever so grateful for the presence of Mother Julia. Her lack of response to my ravaged face seemed to help the men adjust quickly to it. I took a moment to explain that I had fallen into a fire and had been a long time recovering. I gave my name as John, for that is indeed my middle name, and introduced Miss Julia as 'my mother, Widow Julia Gilman.' Robert Hastings—he did not recognize me—offered us refreshment in his house, calling me 'Mister Gilman,' and I took no pains to correct him. Miss Julia was quickly taken in hand by Mistress Hastings. As we walked to their house, I felt the eyes of my wife watching me the entire way. Could I have been mistaken? If not, if she did indeed see me, it is clear that either she did not recognize me or she wants nothing to do with me now that my face is so not my own.

"Oh, no," Maddy said. "He thought John was her nephew."

"A logical assumption," Father John said. "He had no reason to believe she'd married somebody else."

"What did he say when he found out?"

I looked at the next entry. "No idea, Henry. He doesn't write anything else until the middle of October."

Sunday, 11 August 1745

HUBARD LOCATED MARY FRANCES within moments of walking into the church the next morning, that first Sunday he spent in the Martin's village. She stood at the front row of pews, five rows ahead of him, grasping the hand of a small child, a boy, who could not have been more than three or four years of age. He wondered if it was the same child he had seen her with yesterday. As he watched, the child turned his face up to Mary Frances and lifted his arms. She bent to pick him up, and as she did so, a lock of her curls fell forward from under her bonnet. She balanced the boy on one hip and swiped impatiently at her hair, just as he had seen her do dozens of times before. "Mama." The lad's piping voice carried over the rows of people between them before she could hush him. At that moment, as Hubbard's heart began to break, Reverend Anders Russell moved into the sanctuary and the congregation quieted.

Why should she not have married? He had not come for her in all these four years. No doubt she thought he had died in the fighting before the Martins left Brandtburg. No. That could not be, for she had tried to run to him as the Martins left the town. She had known then that he was alive. But he had not followed her. She could not have known how he had railed against the constraints that held him away from her. Now, with a child of her own, she would want no memory of him.

As the import of the situation hit him, he staggered slightly and had to adjust his stance lest he fall against the man who stood on his right. On his other side, Mother Julia quirked an eyebrow but said nothing. He shook his head slightly to indicate that all was well. But all was not well. If Mary Frances had married, as she must have to have had a child, he must never let her know that he still lived, for no woman could be married to two men. Let her believe he was dead. That would be kinder to her than true knowledge.

She must have believed him dead, or perhaps believed their marriage had not been valid. After all, no banns had been announced. There was no record of that marriage in any family Bible.

At Reverend Russell's direction the people began to seat themselves, and Hubbard could see the man who sat beside Mary Frances. His heart seemed to lurch within his chest. Homer Martin? How could she? That illiterate braggart?

As soon as the service ended, Hubbard hurried out the door, desperate to remove himself from his wife's presence. He hardly paused even to speak to the minister. "Fine sermon," was all he said, even though he had heard not a single word of it. Behind him Miss Julia—Mother Julia—veered off to speak with some of the women with whom she had so recently become acquainted. Hubbard knew she would question him later, and he could not imagine what he would say to her. For now, his only thought was to remain out of the sight of his wife. His former wife. His love. How could she?

2000

"DON'T DESPAIR, MADDY." Dee laid a comforting hand on Maddy's shoulder. "We'll get it all sorted out eventually."

"Just think," Pat said, "you might find a juicy murder in here, Maddy."

I knew she was trying to lighten the tone, but I thought her comment was in rather poor taste.

Dave laughed though. "Just think about it. You could bump off Hubbard Martin in one of your books."

Maddy scowled at him, obviously thinking his remark was inappropriate, but all she said was, "I want to get this Hubbard—Hubbard

Brandt—taken care of first."

"Let's let Ida read some more," my mom suggested. "Maybe there'll be some answers there."

Monday, 9 September 1745

He has avoided me in the four weeks since he appeared, although I have seen him watching me, trying to look as if he is not paying any particular attention, as I go about my daily rounds. He cannot be unaware of my supposed marriage to Homer Martin, for several times within his hearing people have addressed me as Mistress Martin. John is still at an age where he wants always to be with me so I know he has seen me with my son. With his son, although he would have no way of knowing that John is his own. If he feels I turned against him, that would explain why he has not spoken with me. Knowing him as I do, he most likely feels that he would be unacceptable to me with his face so ravaged by the fire scars, but how could he believe that? Does he not know that my love for him is as true as it was the night we were joined in holy marriage? More true now, perhaps, for I have John as a living, laughing, constant reminder of my love for my husband. How I long to clasp my arms around him and cradle his damaged head against my breast. I tried to approach him once when there were—as so seldom happens—no other people nearby, but he turned away from me as if the very look of me pained him. As well it might if he thinks I was willing to marry Mister Homer Martin. If only he knew the truth. I could not catch his eyes. His eye. I almost called out to him. It is as well I did not, for within moments, Charlotte Ellis appeared around the side of her house, and any chance I might have had to speak with him was gone.

I yearn, too, to know whether he bears other scars. I learned long ago that not all scars are visible. My heart has long been scarred by Mister Homer Martin, although no one in this village knows it. Does my blessed husband carry additional scars from the so-called accident? Or scars caused by his enforced separation from me? Would that I knew.

"Why doesn't he just tell her who he is?" Dave sounded disgusted.

"He can't," Pat told him. "She's got a kid, remember?"

"Like that would make a difference."

"It would," Ida said before Pat could explode. "He's protecting her."

He brought with him a woman he introduced as his mother, Mistress Julia Gilman, and he said only that his name was John, which it is, of course. His middle name. If the company here therefore assumes that he is John Gilman, it is not due to any untruth on his part. He was ever a man for whom truth was most important. Would that I knew the truth of how he came to be here with Widow Gilman.

I am surprised that none of the men of the town seem to recognize either Blaze or Star, but I suppose it has not occurred to any of them that a Brandt could have tracked us so far. Or that a Brandt would come so brazenly into our town. A third horse, a lovely little mare, trailed behind them on a lead as they came into town, carrying the bedrolls and supply sacks with dainty ease. I do wonder where Ira Brandt is, for he would never give up his prized gelding to a 'mere' woman such as Widow Gilman. I write that word with great indignation, for I know well how little respect Ira Brandt has for any woman.

"But he changed," Melissa said.

"Mary Frances didn't know that."

"I agree, Pat," Carol said, "but I wonder if she found out. I certainly hope so."

Miss Julia, as she has asked to be called, is truly a motherly woman and a fine healer, She has already assisted Louetta Tarkington in several childbirths. Louetta speaks most highly of her. Miss Julia inspired numerous scandalized looks when she rode into Martinsville full astride Ira Brandt's horse. She rode with perfect mod-

esty, for she had sewn her skirts so they form divided legs, almost like a man's breeches, but of course much more voluminous. I must say it looked eminently sensible to me, but Mistress Sarah Russell felt it incumbent on her as the minister's wife to chide Miss Julia.

No one has reported what went on in the conversation between the two women, but Miss Julia still wears her divided skirts and looks so at ease with them that I find myself wanting to emulate her. I wonder if she would share with me how she managed the design?

"They sound kind of like the bloomers that women started wearing"—Rebecca Jo looked at Sadie—"when? Around the late eighteen hundreds?"

Sadie ran her hands up and down her sweatpants-enclosed thighs. "Miss Julia was certainly ahead of her time."

"A century ahead." Bob sounded like he thoroughly approved. Of course he did.

I could just imagine how he and Miss Julia could have been great friends if Bob had lived back then. Or if she lived now. I would have loved to know her, too. "Do you think Miss Julia and Mary Frances ever got to know each other?"

"I hope so," Bob said. "They sound like they'd be well matched as friends. I wish I'd known them both." His echo of my thought was uncanny.

Several times Miss Julia has indicated a wish to speak with me, but always there have been others about. I am sure she would be able to answer many of my questions, but also I fear that she may have just as many questions for me. How could I ever answer her without endangering my son? I do not know, after all, how much she knows about me.

Hubbard may consider her to be like a mother to him, for he has told all the town how 'his mother' cared for him after his accident, but why would he bring her here? Why would he have come here, indeed, if he did not intend to speak with me? Might he have come to tell me that somehow our marriage was not true and that he has released me from his heart? Did he not love me with the intensity with which I loved him? Could that first marriage of mine have been somehow wrong? Perhaps it was not valid since there were no witnesses other than Mistress Atherton, the minister's wife. No banns were read for the Sundays before the ceremony nor was our marriage recorded in any family Bible. I do not know, and I will not rest easy until I receive answers to my questions.

"How sad that she doubted his love," Glaze said. "I hope they get this cleared up in a hurry."

Reebok leaned forward. "Are those bands she mentioned kind of like wedding bands? Wedding rings?"

"Banns," Carol said, and spelled it for him. For all of us. "They were an announcement in church, usually for two or three weeks in a row, that gave notice that two people were planning to marry."

"Gave 'em a chance to change their minds." Dave's loud guffaw brought a frown to Pat's face. No wonder. I sure wished the ice would hurry up and melt.

"Was the listing in the family Bible what made it official," Doc asked, "or was something else involved? Like a registration form or something?"

"There weren't any official rules," Carol said. "Not at that time."

"We're more likely to find out the answers," Ida said, "if all of you will quit interrupting me."

Miss Julia lodges with the Hastings family in their house on the corner, and there is no hope of a private conversation there!

I will not risk the reputation of my son, however. Should it ever be thought that he is a bastard and that his mother lives in sin, the town would scorn him as much as they do the offspring of those shameless Ellis girls. And they would see him that way, for everyone here witnessed my supposed wedding to Homer Martin on the day my father died, and should it be known that my marriage to Homer Martin was not true, then my sweet son, who is believed by all (except perhaps by Charlotte Ellis) to have been begotten by Homer on that wedding night, would be scorned and never allowed to become a leader of the men here.

Ida turned the page. "That's not quite the end of this entry, but I'd like to stop and absorb this for a while." She inserted the ribbon she'd been using as a bookmark.

"Makes me wish Glaze could get out her dowsing rods and find Ira's grave," I said.

Glaze rubbed her hands along her upper arms. "Maybe after the ice is gone."

"Do you think we could dig him up?" Maddy sounded entirely too excited about it.

I made a face. So did Ralph Peterson, but Bob looked interested. So did Reebok.

"Really," Maddy said. "Just think about it. Ira was missing his arm, so if we found a skeleton with only one arm bone, it would be proof. Right?"

I caught a look on Reebok's face that I couldn't interpret. He patted his shirt pocket, but then he saw me looking at him and dropped his hand. What on earth was that about?

"I'm not sure that's a good enough reason to disturb a grave," Easton said.

Maddy stuck out her lower lip. "I kind of doubt Ira would mind by this point."

"He might even want to have a real headstone with his name on it."

I gawped at Easton. Was she being sensitive for a change?

"What I'd like to know," Reebok said, "is how this all ends."

Dee tapped the table. "Patience, Reebok, patience. We still have two more volumes."

Ida rested the journal in her lap and folded her hands on top of it. "Her sentences always seem to get so involved."

"That's for sure," Dee said. "Nobody writes like that nowadays."

I thought about my own occasionally long-winded journal, but decided not to contradict Dave's statement. "She's talking about the Miss Julia that Caroline what's-her-name wrote to. The one who lodged with the Hastings family. Right, Maddy?"

But Maddy had already headed for the stairs to retrieve the letter from the museum drawer.

After she read it to all of us, the men were noticeably impressed with the way we were tying all these loose ends together.

What loose ends? I would like to play with them.

I couldn't stop yawning. "I hate to call it a night, everybody, but I'm tuckered out."

My mom looked relieved. "Good idea, Biscuit." She turned to Dad. "Shall we?"

"Not until we men get this mess cleaned up."

I took a few seconds to instruct the fellas about where to put the big soup pot. It was so tall, there wasn't much room for it on the pantry shelves, so it just lived on the back burner of the stove.

Bob gave me a funny look, and I gave him an apologetic grimace. Of course he knew where the pot went. I was getting as bad as Clara, telling everybody what to do and how to do it.

Luckily, we didn't have to wait too long for the cleaning up. They were amazingly efficient. That was what came of lots of practice. I did wonder if Ralph and Dave would continue to help with dishes once they were back on their own territories. All this practice shouldn't go to waste.

Matthew Olsen's House

CLARA MADE HER excuses early. "I really need to get back to Hubbard."

"But you've hardly eaten a bite," Anita said. "You don't want the food to go to waste, do you?"

Clara didn't give a fig about Matthew Olsen's food. "Hubbard may need me."

"You poor dear," Anita said, but Clara didn't believe for a second that she meant it.

She hadn't been back in the room but half a minute before Hubbard opened his eyes. She saw it clearly. The candle flame on the dresser was magnified in the mirror and threw its light across the bed.

"Why?"

Just that one word. That was all he said. It was so distinct. It made so much sense. He didn't need to tell anybody about not being a Martin. All he had to do was say that Clara had wanted him dead. She'd said so, hadn't she? She'd told him his dead brother had been twice the man Hubbard was. Or had she said ten times better? It didn't mater. She'd made her anger plain. She'd shoved him, up there on the clifftop. She'd shoved him. That's all he had to say, and Clara's whole world would be lost.

Prison? Was she going to spend the rest of her life in prison?

Saturday, 12 October 1745

ALTHOUGH SILAS MARTIN resented his brother's high-handed way of ordering him to carve the doors—with a scene of Homer leading the party into the valley like Moses leading the Hebrews into the Promised Land—he had to admit that the actual carving was going well.

Not that he had progressed very far. He had spent a good deal of time planning out the placement of the design. He had opted for thickly leaved trees, more like the Garden of Eden than anything else, but his trees were taken from his memories of the trees in the north, beech and white birch and sugar maple primarily, none of which—other than a few beech trees—grew this far south. There was a dark-barked river birch that grew in this colony. It had shaggy bark, but it was so unlike the lovely northern tree used for the white birch bark canoes, he chose not to depict it on these doors.

At the base of his doors, he would show the trees growing out of mounds of grasses, as if there had never been a tree felled in this rich valley. He had not yet introduced any human figures into his creation, particularly not the figure of his brother. Perhaps he might simply forget to include Homer. After all, Silas had never had any great success at carving faces.

The lean-to workshop he had set up on the south side of the church building was spare, for naught was needed but two sawbucks to hold one door at a time and, of course, his carving tools and his preliminary sketches. There was ample light, and the simple roof over the three sides of wall provided shelter from any rain. He would have to finish these doors before winter set in, though. The winters would most likely be mild here in this southern clime, but he imagined there would be some snow within another month or two. If not snow, then freezing weather at the very least. Carving was not best done when fingers were in danger of being too stiff to bend.

He took a brief moment to wipe the sweat from his brow and draped his kerchief back across the leg of the sawbuck. There were two newly-filled graves in the cemetery beside the church, but Silas did not mind the companionship of the dead. They never criticized his work. His gaze drifted to the nearby grave of the unknown, one-armed man who had fallen to his death just two months before. He shook his head, wondering as he often did, if the man had had a wife and children who now would never know what had happened to the husband, the father. He breathed a quick prayer of repose for the man's soul and went back to his carving.

Homer had not deigned even to look at the first door yet. He assumed, Silas supposed, that his instructions would be followed. Silas knew there would be an explosion of temper when the hoped-for scene of Homer as Moses did not appear. Silas did not care. He was heartily tired of his brother's arrogance. He was tired, too, of the frequent ravings of his brother against the Brandts.

Although Homer never named them directly, for he followed his own directive to erase the name of Brandt from this community completely, still he spoke stridently—and repeatedly—of the need to remain secreted within this cliff-lined valley lest enemies descend. Last night he had been particularly vociferous as the men gathered around the communal fire in the center of the town. Silas was fairly sure that without Homer's feeding the fires of resentment, most of the men of the town would be just as happy to forget about the Brandts completely and settle into their peaceful life here in this hidden valley. But Homer would not let the matter …

If Silas had been paying less attention to his resentment of Homer and more attention to the direction his knife was headed in, he might not have cut his hand so badly when the knife slipped, but as it was, the wound was deep.

"YOU NEED NOT carve yourself to pieces, Husband," Louetta said later as she patched him up and applied the tight bandage needed to stem the flow of blood.

He flexed his fingers gingerly, causing the loose ends of the tied cloth to tremble. "I will not be able to work more on the doors until this is better healed."

"Is that so bad an idea? Your brother had no right to—"

His hand did not pain him enough to keep him from sweeping his wife into his arms and stopping her objections with a resounding kiss. "This will not slow the work too much," he said when they both paused several long minutes later. "I expect with your expert bandaging I will be back at work soon."

She leaned back in his arms and studied his face. "There is a man in the town who could help you."

"With the carving?"

"Yes." She paused as if to temper her words. "Most likely. The stranger who came with his mother two months ago."

"Oh? And what would you know of him?" He tried to make his voice stern, but Louetta knew him too well.

"I know nothing directly, Husband, but Miss Julia showed me a number of clever animals he whittled for her as they journeyed here."

"The doors need more skill than mere whittling, Louetta."

"His carvings are quite lovely. He made a cup for her that has a twining vine about it. I felt I could almost see the vine shiver in the breeze." She leaned her cheek against his chest. "There are so few men in this town, none in fact that I can call to mind, who share your fine eye, but Miss Julia's son John seems to have the same appreciation you do for …"—she searched for the right word—"… for the exquisite."

"Exquisite?" He laughed and kissed her again. His exquisite wife. "I will speak with him."

In truth, Silas had wanted to make a better acquaintance of John Gilman. There was something about him that called to mind someone, although Silas could not imagine who that someone might be. He knew he had never met anyone by the name of Gilman before this man and his mother had come to town.

Tuesday, 15 October 1745

HUBBARD BRANDT DID not expect anyone to be inside the church. This early on a Tuesday morning, all the townspeople would be toiling away at their morning chores, working the fields, tending gardens, preparing for the upcoming harvest, going about their usual daily routines. Still, he entered the church with caution, not wanting to disturb anyone who might be at prayer, and certainly not wanting to encounter anyone who might wish to converse. Not that people cared to speak with him. Not with his face the way it was. He felt useless. Always before, in Brandtburg, along the trail, staying with Mother Julia and Miss Anna, traveling with his brother and Miss Julia, he had been of use. Now, what did he have to contribute? Miss Julia had seemed to merge into the activities of the women in this community, but he—Hubbard—John—he hardly felt he even had a name anymore, nor was he of value to anyone.

He did chores for Mister Surratt to pay for his board, but what more could he do? Perhaps he could carve cups for the Surratt family, too small a gift for the chance to live near his beloved wife.

He fell to his knees at the short railing in front of the altar, but no word of prayer would come to him. He did not know for what he could possibly pray. He supposed his earlier prayers had been answered. He had prayed to see his wife, his Mary Frances, to know that she had come safely through the journey.

He had seen her.

She was safe.

All his previous resolve not to approach her, since he knew she could not possibly accept him with his ruined countenance, was for naught. Now, there was a greater reason why he could not approach her. She had a child. A child by Homer Martin. Hubbard felt the bitter bile rise in the back of his throat at the thought of that man with Mary Frances. Of all the men who had traveled this way, why had she chosen that one?

Yet Hubbard could not bring himself to leave the village. Not while there was still a chance for him to see her from afar.

He wondered what Mother Julia would say. They had not talked about it, but she knew his wife's name, and there was but one Mary Frances in the entire village. Mary Frances Martin.

MARY FRANCES MARTIN. She hated that name, hated the very thought of it, hated to hear herself called by it, so when the new woman in town, Mistress Julia Gilman, called out to her that Tuesday morning from the porch of Hastings House, she was sorely tempted not to answer. Instead, she set her mouth into what she hoped was a pleasant expression, gripped her son's hand more firmly, and waited for the older woman to catch her up. The woman might be elderly, but she walked with a firm stride indeed.

"Good morrow, Mistress … Martin?" Mary Frances had little time to wonder why there was such a distinct question in the woman's voice. "I planned to spend some time in the meadow above town, for the mullein spires are ripe for the picking, and it is such a fine, dry day. Would you and your son care to join me, since we appear to be headed in the same direction?"

"You seem well-equipped." Mary Frances nodded toward Miss Julia's three empty gathering baskets, one of which was a good deal smaller than the other two.

Miss Julia's laugh was surprisingly youthful. "Indeed, I am. I have hoped for some time to speak with you privately, so when I saw you coming up the lane with your son, I chose three baskets from the stack Mistress Hastings keeps beside her door."

Without answering directly, Mary Frances turned to her left, uphill. They walked in silence for the most part, speaking only when they greeted other women who worked in their gardens, harvesting the late summer crops.

Mary Frances had her own garden to attend to, but first she intended to visit with her sister Constance to see how little Parley was faring through her bout with a high fever. Still, she supposed she could grant Miss Julia a short conversation. She knew she would have to guard her tongue, for she knew not what Hubbard—she would have to remember to refer to him as Mister Gilman—might have told this woman who pretended to be his mother. She longed to ask a hundred questions, but she had to protect the honor of her son. Hubbard's son.

She was relieved when they reached the meadow to find that no one else was there. Miss Julia handed the small basket to John and suggested that he might like to fill it with whatever treasures he found.

"Tweasures?" The boy had a charming lilt to his voice, and both women smiled at him.

"Yes, for certain," Miss Julia told him. "The meadow is filled with treasures, if only you will keep your eyes open."

"Stay away from the cliff," Mary Frances warned him. She waited for him to nod before she let go of his hand. He headed straight toward a tall clump of wild daisies and began plucking the flower heads with calm, gentle deliberation, placing each carefully into his basket. "The base of the cliff is dangerous," Mary Frances said. "Not two months ago, we found the body of a man who had fallen to his death. "

Beside her, Miss Julia drew in her breath. "Had he but one arm?"

Mary Frances studied Miss Julia's face. She saw pain mixed with … with what? Was that relief? No. It was an emotion more complicated than relief.

Miss Julia turned to face her directly. "May we talk frankly with each other?"

Mary Frances nodded. She was not sure whether she herself would be frank with this woman, but she most certainly wished to hear what Miss Julia had to say.

THE CHANCE TO speak with John Gilman came sooner than Silas expected. He passed by the front door of the church on Tuesday, several mornings after his wife had suggested that he speak with the scarred stranger, not expecting to see anyone there. His hand felt somewhat better, for his wife had been diligent about dosing it with herbs and poultices. While he still could not trust it to be steady enough for the exacting work of carving—he needed both his hands for that—he wanted to inspect the work he had done on the previous Saturday.

John Gilman stepped out of the church, stopped so suddenly, and went so pale on the side of his face that was not already white-scarred, Silas thought the man looked like he might have seen a ghost.

"Good morrow, Mister Gilman," Silas said. "I am sorry to have startled you."

"I did not expect to see you … to see anyone here."

Obviously not, thought Silas. "I have not had a chance to welcome you properly to our community. I am Silas Martin." He held out his hand, and the man took it, somewhat reluctantly, Silas thought. "Perhaps you would do me the honor of accompanying me to my workshop." He gestured toward the side of the church. "I am carving new doors for the chapel."

"I would happily go with you," John said, speaking carefully. His mouth was so restricted by the horrible scarring that Silas wondered how the man could speak at all. "I wonder, though, why you want me to see your doors."

Silas smiled. "My wife informs me that you have a deft hand with a carving knife and a fine eye for artistic work."

John's one moveable eyebrow lifted. "Your wife, Sir? How would she know aught of me?"

"She informs me that your mother has been telling tales, showing off the fine animals you whittled for her and a most marvelous cup. Please. It is just a few steps around the side of the church. I would be obliged if you would give me your opinion of the design I have created for them."

John Gilman nodded, and Silas led the way.

HUBBARD FOLLOWED SILAS Martin around the left corner of the church. He wondered briefly what other tales his 'mother' might have told. He surely need not worry. She would hold her counsel and would protect Hubbard's secrets.

Silas had obviously not recognized him, although Hubbard had almost felt his heart stop beating when he stepped from the church practically into the path of the man. He rubbed his chest, for it had begun to pain him somewhat. The result of having been so suddenly surprised, he thought.

He walked behind Silas past several graves to reach the entrance to the roomy lean-to and was taken aback by the beauty of the door laid out there on two sturdy sawbucks. "This is fine workmanship indeed."

"The morning light is suitable here," Silas said, "and I have good subject matter."

Hubbard trailed his fingers across the finely wrought leaves. "Beech," he said. "I can almost hear them whispering in the wind."

He touched another of the trees, unfinished but truly magnificent in its arching beauty where Hubbard could see it rising from the surrounding wood. "White birch." He could not keep the wonder from his voice. "Sugar maple."

"I see my wife was right. You do have a fine eye." Silas lifted his bandaged hand. "I cannot work more until this hand of mine heals."

Hubbard raised a hopeful eye to meet Silas' gaze. "Would you be averse to my helping you?" When Silas seemed to hesitate, Hubbard plowed onward. "I have had naught to do since I came here. My … my mother has begun to be of some help to the healers in the community, but I have not yet found a place where I might be of service, other than the chores I do for Mister Surratt to pay for my room and board."

Still, Silas studied him without speaking.

"I would be happy to show you on scrap wood what I am capable of. If I were you and had a project as fine as this," he nodded to the door before him, "I would not want unknown hands touching it unless I were sure of their talent."

Even as he spoke, Hubbard realized how much he hungered to bring more life to the pattern before him. Not just trees, but flowering vines. Perhaps there would even be a way to join a nearly invisible H with an equally hidden MF. If he could not have his wife with him in life, he might at least join with her here, on the church doors. He cared not if some might consider it sacrilege. He did not care at all.

Still, Silas said nothing.

I KNOW THIS MAN, Silas thought. I do not know how I know him, but he is without a doubt someone I have met before. He searched his mind for any trace of a Gilman family. Could he have met the man in a tavern along the trail? No. He would never have forgotten such a scarred face. But mayhap the man's face had not been scarred before, when they met.

Silas had a good ear for voices, but this man's speech could be of no value in identifying him. Silas doubted not that Mister Gilman's words sounded far different now from what they had been before he had been injured, for where his lips had been on the right side of his face, there was now only a thin scarred line. He sounded as if he spoke always around a mouthful of porridge.

Gilman had lived to the far north, Silas knew. The man had unerringly identified not only the carved beech leaves, but the white birch as well, and Silas had not seen a white birch for the past two years, not since the Martin company had passed into the warmer lands of the south. Nor were there any sugar maples this far south.

He stepped to one side, trying to see more clearly the uninjured side of John Gilman's face, but John turned slightly at that very moment and raised a hand, almost as if he did not want his face to be inspected. He scratched at the skin just above his one seeing eye, which effectively blocked the view of his face.

He knows I might recognize him. Silas took a long breath. *I will find you out, Sir.*

When he expelled his breath, he said simply, "Carve me something, then, that I might see the work you do." He gestured toward his workbench. "Do you need tools?"

John Gilman considered the offer for a moment. "I have the ones I need."

"Shall we meet back here in, what? Five days? After the Sunday services?"

Gilman nodded. "That will be time enough. I thank you, Sir."

Silas turned to the back of the shed and lifted a short oaken plank. "You might as well use the same type of wood as the door itself. This plank was not planed true, but it will make a good test nevertheless." He debated for a moment whether or not to mention Homer's plan for the doors. It would keep John Gilman here another few minutes, minutes during which Silas could continue to study the man's face and bearing. "My brother asked that I carve him as Moses leading the faithful into the promised land, parting the trees before him as if they were the Red Sea."

"Homer Martin … as Moses?" Gilman sounded utterly incredulous.

"Those were my sentiments as well." Silas was amused to see that Gilman had no trouble discerning the unsuitability of Homer as a Biblical patriarch, although he had not observed Gilman talking with Homer since his arrival.

"He seems to have his Bible stories somewhat confused," Gilman said.

Silas grinned. "He may not have remembered that there were

forty years between the Red Sea and the end of their journey."

"I see that you are not following those instructions. Do you fear the repercussions when he discovers your … insolence?"

"I have handled my brother for many years. I believe I can weather this storm." He handed over the oak plank. "I look forward to seeing what you can do with this."

Once again John Gilman thanked him, took the plank, and turned to leave. "Till Sunday, then."

Silas watched him walk away down the path. His gait was slightly uneven, not enough to say it looked unsteady, but there was a curious hitch to his stride.

A curious hitch to his stride. And Silas Martin saw in that moment just where he knew this man from. This scarred and secretive man was Hubbard. Hubbard Brandt.

Whatever was he doing here? Why ever had he come this far?

Silas reevaluated his expectations for the church doors. Hubbard Brandt was a fine craftsman. Silas had seen examples of his work in Brandtburg and had been impressed with the man's ability to capture what appeared to be light in the way he carved truly elegant forms. For once, Silas was glad his own work on the doors had progressed so slowly, for now there was hope that, with the two of them combining their skills, the doors might be true works of art.

But why? Why was the man here?

HUBBARD FULLY INTENDED to walk away from Silas Martin, but he turned his head toward the graves beside the church and caught sight of one phrase on one of the crosses. *Unknown Man.* He stopped so suddenly, he had to fling out his arm to keep his balance, and he dropped the plank he held. That was the trouble with having but one eye. He so often felt as if he knew not how far he was from—or how close to—nearby objects. This grave was fairly new, for the soil had not yet settled much over it. It looked disconcertingly like the mound over his mother's grave in Brandtburg.

Behind him, he heard Silas approach. "One of the women of the town found the body of this man up"—he gestured with his head—"in the meadow above the town." Silas reached down for the plank and handed it to Hubbard.

Hubbard cleared his throat and moved to the head of the grave, so the ruined side of his visage faced Silas. The date *1 August 1745* was too much of a coincidence. “And you know not who he was?”

“There was naught in his bag to identify him, nor any markings on his rifle.”

Hubbard could tell Silas was watching him carefully, but knew also that his scars prevented any sort of expression from giving away his thoughts. He held his breath. Did he dare ask if the man had had but one arm? But surely someone here would have recognized the face of Ira Brandt?

As if the man at the foot of the grave had read his mind, Silas said, “His face was destroyed in the fall from the top of the cliff, but no man we knew of was missing. We searched the land above the cliff and found signs that a horse had been there.” He paused for several long seconds, and Hubbard could tell there was more Silas wanted to say. “The man had but one arm.”

Hubbard put out a hand and rested it on the cross, as much to steady himself as to say a final farewell to his brother. He had feared as much, but could not help the hope he had nurtured, like a small flame, a hope that Ira might some day be found. He reminded himself that Ira *had* been found. After a moment, he turned to leave. “It was kind of you to bury him in hallowed ground.”

“I would want the same for myself were I to die far from my home.”

Hubbard could not tell if it was just a flight of fancy on his part or if Silas had indeed put unusual stress on the word *far.*

MARY FRANCES PULLED her gathering knife from the specially made pocket she had tied around her waist that morning. Bending, she whacked at the stem of a tall mullein spire with more force than she had intended.

“We may not have long to speak before others come into the meadow.” The voice beside her was low but confidant. “It would behoove us, I think, to speak without trying to veil our thoughts. I know about Brandtburg.”

Mary Frances had not expected such directness, even from this forthright woman. She paused with her knife close to the stem of another mullein stalk.

"I know of your marriage to Hubbard."

It took Mary Frances a moment to gather her wits. She lowered the knife, but her grip on it had tightened. "You will not tell?"

"It is not my secret to divulge. I think neither you nor Hubbard wish it to be known, and I will respect that, for Hubbard has become like a son to me." She looked down the meadow to where young John diligently studied something on the ground. "He does not suspect that you bore his son."

Mary Frances felt her insides harden. "I would willingly kill anyone who threatened my son."

"You misunderstand me. May I call you Mary Frances? I dislike using the name Martin, for I sense it is distasteful to you?"

There was a hint of a query in the woman's voice, and Mary Frances nodded, cautiously.

"Hubbard—I suppose I ought to refer to him as John, his middle name, since that is how he chose to mask his identity—was suffused with joy when we finally found you, but he was distraught that you had apparently married another." Her voice held no judgment.

"My father forced the … the marriage on me after less than a month on the trail." Mary Frances could not help the note of bitterness she still felt at this betrayal. "I tried to refuse, but he and my mother both were …"

Her voice trailed away, and Miss Julia reached out to touch the back of her hand.

Mary Frances swallowed, hard. "And then, within months, it became obvious I was with child, and I could not leave, not without risking the babe's life. Everyone assumed the babe had been fathered by …" She felt her face contort. "Why did he not come after me?" She could hear the heartache in her question and doubted not that Miss Julia could hear it as well.

Miss Julia's eyes softened. "He did, my dear, as soon as he was able, but circumstances conspired against him. His brother Ira began the journey determined to extract vengeance for his missing arm."

"It was not missing when we left Brandtburg." In spite of herself, she was curious. "What happened?"

As Miss Julia recounted the long story that John—Hubbard—had told her, Mary Frances found herself gradually relaxing. Although she kept an eye on her son, she sank onto a tussock of soft grasses, still thick and green despite the oncoming of autumn, and motioned to Miss Julia to do the same.

"They were close behind you," Miss Julia finally said, "and felt sure to have caught you up soon, but they stayed one night in an abandoned cabin. That is where the"—she paused, apparently searching for the right word—"the accident happened."

"My husband's … Hubbard's …" It took her three tries to settle on the right term. "John's face?"

As Miss Julia related the events of that long-ago day, Mary Frances found herself clenching her knife so tightly the blood drained from her hand. She had hated Ira Brandt for years because he was the one who had murdered Myra Sue, her dearest friend, but now she felt a new reason for hatred spring up in her, even more powerful than her first rage.

"Ira nursed him for months, there in the rude cabin, throughout the ensuing winter. They would have died but for the deep well and the ample supply of firewood the previous inhabitants had left behind. By the time spring arrived, Ira was ready to go back to Brandtburg, but Hub—John declared that he would not return until he had found you. That is when he told his brother of his marriage and his hopes of seeing that you were safe, that you had survived the journey." Miss Julia studied the back of her hands. "He had no hope that you would accept him as he was."

Mary Frances let that worthless comment settle into the still air. "What did Ira do when he heard of our marriage?"

"John told me that he said little. He simply walked across the clearing to where two graves lay among wildflowers under the edge of the forest, and stood there for a long, long time."

"Did the house have a roof of pine boughs intertwined with saplings?"

Miss Julia seemed surprised by the abrupt question. "I do not know. Why do you ask?"

"We stayed at that same cabin our first summer on the trail. Louetta, the one you have assisted in her healing practices, the woman now married to Silas Martin, lived there with her son Brand. She killed the bear that had mauled her husband …"

Beside her, Miss Julia drew in a startled breath.

"… and joined our group when we came upon her. Those two graves were her brother's and her husband's. She and Silas Martin married last year. A true marriage." She could not keep the bitterness from her voice.

Miss Julia sat silent for a few moments. "John had no wish to show himself to you, for he felt sure you could not accept him with his face scarred as it is." She seemed unwilling to leave this matter unaddressed.

"That is the most hare-brained thought imaginable."

"As I told him, but he could not see the possibility."

Just then, John ran up and hugged his mother. "I wuv the fwowers."

She held him close for a few seconds, took the limp daisy he offered her, admired the lichen-covered stick he placed on her lap, and sent him back to gather more.

"He has the look of his father," Miss Julia said. "Not that anyone else would see it, for they seldom look at John, and he is careful never to turn the undamaged side of his face toward anyone without putting his hand up as if to brush away a mosquito or scratch his eyebrow."

Mary Frances thought about it. She had noticed that, but without understanding the significance of it. "He protects the reputation of his son."

Miss Julia shook her head. "He simply wants to be sure no one here recognizes him. He does it to protect you. He does not know young John is his own. He feels certain the boy is the son of Homer Martin, which is the main reason he does not wish to impose himself on you."

"He believes that?"

"Men can be oblivious at times."

"Hubb—John was ever ready to believe the best of others and the worst of himself."

"What a waste of—" Miss Julia stopped herself. "He is one of the finest men I have ever had the pleasure of knowing, and I am proud to call him my son, but in this"—she motioned toward Mary Frances as if to encompass the woman's last statement—"he is foolish indeed."

Silence descended on them again until Mary Frances thought to ask, "Why was Ira Brandt so close to the edge of the cliff?"

"He had ridden ahead of us to scout the lay of the land while I rested, having twisted my back awry. John stayed with me. When Ira's horse returned without him late that night, John was reluctant to leave me, for we had heard the cry of a painter close by. We both assumed Ira would come stomping into our camp the next morning. When he did not, even during the next few days when I lay in pain from my back, we were worried, but assumed he had perhaps found your path and forged ahead even without Blaze."

"But he had not."

"No. He had not. I do believe we both knew that something … something had happened to him, but we each kept up the charade of believing him to be but lost."

"Charade? What is that?"

"A word I learned from a traveler who came to Harrisburg, the town where I lived. It means a pretense, an act, an untruth masked as a truth."

"Mama?"

Mary Frances turned away from Miss Julia, as much to cover the sorrow she was sure must show on her face as to answer her son. "Your basket is filling nicely."

"More."

"Yes, you may add as many flowers as you wish."

When Miss Julia was sure the boy was occupied, she continued. "John had asked him to search north from where we were, but Ira must have gone south, which brought him to the edge of …" She looked upward at the towering bluff and did not finish her sentence.

"So you came here hoping to find him?"

"No. The longer we searched, always to the north of that camp, the more we felt sure he had gone astray somehow, but there was no hope of finding him in the thick woods and mountainous land. We stumbled finally across the trail your wagons made and came through the gap in the cliff far north of here."

"We call it Russell's Gap."

"I see," she said, although Mary Frances was fairly sure Miss

Julia did not understand the reasoning behind the name.

"Reverend Russell wanted us to rest on Sunday before entering the gap, so we might come into the valley refreshed by our Sabbath."

"I see." And this time she did. "We stayed the night in that same place, and it was there that John told me of his marriage and his hopes of finding you."

"Why, though, did it take so very long?"

Miss Julia told her then of the yellow fever and of the change that Ira had undergone during the year he lived beneath her roof and under her care, as he finally understood that it was his own actions that had brought the delays upon them. "I am afraid I slowed their journey a great deal when we left Harrisburg. Even with my divided skirts, I could not ride as fast as they might have, had there been just the two of them alone. But I think the slow journey and the long nights along the trail served a good purpose. Although Ira left Brandtburg intent on revenge, by the time he came to the edge of this valley, he had determined to beg Homer Martin's forgiveness."

Mary Frances made a derisive sound. "That he never would have gotten. Homer Martin refuses to let anyone even whisper the name of Brandtburg, lest the evil Brandts learn of us somehow and come to slaughter us all."

Miss Julia pursed her lips, as if trying to decide whether or not to say something. "I am not the only reason the journey was slow from the time we left the Susquehanna. Your Hubbard—John—had need of occasional rest along the way, and I sometimes feigned more decrepitude than was true as an excuse to tarry a day or two at a time. I think it happened when he had the … the accident. His heart appears to trouble him."

Mary Frances felt her own heart leap in fear. "His heart?"

"I think it is nothing to be concerned about, but he seems to require more rest than perhaps he ever was used to."

Mary Frances thought back to her wedding night. Her true wedding night. And to the way Hubbard had occasionally paused in—she could feel herself blushing, even though Miss Julia could have no idea what her thoughts were. She remembered how he had held his hand against his chest. "Miss Julia? You will tell me should you see any change?"

Before Miss Julia could reply, other than a quick nod, the women heard a hearty greeting from the edge of the meadow. "The hordes are upon us," Miss Julia said with a sigh, "for this day is a fine one for gathering. Might we find another time to talk?"

"Certainly," Mary Frances said. She smiled at this woman who so obviously loved and respected Hubbard. "Most certainly." Gathering her voluminous dress about her, she rose to her feet. "I would fain have you teach me the way you divided your skirts."

Miss Julia laughed. "With pleasure. Together, you and I will set this town on its ears."

Mary Frances snipped off a large mullein spire. "You have already done so all by yourself. To hear Mistress Russell talk, one would think those skirts of yours were a scandal." Her face grew serious. If Mistress Russell thought divided skirts were a scandal, what would she make of it if she knew Mary Frances had two husbands, only one of them true? And that one true husband, a Brandt?

SILAS STUDIED THE man who leaned against the grave of the unknown one-armed stranger. The supposed John Gilman had a wary look in his one working eye, although with such heavy scarring on the rest of his face, it was hard to tell for certain just what his thoughts might be.

Silas made as if to turn away. "I will see you and your carving in five days' time then?"

"Yes. Good day to you." John clutched his plank more closely, stepped away from the grave, and continued down the path.

Silas waited until he was three or four yards away, and then called, "Hubbard?"

John Gilman turned around. "Yes?"

Silas could tell the moment awareness hit. The good side of Hubbard's face blanched, and he dropped the plank yet again as he stumbled.

"You … you … I …"

"You need not fear that I will betray you," Silas assured him. "Your life would be forfeit if my brother Homer discovered who you are, and I have no wish for that."

"Why …" Hubbard left the question hanging in the air.

Silas glanced around. Three children carrying wooden buckets ran down the hill, headed for the river. "Come back to my workshop where we may talk in private."

Hubbard left the plank lying where it had fallen and followed him, but Silas could hear that the man's steps were slow and uncertain.

I SHOULD HAVE *expected a trick such as that,* Hubbard thought. *Silas was ever the brighter of the two Martin brothers.* He stepped into the shelter of the workshop and squared his shoulders. "It must have been your artist's eye that discovered my identity." He tried to keep any sullenness from his voice, but he could not help the fear that welled up in him. What if Silas told Mary Frances? "How long have you known?"

Silas chuckled. "About four minutes."

Hubbard cocked his head to one side.

"You recognized the white birch, for one."

"Ah," Hubbard breathed. "And there is no white birch here in this colony."

"Still," Silas admitted, "you might have simply traveled far to the north. But the way you walk is most distinctive."

"My gait was ever awkward." He rubbed his hand across the thigh of the offending leg. "I doubted anyone would think about my feet. Not with my face as it is."

He thought Silas looked uncertain about what to say next. There was a long, uncomfortable silence.

"Mistress Gilman is a most pleasant person," Silas finally said. "My wife has become quite fond of her."

Hubbard nodded, still wary, but willing to let the subject stray for a moment. "I can understand that. Both Miss Julia and your wife are most competent healers." He took a deep breath. There was little sense in waiting to address the problem at hand. "My brother would have died without Miss Julia's help."

Silas looked a question at him.

And so Hubbard told him. There was little sense either in denying the reasons for their journey, although he did not—would not—tell of his marriage to Mary Frances Garner. That was not his secret to divulge. Instead he told of the delays due to the loss of half of Ira's arm and later to the accident that had marred Hubbard's face, of the long winter recovering from that event, of the timely intervention of the Indian woman, and then of his brother's bout with the yellow fever and how the expert care of Mistress Gilman had saved his life.

"Else we would have caught up with you months—nay years—before we did." He paused in the telling, and Silas waited quietly. "The interruptions to our journey were, perhaps, heaven-sent, for my brother began our trek intent on revenge, but somehow that ..." He found himself groping for the right words. "... that anger seemed to burn itself out as we journeyed. We came here at last so that he might beg forgiveness of your brother for the death of Mistress Myra Sue Martin."

Silas remained silent, seeming to be lost in his own thoughts.

Hubbard could not bear it. "Your brother has remarried, though?"

"Indeed." Silas shook his head and grimaced. "After less than a month on the trail."

Had Mary Frances been so anxious to put her first marriage behind her? Could she have cared so little for him?

"I have ... always"—Silas seemed to be choosing his words carefully—"thought that my brother's second marriage was ... ill-advised."

Hubbard held his breath.

"Her father was close to dying from a leg wound he contracted during the ... the fight in"—he lowered his voice—"in Brandtburg. He arranged the marriage in order to see his daughter provided for. He died the next morning after she was wed."

Why, why, why? Hubbard could not still the anguish in his heart. He turned away to his left so Silas would not see the unmarked side of his face.

"I should be reluctant to say so," said Silas, "for it is not my place to judge my brother's marriage, but I have never seen any joy on Mistress Martin's face while she is in the presence of her husband."

Hubbard looked a question at him.

"I know what joy in a marriage is supposed to look like," Silas said simply. "There is much deep affection between my own dear wife and myself."

There would have been much joy between my beloved Mary Frances and myself. Hubbard could hardly abide the pain of loss such a thought brought to him. He ran his palm over his chest and pressed it hard against his heart, hoping to still the unseemly pounding.

"So this man, the one-armed man, was your brother?"

Hubbard gathered himself before he could answer. "Yes. It appears to be so, for the date on his marker is the day after he disappeared. Mother Gilman—she bade me call her that on our journey—had injured her back and was unable to ride for nigh on a week. My brother left us to scout ahead and must have fallen to his death. His horse returned without him."

"Ah, yes. Blaze. A remarkably fine steed."

"I am surprised that no one here seems to have recognized either Blaze or Star."

Silas nodded. "I have found that men generally see what they expect to see." He paused, and when he spoke there was an undercurrent of mirth in his voice. "Despite my brother's rants, no one here ever expected the Brandts to find us."

"The Brandts did not find you." Hubbard could hear the reluctance, the bitterness in his own voice. "Only the Gilmans."

2000

My gratitude list for Friday 12/8/2000

1. Glaze, of course, and Tom. I do so hope they'll be happy in their marriage—even if they did get hitched in an attic!
2. All the wonderful things we've found upstairs over these three days—the hoop and those strange instructions from Mary Frances Martin and even that faded old sunbonnet. I wonder what we'll find tomorrow…
3. The wood stove. What would we do without it? Well, I can answer that. We'd be frozen out of our tutus.
4. Bob and his quiet sensibility. How sweet he was to arrange that Mom and Dad and Tom's family could be here for the wedding. Well, there wouldn't have been a wedding if he hadn't done that. I need to stop editorializing and go back to my gratitude list, but really, how could I have been so lucky?
5. All our marvelous friends. I sure do hope the ice melts soon so they can all go home! Enough of this togetherness. However did

the Martin clan endure traveling together for four whole years?

I am grateful for
Widelap and Softfoot
SmellSweet and Fishgiver
the happy chatter of the birds
ListenLady who hears me
window sills to sit on so I can watch the
furries beneath the bird feeders

I placed my journal aside and extinguished the lantern.

Bob and Marmalade were already snuggled under the comforter, and I slid down next to them as fast as I could. I pulled off the wide hand-knitted scarf I'd wound around my neck and shoulders and pushed it up between my pillow and the headboard. It always amazed me how simply protecting my neck could make me feel warmer all over. But with Bob's built-in heating effect, I didn't need any sort of shawl once I was tucked in.

I help warm you too.

And, of course, Marmalade added her furry comfort. At my feet I could feel the long johns, sweatpants, turtleneck, and heavy sweater I'd placed on top of the sheet but under the blankets and the comforter. I refused to start my day tomorrow putting on frigid clothing.

I waited a bit to be sure my little nest was warmed to my satisfaction.

I am warm enough.

"Bob? Did your mother ever feed you cod liver oil when you were little?"

He started laughing—not out loud, but I could feel the vibrations, like an earthquake on its way to the surface.

"What's so funny?"

"There was this one day when Tom and I wanted to go fishing. It was near the end of the school year, and our moms were both planning to go up to Garner Creek to something or other that was going on. He and I decided to pretend we had tummy aches. Not bad enough for our moms to stay home with us, but bad enough that we could promise to spend the whole day in bed and they'd leave us sleeping."

"Yeah? I have a feeling this is going to be good."

"Depends on your point of view." He wrapped one arm around me. "Mom looked at me with that kind of look every kid knows if he's ever tried to get away with something."

"Like she's reading your mind? My mom had the exact same kind of look."

"She went in the laundry room and came back with a big bottle of something. *I'm sorry you don't feel well*, she said. Her voice was incredibly syrupy. *Open up.*"

"Cod liver oil?"

"Yep. She cancelled her trip and dosed me every four hours. I never tried to play hooky again. Neither did Tom. He got the same treatment."

"She kept it in her laundry room?"

"Isn't that where everybody keeps cod liver oil?"

I spluttered a bit. "It was probably next to her blueing."

"Huh?" He brushed my hair away from his face.

"Sorry. Am I tickling you?"

"Just my nose. I doubt I could feel anything through this beard. What was that about blueing?"

"It's a long story."

"I don't have a single place I need to be right now other than here."

"YOU'RE REALLY GETTING into this attic stuff, aren't you?" Dave watched Pat remove several cashmere sweaters from her suitcase. Once she had them piled up the way she wanted them, he blew out the candle, waited for her to slip into bed, and then stretched his legs out, pushing his toes against the confining blanket where it was tucked in at the foot of the bed. "Damn bed isn't long enough."

"It beats freezing to death in the king-size at Melissa's."

"You've got a point." He didn't even bother to cover his enormous yawn.

"I wonder if the two of those are ever going to get together?"

"What?"

Dave's question sounded to Pat more like a reflex than a real question, but she answered it anyway. "I mean Mary Frances and Hubbard, but I doubt they will."

She could feel him pull back and look in her direction, although it was so dark with those heavy curtains over the windows, he couldn't possibly see her.

"I thought you'd be rooting for the two of them. You're such a romantic."

Pat sighed. "It just won't work, Dave. She has her son to worry about. People were a lot less forgiving about things back then. Especially something like bigamy."

"What's a little bigamy between friends?"

She was too tired to poke him in the ribs, no matter how much she wanted to. "I wonder if that Charlotte Ellis—the one from way back then—will ever start blackmailing Mary Frances."

Beside her, she felt Dave stiffen his arm. "Why would she do that?"

"Because she sounds like a horrible person. She's suspicious, and Mary Frances obviously doesn't trust her. I guess we'll have to wait for more diary entries."

"What would you think about Mary Frances if she caved in? If she did pay blackmail money?"

Pat was delighted. Dave actually sounded like he wanted an answer from her. Maybe there was hope for him after all. "I'd think she was a fool," she said. "She ought to shove that Charlotte Ellis off the cliff and get rid of her."

"Read a little farther, then," Dave said. "Maybe she will."

FATHER JOHN LIFTED the lantern and swung it gently almost like a censer.

Henry smiled. "Are you trying to warm the place up with that pitiful little flame?"

"We'd be better off doing some calisthenics," the priest said.

"Be my guest." Henry hopped into his narrow bed and pulled the covers up to his nose. "I'm going to use the time-honored method of shivering."

"Planning to get up at two?"

The silence from the other side of the room lengthened.

"Nope," Henry finally said.

"Good. Neither am I."

REEBOK STACKED TWO more thick logs onto the heavy bed of coals in the wood stove. The Chief was depending on him, and Reebok enjoyed being the keeper of the fire. Keeper of the fire. He liked the sound of that. He adjusted the damper, proud at how well he'd come to understand the workings of the stove.

He thought of all the people settling into sleep above him. Even with heat rising the way it did, it had to be cold in those rooms, especially the ones at the far end of the hallway.

He picked up the heavy fireproof mitt next to the stove and adjusted the fan atop the stove so it would blow more toward the stairs. He was plenty warm.

Right here was the best place in the house to be on a cold night like this.

He curled up in the blanket and settled, expecting to drift off immediately, but a most unwelcome picture of Hubbard lying at the foot of the cliff came into his head. He'd seen dead bodies before, of course. That was part of being a police officer.

But he'd never enjoyed it. He liked remembering them even less. Of course, Hubbard hadn't been dead. But he might as well have been with his brain all askew like it was.

He pushed the blanket away. Maybe he was too hot.

But the couch was occupied by too many faces, dead faces. So he lay there and thought.

He couldn't believe Hubbard Martin had tried to kill himself. It just wasn't like the man.

And then there was all that talk at the table about Ira Brandt and the one-armed skeleton. It reminded him of the bones found by that hunter. He could tell, sleep was going to be a long time coming. He got up and walked to the fogged-up window. He wrote his initials, shook his head, and rubbed them off. It was too dark out there to see anything anyway.

CHARLIE ELLIS HAD a hard time getting to sleep. *It's been such a full day you'd think I'd be more tired*, she thought. All these jaw-breaking yawns certainly made it seem like sleep ought to be right there for her. But it just wouldn't come.

She found herself imagining Ira Brandt falling when the cliff collapsed all those years ago. She couldn't help shuddering. It was too easy to picture what a mess he'd made at the bottom. Sort of like the mess Hubbard Martin had made only a few months ago.

She'd just been returning from an early morning walk when the ambulance passed her by with Hubbard Martin on the way to the hospital. Within a couple of hours, everybody in town was talking about it.

She'd have to ask tomorrow to see if anybody else, besides Hubbard and that Ira guy from the diaries, had ever fallen off the cliff.

No, maybe she wouldn't. It wasn't any fun to think about.

Finally she turned her flashlight back on, found a book on the little shelf on the other side of the room, and crawled back into bed.

She decided she'd keep reading until she heard Easton get up to go to the bathroom, and then it would just take her a minute, maybe a minute and a half, to shut up that Sadie Masters forever. Old people were always dying in their sleep, weren't they? She opened the book. Jane Austen. She hadn't thought about *Pride and Prejudice* in years.

1992

"WE'RE GOING TO begin this semester with *Beowulf*, the first epic poem we have in the English language," Mrs. Van Aken told the honors English class the first day of Charlie's senior year in high school. "Eventually we'll work our way up to the nineteenth century, for which we'll read *Pride and Prejudice*, followed by *A Tale of Two Cities*." She looked around at the faces before her. "I expect great things from this class. You are here because of your outstanding reading and comprehension skills, and I intend to stretch you to the limit."

"The limit of what," the boy next to Charlie Ellis muttered, but Charlie didn't pay him much attention. She thought all of this sounded exciting.

When Charlie went to college the following year, she told Tricia Moody, her roommate, about both books, and *Beowulf*, too, but Tricia wasn't that interested. "I'd like to read *Pride and Prejudice* again sometime," Charlie said. "That's why I brought it here with me."

But there were too many other books to read for classes, too many term papers to write, too many classes to attend, and way too much talking to do late into the evening as the two girls talked about their lives so far. Well, Charlie did most of the talking, but Tricia never seemed to mind.

At the end of freshman year, Charlie packed up Jane Austen's book and took it back home, unread.

2000
Matthew Olsen's House

CLARA RESENTED THE fact that whoever remodeled Matthew's house way back when had put the master bath across the hall from the master bedroom. Not that there was anything grand about this room, nothing to justify the term *master*. She had to remember, though, that this wasn't the master bedroom. That was upstairs. The room Anita was sleeping in. The room with the attached bathroom. The room Clara should have had. It wasn't fair.

At home her bathroom adjoined her bedroom. Hubbard always had to go a few steps down the hall from his room, but then he hardly ever had to get up in the middle of the night the way Clara did.

Here, in Matthew's crummy house, she had to walk across the hall. That stupid bird of Matthew's always squawked as if to announce her intentions, and she knew Matthew and Nick could hear her each time, no matter how quiet she tried to be. Clara did not like to be embarrassed.

She should have taken Hubbard to the Johnson's house. Mary would have given them the biggest bedroom, and the bathroom was right there. But then she would have had to put up with the Johnson's two Irish setters. At least they didn't have birds. Or cats.

Clara shivered. She hated cats. That was one reason she never went to the town library if she could avoid it. Now that she was planning to disband the library board, she'd never have to go in that place again. Horrible orange cat. Gave her the shivers.

The cat that bit her when she was five had been orange, too. All she'd done was step on its tail. And pulled it, too, and maybe she'd kicked it once, but that was no reason for the cat to turn on her like that. No more cat. That was the last time her mother ever allowed an animal in the house.

Enough of that. She swiped her hands together to get rid of those memories.

Just to be sure Hubbard wasn't going to fall out of bed—or try to climb out of it—while she was out of the room, she tucked the sheets and blankets in tighter around him. Made sure they were pushed way up under the mattress as far as they could go.

Hubbard let out a low moan. She stopped halfway to the door and waited to see if he was waking up, but his breathing went back to that dull rhythm she'd come to abhor.

Better that, though, than having him wake up all the way and tell what he knew. About his family. About what they'd been going through. About what Clara had done.

ANITA WANTED MORE than anything for Nick—for once in their marriage—to put his arms around her and maybe push her hair back away from her forehead by planting a kiss on her forehead. He used to do that. Didn't he? She wasn't sure anymore. Maybe she'd just dreamed it.

Of course, now it was better not to wish for that. There was no way she was going to let a hug turn into something more.

She loved him desperately. It had taken her a long time to figure out that Nick was in a world of his own. A world where she wasn't welcome. A world where the only person of importance was … was Nick.

For some reason, she thought about Charlotte Ellis, the woman on the library board. What on earth had brought that woman to mind?

It had always been like this. It didn't seem to matter how much she cooked for Nick, how much she tried to make herself pretty for him, how much she smoothed out all the wrinkles in their day-by-day life, how much of the office work she managed in his dental clinic, he still wouldn't simply hold her. And then, once she'd found out what was going on, after she'd had the treatments, she didn't dare let him. She couldn't trust him.

Nick finished brushing his teeth. Dentists did that. After every single meal. At least, Nick did. She thought back to their wedding night. She'd been fairly naive, but she'd bought a filmy negligee, thinking it would please her new husband. Mrs. Foley. How proud she'd been of that label. She'd taken her time undressing and donning the diaphanous garment, while Nick lay there watching her. As she slipped under the covers beside him, he'd reached for something on the bedside table. A gift? She'd felt her eyes light up and her heart open even more.

Until he handed it to her. "You forgot to floss."

The white plastic container felt like … like a lump of rusty iron.

She tried not to remember that, but something about this ice storm had brought it back. Or maybe it was the sound of him in there snicking the little plastic container closed. At least now he left it in the bathroom instead of on his bedside table.

He walked past her bed and left without a backward glance. She listened to his deliberate tread as he walked downstairs to the couch. It took her a long time to get to sleep in the cold narrow twin bed.

Beechnut House

HALFWAY THROUGH THE night, Marmalade woke us both.

Listen.

At first it took me a moment to figure out what I was hearing—besides her loud squawking.

Squawking?

She must have been trying to tell us something. I needed to take a cat communication class.

"Rain," Bob said. "It's raining."

He pushed up onto one elbow, and I grabbed the comforter to pull it back under my chin. "It may be raining, but it's still cold as the dickens in here."

"I didn't think to tell you. The temp has been rising all day, and NPR said we might get rainstorms, but I have to admit I didn't quite believe it. The clouds looked more like snow clouds than rainclouds."

If I'd been able to see him in the dark, I'd have raised my eyebrows at him, but it would have been wasted effort as dark as the night was. "You can tell the difference between rain clouds and snow clouds?"

"Sure." He sounded astonished. Maybe he was raising his eyebrows at me. He lay back down and wrapped his arms around me. "This rain'll put us right back to sleep."

I snuggled closer. "Love the sound."

So do I.

THE ONLY REASON I knew what time it was when the call came is that I mumbled something at Bob and he told me, "Go back to sleep. It's only two-thirty. Reebok and I have to go."

BOB TIPTOED AS quietly as he could down the stairs in his sock feet. He hated to wake Reebok, but he knew Garner wouldn't want to miss the excitement. As quickly as he could, he explained what was going on. He gathered heavy-duty flashlights and put on his boots while Reebok dressed. By the time he got back to the living room, Reebok was ready.

"Do you think we should take Reverend Pursey with us, Chief?"

"No. Why?"

"Mrs. Martin might need him. He's her pastor, after all."

"Good thinking, Garner. I'll get him."

But Reebok was already halfway to the stairs.

AS SOON AS SHE heard Easton head down the hall, she pushed back the covers and eased her way out the door. She'd just reached for Sadie's doorknob when there were footsteps behind her. She whirled, and that stupid deputy switched on his flashlight.

"Is something wrong, Ma'am?" he whispered.

"No." How had he gotten out of his room without her hearing him? "I … I just had to go to the bathroom."

"It's back that way." He pointed over his shoulder. "I think I heard somebody in there, though. You could always use Miss Biscuit's powder room under the stairs."

She didn't need him being helpful. She needed him out of here.

He waited for her to head toward the stairs, and then he walked on—she could hear his quiet footsteps—toward one of the other bedrooms. She took a quick glance over her shoulder. The ministers?

What was he doing bothering them?

This was ridiculous. Everybody was getting in her way. She might as well go back to bed. No. While she was up, she'd go ahead and use the bathroom. That deputy was watching her, she could tell. No sense getting him suspicious.

By the time she made it back to her room, Easton was just stepping into Sadie's room.

"Good night, Miss Hastings," the deputy said as he lighted the way for the minister along the hall toward the staircase. "Good night, Miss Ellis."

She ignored him. She'd have to wait till tomorrow night.

EVERY ROOM WAS lit up in Matthew's house, and the door opened before the three men even reached the porch. Matthew had gathered the group in the living room and somebody—Bob guessed it was Anita—had made coffee on the wood stove. It felt to Bob more like a carnival than a death scene. There must have been fifteen candles spread out around the room.

"He's in the bedroom," Matthew said. "Clara's the one who discovered … uh … found … it … uh … him."

Clara didn't even look up at hearing her name. Maybe she hadn't heard it. Bob thought she looked rather stunned. As well she might be. He lowered his voice so as not to startle her. "I need to look at Hubbard"—he didn't want to say *the body*—"and then maybe you and I could talk, Clara?"

She nodded dumbly, not raising her head.

Henry sat beside her and took her flaccid hand.

Bob and Reebok headed for the bedroom that Matthew pointed out. They asked Matthew to remain out in the hall.

Hubbard lay on his back. The sheets were tidy, tucked in all around him. Aside from the usual smell that accompanies unexpected death, nothing seemed awry.

Bob felt for a pulse, lifted a half-closed lid and shone the light directly into the eye, eliciting no response. Not that he had expected any. The body was colder than the chilly room accounted for.

"Chief? Do you see what I see?" Reebok pointed, careful not to touch the body.

Bob hated to say so, but he most certainly did.

When he got back from calling Doc, he donned gloves and pulled back the sheet and blankets that had been tucked so carefully, so tightly, under the mattress. No blood. No evidence of a wound. No bruising. There was a bulge in the pocket on Hubbard's pajama top. Bob removed a brown wallet. Why stash a wallet in your pajamas? From what he knew of Hubbard's condition, Hubbard probably couldn't have done it himself, so it must have been Clara.

He looked through it. All the usual stuff. A few ones, a five, two credit cards, a license, a concealed carry permit. He handed it to Reebok, who made the same sort of examination, and then spread his hands as if to say *huh?*

Bob's sentiments exactly.

"Should I give this to Mrs. Martin, Sir?"

"No. It's here for a reason. Until we know what that reason is, I'd rather keep it handy."

"What if she asks about it, Sir?"

Bob looked back at the corpse. "Let's wait and see if she asks."

Reebok slipped it into an evidence bag and labeled it.

"Whenever you get back to the station, be sure you take this along and lock it in the evidence safe."

Reebok tucked it into his pocket. "Will do, Chief."

Bob disliked subjecting the other people to having to be in the room with the corpse, but there was no place else where he could question them individually. He and Reebok spread a sheet over the body and placed two chairs where Bob would be facing the bed, and Matthew—or Nick or Clara or Anita—would have their back to it.

Reebok brought in a third chair for himself and got out his notebook. He made a note to himself on a blank page. *Move Hubbard Martin's index card.*

FATHER JOHN LAY awake. His softly-lighted watch face said it was almost four. Henry still wasn't back from Matthew Olsen's house. Father John didn't know Clara Martin as well as Henry did, but he could well imagine how needy that woman would be. Even someone who liked to run everything around her the way Clara did could be thrown for a loop by something like this.

Whatever in the world could have made Hubbard fall off that cliff? Could it have been a try for suicide? He crossed himself. One of the troubles about suicide attempts was that they weren't always successful and left the person worse off than they'd been before. Of course, if Hubbard had been in such despair that he'd wanted to end his life, maybe being left without much brainpower would have seemed preferable. Still, suicide was never the answer. Not only did it solve nothing, but it left the survivors with so many unanswered questions and—inevitably—with a lot of guilt as well.

Now, for Hubbard to have died tonight when the word was yesterday that he might be regaining consciousness—it didn't make sense.

He'd just managed to drift back to sleep when Henry walked in, his fingers carefully covering the lens of his flashlight, apparently hoping not to wake his friend.

"I didn't think you'd be back tonight anytime."

Henry set the flashlight on the small bedside table and untucked his warm scarf from the front of his sweater. "I never want to have to do anything like that again as long as I live."

Father John waited, but Henry just mumbled an apology for waking John, crawled into his bed, and settled in without saying anything more.

I SHOULD HAVE moved over onto Bob's side of the bed, I thought as I groped for the phone, trying to reach it before it woke everybody. Oh, for heaven's sake, what was I worried about? Our door was closed, so nobody would hear this one. Probably. And the kitchen phone could only disturb Reebok, since I'd turned the ringer on low. That left the phone in the office, where Doc was sleeping, but I was pretty sure I'd turned that ringer completely off.

"Biscuit?" He didn't even wait for me to say hello. "Go downstairs and ask Doc to come next door."

"To Matthew's?" Of course it was to Matthew's. That was the only *next door* we had on this block. "Okay. Is Matthew all right?"

"Do it, Biscuit. Now."

He was never that abrupt with me. Something must be bad.

I was out of bed and down the stairs before my eyes were halfway open.

The End

Not quite.

Thus ends PINK AS A PEONY. The story concludes in the final volume of the Biscuit McKee Mysteries, WHITE AS ICE.

The Original Families on the Trek

MARTIN

(descended from Albion & Lucelia Sabriss Martin through their son William)

Homer (marries 1. Myra Sue Russell / 2. Mary Frances Garner)

John (born to Mary Frances on the trail)

Silas (marries widow Louetta Washburn Tarkington)

Brand Tarkington (son of Louetta)

Louise (barn baby, daughter of Silas and Louetta)

BREETON

Willem Breeton & 1. Mary Surratt Breeton / 2. Constance Garner Breeton)

MaryAnne (marries Thomas Russell)

Pioneer (marries Bridgett Hastings)

Susan (became a spinster)

Willy (marries Nell Surratt)

Parley (barn baby, born to Willem & Constance) (marries Brand Tarkington)

GARNER

Calvin Garner & Augusta Hastings Garner

Nehemiah

Wilbur

Mary Frances (married to Homer Martin on trail)

Constance (marries Willem Breeton on trail)

Able (marries Anne Russell)

HASTINGS

Robert Hastings, innkeeper & Jane Elizabeth Benton Hastings

Charles (marries Edna Russell)

Bridgett (marries Pioneer Breeton)

Lucius (marries Fionella Surratt)

Clarissa (born on the trail)

Cordelia (born in Martinsville)

Robert's father Richard Hastings (the original innkeeper)

Jane's elderly mother

RUSSELL

Reverend Anders Russell & Sarah Endicott Russell
Myra Sue (marries Homer Martin)
Thomas (marries MaryAnne Breeton)
Anne (marries Able Garner)
Abner (bachelor)
Edna (marries Charles Hastings)
Matthew (blacksmith) & Abigail Downes Russell
two sons, Mark and Luke, apprentices

SURRATT

Call Surratt & Geonette Black Surratt
Nell (marries Willy Breeton)
Fionella Surratt (marries Lucius Hastings)
Edward (bachelor)
Barnard (barn baby)
Widow Black & Geonette's siblings (Sergeant & Presila)

ENDICOTT

Chauncey (elderly brewer) & his wife
Worthy Endicott & Eunice Surratt Endicott
Isabelle
Jonathan
Rufus
Ellen (born on the trail)
Herman (born in Enders)
Charlotte Endicott Ellis, widow (first daughter of Chauncey)
Louisa (unmarried)
Jane (born on the trail)
Adele (born on the trail)
Martha (unmarried)
Alice (born on the trail)
Tansy (born on the trail)
Sarah Endicott Russell (Rev. Russell's wife)
Sayrle (bachelor)

Joel (bachelor)
Daniel (bachelor)
Sanborn (bachelor)

EVEREST
Joseph Everest & Arinda Surratt Everest, with five children

FOUNTAIN
Peter Fountain, wife, and eight children
Marcus Fountain (marries Juliana Stickney)
Orra Fountain (marries Colton Shipleigh on trail)
Alan Fountain (fiddler)

SHIPLEIGH
Elias Shipleigh & Anthina Surratt Shipleigh
Colton (marries Orra Fountain on trail)
and six daughters

STICKNEY
Timothy Stickney & Adah Kellogg Stickney with various children
Juliana Stickney (marries Marcus Fountain on trail)

==================================

BRANDT
Ira Brandt & Felinda Merchant Brandt (deceased)
Ira Marcus
Ira Alonzo
Ira Prentiss
Ira Samuel
& 3 daughters
Hubbard John Brandt

Children of Beechnut House

Robert & Jane Elizabeth's children:
1. **Charles** m. Edna Russell
2. Bridgett m. Pioneer Breeton
3. Lucius m. Fionella Surratt
4. Clarissa (born on the trail)
5. Cordelia and Emeline

Charles & Edna's child:
Alonzo m. Margaret DeWitt

Alonzo & Margaret's children:
1. Lydia m. Curtis Sheffield
2. **Reuben** m. Astaline Shipleigh
3. Ethan m. Naomi Russell

Reuben & Astaline's children:
1. Mary Etta
2. Electa
3. **Rose** m. Baxter Hoskins
4. Emma and Caroline (twins)
5. Lilian
6. son
7. son

Rose and Baxter's children:
1. Zenus Hoskins m. Melanie Surratt
2. Kathryn
3. **Arthur** Hoskins m. Grace Surratt (sister to Melanie, Elspeth & Delilah "Dolly")
4. Euston
5. Timothy

Arthur & Grace's children:
1. daughter (stillborn)
2. **Gideon** Zenus Hoskins m. 1. Leonora Martin 2. Eliza Russell

3. daughter
4. son
5. son

Gideon & Leonora's children:
1. son
2. Ellen
3. son
4. Rachael
5. **Young Gideon** m. Amelia Stockwell

Young Gideon & Amelia's children:
1 - 4. daughters
5. **Perry** m. Elizabeth Endicott
6. Myrtle m. Frank Snelling

Perry & Elizabeth's child:
Lyle

Town Council Chairmen

Homer Martin (b. 1721) m. Mary Frances Garner
John (b. 1742) m. (wife's name unknown)
Jerrod (b. 1772) m. Betsy Surratt
Ketchum (1800-1893) m. Janet Russell
Tobe (1822-1912) m. Irraiah Garner
Morgan (1851-1924) m. (wife's name unknown)
Obadiah (1883-1946) m. Irmagarde Hoskins
Leon (1915-1979) m. Matilda Shipleigh
Hubbard (1940- 2000) m. Clara Black

Inhabitants of Beechnut House

Richard Hastings (the original innkeeper)
Robert Hastings, builder of Beechnut House, m. Jane Elizabeth Benton
Charles Hastings m. Edna Russell
Alonzo Hastings (son of Charles) m. Margaret DeWitt
Reuben Hastings (son of Alonzo) m. Astaline Shipleigh
Rose Hastings (daughter of Reuben) m. Baxter Hoskins
Arthur Hoskins (son of Rose) m. Grace Surratt
Gideon Hoskins (son of Arthur) m. 1. Leonora Martin 2. Eliza Russell
Young Gideon Hoskins (son of Gideon) m. Amelia Stockwell
Perry Hoskins (son of Young Gideon) m. Elizabeth Endicott
Lyle Hoskins (unmarried)

Who's in Biscuit & Bob's House

Biscuit McKee, librarian & her husband **Bob** Sheffield, town cop
and, in alphabetical order by first name:
Amanda Stanton, neuromuscular massage therapist
Carol Mellinger, visiting professor
Charlotte Ellis, relative newcomer to Martinsville
Dee Sheffield, employee of M'ville Fdn., Rebecca Jo's daughter-in-law
Easton Hastings, redhead
Father John Ames, priest at St. Theresa's, brother to Maddy
Glaze McKee, Biscuit's sister, head of the Martinsville Foundation
Henry Pursey, minister at The Old Church
Ida & **Ralph** Peterson, grocery store owners
Madeleine "Maddy" Ames, would-be thriller writer and employee of M'ville Fdn.
Melissa Tarkington, owner of *Azalea House B&B*
Nathan Young ("Doc"), town doctor, and **Korsi**, the office cat
Pat & **Dave** Pontiac, guests at Azalea House
Rebecca Jo Sheffield, Bob's mother
Reebok Garner, Martinsville Deputy
Sadie Masters, widow and role model to Biscuit
Tom Parkman, restaurateur and Glaze's fiancé
and me! I'm Marmalade

Latecomers:

Frank & **Sylvia** Parkman, Tom's parents
Esther Anderson, Tom's grandmother
Ivy & **John** ("Mom" and "Dad") McKee, Biscuit's parents

In Matthew's House

Matthew Olsen & his parakeet, Mr. Fogarty
Hubbard and **Clara** Martin
Nick & **Anita** Foley

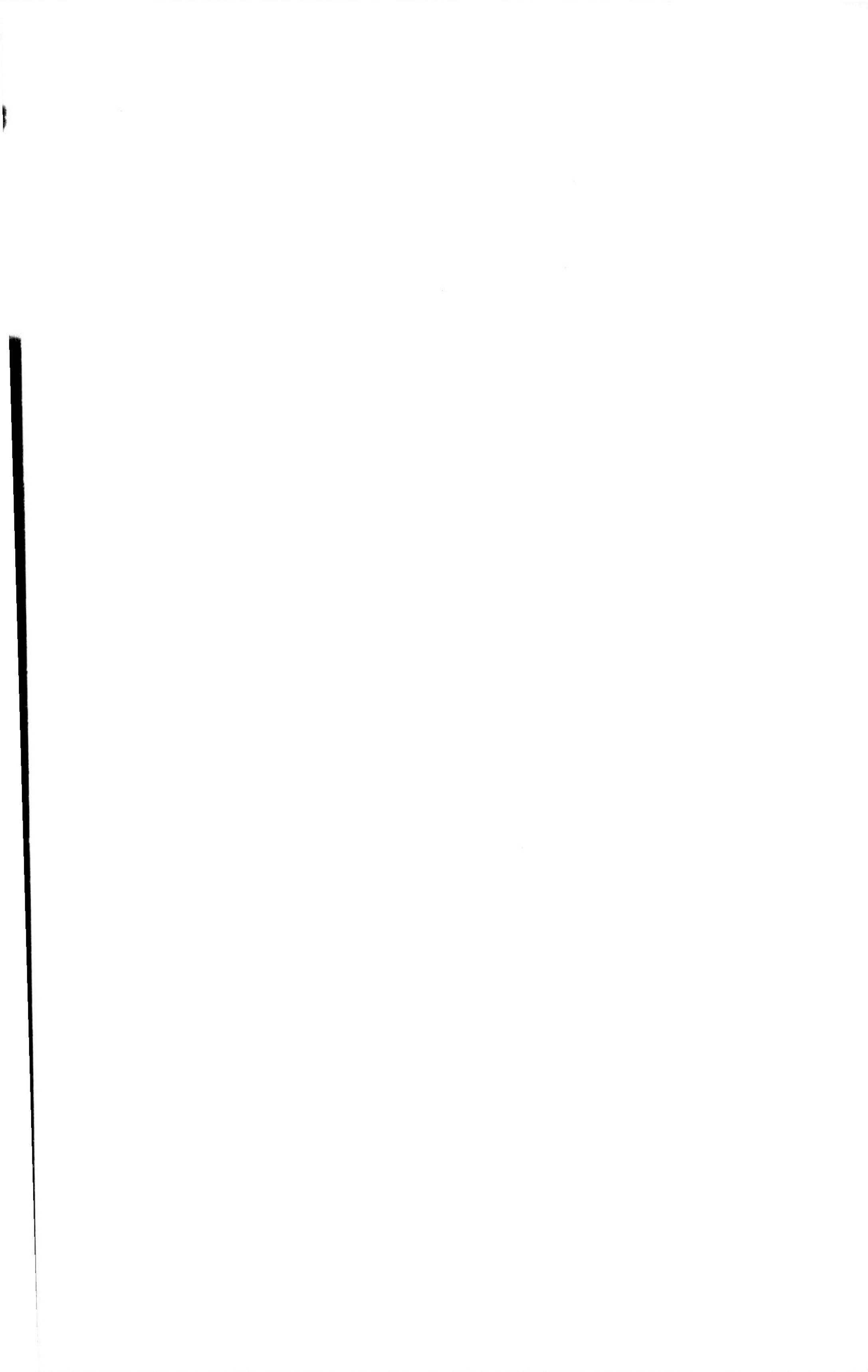

CPSIA information can be obtained
at www.ICGtesting.com
Printed in the USA
LVHW030328210519
618456LV00005B/522/P

9 780989 714297